LOVE DELAYED

Waiting to Breathe
Book 1

LOVE BELVIN

MKT Publishing, LLC

Love Delayed

Book 1 of the *Waiting to Breathe* series

ISBN: 978-1-950014-20-0 (Paperback)
ISBN: 978-1-950014-18-7 (eBook)

MKT Publishing, LLC
First print edition 2014 in U.S.A.

Cover design by **Visual Luxe**

Chapter One

NOW: *May 2014*

Zoey

Sitting in the bleachers, I'm twisting and turning, totally annoyed by what I see when I glance around at my son's soccer game. The women are tapping each other covertly —or so they think—on the thighs and arms as they ogle Stenton Rogers, coaching a bunch of six and seven year olds.

I don't want to be here. Shoot, I've declined my child's invitation all season long to be at games his Dad was able to attend and coach, until I could no longer brush off the glint of disappointment in his little marbled eyes.

Stenton attempts, in earnest, to be a part of every sport our son is registered for. He's even been able to pull off the title of coach, though he can't make each spring game because of work. In my opinion, it's best that he doesn't attend at all. There's always too much fanfare at these events because of his celebrity. All the soccer moms show up with their book club, painting club, line-dance troupe and whatever other organization they belong to, making a spectacle of his presence. This is precisely why Stenton never brings his colleagues to any of the games to watch our son in action. If he did, it would be a zoo. It's enough that these parents must agree, in writing, to no pictures at the top of the season. In my opinion, Stenton should stay home and leave the attention to the tikes on the field.

Again, I'm annoyed.

As I try to put my discontentment aside, I warm at the sight of these small kids in their color-coordinated t-shirts that are supposed to serve as jerseys. My little guy, Jordan, has the number seven embroidered on his back; I'm sure paying homage to his Dad's professional number. I know I said I'd put my unfavorable feelings for him aside, but seeing that number reminds me of how we've arrived at this inimical point in co-parenting. Why I've receded my time around him over the past few years.

I see Jordan running my way with the biggest smile plastered on his checkered-tooth mouth. Even with missing teeth, Jordan lights up my world.

"Mom, did you count my goals?" he asks breathlessly, almost bum-rushing me as I try to step off the metal bleachers to greet him.

I stagger as his dense frame collides with mine. At six years old, Jordan is a solid kid, leading in height, presumably taking after his lanky father.

"Sixteen, JR, but you have to share the ball with your team-mates. This is not a one-man show, kid."

"You sound like Dad, Mom. I'm a beast! Argh!" he literally growls.

I have a growling athlete of a child.

"Yeah, honey, but at this stage in the game, I think you should focus on learning how to be a part of a team."

"That and aggression, all of which you've demonstrated out there today. I'm proud of you, son."

Those tenor vocals poured so smoothly and effortlessly over me. Still on my haunches, talking to Jordan, I peer up to find a set of tall legs belonging to the lengthy creature towering over me. My mouth goes dry, my pulse races. That quickly, I'm disturbed all over again. His smile is filled with pride and total adoration for this little boy, the way that it always is. In an instant, I hate myself for being entranced by his undeniably magnetic countenance.

"Thanks, Dad!" my baby gushes. Then his eyes grow wide as the sun. "Mom, we're going to dinner. You wanna come? It's the last game of the season, remember? And me and Dad are gonna hang out. Please come. Please!"

I fight to keep from dropping my head and shoulders and maintain my smile while being cornered to hang out with Stenton. It's the last thing I want, it's too hard. But when I see Jordan's little lips curl up in plea, I can't say no. Well, not flat out.

"Bernard and I may be going out tonight, JR."

"Awwww, Mommy!" Jordan's crestfallen smile matches his collapsed shoulders.

"May?" Stenton points out.

I stand, regrettably, finally having to face him. My fears are confirmed when I'm squared with his six-foot, seven-inch frame. I can't help but absorb his almost jet-black five o'clock shadow, one of my weaknesses when I stare dreamily into his marbled orbs, yet another feature he's given to our son. Stenton smells delightful per usual, and his casual look of blue jeans and a simple black t-shirt exposing his heavily inked arms is probably what those moms and their friends went crazy over.

I lick my dry lips. "Yes. We may go out this evening." I try to challenge him, I don't think I like where he's going with that question.

Stenton looks at the watch on his tatted wrist. "It's almost seven now. If you two don't have solid plans, I don't see it happening this evening. How about this, come hang out with us Rogers men and if Bernard calls, you can split with us and join him."

When I'm able to pull my eyes from his mouth, I trail them down to an anxious Jordan. The gleam in his eyes can't be ignored. I hate being trapped by Stenton, even if it is with my little guy. It is the last game of the season after all. What child wouldn't want to end it celebrating with both parents?

This is what I've always struggled with, raising a child as a single woman. I came from a two parent home and we did everything together, including struggle; I haven't been able to provide Jordan the security of having both his parents under one roof when he goes to bed at night. There's substantial security in that for a child. Not providing totally goes against the values I grew up with as a child. I try to make concessions where I can and try not to overcompensate in other unhealthy areas of parenting. Like now.

"Okay," I breathe out as I face Jordan. "Where to?"

"Yay! Mommy's hanging out with the dawgs tonight!" Jordan proceeds to do some type of stomp of a dance.

He isn't just referring to him and his dad. Stenton has to travel everywhere with security, most times two. Tonight is no different.

I glance up at Stenton who's grinning and I wonder if it's because he's taught our child this ridiculous dance or because he feels accomplished in roping me into this outing.

"I'm parked on the west side of the park. Where can I meet you?" I try for an imperceptible face.

"We're over there, too." Stenton offers. "We can walk you to your ride and you can follow us."

On my way to the restaurant, I cringe at having to prepare myself for the circus that will be the paparazzi at the door, trying to capture every move we make. I abhor that aspect of being a part of Stenton Rogers' world. It all comes with his package. He hates it probably more than I detest it.

Surprisingly, I'm wrong. There are no paps waiting in the bushes. We enter a small Italian restaurant from the rear. There's a small section in the back awaiting us. The three of us share an amenable dinner that is filled with laughter, all surrounding the one shared happiness between Stenton and me: Jordan.

It's weird trying to avoid eye contact with Stenton throughout dinner. I can't look at him, don't want to become entranced and start my usual befuddlement over my checkered relationship with him. I struggle with so much guilt when it comes to my son's father. I don't want Jordan feeling the effects of the grievance I've developed over the years for his father. Stenton is an excellent dad. Any child would be fortunate to call him Daddy. I'm all too blessed that my child has that benefit, but it is that connection to him that makes my life so perplexing.

And the way that I can see from the corner of my eyes Stenton gazing at me longingly, as he always does, never fails to hurl me into the bowels of confusion and resentment that I've lived with for far too long. The state of bewilderment has been a mainstay as far as Stenton is concerned. The resentment and bitterness I feel for him is a new sentiment. It's caused a shifting in me, changing the core of my optimistic being.

"So, no more Ariana, huhn?" Stenton asks Jordan.

With a bashful smile, Jordan shakes his head.

"What are you going to do when you hit first grade in September? You're going to have to upgrade your G to get the older girls, man. Are you up to it?" Stenton continues to goad.

I watch raptly as Jordan tries to swallow his food, keen to reply. I'm not fond of the idea of my six year old having a girlfriend, but his dad seems to get a kick out of it, so I entertain it.

"You know I'mma make it do what it do, big dawg," Jordan quips. Stenton's head rolls back in laughter. Laughter that lightened the hold in my chest. I can tell he was inciting Jordan for just that type of response.

"Excuse me?" I demand.

"Mommy," he cries, now sounding more his age. "You know I'm gonna do all my school work first."

"That's right because it's books before…" Stenton prompts Jordan's completion.

"Babes!" I can tell this is a mantra his dad has also been coaching him on.

My phone goes off. It's a text from an employee, calling out of work tomorrow.

"Is it time to go?" Why does Stenton have to pierce me with *those* eyes? It frustrates and excites me at the same time.

My eyes swing back down to my phone, and as I reply to the text, I respond to Stenton without the eye contact I know he prefers. "No. It's work."

"Good," Stenton replies smoothly.

"Oooh, Mommy, you wanna come with us to the Gameroom?"

I drop my phone in my lap and glance over at Jordan. *Now, this is too much. I've agreed to dinner, not date night with Stenton Rogers.* It had been sometime since we'd all gone out as a family. Years ago, we'd take exotic vacations together regularly. I had to put a stop to that.

"Honey, it's really late and Mommy doesn't do well with a whole bunch of kids running around in one room. You know that."

"We actually have the place to ourselves. I wanted to be sure to hit up the spot with him since I had to run right after the last game. We're calling it the end of the season celebration," Stenton provides with his eyes penetrating me. "Right, JR?"

"Yeah, Mommy. Just come. We're going to have mad fun!"

Stenton is trying to set me up. He knows Jordan wants me with him tonight. I feel uneasy. But when I hear Jordan talk with missing teeth, distorting the sounds of his words, I have to consider it. By all accounts, Jordan is a well-rounded kid in spite of being raised by parents in two separate households. He's an only child and I think that fact is the cause of his extreme maturity. His father only treats him as a child when he's disciplining Jordan and giving him some golden nuggets of life. Outside of that, these two are like best buds. I struggle with being the witch of a mom. I want Jordan to be surrounded by love.

"Okay," I acquiesce.

I follow them over to Gameroom, which is located in Center City Philadelphia, not too far from my and Jordan's home. Jordan will be staying the night with his father, but at least my commute won't be so far when I leave.

Sure enough, the place is empty with only staff on standby for Stenton and Jordan's needs. We immediately start with video games, something both guys enjoy. Then we move on to pinball machines, and after that, bowling. When we arrive at the miniature basketball courts, of course, Jordan invites me to play, and it is hard not to get caught up in the excitement of the game. The second time I miss the shot, Stenton sidles up behind me and coordinates my wrists so I can have better range with my throw. His scent is so familiar and compelling that it's distracting, making me uncomfortable.

I toss the ball and make the shot.

"Yay! Mommy got skills! Mommy got skills!" Jordan jumps up and down on his toes.

I glance over at Stenton whose pouty heart-shaped lips are too patent and his eyes are slanted a bit more than usual as his heavy eyes rake over my entire face. This happens each time we touch, no matter how casually. It's also why I've opted not to spend time around him over the past year. It clouds my mind and judgment. It also depresses me.

"Zo," pours from his mouth melodically. Stenton always enunciates my name with reverence and bold sensuality. "There's something I need to talk to you about…something we need to discuss."

My heart pounds in my chest and the palms of my hands mist. Why his request to talk causes immediate anxiety, I don't know, but my mouth has gone dry and lips part. Fear lodges in my throat, rendering me unable to speak.

When I'm able to, I whisper, "*Su*-sure." I then try for a cooperative smile.

See, that's always been the thing about Stenton. He's brought out those things in me that are uncharacteristic of my true nature. I've always stepped out of my comfort zone with him and have done things I never thought to do. At one point they were all good traits that modified the core of me. My sense of optimism and unconditional love prevailed where he was concerned. Now, those qualities have morphed into characteristics that are ugly and dark, which is why it's time for me to go.

"I think Mommy's just about played out, baby," I say to Jordan as I turn to him, dropping on my haunches. "I have an early day tomorrow since one of the workers called off. I'll see you in a couple of days?"

My heart twists at that acknowledgement, but I know he's in the best hands. The only person who loves my child possibly as much as I do is his father. He adores Jordan.

Jordan nods, surprisingly not fighting my departure. I offer my balled hand to do our fist bump and he joins me. I can see the slant in his eyes as well. Sir Jordan is sleepy. It's nearing his bed time. I kiss his head and turn to collect my leather jacket and purse that I tossed on a statue earlier.

When my gaze meets Stenton's, his hand drops from his chin and his shoulders square, a sign of him opening up to me. It further coils my heart. *I hate what we've become.* I don't know how to say a simple goodbye. Over the years, I've lost conversation for Stenton more and more. Luckily, he takes the lead in our parting words.

"Good night, Zo. Thanks for hanging out with us tonight. Jordan will be home on Friday."

The brevity of his bidding me goodbye sends a fluttering sensation through my chest. Still, I don't know what to say. So, I say nothing. I nod, turn on my heel, and give one last fleeting glance to Jordan who's now shooting the ball, not paying us any attention, thankfully, before walking out.

When I arrive home, I shower and crawl into bed with a heavy heart and exhausted limbs. I know I should check in with Bernard, but I'm too tired, too preoccupied with images of Stenton in my head. Too troubled about the thoughts of what could have been when I realize I just spent an eventful evening with what, for years, I so desperately wanted to be my family.

Minutes into this internal battle I've engaged in while I beg for sleep to come, I feel my ducts fill with tears. I knew they'd arrived before they poured because dealing with Stenton for the past seven years acquainted me with the act of crying, something I don't recall doing much of before him. My chest heaves from the heaviness my heart bears and my lungs fill with the pain of what I've become. Then the tears. This is exactly why I didn't want to extend the evening with Jordan's dad in the first place.

And so here it is, another night of haunted memories, trying to figure out where I went wrong years ago.

love
belvin

THEN: June 2006

"Girl, aren't you pumped? Yeeeeeeah, baby!" Angela shouted with one hand on the steering wheel and the other, holding a cup of WaWa coffee.

I rolled my eyes. "Yeah." I yawned. "Just ecstatic. Wooohooo," I pushed out wryly.

"Zo, you have no idea what you're in for! And I'll never forget my favorite cousin, who took the journey with me to get my husband! We're going to have so much fun these six weeks! I can feel it!" Angela was so beside herself with glee, she literally exclaimed each sentence.

"How long before we're there?" I asked, yawning again. It was around 5:30 a.m. and I was completely exhausted.

"Not long at all," she answered as we rode in her 2000 Ford Taurus.

She had come to pick me up since Princeton is en route to Moorestown, NJ where we were spending the greater part of our summer.

"Girl, you are going to thank me as soon as you see those tall, rich and fine basketball players! I heard at least six *76'ers* are going to be there and possibly two from the *Knicks*. Zo, we got the best assignment!" Teasingly, she nudged me in the arm as she laughed.

Angela and I had been tight since I moved to New Jersey from South Carolina in seventh grade. We had known each other prior to my move, but when I arrived we became best friends. There were no secrets between us. We shared everything and every detail of our lives.

Angela stole glances in the rearview mirror, assessing her makeup. She was beyond excited about this excursion. Her almond skin came from her mother, though her beautifully carved facial features were all from her dad. Angela and I were fairly the same average 5'5" height. Even with the whopping fifteen pounds she'd put on her last few months of college, she still had a killer body, only now, her figure seemed more mature. And believe me when I tell you she knew how to work her weight, no matter how much or little.

My complexion was less than a shade darker than hers. Some referred to me as light skinned and others brown. I was thin, never being more than a size five, if I was lucky. I'd wished for that surprise fifteen pounds myself, but wasn't so lucky. Most of my weight came from my wild hair. Angela's hair was far more manageable than my own. She was lucky there.

The common thread for Angela and me was that we both struggled to break the mold of the traditional religious restrictions our family put on us. I didn't want to live mundane; go to school, marry right away, have babies, and perpetuate the perception that there was nothing to explore outside the walls of the sanctuary. I wanted to live, to travel and discover what else was out there. I didn't want tradition; I wanted to paint the path *I* created. The one never toured. My first start was school. I would get my degree, secure my family and take off somewhere—anywhere. But I wouldn't be held back by condemnation for wanting more.

Angela endeavored to break away from the same outmoded lifestyle, but her approach was more rebellious. She was a bright student, always having maintained at least a 3.0 grade point average. I always argued that she could do better if she applied herself and went beyond just getting by. However, Angela would always counter that I could work for my 3.8 average alone; her efforts would be made finding a millionaire to seduce. I never understood the long-term accomplishment in that, but admired her boldness and veracity.

I liked a bit of rock and roll; she lived for hip-hop. I appreciated understated beauty; Ang was the cleavage and camel-toe revealer. I studied to improve; she studied to pass. I liked art, appreciated variety; my cousin enjoyed attempting sensual art with her body. We girls had different agendas, but our goals were the same. We wanted to chart our own paths, ones very different from those our parents traveled.

The only thing that could have had Angela up and live at this hour was a man. Although I was enrolled at Princeton University and she was at Rutgers University, the New Brunswick campus, we both applied for the *Working Toward the Stars* program. It was a unique opportunity for participating universities in New Jersey. The program selected top performing students to take on non-paying jobs that put them in the room with top professionals. Our options were theater, music, engineering, baseball, football, basketball, opera, NASCAR, culinary arts and several more. Angela talked me into applying because she had the biggest crush on Stenton Rogers.

Stenton Rogers: NBA shooting guard for the Philadelphia 76'ers, from Newark, NJ, was the number two overall Draft Pick, three-time MVP Awardee, and four-time Champion. *Oh, and his jersey was number seven.* I knew things about this man that were of no consequence to me. I knew nothing about sports, much less basketball. I was simply happy to be spending much of the summer with my closest cousin.

Secretly, I had no idea what she wanted with a man like Stenton Rogers. He stayed in the headlines for his reckless behavior. Either fighting with paparazzi, or losing his cool on the courts, or taking nude pictures with models; Stenton Rogers was a topic at every dinner table in America at some point. Two years earlier, the news, blogs and all things Internet were buzzing with the leaked pictures of Stenton and an unknown woman doing things my untainted mind couldn't conceive. It was the time in American culture when the world finally discovered how far down his tattoos reached.

Again, I didn't follow basketball, but my father and every other man I knew were fanatics of the sport, and almost invariably during each man-talk exchange there would be mention of Stenton Rogers. Mainly, the discussion would be led by his dominance on the courts, but more often than not, his wild and lewd behavior with random women would be the subtopic.

And then there was the two minute clip of a sex tape that was released. Now, that one was stripped from every blogger's site within two days of being leaked. Stenton was under fire by the league and almost let go. According to my dad, he was suspended for the remainder of the season behind that one. My dad also said if Stenton wasn't the premiere player of not just the Philadelphia 76'ers, but also the league, he would have been fired without a second thought.

That incident, mixed with the bar fight he'd engaged in just the night before that video was leaked, had women everywhere in a lustful frenzy over Stenton Rogers. Fawning over him became vogue. I didn't get it. What dignified woman would want a man whose body so many women across the world were acquainted with?

My cousin, Angela.

"Holy mother of Joseph! I'm gonna have his dribbling babies!" Angela's screaming roused me from my daze. "I gave Timmy a parting screw yesterday. All I kept thinking about was how the next man between my legs will be Stenton Rogers! I've been so excited these last few weeks that my cycle has been knocked off." She slapped the steering wheel.

Ahhhh… Timmy. I had mixed feelings about Timmy's mention. He'd recently cheated on Angela with a coworker, Regina. Angela turned volatile at that discovery; showed up to his job physically threatening the both of them, egg-bombed his car and slashed two of his tires. I was surprised there was a recovery period for those two that included sex.

"Oh, my god…my first question for him will be how many tattoos he has. Ooh, Zoey, they're from his neck, all the way down to his waist…even on his knuckles! I can't wait to see each and every one of them." She giggled in delight. "And I've been told he has a potty mouth. Mmmmmm! I can't wait to put mine *on* him," she mused aloud. "Umph…here we go!" she sang as we pulled into the circular driveway of *Moorestown Creek* private country club.

A white gloved valet jogged to the driver's side and courteously asked our reason for being there. Angela airily explained our enrollment in the *Working Toward the Stars* program. Her lengthy words and perfect enunciations were entirely unnecessary, and was all for him to explain that we needed to park our own car in the back lot where all employees did. That didn't pump the brakes on her enthusiasm, though. Ang was ready to lay eyes on her future husband. I, on the other hand, was ready to get through my first day so I could crawl back in the bed to catch a few *Zs* before my night class.

We checked in with the program coordinator, Jeffery, an employee of the facility. He offered us options for the role we'd play for the summer. We could either be courtside bartenders and serve non-alcoholic beverages or collect the balls the players would use to practice their shots. I didn't want to be in too close proximity to them, so I was relieved when Angela enthusiastically opted for the *ball fetcher* role.

We took off for the gym. Along the way, I noticed the prestige of the place. Plush carpeting, stark white walls with built-in frames, real greenery on gold stands against the walls, and the all-white gloved staff.

After a brief orientation of the beverage stand, I was left alone in the corner of a massive gym. There were no bleachers, just a massive court with seats dispersed around the center floor. By 7:00 a.m. tall figures with tight faces had begun strolling in. I'd guessed although this was their normal training time, it was still their vacation period and they weren't so inspired.

From the second lanky figure that walked through one set of doors, I wondered where was Angela's *Stenton Rogers*. I'd seen him on television over the years here and there, but again, I didn't follow sports and his lewd behavior had calmed over the last couple of years, so I hadn't caught a glimpse of him on the newsstands at my local grocery store in a while. And from the considerable distance, he could be the man at the other end of the colossal room, holding the industrial mop.

I spied Angela from across the court and her eyes were already on me, beaming with anxious enthusiasm. I'd wished there was a way I could ask her where was *her* guy. I thought to send a text, but quickly retracted that idea, as we weren't allowed to use our phones in the gym. By ten minutes after seven, there were nearly fifteen people in the gym; perhaps four women, but mostly men.

It eventually became clear to me who was who. Most of the basketball players were amazons with the exception of this one spirited and loquacious short man. He was short, and I don't mean NBA short, but even layman short. He could be no more than 5' 7", but he was fast! I mean, he moved with extreme speed when passing and shooting. Those giants moved like zombies compared to him. And between each successful play he'd have a loud and often brash comment to follow it up.

One of the things I kept hearing him call out was the word *stentro*. I didn't know what that was, but when he stood still, he'd hold his crotch in some form and often say, *stentro*. It wasn't until nearly two hours after their arrival that I'd caught on. A ball went out of bounds and this time Angela went to fetch it.

"Steeeenton," she purred rather loudly, I'm sure to gain his attention.

One of the giants stopped and turned to her. Angela tossed the ball with a girlie flicking of the wrist. The basketball barely made it over to him, but he picked it up and graciously thanked her.

"You're welcome, Stent," Angela shouted sexily again, curving her body into an "S" shape.

Hmmmm…so that's Stenton Rogers?

Things from that point on were pretty eventless. By Tuesday, I regretted taking on this quest with Angela. When Wednesday rolled around, Angela asked to stay until after the guys were through changing in the locker rooms. I didn't want to; I was tired and preferred catching my daily nap. Nonetheless, I'd agreed.

"Oop-oop!" Angela jumped in place while we stood in the hall right outside of the men's locker room. "Here he comes! C'mon," she whispered rapidly with the least amount of conspicuity as she could, then pulled me by the arm and sashayed over to where the men were exiting.

"Oh, look at this," the short guy with almond skin similar to mine tapped Stenton Rogers on the arm. "It's the two caddies." He did his usual groping of himself as he laughed at his own joke.

I looked up to the tree-towering man, Stenton Rogers, and my eyes quickly averted from his glower. I know I must've looked all of eleven years old with that move, but my eyes couldn't stand to look at him for long now that he was in my face. It was like looking directly at the sun on the brightest day.

"Heeeeeey, guys!" Angela sang. "We just came by on our way out to say good day training earlier. I see your passing technique has improved."

I glanced over at her with the look of death. I didn't know anything about basketball, but had sense enough to know you didn't critique professionals when you didn't play.

I watched the flirtatious grin that played at her lips as she pouted them mischievously.

"We 'bout to get into some business thangs, but later we gonna have a few drinks with some buddies of ours. You ladies are more than welcome to join us," the short one offered greasily then swiped his tongue over his lips.

I saw the way he sized up my breasts and Angela's thighs respectively. It made me incredibly uncomfortable. What was more disconcerting was Angela jumping at the opportunity. She literally jumped to face me, begging me to agree. I couldn't believe she bought that as an appropriate invitation.

"I have class tonight," I reminded her.

Within a beat, Angela squinted her eyes at me, clearly seething at my response. This was for her. I enrolled in this stupid program for her. She was up close and in Stenton Rogers' face. Here was her opportunity and if this weak and disingenuous invitation was it, she'd be taking the rest of the journey alone.

"What time and where?" Angela whipped her head back to them and eagerly asked.

The short dude looked up to the tatted tree, Stenton Rogers. "You'll be done with your interview by seven?" Before the lanky guy could reply, the midget answered. "Yeah, seven would be good. We're meeting at a small spot in Philly. Write me your number and I'll have my people text you the address."

Write down her number? *Really?* I watched as Angela scrambled for her purse, in search of a writing utensil. *It's 2006; who still writes down phone numbers when they could easily be plugged into cell phones?*

Someone's phone rang. Everyone went searching for theirs except for Angela who was scribbling her information on the back of a receipt.

"I'll meet you outside. I gotta take this," the tall guy mumbled. His voice was nasal, yet husky, forcing me to steal a glance at him for the second time. He didn't pay us a parting regard before walking off.

"Here you go," Angela shoved the paper to shorty. "Stent is going to be there, right?" No one could miss the zeal in her voice.

"Oh, yeah," he returned, not even looking at her when he answered. He slickly pushed the paper in his pocket and took off in the wake of his giant friend. "It's been real, ladies. Looking forward to seeing you later," he tossed over his shoulder.

Angela turned to me and silently jumped up and down in anticipation once he was no longer in sight.

"You're so going to cut class for this, right? For me," she begged, out of breath.

I pulled her by the hand in the opposite direction to the back parking lot. "Absolutely not. I can't skip class, Ang."

On the ride back to my campus, I listened to Angela give me all the reasons she believed I should go down to Philly with her, even guaranteeing me as the godmother of her and Stenton Rogers' first baby. And all the while I told her no.

The next day at the country club was completely uneventful. On the way back to campus, Angela told me how the short guy, whose name I learned was Alton Alston, asked why we didn't join them. She said she gave him some bogus excuse about having to go to class as a means of not appearing too desperate. She *was* desperate! Angela said she'd come up with a plan for getting into Stenton Rogers' bed soon enough. We only had a few weeks of their pre-training season to make her dreams come true.

That Thursday, I was still at my assigned post, bored out of my mind. It was only 9:30 and my stomach was already growling. I'd only had time to grab an apple and water on my way out that morning because I'd overslept and had to rush out of the door to meet Angela. I was up the night before, writing a paper that made up a good portion of my summer grade. I made sure to knock out a class in the summer since my scholarship generously covered the expense.

I wanted to complete my undergrad career as quickly as possible; I had responsibilities awaiting me. My family. Angela didn't take summer classes at Rutgers. She was fortunate enough to not have to even work. Her parents thought this *Working Toward the Stars* was actually a significant course. The one credit that it provided wasn't worth the five or so hours a day I dedicated to it. I would have much rather been somewhere sleeping or reading.

That morning, as my thoughts ran amok, wishing I was anywhere but at a country club serving millionaire jocks, I recalled Bernard, the choir director at our church, saying he was going to post a video of the regional choir he belonged to, practicing for their submission to the next *McDonald's Gospelfest*.

I was squatting behind the bar, perusing my *Facebook* timeline for it when I heard, "Are you supposed to be doing that or serving drinks?" The tone was brusque, his silky chords poured, not just in my ears, but over my entire body causing my pulse to race.

I didn't think, I only felt the echoing of his vocal chords in my core, then panicked. I jumped from the floor, nearly crashing into the small cart. The last time I'd looked up, they were practicing some type of fake-out passes with some guy named Olajuwon. I only knew this because that's what they called him on the court and he wore a t-shirt with that name printed on the back.

"Can I help you?" I finally glanced up...and I mean *up*.

My eyes traveled his all black jersey. I idly realized no one ever wore official league jerseys to the country club, he was no different. But what jolted my attention was the ink. It was an entirely different experience than that from afar. This man's arms and neck were covered in red, black, and yellow tattoos; from the portion of his chest that I could see, all the way up to his neck, and down to his knuckles.

I don't think I'd ever seen so much graffiti on a body before in my life. There were so many shapes, colors, words, and expressions. There was an embossed star on his neck, just below his earlobe, a meticulously jagged barbwire that was etched around his neck and came around to his chest, expanding into a larger image that his jersey concealed. On his left shoulder was a pair of skulls with red eyes and other fiery ornaments, and just below that was a tribal sun. And surprisingly *to my dismay*, that was all I could observe considering his stance in front of me.

I could easily get lost in isolating each one and discovering the totality of them individually. I found it strange that those markings made his presence extremely...masculine. What was more eerie about this ink encounter was the fact that I was surprisingly drawn to them. Me! Drawn to marks that marred the beauty of natural skin!

My eyes trailed up to his orbs and that was my undoing. Stenton's eyes were a rich combination of brown and gold hues, some even sparkling, snatching the breath from my hyperactive lungs. They reflected like marbles. The cinnamon skin on his face was free of inked patterns. His eyebrows were thick and handsomely bushy. His nose was moderately wide and long reaching just above his neatly trimmed mustache. And his lips were full with the top spread wider than the bottom, making them resemble the shape of a heart. I found myself biting my bottom one, embarrassed by my assessment of this man's assets.

Wow! Angela is going to have some tall and handsome babies!

"I *did* want something to drink, but Facebook seems to be the service of the day," he growled, pointedly glancing at my phone.

I pushed it into my pocket, straightened my shoulders and asked, "What can I get for you, Mr. Rogers?"

His long, inked and corded arm reached toward me, "Your phone, please."

My heart sank. Not that I cared about being released from this stupid program, but I didn't like the idea of failing at something, even something as brainless as *Working Toward the Stars*. His tone made me feel like if I didn't at least cooperate, he'd report me. I chewed on my bottom lip as I contemplated. My eyes scoured the court. No one was paying us any attention. *Yet.* I sighed as I pulled my phone from my pocket and handed it to him.

He handed it right back, "Password."

I rolled my eyes, took the phone to unlock it and handed it back. Stenton tapped a few times and I could tell he was strolling down my timeline. I figured he was trying to see if I'd shared any pictures from the country club recently. He probably went into my inbox, too.

"I could rat your ass out," rumbled from his throat.

I shrugged my shoulders. "And I could show the world your horrible jump shots." My eyes gestured over to the Olajuwon fellow. "I could tell everyone how you need assistance from a guy with a name like that."

His thick brows pinched, and tempting mouth curled into a controlled grin, simultaneously. He held my gaze for a minute before going back to my phone, flicking away. I was incredibly annoyed by his invasion of my privacy to see if I had breached his. Then I caught Angela's questioning glare from across the court. I shrugged my shoulders slyly, or so I thought. When I glanced back up to Stenton Rogers, I was met with a scowl sans the grin as he followed my line of sight over to Angela.

He handed my phone back to me. "If I find any pictures of me in here, I'll know they came from you and I'll have you reprimanded." His tone was derisive.

My heart pounded in my chest. "And if I find you scored a jump-shot, I'll know you're the world's biggest fraud who doesn't have any natural talent." I met his glare.

What in the world was I talking about? I knew nothing about sports!

"Is everything all right here, Mr. Rogers?" I heard just behind me.

I turned to see the site coordinator, Jeffery, headed our way. *Shoot!* I was in trouble. I wouldn't survive the embarrassment of being escorted off private property. And how would I get back to campus? Angela and her Stenton-Rogers-obsessed self wouldn't leave this gig to run me up the highway.

All I could do was stare at Stenton with coldness in my eyes and chin in the air. I would go with my dignity, not giving him the satisfaction of my groveling.

His eyes were stapled to mine as he replied, "I was just asking Ms…" He was asking for my name. Inexplicably besieged, I couldn't think quick enough under his piercing gaze to give it to him. But Jeffery did.

"Barrett. Elizabeth…" Jeffery provided, respectfully.

That answer only further intensified Stenton's glare.

"Yeah…Ms. Elizabeth Barrett here to be sure to keep enough Pepsi products on ice. That's all I drink." Stenton never moved his eyes, so I'm sure he caught my deep exhalation of relief.

"Oh, sure, sir. We have loads of Gatorade, Tropicana and Aquafina in stock specifically for you. We are fully aware and prepared for your contractual obligations, sir," Jeffery eagerly and efficiently advised.

Stenton nodded stiffly, but his eyes never left mine. I scrambled inside the ice box of the bar because the glare he was giving made me uncomfortable. I randomly pulled out a Lemon Lime flavored *G Endurance Formula* and handed it to him. If I wasn't so perceptive, I would have missed the flash of his quizzical gaze.

"Electrolytes," I croaked out. "To help maintain your fluid balance and regulate muscle contractions." I nodded towards the Olajuwon guy, who was waiting with his hands on his high hips. "You need it, right?"

When my eyes returned to Stenton, I watched as his heart-shaped lips slowly twitched into a smile. He took the bottle from me, opened it and turned to walk away as he gulped from it.

"Good job, Elizabeth!" Jeffery gushed as he patted me on the shoulder before walking away. I let out a long sigh of relief.

What a close call.

After the guys were done a few hours later, we got invited to lunch. Well, it was more like Angela got us an invitation to a diner not too far from the country club after we "happened" upon Stenton Rogers and Alton Alston coming out of the locker.

Angela had me drive so that she could reapply her makeup on our five-minute ride there. As we sat in the car and waited for them in the parking lot at Angela's insistence, feeling self-conscious about not being duteous about my appearance, I checked my long-wear *MAC* lipglass that my sister, Ruth, had let me borrow and saw it still glistened, even if less glossy than this morning. I was starving and wanted to eat.

"I wonder how big he is," Angela mused as I pushed back my cuticles with my fingernail. "If he's small, I won't tell him, but damn, I'll be disappointed." She twisted in the passenger seat to face me. "You ever heard of pencil dick men? Girl, I had one or two in my day. They are the worst—or maybe the thick but short ones. Those don't make it past your lips." She let out a frustrated groan. "I don't know which is worse. God, please just let him be big."

I snorted and shook my head as I continued with my nails.

Finally, they pulled up. I was tired of hearing about what Angela wanted to do to Stenton Rogers in bed and guess whether she'd get the opportunity that night. We got out of the car and walked up to the Jeep Wrangler they pulled up in. The guys were still piling out of the truck. They were with three other big, meaty men, one carrying a camera.

"What's with the camera?" I tossed over to Angela.

"You don't hear them talking on the courts?"

I shook my head.

"It's for a documentary they're doing on Alton," she explained.

Great. Another reason I don't need to be here!

We continued toward the restaurant behind the guys. I couldn't help but steal a glance at Stenton, who was on the phone; his tats were so loud. He wore a gray tank with blue stripes stretched across, cargo shorts, and *Jordans*. I noticed he put on a netted baseball cap hat he turned to the back, and brown gradient *Ray Bans* with lenses looking extremely conspicuous.

Alton addressed us, "Oh, y'all made it to eat, huhn?" he jeered, holding his crotch. He did that a lot. "That's one thing you could offer college kids: give their asses food and they will dance!" He and one of the beefy guys laughed loudly.

We paced behind them into the restaurant and already, I was ready to bail. I didn't want to lose my cool with the Alton guy. I hated the *king of wisecracks* type. They hurt feelings. They led us straight to the back to a large circular booth and as we ambled back there, one of the guys yelled over to the waitress by name. I saw how she immediately made her way to the back, picking up menus along the way.

As we sat, I heard Rihanna's track, "Music of the Sun" streaming from the speakers. It was growing on me; a reggae feel. We were seated all of twenty seconds before the waitress arrived with menus. Alton referred to her by name and she blushed a shade of rose as she responded to his familiarity. They obviously came here often. I quickly settled on what I could afford and would enjoy: burger and fries. Angela ordered a steak with potatoes. Did she think we were at a formal restaurant? I knew she was trying to come off as high maintenance. I didn't have the time for that. I wanted to get back to campus for my nap before class.

"Drew, man," Alton called over to the guy with the camera. "You can stop recording. I don't need me grubbing on film."

The guy nodded and clicked off his small hand-held camera. I was relieved; we hadn't signed anything consenting to be filmed.

"So what do you ladies do when you're not catching balls?" Alton jeered.

The table went up in laughter. Even Stenton broke from his telephone conversation to express his amusement. I was annoyed already. Even more irritating was Angela's contrived cackle for the joke.

"Well, you know…" Angela purred as she twisted her curls with her index finger. "I'm a Rutgers student, majoring in hospitality management."

I rolled my eyes, wishing I wasn't sitting next to her in that moment. In the circular booth, Stenton Rogers and I had the end seats with the others in between. I was sure Angela strategically sat to the right of me, believing it was closer to Stenton. Everyone with the exception of Angela and me were on their phones.

"Hospitality, huhn?" Alton supplied. "Just how hospitable are you? What kind of hospitality do you serve up?"

"The type that Stent likes," she purred.

Ughhh!

"Oh, shit!"

"Damn!"

"All right, now!"

Everyone seemed to have a reaction except for Stenton. He did look up from his conversation, I guess caught off guard. I had no idea why; I'm sure he got this all the time.

Angela continued with her hair twirl, her eyes set on Stenton. It took him a few seconds, but he went back to his conversation, leaving her hanging. Angela needed to hook this man and soon, because I didn't do chicken head, or bird, or thirst.

"And what type of hospitality do you serve up?" I heard Alton ask, directing his question to me.

I swear, I didn't want to look up. I didn't. Because looking up would have meant that the time clock on me having to use my sarcastic wit to tear into him would start, and I didn't want to ruin this for Angela.

"Oh, you must not be college material," he continued when I didn't jump to answer or acknowledge him.

"No!" Angela nervously laughed. "Zoey here is a Princeton Tiger. She's there on full scholarship. My family has brains, beauty, and body," her tone turned husky.

She didn't have to speak for me. It would've taken just a few seconds for me to devise my own retort.

"So, I ask again, brains-beauty-and-booty queen…" The guys laughed. But not Stenton. "…what's your hospitality…today?" Alton amended.

I could have been wrong, but I could swear he was propositioning me. This was what these pompous athletes did to desperate women. That wasn't me.

"Mmmm…" I tapped my chin. "Well today, my hospitality involved serving a refreshing beverage to a tiny floor mopper."

"Floor mopper?" he asked confused.

"Yeah," I replied. "You're so petite compared to your contemporaries. If I wanted to locate you all I had to do was look at the floor."

Angela kneed me under the table. I saw her eyes stretch wide, clearly appalled. My eyes raked over to Alton, preparing myself for a war. There was sputtering from the three random men at the table. Stenton stared at me, sheer humor in his eyes. And Alton gave me a blank stare.

I excused myself for the bathroom. As I stood to skirt out of the booth, I didn't miss Alton's gritty gaping, trying to catch a view of my rear. I made sure to take my time in there. The thought of hanging out, at least until the food was served, did pop into mind. But I didn't give in. I'd already pissed Angela off with my temper.

When I got back to the table, I kept quiet and hoped Ang wasn't too pissed with me. The Alton guy didn't say much to me. Hopefully my teaspoon of humor was a repellent to his crass behavior. I wouldn't hold my breath. As their conversations flowed, Angela tried to pull in Stenton, who eventually got off the phone, with flirtatious banter.

"So, you think you're ready for another All-Star season, Stent? It'll make three for your career," Angela attempted.

"For him?" Alton shouted, seemingly offended. "You think Stent is the only man on that court? Who do you think gets him the ball for those baskets?"

When the waiters arrived with our food I was so relieved. I was starved, and dug in immediately, tuning them all out. I checked back in every once in a while when Angela's inflection changed to express interest or coquetry.

"So what—or should I say who—do you do at night, Stent?" Angela asked.

My eyes shot up from my plate in horror.

"Oh, shit!" Alton shouted. "She getting straight to the point, StentRo!"

There's that moniker again.

Stenton wasn't as spirited in his response as his friend. "My girl," he answered as he poured ketchup in his plate.

I then noticed his huge salad and small side serving of fries.

Weird.

"I didn't know you had a girlfriend. Anyone I know?" Angela pushed.

Stenton shook his head, still not facing her. That rubbed me as strange. Did he or didn't he? Either way, he didn't seem to be checking for Angela.

"Well, sweetheart, if you're looking for someone to practice that hospitality on, I'm your man. I ain't got no girlfriend," Alton announced.

I rolled my eyes again.

"What happened to Tynisha?" Angela inquired. "Last I saw her reality show, you had flowers delivered to her."

Alton clapped his hands together. "She's the mother of my kids. I treat her like the queen she deserves to be treated as. That's how I let them other jokers know what she's built for, know what I mean?"

That was such a weak answer. Unless you were living under a rock, everyone knew Alton and Tynisha had an on-again-off-again relationship. He was likely the reason she got her show. Apparently, she was a fashion stylist. I didn't know who Alton was initially: I'd seen a few pictures, but wasn't that familiar with him. And from being off the court at the country club, I couldn't exactly see the faces of those on the floor. He'd come over a couple of times for beverages, but it never clicked until last night when I was online and came across a picture of them coming out of a fancy restaurant in Edgewater. When I Google'd him, I quickly gathered his reputation as a habitual cheater.

"So, Stent has a girlfriend?" Angela practically sang. "Is it serious?" She held her fork to her mouth sensually.

Stenton glanced up from his plate and smiled sardonically as he chewed.

Ang! Stop it…he's not interested!

"This man is damn near married," Alton scoffed. "That's who he was on the phone with earlier. He just don't want the world in their business. He keeps his shit on the low."

So why are you *sharing it with strangers?*

"But everybody needs a friend, right Stent?" Angela forged ahead, ignoring Alton. "My parents have been married for twenty-three years; I know how…tight things can get." She was twirling her hair again.

"If I were a boy…" Stenton remarked.

The table went up in a roar. In my typical hyperactive mind, I sensed a double entendre at the reference to the Beyoncé track that had been released this year. If he were a boy, he'd cheat on his girlfriend…or he wouldn't cheat because he'd be hurt if his girlfriend did it to him? I didn't know. One thing was for sure and that was he was playing Angela and I couldn't stomach much more of it.

I pulled out a twenty dollar bill, placed it in the center of the table and nudged Angela. "I have to go to the bathroom and then I have a call to make. I'll be outside when you're ready."

"Damn! You got the shits, girl?" Alton yelped. "That burger gave you the runs?"

"If it did, you gave me a double portion with the way you were dragging on the courts today," I hissed and left the booth.

Twenty five minutes later, as I sat in the small waiting area, they all came out of the diner, loud and boisterous as I'd left them. Goodbyes were made—or should I say, Angela gave her goodbyes to a disinterested Stenton, and Alton answered for him. I got told off the entire ride back to Princeton. Angela accused me of being standoffish.

"You didn't have to pay for your own food, Zo. You looked like such an amateur. Everybody knows that when you go out with ballers—pun intended—you don't pay for anything."

"It was my food. It was only a burger and fries," I argued.

"Ughhhh! That's not the point, Zo! You didn't have to pay. Then they expected me to follow suit!"

I was sure they didn't. Angela's conscience did.

"I could've covered you if you didn't have it, Ang."

She banged her head against the steering wheel, exasperated. "Tomorrow—*if* we're lucky enough to get to hang out with them— you don't give Alton any shit, and you don't pay."

"Okay, Ang, but do you think your chances are better with Alton than Stenton? I mean, he seemed pretty adamant about being faithful to his girlfriend. And Alton practically begged for your attention. If you're going to have a willing adulterer, Alton seems to be your man."

Ang let out a hard laugh. "You can be so dense. Please, Zo! They all cheat! There is not one faithful man in the NBA, NFL, MLB or any other sport. They all fuck around!"

I nodded, taking in all of her words. I didn't argue. I never challenged Angela on things she professed to know and I had no knowledge of. The subject of men was a topic that she could run circles around my head with. I wasn't as experienced in relationships as she was.

After wrapping up that scolding conversation, I took to my dorm and engaged in a much needed nap. I slept for three hours, waking up in just enough time to get to class.

While walking back to my dorm for the night, I went into Facebook, still hoping to catch that video from Bernard. What I found immediately was a friend request and a new inbox. The friend request was from a *Notnet Srego*. That was a strange name and I initially thought it was spam until I went into the inbox and found a message from this person.

Have you taken that philosophy course yet?
Huhn?
I replied: **What's up with the profile name?**
Anonymity.

That was a bit strange to me. Because it was school related, I decided to accept it and hold off on replying. I then went into my timeline and found the video finally. I watched it several times before passing out that night, so proud that a piece of the talent in the choir's harmonious sounds came from my church.

27

Chapter Two

Zoey

The next day, we got invited to lunch with the guys again. And that day, I did temper my words and reactions to Alton's crassness at the diner.

"Yo, last week, I had this squirter!" he announced with so much emotion that he seemed pained, as we sat in the same booth.

"Fuck, bro, them squirters be the shit!" one of the two random guys, whose name I just learned was Travis, chimed in excitedly.

I had no idea what a squirter was. In fact, there were lots of topics they discussed that I had no clue of. It was as if we weren't there. I thought the purpose of going out with them was to interact with them—well, at least for Angela. We all sat in the same seats for the most part. Only today, Alton sat right next to Angela. Something was in the air.

"That bitch had *me* screaming when she was coming in my face," Alton croaked on a laugh, as did his friends. Stenton even chuckled at that comment. Alton tried to come up for air. "I...c-couldn't...keep...up, my dude!"

Angela and I gave each other quizzical glances. What in the world was a squirter and how could a woman do it in his face?

"So," Angela twirled her hair as she smiled sheepishly. "What's a squirter?"

The whole table went up in laughter. Even Stenton bashfully laughed and tried to hide his face. From the second of it I caught, I could see the sun shine through his smile. It was the most surprising thing I'd experienced. The camera guy, Drew, started banging the table and had the dishes clanging. Once again, Angela and I glanced at each other gravely confused.

"You must not be one," Drew choked out.

"Either that or you've been fucking jackasses," Alton plugged, sobering. "I can show you better than I can tell you. Holla atcha' boy."

They were like a bunch of twelve years olds at the table. Whatever a squirter was, it was a sexual reference and I didn't want to take part in a conversation like that with these clowns.

"Aye, Tiger," Alton called over to me, referring to my school's mascot. "I do twinsies. I can assess your squirting capabilities, too. I won't even charge you." He could no longer hold on to his mirth. He laughed until tears dripped from his eyes.

There was another bout of laughter. My eyes darted over to Angela, who was giggling herself. I couldn't do it. Wouldn't sit there and be demeaned by a pint sized jock. I promised Angela I wouldn't come back for him, but I didn't say I would stay and endure it. I peeled my last twenty from my purse, slapped it on the table and left the booth. This time I didn't give a bathroom excuse.

I went straight for the bench in the waiting area and parked it there. I must have been out there for almost ten minutes when I noticed Stenton Rogers coming through the double doors that let out to the waiting area. He stood by one of the doors, facing the glass. He wore army fatigue carpenter shorts and a salmon, V-neck cotton t-shirt with white *Converse* sneakers and a baseball cap. His style of fashion was…eclectic. I was not the one to critique fashion; I had not an ounce of creativity in me as far as that was concerned. This look worked for Stenton Rogers and his tattoos.

Those tattoos…

I was growing captivated by them once again and caught myself. I took a deep breath and shook my head, remembering why I was at this diner in the first place. My phone chirped an alert from Facebook. I checked to find a message from *Notnet Srego*. I'd totally forgotten about getting back to this "anonymous" new friend. I'd hoped it was a tutoring prospect. I could sure use the money.

The message read:

You never got back to me about the philosophy class.

I returned: **That's because I don't know who you are.**

The phone chirped. **You accept requests from random people?**

I didn't know how to respond to that. I didn't like how this jerk was questioning me.

I do it because I get a lot of requests for tutoring this way. You mentioned philosophy. What about it do you want to know? I tried being more direct.

I looked up, absentmindedly glancing over to Stenton's back, which was facing me. His head was still down, zoned into his phone. I diverted my attention to the other side of the area. I didn't want to get caught gawking at him—not that I was—but I just didn't want to give him or Angela the impression that I wanted him.

As I waited on Angela to finish up, my phone chirped again:

Is it true that we have no perfect idea of anything but of a perception?

Huhn?

I typed back: **David Hume? What about it? Do you need help building an argument... Pro or Con?**

Then the doors opened and Angela was the first to come through, wearing a conspirator's smile. Strangely, I was relieved. That meant I wouldn't be getting told off for walking out again.

"Ready, StentRo?" Alton called out.

Stenton turned to the crowd. I noticed his eyes glided over me briefly before facing Alton. His messy brows narrowed as he clapped hands with Alton.

"Yeah, man. I got shit to do. Gotta get across that bridge," Stenton murmured.

"Cool, man. I just got into something. I may be crashing at your place tonight," Alton spoke in a low tone.

I didn't hear much after that because I'd begun my trek out of there, but I noticed Drew was filming Alton again.

On our way to my campus, I discerned Angela wasn't as talkative as usual. Although I was grateful to have missed her wrath, this was strange for her.

"Everything all good?" I probed tepidly, not wanting to open Pandora's Box.

"Yeah," she let a long sigh escape.

My brows hiked. "You sure? You look like you were just charged with cleaning the sanctuary for a month."

"Yeah…" she sighed again, but more audibly behind the wheel. "I guess I'm feeling a bit blue because I'm finally convinced that I won't have Stenton."

"Why? Did something happen?" I was eager for answers now.

Is that why he came out in the waiting area before everyone else?

"Yeah," she sighed again, this time her shoulders sunk. "I've decided to mess around with Alton." Her eyes never left the road.

I almost gagged. "Why? How?"

"You were right." She shrugged. "He's been throwing hints since yesterday…well, actually all week. I guess I was so set on Stenton Rogers that I never paid much attention. And when Stenton tried to go all *one-woman-man* on me, I just gave up. Hey, if you can't have Prince Charles, Henry is always a viable stand in, right?"

Ang's voice was soft, dreamy even, which meant she'd given this some thought and there was no changing her mind, even if I mentioned the Tynisha woman to her. I knew this and I still attempted it.

"But Alton is still involved with the Tynisha Lang girl. Do you want to get into bed with a man with baggage like that, Ang?"

This time Angela did look at me. Within seconds, she exploded in laughter; her face turned red and all. "Zoey, I told you they all cheat. This is par for the course for Tynisha just as much as it is

Alton." Her eyes went back to the road. "But damn, I sure had my heart set on Stenton Rogers."

My phone pinged again. I opened the Facebook app and saw there was a new message from the anonymous philosophy inquirer.

I'm asking because I have no idea why someone like you hangs out with a girl who throws herself at men. I've been trying to figure it out. This time ol' David had it wrong. Not even my perception is perfect.

I dropped the phone like it burned my hands.

"What's wrong with you, Zoey?" Angela sounded alarmed next to me.

Is that—

I scrambled to get my phone from in between my seat and the door. I tapped the screen until I got to the profile of *Notnet Srego*. I mouthed the name until it clicked.

Notnet Srego is Stenton Rogers spelled backwards without his first initials!

Stenton

So fucking pretty. That was the only way I could described the girl. Fucking pretty. I could use the adjective beautiful, but it wouldn't accurately describe a female of her age. Of course she was beautiful, but there was something innocent and unblemished about her persona that kept her in the *pretty* lane. Maybe it was her untarnished honey skin that she wore naturally. Perhaps it was her long hair that was so natural and unkempt, but went with her style so well. It could have been her thin frame that was always covered in loose clothes, even when she wore short shorts.

I had no intentions of contacting her, or seeing her beyond the hours of my pre-season training. She was cute, but so were millions of women I'd encountered in my life, like her friend. I could never remember her friend's name, but her name I did. She had two: Zoey and Elizabeth. I didn't get the correlation, but couldn't forget them. On Facebook she was Zoey B. It wasn't until the dude at the club gave her whole government that I knew her formal name must have been Elizabeth Barrett. Maybe Zoey was just a middle name. Either way, it was a perfect name for her. It was innocent and carefree.

She was tight almost every time we got up after training that first week. Alton begged me to stick around while he pursued them, or let them catch his sloppy ass. I didn't want to. I wanted no parts of that type of energy. Not anymore. Her friend was aggressive as hell. I appreciated the ambition; I just wasn't interested. Alton was all for it. He enjoyed that fanfare. And me, from the moment I saw Zoey's eyes when I'd busted her ass on the phone, I enjoyed the intrigue. I'd been over to the beverage cart once or twice before then, but I never paid attention. When I'm training or practicing, I'm in a zone. The last thing I'm thinking about is ass. And from what I saw of both girls, they were young.

I didn't do young girls anymore. Contrary to what many think, young girls aren't the best fucks. When you reach a certain age, you realize the best sex is with a woman who knows how to use her body to bring you both pleasure, not just you. The ones who attempt to just bring *you* pleasure are empty. What makes you feel like the shit is a woman who is fucking your brains out while you're giving her the best dick she's ever had. Years ago, when I'd entered the league, I didn't get that piece of significance. I do now. And that young friend of Zoey's could offer me nothing more than decent head *if* she had skills. I had fuck partners. Those with talents I was guaranteed and discretion that I'd pledged years ago.

As I sat in the back of the Jeep, I waited for an answer from Zoey about my question of her hanging out with the likes of her friend. They were obviously not of the same agenda. I'd spent several days with them, eaten out with them the last two and it was clear Zoey didn't want to be near me or Alton. But why the fuck did she sign up for the program? I'd only known about it because the director of the country club asked our permission for them to work around us, for privacy reasons. I didn't have a problem so long as they didn't take pictures or talk to the press. They were signing the same confidentiality agreement as the rest of the staff, so that area was covered.

When I realized she wasn't going to respond right away, if at all, I got off of Facebook and went about my day. I had a busy schedule ahead, which wasn't anything new. My fucking summers never belonged to me. Of course with work, neither autumn, winter nor spring belonged to me either. It was just my busy yet mundane life.

As we pulled up to my ride, I grabbed the handle to get out. "Let me holla at you for a minute," Alton called from the front seat.

As we neared my car he murmured, "Listen, man, I appreciate you for hanging close these past two days."

"Ain't nothing, man." I went to give him some love.

He took it, but his face was balled up, he was struggling with something. I knew Alton. He was a fucking man in heat with a heart. I knew he'd be speaking about how he flirted with the young jawn over the past two days.

"Nah, man. I just appreciate you for not judging me. It's just that things with Ty and me are complicated, man. You know how that is," he attempted an alliance.

Never once when we agreed to off-season training together this summer did I imagine getting into sticky shit with him. We'd had a mediocre season and didn't make it to the championship, so we vowed to bring our best game next season. That preparation started just a couple of weeks after we were done with the previous season. We took no extended vacations. I'd barely celebrated my birthday. We kept our focus, but then there was this.

"Look, Al, what goes on between you and Ty is between the two of you. I know that you love her—and shit, the whole world knows she loves the fuck out of you. I've not been in your shoes. I don't know what that commitment shit feels like. My only advice to you is to be smart about this shit. That Tynisha is a rider. It ain't too much of that around and it damn sure ain't in those young ass girls. Just be careful. Be safe." I extended my arm and shoulder to buffer my sermon.

He took it with a wry smile. I knew Al. He was an emotional man; one that couldn't keep his dick in his pants. And because of this, Tynisha's hands always stayed in his pockets. They were three kids and six years in and still couldn't get shit right. When he fucked up—and that was a lot—his apology would always involve an insane expense. His lawyer always stayed in his ass about the sports cars, vacations, homes, shopping sprees, and jewelry he'd apologize with. Seemed to me it was cheaper to be single if you preferred variety like he did. But I knew there was something deep within that had committed and connected him to his lady that was not the case with any of the other women he fucked.

"I'm gonna get my shit together, man," he whispered, I was sure, so no one could hear his crying ass.

Alton had a gregarious and crude sense of humor, but his personality was far more sensitive. Very few saw that if they weren't paying attention. Al was good peoples. Many couldn't stomach him because of his asshole tendencies. I saw straight through that shit. It was something he did to appeal to others or to ward off threats. I didn't need the appeal, neither was I a threat to him.

"You all right with me, man. Don't sweat that shit."

"I'm gonna get that Angela. Give me to like tomorrow. She with it," he gloated.

That Al could sure switch it up. He couldn't help himself.

I laughed at his silly ass and checked my watch. "I gotta get outta here, man. Got shit to get into." I hopped into my truck and took off to Philly.

I headed straight to my place, an apartment in Bala Cynwyd, not too far from the job. There was paperwork I needed to go through before meeting with my attorney the following day. I had to be on top of my game for that shit, and knew he'd grill my ass for facts that would be found in these documents he had sent over a couple of days ago.

That Friday, I found myself at lunch with Zoey. It was somewhat coordinated seeing that Alton was finally fucking her girl, Angela. We sort of ended up waiting on them and had to preoccupy ourselves, and why not over food. I was sick of the diner. That was Al's speed. I'd had too much of that shitty food. We ended up at a *Sergue*, a restaurant I had my assistant arrange to open early so I could eat somewhere decent. It wasn't the fanciest of places; I wasn't on a date. Just somewhere I could have privacy and use as an alibi in case Al got caught again with another girl. One armor went with Al and the other stayed with me and sat at a nearby table.

Zoey sat across from me, just as irritated by the idea of having to wait on her girl to get fucked as I was. She was so damn pretty though. Her hair was straight today, but still unstyled and she wore small gold stud earrings, making me wonder how her understated look would pair with diamond studs instead of the beads of gold. She still had on her club uniform shirt and little khaki shorts that showed off her slender yet long legs. And although I was grateful to not be with yet another eager individual who wanted to put me on the running wheel, under the spotlight to perform, I couldn't help but notice her less than appealing disposition.

I had to spark up a conversation or I'd bail on Al's trifling ass. I couldn't lie, as much as I wasn't one hundred percent decided on her motive, Zoey still intrigued me. She was like a closed book and I figured I could use her as entertainment while I did this childish ass high school cover up shit with Al.

"So," I started, not knowing how to initiate a conversation with this young girl.

A young girl who I oddly found attractive.

"So," she parroted.

That tickled me.

"So," I sat up in my seat. "…you never answered my question."

"What question is that?" Zoey plucked at the table cloth.

"Why is it that a girl like you hangs out with a girl like Angela if you guys don't have the same agenda?"

I took notice of the ice on my *Audemar*. *It's time to have it cleaned.*

She sighed, "Well, that *girl* is my cousin."

My eyes rolled over to her. "Really?" My face fell towards the table. "So we have another set of young girls claiming to be related, thinking it's a way to express allegiance to one another. I'm from Newark; heard it all before."

Zoey rolled her eyes, "Try *my mother and her father are blood siblings* kind of cousins." She shook her head like she was frustrated and let out a breath. "Listen, I know Angela can be racy; I view it as charm, but she's a good person. We've been close since we were little and she's the realest person I know. She has a really good heart."

I snorted, "She has proclivities for chasing ballers with paper is what she has."

"No. That's not it. She's just been obsessed with 'Stenton Rogers,'" —she used air quotations—"…since we were in grammar school is all. She was excited when she learned you'd be local in Jersey this summer and could meet you." Zoey shrugged her shoulders. "She jumped at the opportunity. Proclivities…no. Overzealous fan, perhaps."

I motioned the space between us. "Being an overzealous fan will get you this: An opportunity in the program you're enrolled in this summer. A chance to chat. A proclivity will get you in a hotel room where she is with Al, doing exactly what they're engaged in right now." I pointed behind me towards the entrance of the restaurant. "So, you've explained to me how you're hanging out with the likes of Ms. Angela. What you've yet to share are your motives for tagging along."

Her head jerked. "Listen, I don't have ulterior motives. I simply won't leave my cousin hanging while she's with a man who could take advantage of her. And while I don't share the same desire to do what she's doing now, because I actually only allow men who give a crap about me to touch me, I don't judge her." Then her head cocked back and eyes squinted. "And if I recall, you have no room to pass judgment either. Every woman on the planet has seen all of your tattoos!"

Zoey inclined in her seat, coming close enough that I could smell the coconut of her fragrance, but not enough for me to taste it. I couldn't believe the excitement that spiked in my chest.

"Me, I get my men the old fashion way: boy meets girl...boy's attracted to girl...girl so happens to be attracted to him, too. Boy and girl do whatever they want together...mutually-consenting, mutually-desiring, and mutually-pursuing. I bet my situation is a lot more genuine and uncomplicated than yours. Unlike you, when men pursue me, they see me. They can experience my essence with no façade that I create to attract or maintain their interest. With you, women are drawn to those materialistic things you've acquired and never look within because they're too preoccupied by your manufactured exterior reeling them in. I don't have to be concerned with that. So, good luck to you, sir."

She was pissed. *And so fucking pretty.* I'll be damned if my dick didn't harden under the table at her jibe. I couldn't contain my chuckle. Later I would consider the truth in her rant. Right then I just wanted to enjoy her. She was like a little ball of energy with so much fire in her.

A Niña.

I took a swig of my water then asked. "What are you studying?"

Her neck twisted to face me. "Huhn?"

"You're a student at Princeton, right? What are you studying?"

"Finance," she tossed over. "Just ended my second year." Her voice was much lower now. She was affected, still fighting her anger.

"How old are you?"

"Twenty."

Fuck.

"What's that face for? Why did you wince like I insulted you?"

Because you haven't lived yet and have shown more substance than women I encounter that are twice your age.

"How old are *you*?" she pressed.

"Twenty-nine."

"Well, don't be concerned about me wanting you. Remember, I'm void of ulterior motives here." She slightly rolled her eyes over her folded arms.

So fucking pretty.

"So, tell me something about you," I forged ahead, finding myself entertained by this conversation.

"Hunh?" she asked again, confused.

"I'm sure you know everything about me. Shit, my life is laid out for the world. Tell me something about you."

"I know everything about *you?*" she scoffed. "My. How presumptuous we are."

"Yeah…isn't that why you chose this summer program?"

"No. And I only know what I need to know about you."

"Which is?"

"Your name, your height, the team you play for, and my cousin is going to have your babies—or *was* going to have your babies," she corrected herself just as the waiter came with our food.

I laughed. I mean, I cracked the hell up. *My babies? Me…kids?* Parenthood for me wouldn't be for another ten to fifteen years. I thought I'd be the type of father that would be rolled into my child's high school graduation in a wheelchair because that's how far off in the distance it would be for me.

"What? What's so funny?" Zoey frowned. "See, you don't know the other side of it. You just dribble the ball, smile every once in a while, and show off your fancy tattoos, but there are actually some women…and young girls, who take to that and they include you in their dreams."

Hmmmm…

"Well…we have no perfect idea of anything but of a perception," I say under my breath, not intending for her to catch it, per se. *No one knows me.* They all swore to have wanted to. "People just know what they want to know."

"And what is that supposed to mean?"

I glanced over at her. "It means that's all your cousin told you about me because that's basically all she wants to know."

And the fact that I'm paid out the ass.

"No. She knows about your tattoos. She knows what the ones on your arms mean, at least."

"Yeah," I agreed dismissively. "But that's not the totality of me. She doesn't know the essence of them. She doesn't know what ideas they were born out of, the significance of them, where they came from. She has no idea the state of mind I was in when I got them."

"She knows you're from Newark," she argued.

"Yeah, because those are easily obtained facts. But what about truly knowing people for who they are…through conversation and really getting to know them?"

"Well, people don't have the luxury of opportunity to do that with folks like you. You can only get what's accessible through Mr. Google. Besides, it's not like you're willing to give every interested person the opportunity to get to know you. You're a celebrity for crying out loud."

"I can't be too inaccessible if *you're* here, having lunch with me."

"Yeah," she rolled her eyes. "But that's because your bestie over there—"

"I don't have a bestie," I cut her off to clarify.

"But you and Alton are always together from what I see."

"That's because Alton is a good friend. We're teammates…partners in many respects, but I don't have a best friend."

"Well, that makes two of us," she uttered with her chin slightly in the air, appearing stubborn, and cute as hell.

"Angela isn't your best friend?"

She shrugged, still not facing me. "Angela has been my partner for years, but we're not the same people, we just have the same goal."

"Which is?" My interest was piqued.

There was a long pause. "I don't want to get into that." She picked up her fork. "Let's just eat." Then, with her head still toward her plate, her eyes coyly rolled up to me. "Oh, and I won't be using Google to get to know you."

Amused, I chuckled at that one as she ate her food. Did that mean she'd be trying to get to know me?

So fucking cute…

The following Tuesday, after training, I found myself alone with Zoey again. Alton and Angela took off to the hotel, but today, Zoey and I agreed to wait at the club for them to return, seeing that Alton and I drove into Jersey together. There were several amenities on site and somehow Zoey and I agree to swimming. I knew it was against the club's policy to have employees patron the grounds, but I admittedly threw my weight around for Zoey's clearance. She initially declined, saying she had no swimwear, but we were able to get her one with the assistance of the accommodating staff.

I was done changing and in the pool before her, taking a few laps. When I came up and wiped my eyes, I saw Zoey tiptoe in, wearing a bikini. My eyes strained. I'd never seen much of her body outside of her legs when she wore those khaki shorts, but this day I saw it all. And I do mean all; the bikini hid nothing. Zoey may have had slender legs and likely no ass in her clothes, but in true form, she was very busty. I mean, Cs type of busty. Her waist was small and hips somewhat narrow, yet undoubtedly feminine, and when she turned away from me to put her towel down on the bench, I saw her ass. Zoey had a nice plump ass. Not the type you saw when she approached you, but the kind that swallowed the small bikini bottom. One side of the cloth was wedged in her ass and I noticed the little dimple on her right cheek. I wondered was there a matching one on her left.

I found myself swallowing hard. When she turned around, I redirected my line of sight, suddenly feeling like I was invading her privacy. Shit, Zoey had a fucking body. Her hair was out and wild as she walked to the opposite edge of the pool and sat. I couldn't help but notice the wide belly button of her flat belly. The bikini they managed to find her either fit her perfectly or was a size or two too small because her breasts looked to be screaming for release. My dick twitched at that thought.

"Is it cold to you?" Zoey called over. "It feels cold to me."

I needed to switch gears here; it wasn't that type of party.

"You're just gonna have to jump in," I returned before throwing my own body in for another lap.

Minutes later, after Zoey got acclimated to the water and swam a few laps herself, we found ourselves in the same area of the pool. I was on my back floating on top of the water.

"How did you learn to do that?"

I stood straight. "Pardon me?"

"How did you learn to float?" she asked.

"Do you know how to back stroke?"

She nodded her head, yes.

"It's the same concept."

She shrugged. I didn't know what that meant. I didn't want to offer to teach her because that would have meant touching her, but she wasn't giving me any clues as to what the fuck she was asking.

I motioned my hands above the water to gesture my confusion.

"Well...show me." Zoey's tone wasn't salacious. She even seemed a bit resentful for having to ask.

I waded over to her. "You have to try to lay flat on your back. I'm going to hold you from beneath the water to be sure you don't sink. Is that okay?" I asked, looking directly into her eyes, trying to avoid her bountiful breasts.

Damn, they're beautiful.

Zoey nodded and managed to lay on top of the water. I immediately took her between her shoulder blades and the back of her thighs.

"Straighten your spine and extend your legs to lengthen your body. Stretch out your arms, too, but not over your head." Zoey did as I asked. "Your body's alignment affects your ability to float. The human body is made up of about two-thirds water. This means your body's composition...its density is similar to the water we're in now. Anything with a higher density than water will sink. That being said, you don't have to do much to get your body to float on top of the water. Your body's natural inclination in water like this is to float."

She stared at her toes while I spoke, and I could feel her trying to relax.

I continued, "You're doing a good job at trying to relax. That's the first step. Look up. Good. Now, slowly fill your lungs to capacity with air. That's going to help balance you."

As Zoey pulled in air, her breasts pushed out of the water, and seemingly into my face…maybe not so much, but at least that's how it seemed.

"Good," I continued. "Now let it out and do it again. Slowly. Put more weight into your shoulders until your head floats naturally. Okay, now your arms can extend over your head…just slightly."

Fuck. Looking at her arms coming together over her head was almost my undoing. I needed to get it the fuck together. *She's a young girl—fucking twenty!* But Zoey didn't seem shy or embarrassed to be almost naked and alone with a man in a pool. She didn't seem the least bit self-conscious about her body, neither was she flaunting it. And that fucked with my head.

"Use your abdominals; they'll help with the balance. Don't forget to kick your legs, but not wildly." I kept with my instruction until I could see her progression in staying above the water. I tried to keep quiet to allow her to focus on her balance.

When she was damn near floating alone, I asked, "Do you have a boyfriend?"

Zoey's eyes shot up to me, but she didn't lose her balance, neither did she change her breathing pattern. I wasn't planning on asking her that, but so many things about her intrigued me. Between Zoey paying for her own lunch at the diner last week and our conversation at the restaurant, I was somewhat fascinated by her.

"Yes," she answered evenly.

"Where is he when you're here, playing sidekick to your cousin during the day?"

"He works," she supplied quickly, trying to maintain her breathing pattern. "He's kind of sort of not my boyfriend."

That statement took me by surprise. I found my face wrinkling. Zoey released her weight over the water, losing her balance to stand.

"Thanks for that," she offered with a smile. "I think I finally get the idea. I'm going to practice. I'll have it down pat before you know it."

She sidestepped my question and reaction to her answer to it. I didn't get the impression she did it deliberately; she just didn't find her response significant enough to dwell on, I had supposed. But I, for some stupid reason, wanted to dig.

"What do you mean he's not your boyfriend? Either he is or isn't. I didn't know there was an in between."

Zoey paused to consider my comment. She shrugged before sharing, "It's just something that we fell into. Someone I found myself dating." She quieted for a moment, contemplative again. She shifted next to me, resting her elbows on the ledge of the pool. "He's a nice guy…"

"But?"

"But…I don't know…there's not that *wow* factor there. I want that *wow* factor…," she gestured with a swing of her arms, "…with a guy. I've had it before and know it exists." Her eyes fell. "It just doesn't exist with him. He's really nice, very responsible…good man of God. So, we just hang out." She stretches her eyelids.

Man of God. She'd mention God and church before. *Is that important to her?* And what was up with that *wow* factor? Was that code for simple attraction or sexual chemistry?

"So, have you had a lot of those *wow* factors?" I attempted covertly. I found myself desperate with wanting to know.

I didn't mean to pry, but Zoey was throwing me off with her signals. It would have been easy to dismiss her as a groupie, an opportunist, but that didn't match her actions. I'd given her several chances to out herself. But nothing.

Although she didn't call me out on my prying, the way Zoey lifted her brow told me she had a clue as to the nature of my inquiry.

"I've had enough," she answered and swam off.

I stayed in place for a while, stumped while Zoey took more laps, appearing content in solitude. Eventually I decide to do the same. *This girl is an anomaly.*

At one point when I came up for air, I heard, "So where's *your* girlfriend?"

I swiped the water from my eyes and saw Zoey floating while holding on to the ledge. "Huhn?"

"Your girlfriend. Where is she? And is she okay with you hanging out at the country club after training while Alton cheats on his girlfriend?"

Oookay. "Well, first of all, I don't know what the situation is between Alton and Tynisha."

"The world is confused about the situation with Alton and Tynisha," she quickly returned.

"I don't think Alton and Tynisha are quite in the know about the situation between Alton and Tynisha, in spite of that reality show bullshit." I detested that fucking show. They're horrible for relationships. "But *I* don't have a girlfriend."

Zoey's arm slipped from the ledge and she lost her balance. We were in ten feet so she had to catch herself quickly.

Her eyes were wild and her breathing matched. "But you told Angela—"

"I didn't tell Angela shit," I quickly and calmly retorted. I had a feeling this would come up the more time we spent with each other. I don't lie, but I also don't rat.

Zoey issued a long and nasty glower. I decided to give her a moment. I was prepared. She then started to shake her head, exasperated.

"What's the problem? Why are you looking like it's about to be a *murder was the case that they gave me* type of situation here?"

"Because the only reason she's with Alton now is because she's under the impression that you have a girlfriend and there's no chance with you…because you won't cheat on your girlfriend. But technically it's Alton that's cheating on his girlfriend and…" she shook her head, out of breath. "This stuff is so messy. *I*-I just don't understand it." Zoey pinched the bridge of her nose.

"I simply wasn't interested in Angela." I found myself wanting to argue my point to this…*damn-near* teen. "And Alton picked it up…and he also picked up she was game for anything. That's why she's with him." My voice was even, but my tone choppy.

"So you don't have *any* girlfriends…no one of significance?"

"No."

"Well, are you dating anyone?"

"Well, yeah. I'm a healthy man. I date."

"Are you dating anyone serious?"

How many times was she going to ask the same question?

"No. Not really."

"What's *not really*—no?" she transitioned in thought. "Answer this: Who was your last date?"

"A woman…from the industry. We've been skirting around the idea of formally dating, even went out last week. It's taking time, but time is necessary for this type of set up."

"What's *formally dating*? Either you're dating or you're not."

"Formally dating is announcing it to the public. I hate that shit."

"Why?"

"It's manufactured. My real life isn't for public consumption," I more or less mumbled. Truth be told, I didn't have much of a personal life. I'd been too paranoid about having it dissected by the public.

"So, this woman…," Zoey continued. Her eyes far softer—timid even—expressing vulnerability for switching gears. "…what are your reservations? Why are you stalling?" Zoey looked away, trying to appear less interested than I knew she was.

Great question.

"I don't know. She's been around. And while I don't really trip off a woman's track record, I certainly don't want the world to know who my lady has fucked."

"And?"

Damn. She could sense my apprehension.

"*And* I don't like arranged relationships. If I'm going to pursue a woman, I don't need my publicist or hers involved."

"So, this would be for publicity?" Zoey didn't mask her curiosity this time.

"For me it would. For her, maybe not. She's been consistent over the years in expressing her fixation with *Stenton Rogers*."

"And that's not the real you," Zoey noted pensively.

She's a quick study.

She shrugged. "Then give her the opportunity to get to know the real you. You can't hide behind that *woe is me* cry forever. You already have her earnest attention. That's half the battle. Make it work for you." Zoey glanced down at the water, withdrawing eye contact. Her eyes slanted as though she'd been struck with a thought. "Your fears are greater than your reality." It was delivered like more of a statement than a question. "Sometimes we allow our fears to stifle us. If you want companionship, you're going to have to lower your guard, just a smidge, to give it a try. If you hide up high on your mountain of fear and paranoia, no one can reach you."

Her statement jarred me. I couldn't believe that nugget of wisdom was executed by a damn youngster. I'd never had a woman encourage a relationship with another woman; they were too busy making an opportunity for themselves. I had been struggling with fear of trusting women. Women with access to my realm of lifestyle were bred. Their faces, color and shapes varied, but their motives never did. Men were the same for that matter. Everyone had a fucking agenda. Since cleaning up my image, I've cleaned up my contact list, too.

Even Erika was schooled by her mother on how to bag an athlete. She'd had one or two in her day as well. I wouldn't be the first baller Erika fucked with and I doubt if I'd be the last. What I did know for sure was that I didn't want to be a part of that circus. Especially having run into this… Niña.

I studied her lips. Images of them *and my* body parts ran through my mind in rapid succession. They were all immoral…for this young girl.

"You think your cousin would approve that message?"

Zoey snorted, "No more than I approve the one she's giving your boy, Alton Alston, right now." She rolled her eyes softly.

Fucking pretty.

Our phones went off almost simultaneously. Alton and Angela

were done. And unfortunately, so was my time with this Zoey girl. I left the pool having made a sound decision. I'd be putting Erika's ass on the back burner. Her body may have acquired several accolades and titles, but her conversation and intellectual measure couldn't hold a candle to this young girl, Zoey. My quandary was what I felt having spent the past two days with Zoey and how that fucked with my head, because wanting Zoey was ridiculous.

Two days after swimming with Stenton, we found ourselves at one of the restaurants at the country club. And while the atmosphere wasn't as charged with coldness and mutual resentment at having to babysit each other, Stenton and I weren't exactly friends either. At least not until the end of that day.

As I ate chicken parmesan that had a bit too much sauce and not enough cheese, I kept my head in my plate. We'd been spending lots of early afternoons together and I still wasn't able to give him direct eye contact unless I was reaming him out for one of his back-handed remarks.

Stenton wasn't disrespectful to me, at least not like I felt Alton was. He did however, have a potty mouth: the type of vulgarity that matched his scandalous tattoos. Even with that observation, I secretly thought fondly of how he expressed himself unabashedly. He was brutally honest about whatever we discussed, and there was something comforting about that characteristic.

And his body...*whoa!* I'd hoped he didn't catch my stumble

when we got out of the pool that day. His chest was wide and defined, but not bulky. His tattooed torso glistened from water running down his chest and abdomen. I'd gotten an up close and personal opportunity at viewing the various scripts, Chinese lettering and other graphics driving my curiosity. His trunks hung low…*like really low*…and I saw the muscular outline of his pelvis. I felt throbbing between my legs and nearly jumped a 180 degree turn to stop my ogling. I'd never thought I'd be privy to his body like that. It felt invasive—more invasive than the conversations we'd taken on in the pool.

It stung when he told me he didn't have a girlfriend. I felt like Angela and I had been duped into something we didn't sign up for. But the more I thought about it, I realized what Angela had going on with Alton, we did ask for; it was the very thing she was seeking with Stenton, only he wasn't interested.

Then I debated telling her. My mind raced for hours after the revelation. The decision not to, ruled out. I thought telling her that Stenton and Alton lied would cause her to feel less appealing. I didn't want her to think she wasn't good enough for any man. Stenton was not God. She could move on and she did…with Alton.

My phone rang, calling my attention back to the table. I checked the number and saw that it was Bernard. I sent it to voicemail, figuring I'd call him back when I was alone. I wasn't exactly prepared to share that I was at a country club, having lunch with *Stenton Rogers*. He'd likely think I'd lost all my scruples. *I* wouldn't have even believed me.

I turned all of this over in my mind as I forked through my food.

"Linkin Park, huhn?" I heard from across the table. It annoyed me to no end what I felt when I heard his tenor most times. My throat would close up and pulse would race simply at the sound of his voice.

"I didn't catch that," I replied.

"Your ringtone…"Numb"." His chin was angled to the table, but his eyes were on me.

My body was inclined to my plate as I peered up at him. "Oh, yeah. I like them," I offered noncommittally.

"You must more than like them if you've selected them as your ringtone."

"What's wrong with me liking them? Because I'm a black girl and they're a rock band?" My tone was derisive.

I got so annoyed with people finding it unethnic of me to like genres other than gospel, R&B and rap. I mean, isn't there more to life than those three groups of music? Are they the only ones blacks subscribe to?

Stenton's mouth drew up as did his eyes when he shook his head. "Do you like Coldplay?"

"Some of their stuff. They can be a little too soft melodically for my taste. I like some of the harder stuff...the ones pushed from the gut." I wasn't ashamed to speak about my peculiar interests.

"Funny...I just knew you'd say "Yellow" is your favorite."

"It's...cute. "Harder to Breathe" makes you feel. I prefer angst to my rock, or at least something that makes me feel."

Stenton scoffed. "I don't consider Maroon 5 a rock band. They're dope and all, but they can go too soulful."

"And what's the matter with that? All music can be soulful." I found my neck jerking.

He scanned the ceiling, letting out a silent chuckle. My stomach did flips when his teeth unveiled. I hated how whenever Stenton smiled, it felt like the sun moved beyond the clouds. And when he smiled with his eyes on me, I felt the cascade of water from the most refreshing spring. I saw the oasis where the sun met the water and created the best ambiance nature had to offer. I saw every detail of it. His smile was that beautiful.

"Right now "Secret" is what I feel," he shared, sobering his voice and descending his cheeks, but the slant in his eyes remained.

His tone was unmistakably scandalous. I had no idea how to take that comment.

"Is that what you feel about the girl you took out last week?" My eyes fell to my plate and I pushed my food around.

"Definitely not," he answered before taking a short breath. "Where did you pick up rock?"

I lifted my shoulders before releasing them. "My mom cleaned houses in the summer in Baskin Ridge. Her customers had children who were having trouble in school. She mentioned how I could probably help. One summer, I made $500 doing something that came natural to me. I kept going back at the request of the parents. Their children listened to a different kind of music and I caught on to it quickly. One year their dad brought home *KISS* t-shirts signed by Gene Simmons himself."

"Dope." Stenton nodded. His hands were in his lap, and his eyes were in his plate. "So, you tutored?"

"Yeah. Still do. Make a few pennies from it, too."

He nodded again, appearing to absorb my words. It was weird…like he was really interested. I figured everyone had a story.

"So how do you know rock?"

He exhaled as he sat up in his seat. "When they learned I could ball, the first thing they determined was they needed to keep my black ass out of Newark outside of the school year. So, during summer and spring and winter breaks I'd stay with families of coaches to train in upstate New York, Connecticut, Delaware…all over. I learned lots of shit; music, art…a few languages. It felt like being passed around, but I got exposed to different cultures and eventually learned how to use it to my benefit."

"Do you listen to hip-hop and R&B?"

Stenton lowered his chin. "Zoey, I'm from Newark, NJ; of course I listen to rap and R&B. They just aren't the only two types of music I enjoy. I really dig rock. It allows you to lower your inhibitions. You don't have to dance to it, and if you do, you don't need rhythm. It's also all-inclusive. Whenever I go to rock concerts, I'm always welcomed and not because I'm *Stenton Rogers* either. It's because they are a group of misfits who were once the cast-asides of society. So they take to underdogs. They accept all people."

"Is that why Angela said you're referred to as the NBA rocker boy?"

He nodded. "At first it started off as a locker room jibe, but as the years passed, and…incidences occurred, the moniker seemed to fit. And I never really gave a fuck about what people thought of me anyway." He tossed his lips into the air.

"So, how do you know about philosophy?"

He went for his glass and took a gulp. "I know a little bit about everything. When you're a promising all-star player, you're given tools most kids from your city are incapable of dreaming about. When my talent was discovered, I was provided tutors to keep me afloat in school. I had curriculums that covered the state requirements and were catered to my learning ability."

"Nice. Having everything handed to you." I tried to hide the sarcasm in my voice.

"Nope. I had to go to class. I had to perform well academically. I only had two responsibilities: maintain my studies and maneuver the ball. My schedules were set for me and that's all I did for years. I knew guys in some of the ball camps I went to who didn't fare well with school." He shrugged. "I so happened to be a sponge and soaked up everything, but only retained what interested me. I didn't have much of a life outside of *dribbling a ball*, as you so eloquently put it last week at the restaurant. Sometimes it was my escape from the court when there was too much pressure from others' expectations. I had great tutors, which is why I can respect what you do. If it weren't for them, I wouldn't have made the grades that I did because I put in so many hours on the court."

"Hmmm…" I chewed on the inside of my lip.

Stenton angled his head to the side. "What's never brought up is the controversy during the summer I got drafted. America had so much to say about my decision to skip college. I had been offered a full ride to Rutgers, UCLA, Howard, Florida State and a few other schools."

"For basketball," I asserted.

Stenton shook his head. "Those schools were for academic achievements. I didn't name the ones for sports. But everyone seems to Google those offering scholarships for balling. The same info can be found about my academic accomplishments. I could have gone either way. I simply went with my passion. Why not circumvent the journey and go straight to my passion?"

Why did I suddenly feel like crap? Who knew he was more than a dribbling jock? The man with the filthy mouth, whorish behavior, and tattoo shell had a brain, too?

"What do you know about…trigonometry?" I quizzed.

"Ah, man, that sine, cosine and tangent 'where a D is constant' bullshit bored the hell out of me. I was a *B* student at best there." Stenton chuckled.

"Okay. What about…quantum mechanics?" I took it up several notches.

"That's the more modern science. I'm from the old school where we learned elementary particles, atoms, molecules, substances…metals, crystals and other groups of matter. Not that New Age shit."

I took in a forkful and chewed while looking him directly in the eye. "You never answered my question though," I challenged slickly, feeling the need to get one off on him. He was probably okay in school, but he wasn't Zoey type of good.

Stenton rolled his eyes as he sighed and dropped his fork onto his plate, making a clash of it. "Quantum mechanics pretty much provides an extensive framework for several features of the *modern* periodic table. One thing it encompasses is the activities of atoms during chemical bonding. That *bullshit* has been substantial in the development of many modern technologies. Blah…blah…blah."

My mouth dropped. "Jeez Louise! You're a geek!"

Stenton snorted. "I'd much rather be called a cerebral rocker baller," he murmured as he went back for his food.

I realized from that conversation that there was more to Stenton than just his tattoos and a ball. Why was it that no one talked about that aspect of his abilities? Why was he never quizzed on trivia during interviews? It would provide a great spin for shows and make their talk a lot less mundane. I'd guessed that Stenton was right when he said people only know what they want to know.

I, on the other hand, wanted to know more.

My fixation with Stenton took off at that point. I found that he occupied my thoughts throughout my day, no matter where I was or what I was doing. I could be in class and found myself etching his name, at church and itched to check his timeline, and/or out with the guy I was seeing at the time, Andrew, and wondering what Stenton's conversations were like while on a date.

Almost immediately, our friendship seemed to have evolved to written communication via inboxes on Facebook. They were random, fun, and exciting all at once. I'd nervously initiate mine and hold my breath, awaiting his response. I knew he was a busy man doing I had no idea what, but busy.

Me: **I have a question that you can't be offended by.**
I waited for his reply.
Stenton: *I'm game. Do you.*
Me: **Ummmm... Are those your real teeth?**
My heart beat wildly in my chest. It was a burning question I'd had since the first time I'd seen his smile. His real smile. Not only was I struck by how long it took to experience it, but also by its radiance. The brilliance of Stenton's smile was blinding. I was growing attached to it. He was generous with sharing it with me. Experiencing that man's smile was like discovering a crisp well on a parching pilgrimage. It instantly decompressed all stressors.
Stenton: *What the fuck Zo? LMAO*
Me: **IJS! They're kinda big...too nicely aligned.**
Stenton: *And so are your boobs but you don't see me inquiring about their authenticity.*
Me: **Don't be pigheaded, you dork.**
I wouldn't speak on the sensation that flashed in my core at his

comeback. That was private along with the rest of the inexplicable things he caused me to feel without his hands...or mouth.

Stenton: ***Don't go getting all prudish. I used to get teased a lot as a kid about my big ass choppers. Trust me when I say I've grown into them.***

Me: **I don't believe you.**

Stenton: ***Don't believe what?***

Me: **That your teeth are real.**

Stenton: ***I'll prove it to you.***

Me: **How?**

Stenton: ***I don't know. I'll think of something. And then you'll prove your boobs are real.***

Me: **Dude! I'm poor. My parents can't afford a boob job!**

Stenton: ***But you studied around rich people. Who's to say you didn't have a sponsor?***

Me: **Touché**

I tossed my phone in my purse before Andrew returned to the car and found me entranced in it. He stopped in *WaWa* to get cash for our date this evening. The entire conversation with Stenton had me blushing so hard my face hurt. Too many racy thoughts were running through my mind to continue this conversation. The first being how I would inspect this man's teeth.

Me: **I did it.**

I typed and hit *send*. Butterflies took flight in my belly. I was taking a risk, but he was the first person I wanted to share this news with for some crazy reason.

It would be over an hour before I got a reply.

Stenton: ***Did what?***

Me: **I broke up with Andrew.**

Stenton: ***Who the hell is Andrew?***

Me: **My boyfriend, you geek.**

Stenton: *Still no wow factor?*

He remembered? Excitement kindled throughout my body.

Me: **None.**

Stenton: *LMAO What finally did it?*

Me: **We were at his place and he was flipping through the music channels. He was trying to find music to set the mood I guess and skipped over the rock channel (btw "Love Somebody" was playing) to find another genre. I asked him to turn back. He said no and that he wanted jazz. I grabbed my stuff and left. I mean, who doesn't feel like getting "wowed" off Maroon 5?**

I held my breath after hitting send, wondering if I gave too much. I must have read my message twice before Stenton's response came through.

Stenton: *Maybe he thought you wanted to get messy like they did in the video. All jokes aside... Who in the hell needs music to set the mood? You can make your own sounds to get off. He's a fucking asshat...an asshat that doesn't like to get messy apparently.*

My head dipped back and I laughed to the point of tears, never mind the bit of arousal I felt when I momentarily allowed my mind to wander to the sounds Stenton alluded to.

Me: **Are you busy?**

Stenton: *Kinda. In a meeting with my McDonalds reps.*

Oh, noooo!

Me: **Stenton! That's pretty important. Go! Stop inboxing!**

Stenton: *My lawyer's a fucking pit bull. He's here putting fire under their asses.*

I didn't know how to respond to that. He was busy. Although I wanted to chat more, had endless questions and topics to explore, he was in fact busy. My fingers tapped the wall to the right of me, contemplating.

Stenton: *I know you're making that clicking sound with the back of your mouth. It's cool Zo. The conversation is flowing. I'll end our conversation here but let's hang out tomorrow. You can give me more details on your breakup.*

I stopped the sound when I realized I was making it. It was a bizarre call on his part. It felt like a small and intimate fact only someone who paid attention would catch. *Did Andrew know I had that bad habit?* My mind raced with what that meant.

Me: **Okay.**

Stenton: **And Zo...you could've text me with this. You would've gotten a quicker response.**

Okay. This is my last message to him.

Me: **I don't have your number, geek!**

Stenton: **215/555-9658**

Chapter Three

Zoey

It was the middle of August, only a week before we were due to complete *Working Toward the Stars*. When Angela was done with whatever she was doing with Alton, we drove her car to church. Our cousin, Karen, texted us the night before asking to meet her there when we were done with our summer internship.

Of course, she wouldn't know we were done hours earlier, but had to wait for Ang's extra curriculum activities to conclude before we were actually considered done for the day. What concerned me was her demeanor. Ang wasn't her usual chatty self. She seemed preoccupied as her oscillating eyes faced the road.

"Was it that bad?" I teased.

"What was that?" she barely paid me a glance.

"Today…with Alton. Was it that bad that you don't have much conversation for me?"

"Oh, that asshole?" She sucked her teeth. "Not only is he selfish, not wanting to go down on me, he also likes to try the most awkward positions. He's a total bust, that little guy."

I couldn't fight my grimace.

"TMI, Ang," I warned.

Ang waved the entire conversation off. "Nah, I'm just thinking about what this meeting could possibly be about. You know Aunt Jenny and Uncle Al are going to flip when they find out about the pregnancy."

"Yeah, but we've talked to her. I think we were pretty successful in our encouragement," I reminded her.

"Yeah," Ang sighed. "I hope so."

When we arrived inside the dining room of the church, we learned how wrong we both were. Karen was there with our aunt, Jenny, who wasn't as bubbly as usual. As soon as Karen laid eyes on us, she leaped to her feet and made her way over by the door of the large room.

When she was just inches away, Aunt Jenny called out, "Hi, ladies. I know this is short notice, but we need to get this wedding planned and done." Her chunky arms waved animatedly in the air when she finally approached us. Karen looked mortified. Her eyes were swollen and red. Whatever she was going to share with us, Aunt Jenny intercepted it with her own agenda. "Now, Karen here couldn't decide on which of the two of you would be her maid of honor. I have a feeling she doesn't want to hurt anybody's feelings, but I don't have time for this. I wasn't given proper notice, ya' know. Let's flip a coin. Call out heads or tails," she charged while rummaging through her purse.

Angela and I turned to each other, now appearing just as mortified as Karen. She did it. She let them set the path for her. Our pep talk did nothing, or not enough. Karen was just a year younger than Angela and me. We grew up in the same church community whose views on marriage being the answer to pregnancies outside of wedlock were outdated.

Karen and her boyfriend, BJ, had been together for three years and were in love, but hardly ready to commit to marriage. She'd been keeping the pregnancy from her parents for almost a month.

She had only told us last week. Karen pretty much shared our views on delaying marriage to explore life. But she was also still in high school.

BJ, on the other hand, was the organist at our church and was in his second year at Middlesex County College. Her parents thought she was too young to date him at the beginning of their relationship, which in hindsight was true. Nonetheless, they dated and got pregnant. When she broke the news to Angela and me after Bible study last week, we took her out for dinner and attempted to give her arguments to present to her family in the event they tried to force marriage. When we'd left Karen that evening, she seemed determined and unwavering, Angela and I both agreed in a subsequent conversation. We were wrong.

"You got it, Zo," Angela sulked, unable to squeeze those words out.

I didn't care about the title. I was devastated by this centuries-old practice of marrying young people off simply because an unexpected pregnancy had occurred. I was seething, so upset that I didn't respond. Instead, I made an about-face and left them in the dining room.

This can't be the cloth I'm cut from.

As I stomped my way to Angela's car, I heard ruckus behind me. I turned to find Angela on my heels, wearing a similar scowl. Her flip-flops flapping up dust in her wake. Then I saw my Aunt Jenny burst through the side door, clearly angry.

"You don't talk to me like that, young lady! I am your auntie!" Angela didn't even glance back before she reached for the door. "I'll call your momma and see what she has to say about this, young lady!"

"Let's go, Zo!" Angela screamed, waking me from my stupor.

I jumped in the passenger seat, and before I could strap up, Angela was peeling out of the parking lot.

"What in the world happened in there, Ang?" It was my turn to flog my arms.

"I cursed her ass out three shades of Sunday," Angela hissed as she kept her eyes on the road.

I knew we both shared the same vehemence against our family's archaic practices, but never had we disrespected anyone. The rims of Angela's eyes were pink. She was about to cry.

"What's going on here, Angela? What would make you curse at Aunt Jenny?"

"Because I want her to prepare my mother for what's waiting for her if she tries to pull that marriage shit on me!" The first tear spilled. Less than a half a second later, the stream came.

"Ang, how long have you known you're pregnant?" At this point, I was struggling to keep my food down. There were just too many surprises in one day.

"Long enough to get this over with. You're the first to know. I have to tell everyone else now."

"Whatever it is you're writing must be pretty important," his voice held its usual gruff and heaviness.

My mouth collapsed as my eyes focused in on Stenton. I was squatting against the wall, staring up at his fierce visage. He was freshly showered and in a grey t-shirt and cargo shorts with a baseball cap turned to the back. Having less of his tattoos exposed and two large diamond studs pinned to his ears, Stenton resembled a rapper rather than a rocker today.

And his scent… *God help me.*

I must have been that engaged to not catch him coming.

"What do you mean?"

He gave me a one-sided grin. "You're making that clicking sound with the back of your throat."

Great.

I collapsed my face into my hands. The last thing I expected to happen, happened in that instant; I realized I could no longer deny my extreme attraction to this man. My life couldn't get any more chaotic.

"Hey...hey," he softly sounded off. "What's going on with you? And why are you over here in the corner like you're hiding from someone?"

I am! From you.

I brought my head up to meet his quizzical gaze. Confusion etched his face and I couldn't say I didn't know why. I was being awfully dramatic. Then he took me by the wrist, igniting fire in my core. He'd only touched my arm with his calloused hands and I was able to feel it all over.

"Let's chat about it over a meal." I managed to stand without giving away my weakened knees. *Stupid body!* "I know you're starved. Your hungry ass always is."

"I was waiting for Angela." I sort of lied.

I was waiting on Angela. I'd assumed she was saying her final goodbyes to Alton...in the moral manner. I'd hoped. But the other truth was I was avoiding Stenton.

"She and Alton were in a heated conversation when I passed them. He knows I'm going to grab a bite. They'll find us."

"Mr. Rogers!" I heard someone call just beyond Stenton. "Mr. Rogers..."

Within seconds Jeffrey appeared and you could see the revelations—accurate or not—visibly running through his mind. "Oh," was all he could say initially.

And initially I panicked, but then I remembered that I'd made it to the end of the summer and didn't need to care. I was so stressed that I didn't realize getting kicked out wouldn't have had the same effect as it would have earlier on.

"Ms. Barrett," Jeffery greeted pointedly, I'd guessed indirectly asking for an explanation for me speaking with Stenton Rogers "after hours." That explanation would never come. I was too preoccupied to care that I didn't care.

"Jeffery?" Stenton called his attention from me. "You wanted me for...?"

"Oh...oh!" He chuckled, pushing up his frames. "I'll be on vacation all next week and I know you'll be done here when I return. I was hoping you could sign this jersey for my son, Christopher Peter." Jeffrey held up a toddler size *76er's* jersey.

Stenton smiled politely as he took the jersey from Jeffrey. "It'll be my pleasure. And I'm sure Elizabeth here won't be penalized if I take her to lunch. She's been extremely gracious my entire time here. I'd like to thank her."

I couldn't help my gasp. What was Stenton doing?

Jeffrey's pleading eyes shot over to me. I guess he didn't want me to decline Stenton's offer. "*Su*-sure! That's perfectly fine. Please… enjoy, Ms. Barrett."

As soon as Stenton was done being Stenton Rogers, we headed over to the restaurant. Once we were seated with menus, Stenton didn't hesitate.

"So, what were you documenting in the gym?" He gave a reverse nod, gesturing where we'd just left.

"It's called journaling, geek." I rolled my eyes.

"Okay," he muttered as he straightened in his seat. "May I ask what has you so affected that you're journaling here?"

I fought with if I should share. The battle had a short life. Once I whispered the first word, the remainder came out spiritedly. I told him about my family's obsolete beliefs and how it had caught up to my generation with Karen. I left Angela out of the conversation feeling she was too close to an associate of Stenton's—or more like it was a sore topic. When I was done, I exhaled. I don't know what I expected, but it felt odd when Stenton sat back in his chair and didn't utter a word for a while.

I'd wondered if he'd paid attention until he asked, "What are your aspirations?"

Wa-what?

"Aspirations?"

"Yeah…" The waiter came to take our order, but Stenton raised his finger dismissing him and the uniformed man scurried off. "When we were at *Sergue*, you mentioned your goals and that they mirrored Angela's."

He remembers that?

"Oh…ummm." I was floored. He had been listening. I wasn't expecting that. "Well, to break this cycle of…societal norms in Christendom. The ultimate goal of a woman shouldn't be marriage, having babies, and making a home for her husband. I want to travel the world, explore the wonders of it. I want to find who Zoey is and why God put her here. I know my purpose supersedes the small box my family and church leaders try to put me and other young women into."

"So, how are you going to prove it? What's your plan?"

"First, to stay away from marriage long enough to find out if it's even for me. Second, to finish undergrad, move on to *Wharton* for my MBA, and get a good job to help my family out. I want to provide relief for my parents, and that can't happen if I'm in some man's house, cooking, cleaning, and making his babies."

Stenton nodded meditatively. Maybe because I needed to make my voice heard, but for some reason, I felt like I'd connected with him.

"Let's get you something to eat. You'll need your energy to lead the next wave of the feminist movement." He cracked a playful smile.

"I'm no feminist, Stenton!" I feigned being offended.

"Good, because if you were, I'd have to insist on you paying for this expensive ass meal we're about to partake in."

I laughed so hard that I snorted like a pig, unabashedly.

"Nah," he attempted to sober up from our laughter. "I think you can do whatever you want, Zo. If you have plans to assist your family instead of pursuing what your family views as traditional goals, go for it."

"I know I have to strategize better, but I at least know what I don't want."

"You may not have your plans organized from A to Z, but you have a vision and passion. That combination is what brings dreams into fruition. You're a spitfire." He snorted and then inclined in his seat. "My mom used to have this little mutt. She couldn't have been more than six inches off the ground and weighed less than five pounds. Mom called her Niña. And she would fuss every dog out in the neighborhood…I mean even the biggest Rottweilers that were chained to their yards. My mom used to laugh and say if she came face-to-face with one of them without leashes being involved, Niña wouldn't have much of a bark."

He chuckled as he stared into the distance, I assumed, visualizing the memory. I was captivated. "One day, a big ass German Shepherd got loose and chased my mother. I saw my mother hauling ass up the walkway for the house when I opened the door. Somehow little Niña came charging past me then my mom and toward the German Shepherd. I saw that miniature mutt sprint so hard that when the German Shepherd saw her, he skidded his brakes and made a U-turn to his yard with Niña racing after him. By the time I caught up with them, she had her canines pierced into his left front leg. She only punctured his skin, but scared the shit out of him with her ferocious determination." His eyes rose to mine. "That's you: small in size, but big in bite. Fiercely determined."

I don't think I'd ever been complimented so. An intimate story from Stenton—not Stenton Rogers—changed the course of my day. I was sure I'd read too deeply into it, but didn't care. I chose to view this encounter from rosy lenses.

"Niña is a Spanish reference." I observed.

"My mother is Dominican," his voice was uneasy and I'd lost his eyes. I felt a pang of disappointment. He lifted his menu.

"I'd like to hear about her someday…I mean whenever you're ready." I stumbled over my words.

"Perhaps. If you agree to be my Niña." Stenton's eyes peered over his menu.

I narrowed my brows. "And what does that entail?"

He placed the menu down on the table and straightened his shoulders. "You pledging your friendship. And you must swear to no piercing of my skin…or my heart."

I choked on my spit…like really choked. My eyes watered.

"Calm the hell down, Zoey. We're not pledging love; just friendship." It took a minute, but I was able to clear my throat. I threw him a dubious regard. "You've pointed out my trust and paranoia issues; I'd like to use you as a guinea pig. Deal?"

Still, I was too stunned for words. *When did we turn this corner?*

This was Stenton Rogers…*Number 2 Overall Draft Pick, three-time MVP Awardee*, and *four-time Champion,* Stenton Rogers.

"Damn it, Zoey." He chuckled…beautifully, melting my core. "I'm not asking for marriage, just permission to let down my guard when we talk."

I gasped. "You better not be! Ughhhh!" I grimaced, earning a hard laugh from Stenton. It was infectious. I really needed to chill out.

"Yo, man! It's time to go!"

My smile faded as I peered up at a glaring Alton. My anxious eyes returned to Stenton, whose expression mirrored mine.

Stenton looked back, I assumed for Angela, just as I did. "What's up, my dude?"

"We just need to get the fuck up outta here, bro." Alton was seething.

"Alton, where's Ange—"

He put his index finger in my face. "Don't even ask me about that bitch."

Stenton shot from his seat almost as if to cover me. "The fuck gotten into you, bruh?"

My eyes enlarged. As crass as Alton was, he'd never taken that tone with Angela or me.

"Like I said, it's time to go!" Alton shouted then charged out of the restaurant as seamlessly as he'd come in.

Stenton offered regretful eyes. I knew he was just as confused as I was. He went into his pocket and pulled out several bills of cash. "Zo, I'm sorry. I don't know what's gotten into this dude today. Rest assured I'll find out." He grabbed my hand. "Lunch is on me." And then he made his exit on the heels of Alton.

While I watched him jog out of the restaurant, Angela appeared in the doorway with tears flowing. I knew in that moment her tears had derived from the same place that had pissed Alton off.

When she arrived at the table she cried, "He's an irreparable asshole."

"Why?"

"Because he doesn't want to accept responsibility for this!"

"Angela!" I gasped.

"What?"

I browsed around the table to be sure we weren't drawing any more attention than Alton had.

"Because you know it wasn't Alton who got you pregnant. You were just with Timmy the night before we started *Working Toward the Stars*." I couldn't believe she'd lay aside that inconvenient fact.

"So?" she kept her arms crossed protectively over her belly. I knew she was feeling more vulnerable than she wanted to let on.

"So, Ang, you can't just pick and choose whose baby this is. You have to recount facts. And the biggest of them all is that you'd missed your period *before* you and Alton."

"Whose side are you on anyways?"

"Yours, Ang. Always yours," I struggled to keep my voice low.

"I can't tell. You sound like a PR rep or lawyer from his entourage. You can't have my back for once?"

I jumped from my seat, no longer caring who saw us, and invaded her space to get into Angela's face. "I've spent almost my entire summer in the face of a man I didn't want to be within a hundred million feet of, trying to prove I'm not something he thinks I am because you've been with his boy, doing the very thing he thinks I'm about." I pointed in the chair across from mine, referring to Stenton. "The thing that I'm not."

Ang's face hardened and her eyes narrowed. "A whore? Is that what you think I am? Well, I got news for you, Zoey: Not everyone aspires to be a goody two-shoes like you. Funny. I thought that was the one thing that bonded us. I see I was wrong."

My mouth collapsed.

"I'll meet you at the car." Angela turned to leave the restaurant.

Angela's pregnant!

Needless to say, I didn't attend my last assigned week of *Working*

Toward the Stars. Angela sent me a text saying she wouldn't be picking me up because she wasn't going back. If she wasn't returning, there was no need for me to because I didn't want to do the stupid program in the first place. I realized I didn't inform Stenton of this decision until Friday, the last morning of the program.

First thing that morning, around 9:00 a.m., I received a text from Stenton asking of my whereabouts. I explained with few words that I wouldn't be making it because of the blowup with Angela and Alton. In so many words, he said he understood. Then a few hours later, he texted again, asking to meet at the diner for lunch. He mentioned having to catch a red eye and leaving town for a few days. I told him I had a few things to do before church that evening and the best I could do was meet him for dessert later that night. I didn't think that would work for him. He did say he was flying out that night. To my surprise, he agreed to it.

Around 9:30 that night, I sauntered into the diner. Heading straight for the back of the dining area where I expected to have to wait for Stenton, I was surprised when I saw his two security guys sitting at a table, closer to the front of the rear area. Behind them, way back in the rear, I saw Stenton seated in a booth. They nodded without friendly smiles, granting me entry to where their boss was waiting. That small occurrence reminded me of his stature. I couldn't believe I was meeting with Stenton Rogers.

What a summer!

"Wow! Don't you look...reserved," Stenton jibed as he gave me a onceover.

I wore a long black skirt, with a plain white blouse and kitten heels. I had to usher that night during a revival my church was participating in. One of the bishops from the upper echelon of our organization was ministering that night and I'd helped prepare the church for the large crowd that was expected. Exhaustion was a word that paled in comparison to what I was feeling.

"Yeah, *Jet Beauty of the Week,* I know," I replied wryly.

With an amused expression, he extended his arm, inviting me to sit across from him. I did, feeling a bit insecure all of a sudden. I hadn't stopped home to change for fear of holding him up. I didn't give much thought to my appearance, or considered that he would either.

"So, a mess, huhn?" Stenton asked, and I knew he was referring to Angela and Alton.

I sighed heavily. "A complete one."

Stenton nodded.

"Do you know his lawyer contacted her this morning, asking for her medical history and that she take a test at a doctor's office of his choosing? They're threatening a DNA test in utero. Do you know how detailed and involved that is? He even wants her to sign an NDA agreement—" My eyes grew upon a revelation. "Is that why you asked me here? He wants me to sign one, too?"

My first thought went to my mother and how I wished she was here to help with this. I didn't know much about legal matters. *I've gotten myself into quite a quandary following behind that Angela!* What in the world was I going to do?

Stenton chuckled. "I don't want any parts of that bullshit. Alton and Angela are two adults that are going to have to figure out their affairs alone. That's what I've told Alton…and Tynisha."

My eyes squeezed shut. I'd momentarily forgotten about Tynisha. But that Alton had some nerve. He was eager to retreat with Angela after training, all summer.

"So, you're being forced in the middle, too, I see."

"They tried. I didn't accept it," was all he shared.

I sulked. "I wish my resolve was that titanium. I've been miserable since it went down. According to our cousin, Karen, Angela feels that I don't have her back and isn't speaking to me. And that's completely insane, considering the reason I applied for this dumb program in the first place was for her. We've been tight since I moved here from South Carolina. My parents were broke and couldn't find many opportunities down there. Angela's mother invited us to stay at their place until my mom and dad got on their feet. We lived with Angela's family for a little over a year before moving out into our own apartment in New Brunswick. Right away, we joined a church that was a part of the C.O.O.L.J.C. organization."

I chuckled, staring at the table. "It was funny how our lives came together once we moved. My father had always owned his small rubbish company, and brought it along with him to generate new clientele, and he did in due time. My mother got a job as a cafeteria worker for a company the board of education contracted out to. While they were busy settling us, Angela and I were busy bonding." I shook my head, exasperated. Stenton's big inked hand reached over to cover mine in comfort. "Angela should have used better judgment!" I stopped to compose myself. The situation had been heavy on my heart more than I realized up until that point.

But I couldn't stop there. I had more to upchuck and Stenton had this patient air to him, facilitating my need to vent. "We just ended a huge week-long revival at my church...prepared for this for months and when it finally arrives, our church community is in the middle of a fornication scandal," I giggled, mostly from how ridiculous that statement sounded, yet how true it was. "And then my family, with their archaic views, are demanding marriage, and with Alton that isn't exactly practical." Stenton had to laugh at that one. "Needless to say, it's not a good time in my family or church. And now folks are looking for me to drop the next bomb!"

"How have you been able to not fall into the traps?" he asked as he took a sip of his water. I couldn't keep myself from ogling his lips. They were the shape of a heart. A full one.

"Traps as in *pregnancy*?"

He nodded.

"Oh, that won't happen," I snorted and delivered unequivocally. "I do things to protect myself. I don't mind the idea of motherhood. I think it's the most precious gift on the planet, but in my culture, it has to be accompanied by marriage and I want no parts of that. So, rubbers for me," I sang off key.

Stenton shook his head, amused.

"No, seriously!" I continued my rant. "I've put things in place to avoid pregnancy...and even STDs. It never hurt anyone to use condoms. What's the big deal? There's no difference in the feeling. Just use protection."

Then he belted out a full on laugh, breaking the wind from my sails. I then decided to bring it in, possibly having put my foot in my mouth. *Just stay away from that topic.* It was our first time out without being on the stealthy agenda of Angela and Alton and I didn't want to make a fool out of myself.

I had no idea what I was doing alone with Stenton Rogers. Angela would kill me if she knew. *She's been in love with this guy since he was drafted.* She'd still not made it clear that Alton wasn't the father of her baby, and I'm sure she'd question my loyalty even more if she knew I was here with him.

What was even more traitorous on my part was that Stenton and I connected on social networking sites, and more recently via text messages. I thought my budding friendship with him ended that afternoon at the country club when Alton came through like a tornado, but Stenton surprised me when he asked to see me again. What he didn't know was since I last saw him, I'd stalked all of his profiles.

"You take lots of selfies," I mentioned casually.

"And you don't?" Stenton replied just as coolly as he dipped his middle finger in his cup of water, swishing it around.

"How do you know?"

"Because I've seen your profile and photo albums."

"Are you stalking me?" My heart stammered in my chest. Why that made me paranoid was beyond me.

"No more than you are me," his voice remained even as his eyes slowly aligned with mine. "You noted my massive amounts of selfies."

"I was simply pointing out your vanity. You know they associate excessive amounts of selfies with narcissism, right?"

Stenton picked up his drink as he chuckled. "Well, in my case it's called business; more specifically, marketing. My publicists pushed for more candid shots on social networks to give the illusion of intimacy. It makes fans feel closer to me...like they actually know me. But if you, my perceptive Elizabeth, look closer—at each picture— you'll notice they don't give away shit about me personally. I'm just a sideshow act. I'm not expressing myself; I give the people what they want to see."

Hmmmmm…

Expressing narcissism to give the illusion of intimacy? *Is that what celebrities do? Is it necessary to protect who they really are?* This was a hard theory to swallow considering all of the selfies and candid shots I'd seen of him. He seemed to be in his home, the gym and public places, but he was right; they never gave a clue as to who this man was other than his alleged vanity, something I didn't pick up at all when with him. *Who is the real Stenton Rogers?* Was he the guy in all the pictures, smiling and appearing well socialized? Or was he the man who secretly invited me to a diner close to midnight in Kingston, a place I'd never heard of until then?

As we were seated in a small booth in the back of an empty section, I'd noticed he'd been quieter than usual tonight. I assumed he was preoccupied with something. I didn't ask, though tempted to. I wondered if he felt the twinge of guilt that I had, knowing how Angela would feel about us being there together without her knowledge. No. That wouldn't make any sense, considering he couldn't give two craps about Angela. He'd only brought her up to express his confusion about our friendship now that he knows we're actually family.

All of that aside, I needed to get honest about why I was here. I liked Stenton…in a friendship manner. He was funny, engaging and really smart, very much a hidden treasure. And if I was *really* honest, I'd admit to feeling a surge of excitement at the possibility of being one of the few who *knew* this side of him. What he saw in me, though, I had no idea. Maybe he felt sorry for me because of how I reacted to learning he dismissed my cousin's advances via a lie about his relationship status. I still couldn't believe that. He'd lied. To her. But with me…he seemed very transparent, no matter how annoying he was.

"I'd like to see more of you, though."

I looked up from the table and saw *that* look in his eyes again. Stenton guarded his smile around me most days. I finally realized he didn't trust me. And I got why, eventually. The more we talked, the more I could identify his problem with people always having an agenda and their hands out. I didn't attempt to prove myself otherwise. My mother always taught me not to fight at getting people to know the real me. She would always say, with time they would know me better than any words could assist with. And that's what I did with Stenton.

Could that be what the glint in his eyes as he sat across from me was all about?

"Huhn?"

He inclined in his seat, bringing my attention to those full heart-shaped lips that had recently begun haunting my private thoughts.

"I think you should take selfies. Converse to my practices, you can show people who you really are. Remind them of your natural beauty and introduce them to your incredible sense of humor," he murmured with squinted eyes.

"Sense of humor? I have a sense of humor?" I couldn't believe his observation. I'd been told about several of my alleged character-istics, but a good sense of humor—or one at all—wasn't one.

"Yeah, like when you clown my wardrobe all the time. What was it that you called me? A—"

"A ghetto rocker?"

"Yup." His lips twitched into an easy grin. "That's one. A bootleg hood model is another."

He let out a full laugh with that one. I joined him.

"Well, your style is a bit different. That's evident in all of your selfies." I busted out laughing at the recollection of some of them. "But then your poses can be so suave. You be like this."

I squared my shoulders, straightened my neck and angled my head a few ways to mimic Stenton's various poses. He tossed his head back and hooted hard. One of his security guys turned to see what was causing the ruckus. When they saw me sit on my knees and snatch Stenton's baseball cap from his head and attempt my Stenton Rogers impersonating, even they cracked smiles.

Unable to breathe, Stenton yelped, "Give me my damn hat back. You can't rock my shit and clown me at the same time. Fashion is subjective, man."

He came over to my side of the booth and tried to grab his hat from my head. I argued, "No, what's subjective is how appropriate those tuxedo shorts were you wore to that party last month."

I laughed with him while continuing with my antics. When he was successful in getting the cap off my head, he then grabbed my phone and handed it to me.

"Here. I'm about to coach you on how to take silly pictures."

I took my phone and went into the picture app. "I'm ready."

Stenton instantly widened his eyes and stuck out his long and broad tongue. I mean…his tongue darn near reached to the bottom of his chin. I'd idly wondered could it extend longer. And then my curiosity caused me to wonder what it would feel like against my—

I clicked the camera then slammed the phone on the table.

"Got it. Enough of that. Hope you're happy," my voice was uncharacteristically low before I forced the straw from my drink into my suddenly dry mouth.

The trail my thoughts were leading down was not holy.

Stenton knowingly shook his head as he turned away from me.

"C'mon. It's late." He stood from the booth and offered his hand. "I've taken up enough of your time," he muttered.

I wiggled my phone as I scooted off the bench to stand. "And memory."

Brain memory, that is.

When his security saw us coming their way, they stood and walked ahead of us. I followed behind Stenton, who adjusted his hat on his head, and studied his body. His walk wasn't as ponderous as other tall men. He had a bit of elegance about his stance and stride.

"Where are you parked?" Stenton called back to me.

"Ummm…all the way in the back, by the gate."

When we arrived to the back of the parking lot, I took the lead to my car. My mind churned with what this farewell experience would be like. I mean, what would I say to him? I thought this would go down a different way, like a quick *nice meeting you* in the early afternoon hours at the country club. I spent most of my summer with this guy: the guy everyone knew as Stenton Rogers. And now we were preparing to say goodbye. As much as I resented having to spend time with the insufferable man, my heart had evolved in terms of him. It had softened to him. At this point, I really liked him as a friend. But I didn't think I'd ever see him again outside of a television screen or print ad, so how would I express *it was nice meeting you*? My mind wouldn't slow.

I was so flustered that when we arrived at my car, I turned to him and buried my face in my palms. "I know…I know…I know I'm supposed to be polite and come up with parting words…use proper etiquette." My voice turned apologetic, pleading even. "But I really can't think of anything, except for it's been really cool getting to know you without the assistance of Google. It's sped my summer up, and made what Angela did that much more bearable because at least I had someone to suffer with me. Uhhh…"

My eyes swept the ground below as I tried to think of something more.

Oh!

"It was cool meeting a fellow-rocker. Now, I'm really going to look for that *KISS* t-shirt signed by Gene Simmons. Uhhh… It's great to have that genre of music in common with someone who shares the same skin tone…or ethnicity…well, not so much of the latter because you're mixed. And…uhhh…don't worry about me stalking you. Here…" I pulled out my cell phone.

"Zoey."

"I'll delete your number. I swear I don't have it memorized or written anywhere. You can go on ahead and delete me from Facebook and other sites now that we won't be seeing each other. I appreciate you giving me the opportunity to get to know—"

"Zoey," he called out again, pointedly. "Shut up." I didn't see a smile or hear humor in his tenor.

"*W*-why are you telling me to shut up?"

"Because I didn't ask you out here tonight to say goodbye, per se —or at least I hope we're not saying goodbye." He changed his stance, lowering himself to align his gaze with mine. "I wanted to see you tonight because you challenged me with proving that my teeth are real."

I stood there with my mouth facing the ground, trying to process what he'd said. For a moment, I was lost, unable to comprehend his intent. Just then, Stenton took me at the back of my head, aggressively pulling me into his hot hard frame, and positioned his lips to align with mine. Immediately, my body melted into him.

His long fingers raked through my hair at the roots, gripping my scalp as he held me. On my tippy toes, and with my elongated neck, I stood enraptured as his lengthy and wide tongue swirled in my mouth, tasting every inch of my cavity, even the front of my teeth, between my gums. My belly stirred with carnal desire and my entire frame vibrated with sensual energy. I didn't know how long he explored my mouth, neither could I think straight to measure. But I knew I didn't want him to stop. I'd never been so thoroughly kissed. Never knew so much could be expressed and experienced through a kiss.

Stenton retracted his tongue then full lips, suddenly leaving me bereft. My eyes flickered open and caught his darkened orbs.

"That's how you can assess my teeth," he informed hoarsely.

Though he attempted humor, his eyes were slanted, heavy with need, his proximity dizzying me. I don't think I'd ever smelled anything so virile in my life.

When he moved in again; I threw my hands up to the back of his head, feeling the soft and natural curls of his mane, meeting him half way, and my tongue was in his mouth before he could think about changing his mind. I didn't go straight for his teeth, I went for his tongue. It was sweet like nectar and agile like the neck of a heron. I wanted more of it. And I took it, liberally.

There was a strong spurring sound that hurled from the back of his throat and even that tossed into my mouth deliciously.

"Yo, Rogers!" I heard in the distance, but didn't allow it to interrupt my sensual and explorative adventure. "We gotta roll!"

Hearing that reminded me of his impending departure. It was then that I used my tongue to inspect his teeth, but no longer questioning the realness of them, just not wanting to leave an inch of his mouth undiscovered.

I don't know who pulled away first. I only understood neither one of us wanted to. My breathing was ragged, and Stenton's composure mangled. He thumbed his bottom lip as he looked out into the distance. When his eyes returned to me they were sharp, piercing with preoccupancy. He didn't say anything when he walked off.

I stood there dazed for moments long, not understanding what had just taken place. It wasn't until I realized the headlights from his truck were still illuminating the dark corner of the parking lot where I stood that I grasped they were waiting on me to safely get into my car before pulling off. So I did. I managed to move my aching body over to my *Kia Rio* and pull off.

On the way home, my phone chirped. When I stopped at the next light I checked the text.

Stenton: **What's your assessment?**

Me: **Of what?**

Stenton: **My teeth.**

Oh! Those! That trivial curiosity paled in comparison to the real discovery of how great a kisser Stenton was. I'd never felt anything like that. At the next light I returned his text.

Me: **I guess they're real. You rich people can afford good cosmetic procedures.**

Stenton: **Well I guess we're even.**

Me: **How so?**

Stenton: **Because your boobs are perfect in size and feel good as hell against my abs and chest.**

Just when I thought my already sodden panties could endure no more liquefaction, I felt increased moisture down below. My breasts felt heavier in their holdings, too. *This is insane!* I waited until I arrived home to respond. I didn't know how to.

Me: **Ummm... Thanks?**

Stenton: **LMAO! GN Nina.**

Days later, I heard a ping from my phone. I reached over to the bathroom sink as Ruth stood over me while I was squatting on the lip of the tub.

Stenton: **What are you doing?**

I typed back: *Just got my hair pressed out by my sissy.*

Stenton: **I wanna see.**

I quickly snapped a picture and sent it: *Cheese!*

He didn't respond right away. *Why was I getting so nervous?* I wore a maroon long sleeve cotton shirt. *But it had no holes*; just a house shirt. Still, I buzzed with nervous energy, awaiting his response.

We'd been texting back and forth, intimately, and sometimes topics got deep. Deep…not necessarily in a sensual nature, but about our pasts, our fears, and our ambitions. So when texts like this came through, it wasn't odd.

Then I heard a chirp.

Stenton: **But what's up with the shirt tho?**

Me: *Shut up! What are you doing?*

Stenton: **Getting ready to workout.**

Me: *Send me a pic…*

Stenton: **Blah**

Then his picture came through. It was just his face. He hid his eyes, which robbed me of so much. There were so many things I experienced when looking through them. So much he tried to hide from the world.

Me: *You're whack…*

I replied, but cunningly, not for the reason I wanted him to believe. My dig was because of him not giving me more. More of what I'd been growing attached to. Him. The real Stenton Rogers.

Stenton: **Yeah…yeah…yeah! Chat lata…**

"You just can't do it."

"Why?" Angela yelled at me from her sofa. Her nostrils were flared and cheeks red.

"You know why, Ang," Karen sighed. She was fragile and had less stamina in this stage of her pregnancy.

But not me.

"Yeah, you do, but in case you don't want to remember, it's because it is a lie, and for us Christians, lying is a sin. I know you've been upset about Timmy cheating on you with that girl, but you need to forgive him and move on."

"Move on?" Angela jumped from the couch as she yelped. Good thing her parents weren't home and we could hash this out without alarming them.

"Yes! Move on, whether that means be with him or move on without him, you must start with forgiving him."

"Forgiving him for cheating on me?"

"Yes! We've all done wrong, Ang. And I'm inclined to believe you would've moved on with Stenton Rogers this summer even if things were good between you and Timmy."

"Oooh…" Karen cupped her mouth. She knew I was right. The elasticity in Angela's panties were worn. They never stayed up.

"You sound ridiculous. I would have never done that to Timmy! Stenton Rogers or no Stenton Rogers!"

"Yeah, but you did it to Alton Alston's fiancée," I charged.

"Alton Alston did that to his fiancée! I don't owe her shit!"

"But you do. As a woman, you are obligated to protect other women with bleeding hearts just like yours. You were just as wrong for getting involved with an engaged man. Your offense may have been different than his, but the game of cheating is still the same. You provided the playground for him to cheat. Just like Regina did Timmy."

"Regina is a bitch. Everyone knows that."

"And you're different? You're putting a baby on Alton that you know isn't his, Ang," I pushed.

Things got quiet. I was losing my patience, but had to forge ahead. We always vowed to be responsible for each other. I had to convince her to drop this bogus paternity claim.

I grabbed my forehead. "Listen, Ang, the thing about anger and resentment for someone who has wronged you is it festers. Just like the bishop said last night in his sermon: you have to view forgiveness as a natural part of life while we're on this journey. As sure as we live, people will hurt and disappoint us. But if we can keep in mind that our time here is short...a blink of a passage; just like Jesus forgave Judas, we'd understand that it's a minor detail in our journey here."

I moved closer to Angela and saw the tears cresting her eyes. Karen sat Angela back down on the couch and wrapped her arms around her. I kneeled in front of Angela, gently gripping her knees.

"You accusing Alton of fathering your precious baby affects everyone in the picture. The real target is Timmy, the person who is the father of this child. Address your issues with him, release Alton, and decide on your next move. If you do not, you will have years of anger, bitterness and resentment that will gravely affect you..." I placed my hand on her tight stomach. "...and your child for years to come. No one is worth your misery. Forgive Timmy and move on."

We stayed in that position for a while. My mind racing, wondering what was going through Angela's head. Eventually she shifted in her seat, so we all did. Angela stood, and we all followed suit.

"I'll drop this paternity thing with Alton," she murmured. But there was more behind her eyes. "I'm also going to figure out what to do about Timmy. But let me tell you this: whatever I decide isn't for you to approve or to judge. Until you have lived...done something bold for once in your life, you have no authority to advise anyone on the art of living."

Then Angela brushed past me, nipping my arm roughly. I turned to watch her storm out of the living room. When I turned back to an aghast Karen, I knew my confusion about what just took place wasn't unfounded.

Chapter Four

Stenton

I rang the doorbell, not understanding what the fuck I was doing there. I knew she texted me, asking me to shoot by because she had something to show me, but that still didn't explain why my dumb ass went to this girl's house on Christmas day, who I'd only known since the summer. I could hear the chatter from inside and sounds of a television. I had no idea if this was a dangerous set up or not. *Shit!* This was some risky shit. Some shit that I'd never done. To add insult to injury, I had my security stay in the truck because I didn't want to come off as supercilious. Zoey wasn't with that shit, so I wouldn't be either.

On the third ring, I heard movement beyond the door. When it pulled open, I recognized the exuberant smile of the little lady wearing it. Zoey looked far more innocent than that vixen I'd last experienced with her tongue down my throat. The thought of that made my dick twitch in my pants. Her hair was in a messy ponytail, she wore an oversized Princeton sweat-shirt and loose gray sweats, and her feet covered in black knitted socks. She looked homely, but her beauty was glaring through all the loose clothes. I didn't need to be reminded of what was under those layers; I'd committed Zoey's sexy ass body to memory.

"You came!"

Suddenly, I couldn't fight my spouting grin. "Yeah. My uncle was sick of my ass laying around his crib. I told you I'd stop by on my way home if it wasn't too late. I hope it's not."

"Oh, of course not," she breathed and appeared somewhat nervous. That made two of us. "Come on in." She backed away to give me entrance into the small home.

I entered straight into the living room where a game was playing on the television. The walls were covered with photos, a few I noticed immediately were of Zoey. The fragrance in there was a miscellany of an aged home, Zoey, and soul food. The lighting was a bit dim because of the dulled bulb. I heard muffled voices from a distant room. *Shit!* I wasn't up to meeting people. I'd hoped that wasn't the plan for the visit. There, in the living room, was a young girl on the phone, chatting spiritedly while holding a small baby.

"I hope you're paying attention to what you're holding, Shemma!" Zoey scolded as she led me into the short hallway that connected to the kitchen.

The little girl shot back over her shoulder, "I am, Zo. Dang!" That's when she caught a glimpse of me, possibly recognizing me. I didn't stay around to know for sure. I stayed on Zoey's heels.

"Ruth...Zo, where is your Daddy?" A woman with a soprano tone called out as she bumped into Zoey in the hallway. The three of us damn near collided, I was so far up on Zoey's ass feeling a bit wary about voyaging through a strange home...without security. "Oh, my!" the woman's eyes batted in a bashful manner. I could tell my presence had caught her off guard. "Who is this?"

Shit. Here we go.

"Momma, this is my friend, Stenton. Stenton, this is Sarah Barrett, the bestest Momma in the whole wide world," Zoey charmed. I could tell it was something she did often.

"Oh, girl!" her mother swiped her away with her hand as Zoey tried planting an endearing kiss on her cheek.

When Zoey pulled back, I proffered my hand. "Mrs. Barrett, it's an extreme pleasure to finally meet Zoey's mom." And I meant that. The strength Zoey exuded could have only come from a woman who positively guided her. I'd meditated on that since our first one-on-one conversation. Zoey's maturation could not have been totally organic. It had to have come with wise impartation.

"Why, thank you…" Sarah struggled to remember my name, which explained why she didn't have that gleam of recognition in her eyes. But there was one of trying to figure out where she'd seen my face before. I'd give her some time and hoped the revelation would come once I'd left.

"Stenton, Momma," Zoey assisted her mother.

"Oh, yes, Stenton. Thank you." And that was it.

No prying. No questions. No awkward staring to try and figure me out. I was grateful because learning my identity could have easily led down a road I wasn't in the mood to travel. Although I didn't know what the fuck Zoey and I were doing, I did view her as a part of my personal life. We'd had way too many intimate conversations not to.

I think in that moment I fell for Zoey's mother. There was something powerful yet cautioning about her aura. I could tell that quickly she was kind, with a degree of meekness, and respectful. There was a hidden grace to Sarah that suddenly illuminated where Zoey got her confidence from. It had all clicked in that brief and awkward moment. My guard had lowered just a bit.

"We're going in the dining room. It's empty, right?" Zoey asked. Before Sarah could answer, she continued, "Oh, and Daddy's over at the Johnson's praying for the sick and shut-in with the rest of the deacons."

Then she moved left and traveled a short distance into the dining room.

"Sit right here, I have to go grab it, okay?" Zoey asked, damn near bouncing out of the room, leaving me alone. Again, she didn't wait for a reply before proceeding.

I tapped my fingers as I inspected the room. While I wasn't as nervous as I was when I'd rang the doorbell thanks to Sarah, I was still on edge about being in a stranger's home without protection. There had been too many horror stories of dudes in my line of work getting set up, chasing ass. While I wasn't exactly chasing ass, I still didn't want to fall victim to that.

"Here we go!" Zoey sang as she entered the room with a small Christmas style gift bag. She handed it over then took a seat next to me, at the head of the table.

"What's this?" I asked, inspecting it.

"Open it up and see, you dork."

I went for the small ribbon tied around the handles and loosened it, then pulled out the green tissue paper inside. I stopped.

"Zo, you have to stop with the clicking sound. That…" I whispered my profanity with her mother in mind. Something about Sarah rang *respect* in my contaminated mind. "…shit gets to me."

"What?" her eyes bulged. "What sound?"

"The one from the back of your throat."

"Oh! I didn't know I was doing it. *I*-I don't know when I'm doing it. Sorry! I'm just a little—"

"Nervous?" I interrupted her.

"Yes."

"About what, Niña?" And there was that pet name rolling off my tongue so naturally.

"Well, about this. I hope you like it."

"Is this a gift?" I asked before going back to the bag.

I pulled out a cotton piece of clothing. When I unrolled it, I found a *KISS* t-shirt from their *2000 KISS Farewell Tour*. On the back, sure enough, there was Gene Simmons' signature with Zoey's name.

"Holy shit," I murmured in awe. I couldn't believe she'd remembered to prove she owned this.

"Cool, right?" Zoey's grin wasn't haughty, it was giddy. She was excited.

"Yeah, it is." My voice still almost a whisper.

"Can I offer you something to eat, seeing this child of mine has forgotten her manners?"

I looked up to find Sarah in the doorway. Still no glint of a fanatic in her eyes.

"Ummmm… Momma, Stent has to go. He only agreed to stop by for a few minutes."

"Oh, okay. Are you sure I can't get you some dessert to go, at least?"

This woman, who it still appeared to not know who I was just yet, was offering me food from her kitchen. I was taken.

"I have a few minutes to spare for Zo's mom's cooking." How could I decline authentic hospitality?

Sarah nodded and took off for the kitchen.

"Dude, can you really stay?" Zoey whispered dubiously.

I shook my head. "Probably not, but fuck it." I wanted to chat about this t-shirt. "This smells brand new. Have you worn it yet?"

"No. It's too big, which is why I'm giving it to you."

"Giving it to me? If the size is the problem, why not give it to your dad?"

"Please! If it ain't John P. Kee, Paul Morton or The Rance Allen Group, my parents aren't wearing it. To them, this is the devil's music. If they had it their way, this would have been in the trash before it made it into their home." Zoey giggled.

I was still in astonishment. I'd met Gene several times before, but strangely found this t-shirt impressive. Zoey always reduced me to a layman when I was around her. That was one of many things that drew me to her.

"You like that crazy metal music, too? Or is my Elizabeth here trying to force it down your throat?" Sarah asked as she placed a large plate of food in front of me.

There was greens, cabbage, yams, potato salad, macaroni and cheese, stuffing, ham, chicken and BBQ ribs all packed on my plate. How she was able to fit it all was anyone's guess. Next to it, she placed a tall glass of tea.

"Momma," Zoey appeared nervous. "I hope Stenton can eat all of that food."

"He's a growing young man. I'm sure he can." Sarah turned on her heel and walked out of the room, then called over her shoulder, "Oh, and I'll be back with some dessert to go."

I looked over to Zoey. She apologetically mouthed, "Sorry."

"No worries at all. You think I'm gonna complain about this feast? You're crazy," I tried to assure her.

"Thanks, Stenton. I know how you are about being out in public. I didn't expect to keep you long, but it's good seeing your dorky face again." Zoey's smile was warm. Her cheeks turned a shade of pink. She was blushing.

"My face or my big ass fake teeth?" I asked before I placed a forkful of food in my mouth.

"Stenton!" she gasped. "Let's not go there again. I know they're real now. Okay?" she tried whispering.

So I did, too. "Good, because I'd like nothing more than to prove it again to you before I leave."

Zoey's head fell back in laughter. We did a lot of that for about a half an hour before I left. Sarah packed up my dessert as promised.

"How was your cousin's wedding?"

"Oh, Karen's?" Zoey shrugged. "It was a wedding...you know...the traditional vows recited that no one upholds past when they slip from their lips." Then her eyes grew large in excitement. "But her baby is gorgeous! Here, let me show off my nephew!"

She pulled out her phone and showed me countless pictures of a colorless newborn and followed up the pictures with insignificant details of meeting him. With anyone else, this would have been painful to the point of my ears bleeding, but with Zo, everything was filled with wonder. She had a talent for that. I listened and dug into my plate.

When Zoey walked me to the door, the living room was empty.

"Thanks for dinner." I raised my right hand. "And the gift." I then raised my left. "This is really Christmas for me. I feel bad it's one-sided."

Zoey shook her head and whispered, "No it isn't. Here, I'll make it even." And she pushed up on her toes and kissed me.

At first it was a lingering peck, but then she came back for more and threw her tongue in the mix, twirling it, releasing a bunch of fucking butterflies in my stomach. I'd never had such a reaction to a kiss. Zoey did shit like that to me. She fucked with my head. My phone buzzed and she pulled back. Once fully on her feet, she timidly wiped her mouth as she sucked in her lips. That was a move uncharacteristic of the Zoey I knew. She never seemed to second guess herself.

"Goodnight, Zoey." I'd lost my voice in that kiss.

"'Night, dork." She smiled softly.

I moved so she could unlock the door, then opened it.

It was fucking hard leaving her without knowing the next time I'd see her, but I didn't know how to address that. I still didn't have a handle on this young girl.

"Keep in touch," were my last words before I left her New Brunswick home.

I gotta get my shit together. She's too young!

January 2007

Stenton

"You meeting up at *Delilah's*?" Alton asked, holding his duffle bag, about to leave.

I turned toward my locker to grab my watch. "Nah," I answered, not really looking at him.

"What the fuck is up with you? You ain't seen them golden tits and ass in months, man." Alton's 5' 6" frame was facing me, awaiting a response.

We were the last in the locker room, having had a long conversation with the coaches right after leaving the court. I was drained and just wanted to be alone with a cold brewski. I realized Alton was still there and therefore not dropping the subject, whatever the fuck it was.

"Your point, man?" I asked, now turning to give him my undivided attention.

His neck snapped back. "*My point is* what the fuck done crawled up your ass and is holding your balls? The whole crew is going to be in the building tonight. Don't sweat the trading leads from tonight. We won. Bottom line." He pumped his free fist. "Now let's go celebrate with hard nipples and soft asses!"

I chuckled. "I'm good for tonight, man."

My phone went off as I spoke. I grabbed it from the locker shelf and saw it was a text from Zoey. I felt a fucking million butterflies in my stomach at the sight of her name across my screen.

Zoey: **Hey! I know you're busy in your season and all (by the way, great game tonite) but I just realized I have no winter break plans. My parents are going to a prayer conference in D.C. and asking me to attend. I'm sooooo not interested. So now I'll be bored and alone.**

"What the fuck you smiling at? I hope that's Erika Erceg, finally wearing your biker-boy ass down." My head shot up at the sound of Alton's voice. I'd totally forgotten he was there.

"The fuck you talking about?"

"You, fool! You smiling like a lil' bitch at your phone, man." Alton's one peaked brow matched his tone.

"Fuck outta here, man," I rumbled as I typed back.

Me: **When exactly are you talking?**

I couldn't believe I was considering this shit. I didn't want to taint this girl. She was everything I wasn't used to: smart, funny, lighthearted, fun and...fucking sexy. My Niña was so much the women who ran in my circles were not, which is why I did entertain her idea of spending time together. I'd missed her quirkiness.

Zoey: **Well when do you have off, dork?**

I found myself quietly chuckling at that.

Me: **My professional schedule is online. Is yours?**

"Man, fuck this. I'm out!" Alton huffed. "I hope that's golden ass you arranging right now, my man." He turned and left out the main area.

Zoey: **Hang on. Searching your schedule now...**

I finished tossing my things into my bag and made my way out of the locker room. I could now feel the smile plastered on my face. *Shit!*

Seconds later, my phone pings again.

Zoey: **Christ! You have no life between October and June! So I was able to find three days in the second week of January. Do you have personal plans?**

She was determined. And I was nervous as hell. I didn't want to fuck this up. I wanted to spend some time with her. Hell, I could see myself coming home to her every night. Hanging out for a few days meant more than she was proposing. Was it something she understood she could be getting into? Was *I* ready for that shit?

Me: **I do now. Send me the dates and we'll make it happen.**

After hitting Send, I felt excitement like never before. This girl had no idea how much she got under my skin.

Zoey: **Yippee! Guess who won't be bored the entire winter break? #Zoey! Yeah, boy!**

I laughed my ass off at the door of my car.

Me: **Wait. What are we supposed to be doing exactly?**

I couldn't deny the anticipation. I felt like a fucking kid, talking about Christmas morning expectations.

Zoey: **Does it matter? Can't go far because of your demanding job. I dunno. Somewhere low key because of your stalkers.**

I could see the sarcastic grin across her pouty lips. Lips that I'd been dying to touch again since Christmas. I swore to myself I wouldn't cross the line with her. I just couldn't resist her company. She was so cool to just chill with.

Hmmm...

Where could we go on the low for just a couple of days? It wasn't until just before I was going to call it a night that I replied.

Me: **We can go out to my place in Jersey.**

We pulled up to the gate where I scanned my card for entry. As the metal doors opened, I looked over at Zoey, who was uncharacteristically stumped. It was almost midnight. I'd picked her up as soon as I left the arena. I was uneasy about bringing her here, but with her it felt right. Zoey was cool.

I rarely went home; I practiced so damn much, keeping me in the South Jersey/Philly area. I didn't have all the bedrooms there furnished because no one hardly came over unless I was having a big ass summer party.

As we rounded the fountain to get to the front of the house, I saw Zo's jaw drop as she spied it. I parked the car and turned to see her sights were still beyond me, observing the grounds. It was hard not to focus my attention on her damn breasts that were bulging in a tight ass blouse she wearing. I'd wondered why she didn't have her coat zipped up. And her jeans. Fuck! They looked like they were painted on. I knew she had curves, but I learned that night they weren't as modest in clothes as I'd assumed. Her pouty lips looked dipped in gloss. I was getting cold feet again about this trip; those nervous waves had been coming every day in my stomach since I agreed to this.

"Zo," I called out to her.

Her brown eyes quickly zoomed in on my face. "Hmmm?"

I lifted a brow. "You good?"

Her neck jerked in response to my question. Her mouth opened and closed along with her eyes. Then I saw the humor rise in them.

"*W*-what? Boy, please! I done been to many mansions in Alpine! This is modest." She rolled her eyes and turned towards the front of the house. "I just remembered that I have a tutoring call first thing in the morning."

She held on to her giggle for a few seconds. I shook my head and laughed at her as I got out of the car and pulled our things from the trunk. I let us inside and disarmed the security system.

Then I turned to her and observed her eyes assessing the vestibule.

"I would show you around, but it's pretty late. I guess we can do that in the morning."

Was I tired? No. My body was bursting with nervous energy. I had Zoey alone in my place and I didn't know what to do or expect. If she were just any woman, I would be counting down the minutes to fuck her. But she's not; she's my little angel.

She turned to me excitedly, damn near bouncing on her toes. "What are the sleeping arrangements?"

I cocked my head and wrinkled my forehead, unable to hide the smirk on my face. "What do you mean?"

Zoey slowly walked over to me and stopped just at my chest and mischievously lifted only her eyes. "What do you think I mean, dork?" Then her chin rose and I had a perfect view of her lips that parted.

My dick got hard. Damn. I couldn't think of her in that manner. I had to get my shit together. I backed up to grab our bags and headed for the staircase.

"Wherever you find a bed. There are six bedrooms, but not all are furnished. Pick one and make yourself at home." I was midway up the twenty five steps by the time I was done.

Later that night, I changed into more comfortable clothes and posted up in the theater room. Zoey wanted to watch horror films and eat popcorn as though we were at a sleepover. Picture that. She even parted her hair into ponytails to add to the experience. It was cute.

What was not cute was when she'd showered and changed, she met me downstairs in tiny ass retro-basketball shorts that stopped at the bottom of her ass cheeks, a tight tank t-shirt that showed the impressions of her bra, and long socks that came above her calf muscles. Upon seeing that, something hit me: Zoey wasn't that cool, laid back beauty that I revered as *cute* last summer. She was still funny as hell, more aggressive, definitely cool, but undeniably sensual now. More sensual than I could trust myself to be around.

While watching the second flick, "Resident Evil," I realized she was damn near underneath me with her legs curled beneath her. She stopped eating her popcorn, which thankfully I did have in stock, during the first flick. Horror films didn't do much for me. I'm more of an action buff, but I preferred this predictable shit to that fluffy romance crap. Zo seemed all into it. I looked down at her and noticed the glow from the big screen casting a bright light on her wide eyes and mouth. Her hair smelled like flowers and I could even pick up a secondary vanilla scent from her body. She was sexy as hell. But no matter how *mature* she looked in that moment, the way she was curled beneath me reminded me of my old Niña.

Her head popped up and she caught me eyeing her. Our eyes locked for a minute before she wiggled into a taller position and then kissed me. Her tongue remained in her mouth, but her lips parted to pull at my lower one. I felt the hike in my breath at that move. She had to have caught it, too, because it damn sure was audible enough. Then there was that smoldering look in her eyes again. The one I'd seen the first time we'd kiss and hours ago at the front door when she'd asked about the sleeping arrangement.

Zoey took to my mouth again. This time she did insert her tongue, swirling it around and around. She changed the angle of her face as our mouths dipped into each other's. I commanded my hands to stay off her body, even though her perky breasts were rubbing against my chest. Even though her hands perused my pecs and then abs. Her fragrance took on a new experience at this proximity. I didn't know how long I'd be able to hold out. When Zo's little hand slipped beneath the elasticity of my waistband, I caught her wrist and pulled my mouth back.

"Zo, we can't do this." I didn't recognize my own voice.

Hell, I couldn't believe she wanted me...and that my dumb ass just shut it down! My cock wanted to be buried deep inside her, proving to be the best lover she'd ever had. But something else deep within wanted to hold off on sex. I wanted to hold on to our friendship just a little longer.

"Why not?" she asked, her eyes pleading with me.

"*B*-because," I exhaled, rubbing my face with my hands. I felt like a damn sucker because I didn't have a legitimate answer. I couldn't believe I felt pressured by ass; Zo's pretty one, no less. I took another breath, willing an answer to come. And it did. "Because I don't have any rubbers," finally came out, *sounding convincing as hell, too.*

She paused, now resting on her knees next to me. *Please don't say you're on the pill so it's okay...* She sat back letting out a sigh. *Whew!* That was my out. It was also my cue. I stood, grabbed the various remotes to shut down the system and turned up the lights.

I walked her to the guest bedroom nearest my suite and kissed her head. "Goodnight, Niña." I yawned. "I'm up at five for a workout downstairs in the gym. I'll be done around eight."

My chest tightened when she turned into the room, visibly moping as she headed to the bed. Each step farther into the room she took, I watched her little ass jiggle. My dick was so hard the shit was painful. I don't know how, but I found sleep at some point after twisting and turning much of the night with Zoey's scent still in my nostrils.

Later that night...or early morning, I rolled over and was stopped by something small and warm. I opened my eyes to find Zoey, quietly snoring with her lips parted. She appeared so innocent and calm, even more than I knew her to be before we arrived here in Alpine, where her seductress persona materialized. This was the Zoey I knew; soft and drama-free. After staring at her for a few minutes, I was able to fall back asleep. But my lewd dreams of her were something I couldn't control.

The following morning, I was slamming refrigerator and cabinet doors while trying to time the stove. Grease was popping everywhere and my fucking pancakes looked nothing like I'd ever been served. The bacon had burned to a crisp just as I was searching for a bowl large enough to whip the eggs in. And to top it off, I'd be damned if the bread didn't pop from the toaster black as tar. I'd fucked up big time and I had little food to start with. I already knew the first thing we'd do this morning was hit the grocery store. Where was Emilda when I needed her? Out of nowhere, I felt the damn spatula being snatched from my hand.

"No, Leo," she sighed. "It wasn't Lewin's research on conditioned reflexes that influenced the rise of behaviorism. It was Pavlov's experimental methods that helped transition psychology from introspection and subjective assessments to objective measurement of behavior."

That reminded me of the tutoring call she said she had this morning. As she spoke, Zoey removed the pan of bacon from the eye and turned the stove off. She rotated, in search of something and then took long strides over to the refrigerator. I couldn't help but notice she was irritated, certainly not my cool and funny Zoey.

"*Lewin* was groundbreaking in modern social psychology because of his work that used scientific methods and experimentation to explore social behavior. Remember," she paused, scanning the contents of the refrigerator. "Uhhhhh...he was a seminal theorist whose great influence in psychology still makes him one of the most distinguished psychologists of the 20th century."

I stood back from the open area to give her space. Zoey wore fitted jeans, a brown sweater and ugly ass Ugg boots. She tapped on the fridge door, humming. "No, that would be JP...Jean Piaget. Yes..."

She pulled out the nearly empty carton of eggs, shredded cheese, a half cut green pepper and deli sliced ham. Then she started opening and *damn near slamming* cupboard doors, making me flinch. Finally she found another frying pan.

"Hang on Leo, I need to put you on speaker while I cook."

She punched a few keys and then I heard the voice of young Leo. He sounded like a jock. I'd hoped he was paying her a fair wage. All of sudden I didn't like sharing her time with a frat boy. They exchanged words as she continued rattling off names and theories. A crazy sensation ran through my chest when I realized she never paid me a glance since walking into the kitchen. I'd hoped she wasn't hanging on to my rejection from last night.

"Yeah...well, I know his work is in psychosexual development. No one can forget Freud!" Leo informed, just a little too excitedly, bringing my attention back to their conversation. "Do you think if he were around today, he could help me score with you?"

My ass bounced off the counter. Zoey's neck snapped to find

me. Her arm slammed into my chest when I went for the phone. I stood in the middle of the kitchen flexing.

"Uhhh…" she eyed me warily. "Leo, it doesn't seem that I'll be scoring…with *anyone*." She rolled her eyes away from me on that. "Listen, go over the ones we've discussed today and we'll plan a time to meet and get you acquainted with the others when I get back on campus." She sounded even more aggravated.

When she hung up, she transferred plates of omelets and toast to the island then went looking for utensils. My Niña was obviously frustrated.

"The last on the left," I advised, feeling like a useless ass.

She got forks and knives and we sat down to eat. The omelet was delicious. I was grateful she was able to pull a rabbit out of a hat for breakfast. I hadn't planned on being at the house these few days and didn't leave any notice for my housekeeper to stock it with food. We were lucky to find what we did. I'm usually in Philly during the season. Not much got me off schedule. Until…

I glanced across the island. Zo was quiet.

"You okay, kid?" I tried, adding a smirk to lighten the moment.

"Mmm-hmm," sounded from her throat after filling her mouth with a forkful.

"Then why the hell won't you look at me?" I was now getting a little irritated.

Her eyes slowly rolled up to mine. "Happy?" she snapped her neck.

There was my smart ass Zo. I chuckled and in spite of herself, so did she.

"You meeting up with the kid, Leo, when you get back?"

Yup, I'm sitting on a fucking maxi pad.

"That's how I make my money." Her sarcasm was thick.

"Talking about psycho-development…specifically sex?"

She shrugged. "You know what they say: those who can't have sex, talk about psychosexual development." More sarcasm.

I dropped my fork onto my plate. "Zo…" I called apologetically.

"I'm just kidding, you dork!" she giggled. "Calm down."

I didn't know if she was kidding about kidding or serious about both. Zoey was fucking with my head. I didn't exactly know how to proceed with her after last night. I felt sexual tension, something I knew nothing about. Sex was never a big fucking deal for me; when I wanted it, I got it. And don't get me wrong, I wanted it, but, I didn't fuck friends. Problem was, Zo wasn't a typical friend. I didn't know what the hell she was.

When we were done, she took our plates to the sink to clean. I stood, resting my hip on the counter next to her, watching her like an idiot. I've fucked more women than I care to think of, but this young jawn had my fucking panties in a bunch.

"So, what are we doing today?" she asked, still not looking at me.

"I think we need to get some food in here. We can start with that," I offered.

She grabbed the towel to dry her hands. "Fine, let's go while it's early. I know how you are with crowds. Don't want to get you mobbed," she mumbled.

"I can actually visit this local grocery store with little fanfare."

"Okay. I'll go grab my things then." Zoey turned to leave the kitchen.

I grabbed her arm, yanked her little body into mine, took her by the face, and pushed my tongue in her mouth. It took her a while to kiss me back, but she did after some time. Her hands clutched my lower arms for balance. I didn't stop until I felt she got the message.

"I don't want to beef with you, Niña," I whispered to her as I held her head in my hands.

She sighed and closed her eyes. "We're not beefing, Stent. We're fine." And then she pulled away from me, leaving the kitchen.

Twenty minutes later, we were at the grocery store, and rolling the cart down the aisle. Actually, I was pushing it and Zoey was rambling about ingredients needed for things she would cook while we were out there. When she asked about my diet restrictions, I told her I eat everything, but just nothing too heavy during the season; I was still on the clock, so to speak.

"What does your chef usually cook for you?" she asked while we were in the produce area.

"I dunno, shakes, vegetables, lean meats. Shit with lots of protein," I answered while reading scores on my phone.

"That doesn't help," I heard from just ahead of me. "But I think we have enough to survive these next two days."

I glanced up to find her staring at me, I guess for an answer.

"Okay," I answered like the dork she often accused me of being.

"You can start off to the register. I just remembered *Adobo* seasoning. I don't know if your chef has that at the house." She started off in the opposite direction. Zoey called over her shoulder, "Don't wait for me. I can pay for the seasoning!" She winked as she sashayed, I'm sure purposely, for humor.

On the way back to the house, the snow started coming down. It brought out an animated Zoey. After putting away the groceries, we found our way to the formal living room, in front of the fireplace, roasting s'mores. It was something I'd never done, but had always seen on television. And my determined Zoey had my ass holding marshmallows and Hershey's chocolate bars in between two graham crackers, laughing my ass off.

She sat with her legs crossed, this time in tights, a long t-shirt, and thick socks. Her eyes were big and smile was bright as she made jokes about the annual women's retreat at her church and how Angela would put melted chocolate in the elderly women's beds, making them think they shitted themselves in bed at some point in the night because they somehow never found the chocolate when going to bed. The stories didn't stop and neither did the laughs. My cool Zoey was back.

"So, tell me: What is the stupidest thing you've ever done?" Zoey asked. "I think for me it was letting Kaleemah Brown cheat off my math test for the whole school year in high school. I never had the heart to tell her no. Angela scolded me for that all year until she convinced me to trick Kaleemah during our finals."

"What did you do?" I lifted a brow, genuinely interested.

"So, I started writing down bogus answers and equations, giving Kaleemah the perfect view of my paper so she could copy it. Then when she was finished recording them, she handed in her paper. I stayed behind, waited until she left the room and told the teacher I needed a fresh exam paper because I'd confused all of my equations for different applications." She shrugged. "He believed me, seeing I was an honor student. And of course, I turned in the correct answers."

"What happened to Kaleemah?" I asked as I bit into my third s'more.

"It was the end of the school year. For all she knew, I flunked along with her. She didn't fail that semester, but she did flunk out of the honors program because our finals counted for such a high percentage of our grade."

Zoey reached over and wiped my mouth. "You're just s'mores'd out, Stent. Your turn. What was the stupidest thing you've ever done?"

"Hmmmm…" I thought for a moment. "I've done lots of stupid shit in my day, kiddo. I think the stupidest was back during the summer when Alton and I got drafted." I put my sandwich down on the plate and took a sip of the milk she insisted I drink with it. "We were at a country club in Mullica Hill doing off-season training—back then we trained in random places. One morning, Al and I woke up and made a pact that we were getting off the property to have some fun before we checked in for official training. I told him I was craving *White Castle*, and he said he'd never had it before. So, I made it my mission to take him to experience his first double with cheese. We bummed a ride up to Newark with a trainer who had a hoopty and we barely made it to the one on South Orange Ave. The trainer left for a car repair shop we passed on the way up, saying he'd be right back once he got his joint fixed.

"Well, after we ordered our food, we walked a few blocks to a park that I knew we could chill at until our ride came back through. But when we got there, dudes from the Westside was there and knew who we were. They wanted a challenge. Now as employees of the NBA, we're not allowed to play street ball, but two kids from Newark and Bridgeton would never be played like fucking suckas. So, we dropped our shit and balled the hell out. People always slept on Al because of his height, but was blown away by his speed and rebounds. We burned their asses on that court. It was so bad that dudes wanted to fight. Again, the two of us being from these cities, weren't new to street fighting, so we were 'bout it. That was until more of their Westside clique showed up flexing because they knew we'd just gotten signed.

"I've never shied away from a fight. When you grow up in the hood, you know you gotta do what you gotta do, but when I thought of the bright future I'd just signed up for, it wasn't that simple. Shit, there was no way I was going to punk out. Well, just as it was about to go down, the trainer pulled up, beeping the horn like a fucking maniac. It somehow got our attention and Al and I locked eyes, quickly agreeing to our next move. We hauled ass out of that little park so fast and barely made it into the car before it spun off. Dudes was chasing us for blocks. Throwing bottles, rocks, sticks…anything they could find, but we made it."

I turned to look at Zoey. She was totally engrossed in the story by the way her face appeared frozen. I'd hoped I didn't scare her with a story that happened years ago.

I chuckled then waved my hand in her face. "Earth to Zoey," I teased.

She blinked and finally hummed, "I guess poor Alton never got to taste those doubles with cheese. Such a sad story."

I fell back, laughing hard as hell, holding my stomach. There was never a dull moment with this girl. Leave it to her to make light of Al and me damn near losing our careers and lives over a stupid challenge.

After she calmed from her laughing spell, she suggested, "Let's play a game." There again was that devilish twinkle in her eye.

"Ah…shit," I grunted. "What type of game? You already have me here eating s'mores at the fireplace like a damn suburban camper."

She giggled, and then started cleaning our mess from the hearth. As she began stacking the crackers, chocolate and bag of marshmallows, she explained, "Okay, the game is called, "Play the Game You Want to Play"."

As childish as the name and request for this game was, this girl could get whatever the hell she wanted from me. I was intrigued.

"What the fuck?" I barked as I followed her to the kitchen after grabbing what she couldn't fit in her arms. "I've never heard of said game."

She waited until we arrived at the kitchen to start explaining. "It's simple. You just tell me what fun thing...or play you want to engage in and we'll do it. Then before we turn in for the night, I'll pick the game I want us to play."

"I don't know, Zo. This seems fishy." I balled up my mouth.

"It's simple." She pushed out as she moved to stand in front of me, wrapping her arms around my waist. Zoey loved to touch. "Name one thing you want to do together right now." Her little head was at my chest with her chin in the air so she could see my face. I'd hope she didn't feel my dick inflating.

My eyes scanned out the window, straight ahead and saw the snow had come down pretty quickly since we'd returned from the grocery store. I wanted to ruffle her feathers, so to speak.

"I want to go outside in the snow." I squinted my eyes, seeing if she'd bail out of her own proposal.

"Okay," she perked up. "Meet you back down here in ten!" She smiled and damn near ran out of the kitchen.

Less than twenty minutes later we were out in the back, flinging snow at one another. Zoey jumped on my back, trying to get me to fall into the snow. She was very physical; always touching and trying to roughhouse with me. It was cute. Maybe because I knew she could never overpower me, even when I conceded and let her take me down. I found myself making animalistic noises to scare her as she ran for cover. We played out there for over an hour before calling it quits.

Zoey showered, and while I went downstairs to run, she cooked dinner. After my time on the treadmill, I showered and slipped on fresh clothes. I went looking for Zoey and found her in the guest bedroom. She was lying on the bed, looking at her phone.

"Hey, you bored yet?" I asked from the door.

She glanced up at me, but didn't have the smile or sneaky grin she usually wore.

"I thought you got lost in this place," she noted on a yawn as she stretched in the bed.

"Funny," I chuckled. "Is dinner ready? You ready to eat?"

"No. I'm not all that hungry yet." She sat up on the bed, then *that* smile slowly appeared. *So damn pretty.* "And we can't eat yet. I haven't gotten my turn at the game."

I had to take a second to think of what the hell she was talking about. Then it hit me; the damn game she proposed earlier. She must have been able to see me registering it from the look on my face because her cocky grin appeared.

"Mmmmhmmm!" she confirmed smugly. "Don't think I forgot."

Her expression was sly, but seeing that she hadn't tried anything since last night, I couldn't believe it was suggestive. All day, I'd been questioning my decision of turning her away. Suddenly, there was nothing I wanted more than to explore that delicious body of hers. *Shit! I can't think about that right now!* I didn't want to ruin my friendship with her, no matter how much it made me feel like a bitch.

Zoey jumped off the bed and met me at the door. She nudged my arm with her fist. "My turn to play "Play the Game You Want to Play." And my game is *Hide-and-Go-Seek*!"

Zoey's eyes grew big as lemons, she was so fucking excited. I thought it was funny and busted out laughing.

"Hey!" She punched me this time. "I don't see what's so funny!"

"*Hide-and-Go-Seek* in the house, Zo? What are we…three years old?"

"Did I laugh when you wanted to go play in the snow?"

Trying to slow my breath, I argued, "That was more like a physical activity." She had to be kidding me.

"Well, this one is more mental." She crossed her arms over her chest and pouted. She wasn't kidding.

"Okay," I exhaled. "When do you wanna get started?"

"Now!" she bounced on her toes in delight. "And to show forgiveness for your lack of appreciation of my game, I'll let you go first. The only rules are you cannot leave the house and cannot hide behind locked doors. Deal?" She extended her little hand.

I took it and gave her a firm shake. "Deal."

"Yippee!" she jumped up and down on her toes again. I couldn't ignore her boobs bouncing in her thin t-shirt. "Now, you go and I'll count to fifty."

She turned back into the room and started slowly counting. I stood there for a few seconds, watching her round booty jiggle, remembering why I decided to go along with this ridiculousness in the first place. By the time she got to twelve, I hauled ass out the door. I ran down the spiral staircase and hung a left. I couldn't believe how giddy I felt about hiding at my age. But as my socks slid against the shiny marble floors, it took my interest to a next level. I glided towards my study, but quickly decided that was too easy a location. I needed to make her search more difficult to end this game prematurely. *She'll get so frustrated that she'll forfeit her turn and call it quits.*

I opened the door to the basement level and ran past my gym, sauna, wine cellar, basketball court, and pool room. I didn't stop until I got to the storage room where the boiler was. Then I went deep inside the room and hid underneath the small window. From there I had perfect lighting to view the door *in case she was smart enough to find me all the way back here.*

My damn phone went off in my pocket. Quickly, I jumped to pull it out and switch off the ringer clip. It was a message from Alton.

Coach wants us early Wed morning.

I snorted. **Don't you think he told me dumb ass.**

O yeah. I guess so. LMAO. Im just bored as fiduk. What ass u into tonite?

How ironic a question. You mean whose ass *I* want to be *into, but can't man the fuck up.*

Just chillin' at the crib. I decided on.

U down the road or up the block?

Up the block. I replied.

Shit! Why the fuck did I tell him that? Now, his ass will be over while Zo—

"Here you are!" Zoey whispered hard, scaring the shit out of me.

"*Muthafuckin....!*" I damn near jumped out of my fucking socks.

Zoey held her stomach as she fell over laughing. I was mad as hell. Thanks to fucking Alton, I lost a game of *Hide-and-Go-Seek...in my house*...to a damn girl! Zoey couldn't stop laughing. She had tears falling from her eyes and could barely breathe. As fuming as I was, there was something about her laughter that nulled my irritation.

"Stent!" I heard like a balloon popping. I found Zoey, whose breaths were now coming in longer draws, looking at me.

"Huhn?" I asked.

"Who was that?" she asked in a tone that told me she was repeating herself.

"Oh! Ummm...Alton's dumb ass!" I grabbed my phone from the floor where it had landed.

"Well, give him my thanks for making this so easy. You didn't even hear me open the *d*-door!" she choked on her laughter.

Yeah, I damn sure will be telling his ass something. Even unknowingly, he put my ass out there.

"Your turn!" she yelled while she headed to the door, still laughing. "You have to count to fifty!"

I glanced down at my phone and found Al's last message.

Cool. Im cumin thru tomar

Don't even waste your fuckin time! He'd probably interfere in something else.

Whada fuk crawled up yo ass?

Before I could answer, my phone lit up with a call.

"Yeah, Zeek," I answered.

"Stent! I'm glad I caught you," my jeweler damn near shouted in my ear. "I wanted to know if you approved that design I sent over last week. I want to get started on it before the Valentine's Day crowd, man."

I took a deep breath, trying to calm myself from being scared the shit out of. I headed towards the door believing it had been at least fifty seconds. As I searched each unlocked room of the basement I spoke about the details of a diamond chain I was having made. Thank god there were just a few unlocked rooms down there; I could have been searching for hours.

I made my way to the main level, going room to room like a damn fourth grader. Midway through the house, I got discouraged, believing my conversation with Zeek was distracting my manhunt. He was asking me to recall details from his sketch.

"Let me go grab that from my bedroom. I'm on my way there now," I informed as I trekked the steps, two at a time.

"Okay, Stent, man, but it's on the edge of the cut that I altered. What you were asking for could compromise the security of the diamonds," he replied, still trying to make his point.

"All right, I see what you mean. I just need to see—"

My words were clipped at the sight of Zoey's naked body in front of my bed. Her face was blank. Her hands were clasped behind her...*expressing restraint.* Her toned right leg was crossed over her left. Her striking dark chocolate nipples were peaked. And there was something about the close cut bed of hair in her pelvis, neatly shaped that made my tongue curl my mouth.

Initially, it felt like a set up. Well, I'd been in the game long enough to know it *was* a set up...but not like the fucking vultures that come with being in the league. This was my sweet Zoey. The Zoey that had no damn clue of my salary. The one who probably didn't even know what position I played. Zoey didn't know about my *Pepsi* contract, or the *McDonald's* endorsement deal I'd just renewed, or about the sneaker line with *Nike*, or the *Cobalt* investment deal I'd just signed with Azmir Jacobs.

This was a different type of plotting.

But what the fuck?

Chapter Five

Zoey

"Yo, Zeek, man, I'mma hit you back," he spoke throatily into the phone before dropping it from his ear.

Expressionless, he stood there, staring at me from head to toe, not moving an inch. It wasn't exactly what I was expecting. *What was I expecting?* Eager anticipation perhaps. But not this.

His mouth finally opened and my heartbeat sped up. Then he closed it again and my breathing stopped. Stenton looked pained...certainly not up for what I was offering.

His mouth opened again and I refused to give him a reason to say no.

"We have condoms...all different brands and sizes for your choosing," I blurted out and then tried to smile.

He licked his lips and roughly brushed his face with a hand, looking away momentarily before returning his gaze to me.

"I wasn't going to say that," he informed, gruffly.

"Well, what were you going to say?" *Why did I ask that?* I told

105

myself going into this plan that I wouldn't give him even a window to exit again. We were doing this tonight. *Now!*

He closed his eyes while taking a deep breath. My heart stammered in my chest and my palms grew clammy.

"I was just gonna..." He shifted in stance. "I don't get no lingerie or nothing? I was looking forward to ripping it off."

I cracked a quivering smile. Still unable to move, I let out the air I'd been holding. *I don't own lingerie.* The closest thing I had to it were slips for church. I wore them under my usher uniform, and even those I shared with Ruth.

But still, Stent made not one advancement toward me. He didn't smile either. I arched a brow, goading him. *Why did I do that...*and so naturally? Stent brought out wanton behavior in me, forced me to push the barriers of my normal conduct. Apparently, it worked. In seconds, he pounced on me.

"*Uhhhhhh!*" flew from my lungs as my back slammed into the firm mattress, and in an instant, Stenton was sucking my tongue from my mouth.

White-hot excitement blossomed in my belly as his delicious virile scent assaulted all of my senses, causing me to shiver. I almost couldn't keep up with his rapid movements. My hands ran through the small and soft curls of his hair as I greedily pulled him into me. Then his clever tongue moved down my chin, my neck and then over to my clavicle. I lost it. My moans were involuntary, desperate. My pelvis pumped his waist with no particular cadence, and I began to resent the fabric of his clothing providing a barrier between us. Stent's mouth moved sinuously to my breasts, sucking and pulling and gently scraping my nipples, almost to the point of pain. Never before did I teeter on pleasure and pain. My head lobed left to right in my torment. I didn't know how to express my uncontrolled pleasure. I'd never experienced such unadulterated bliss. But I knew how to demand what I needed.

"Stent...I can't wait. Take off your clothes," I cried out. Then I started patting the bed around me in frantic search of a condom. "Here. Choose one." I handed him the first I could feel. "Hurry!"

Stenton's head rose from my belly and the glower of confusion he wore couldn't be missed. He contemplated for a minute before shuffling to his knees and dousing his shirt. Then he bent to rid himself of his basketball shorts and boxers. His swollen pelvis came into view, and underneath his bush of hairs, his long and thick erection sprung out like a miniature baseball bat. Its ridges were prominent. Its crest, wide and engorged, with a bead of liquid at the head. I swallowed hard, unprepared for this part.

How is he going to fit all of that into me?

"You cool, Zo?" The tortured squeak in his baritone caused my head to jerk up.

I bit my bottom lip and nodded my head casually, not wanting to ruin this. I was ready for him. When I observed the twitching of his appendage, I knew he was ready for me, too.

As he applied the condom, I watched absorbedly. My clitoris throbbed a rhythm and speed that echoed in my core. My eyes dipped back down below and I studied the ink that went into his pelvis, finally getting the full view of the collage. His thighs were surprisingly muscular unsheathed. They were columnar: strong and dense with wirehair sprouting indiscriminately. I'd never witnessed anything as male. His waist was narrow and when I angled my head just inches, I could see the curvy muscles in his glutes.

"Zo," he almost whispered, voice still seemingly laden in despair. "You're making that clicking sound with your throat again, baby."

I felt my chest rising and falling. The sight of my pebbled nipples and his throbbing erection in the same view, just centimeters away, nearly sent me adrift.

"Zoey, look at me," his voice was now impatient, thick, and raw. My explorative eyes met his. "We don't have to do this now. I don't want you to think this is something you have to do to be in my world. I-I care about you…a lot." He hesitated. "It's not like that between us. You're different—"

"I love you." I didn't recognize my own voice. I sounded desperate and overcome like a sex pet. "I've never loved *anything* like I do you," My voice flowed more sensual and brazen than my nerves were composed at the time. "I'm crazy about you and I want it all. I want this." I observed the deep caving of his chest at my confession. "And I want it now."

As Stent drew in a sharp intake of breath, his eyes grew. His long and wide chest nearly crashed into mine as his tongue hungrily flew into my mouth, ravishing me. I pulled him into me again by the back of his head and pushed my pelvis into him. When I felt the head of his thick erection rubbing against my slickened lips below, I knew there was no turning back. Instead of giving room to my escalating anxiety, I thrust into him. That's when I felt the start of him, but it was like he hit a wall. My back bowed over the bed and head pushed into the mattress. My bottom lip remained in between Stent's teeth. My breathing accelerated and I was panting, feeling dew sprout from my body. I saw his eyebrows knit together.

"Go!" I urged, not wanting him to think I was backing out. *Or that he should.*

He raised his hips and gently circled them; I assumed, trying to gain deeper entry. It wasn't working. *No!* I felt the tears rimming my lids. I had to do something and quick, too many factors working against my mission. I threw my arms around his neck and kissed him hard. Then I wrapped my legs around his waist and lifted my pelvis into him. Stenton grunted and plunged into me again, not making much progress. Fire shot through my belly and my legs trembled around him. His head flew up from my mouth.

He knew.

"Zoey!" he barked.

"Shhh! No...no...no! It's okay," I panted, trying to soothe his abrupt alarm.

He rested on his elbows, plank style above me. His labored breath, hitting my face at a rapid rate.

"Why didn't you tell me?" he implored.

"I didn't think it was a big deal," I whispered through the palpitating pain shooting through my groin.

"That's not a good explanation!"

I exhaled. "Because I didn't want you to turn me down."

"Turn you—" he sputtered. "Why would I do that? Did you plan this?"

Since that first kiss. I nodded my head. Stenton blew out another breath. My legs still gripped his waist to hold him in place. He was *still* inside of me, throbbing. I was *still* in pain, impatiently waiting.

He's going to stop this.

"I'm not your little sister, Stent. At least, that's not what I want to be anymore."

His angry eyes were like a smack in the face. "Is that what you think you are to me?"

I nodded firmly.

He snorted and I saw a lewd flash in his eyes. "You've been a lot of fucking things in my mind since last summer; a little sister has never been one of them."

Relief settled upon me like never before. Then I felt my panting return. My excitement resumed and determination reignited. But Stent was still motionless. I didn't want to waste another moment. I felt stretched beyond capacity in my groin and even considerably pained, still I was ready to see this through, to give Stenton something from me that no one could take away from us, and I couldn't get back.

I tried to wiggle in spite of the ripping sting below. Stent sucked in a breath and his eyes fluttered.

When they opened, he muttered inches away from my nose, "Now, I'm going to finish this because you seem to be so damned determined for some foolish ass reason." He rocked into me and my breath caught in my throat. I thought that was a bland reason, but wouldn't dare utter a complaint. He reared slowly and pushed in again. I could hear a groan from the back of his throat. "And because your pussy is so snug and warm and creamy that I can't stop."

That was it. I leaped up, pulling him into my arms and began to rock with him through the pain. With each thrust, the sting subsided. It took a minute or two, but he was eventually suctioning in and out of me with more ease. I started to feel the sweat on his arms and wiry back, his delicious scent blanketed me. Stenton lowered himself on his elbows, wedging my head into place and took my lips into his, wildly lashing through my mouth with hunger.

This was a different side. Here was a level of intimacy I quickly understood could only be experienced through sex. In this act, he was giving me a different passion than he gave on the court. His biggest fans would never experience the outpouring of his innermost like I was in that moment with him. This was a different greatness, and we were making it together.

Stenton's moans grew to generous proportions. He was vulnerable, needy. His body rocked into me and several muscles held on to mine like he needed me. And that's what I needed from him. I yearned to feel connected to him far beyond telephone conversations and text messages. I wanted a deeper bond. An exclusive attachment to him. I wanted inside of his very being, even if that meant allowing him inside of me.

Wracked with pain from rubber chafing my rawness, I felt pleasure like nothing that was described by any of my peers who shared their sexual experiences with me. As we smacked into each other, the world turned off and an exclusive piece of Stenton came alive inside of me. Our heads lay side by side as his hips rolled over mine, in between my quivering thighs. His ragged breathing into the side of my face as my lips literally touched his ear. In no time, Stenton's pants grew violent and uneven.

"I can't hold out," he cried desperately.

I didn't know what that meant. It made me a tad nervous. The only thing that didn't have me leaping from underneath him was that he was *inside* of *me*, and whatever it was causing this urgency in his body had emerged from our actions.

"I can't hold—" ripped from his lungs. I grew panicked. My grip on the wings of his broad sinewy back tightened. "Niñaaaaaaa!" he whispered in my ear like a carnal dream.

I clutched him closer to my chest as his body quivered and then stilled, then his pelvis jerked a few times again before collapsing onto mine. I felt his wildly racing heart against mine. I felt the burning at the surface of my vagina. I felt him pulsating deep in my womb. I felt ecstasy.

We remained that way until Stenton moved to alleviate his weight from my frame. I didn't mind his heaviness at all. He'd now calmed down. He was no longer in duress. Still, I wanted to soothe him. When he rose to his knees, my eyes trailed from his glossy face, neck, chest, and down to his semi-deflated penis that was covered in a pink condom.

"Is that…my blood?" I croaked out, feeling lightheaded by the consequences of my *bright* idea.

Stenton scoffed as he pulled my arm from over my eyes. "Don't go schoolgirl on me now. You weren't so bashful when your hot ass was seducing me."

I braved another sight at the small puddle that I discovered beneath me. I felt my mouth collapse.

"Uhn…hnnn. Look at the mess *you* made," he continued to tease in a tone that made me want to cause more of a mess by him taking me again.

I rolled my eyes. "It's not that big of a deal. You act as if you've never seen a little bodily fluid before," I shushed as I struggled to sit up; my muscles seemed to have locked into place.

"Hold!" Stent ordered as he pulled the condom off then jumped from the bed, seemingly with a totally opposite disposition than my languid one.

Within seconds, I heard the tub running from the other room. I maneuvered around, trying to assess the damage. No matter how gruesome the blood scene appeared, I couldn't ignore the happiness blooming in my heart. I'd finally made love with Stenton.

Or is that what we'd just done?

Stenton jogged back into the main area of the room and held his hand out to me. Lazily, I wiggled off the high bed and wobbled into the bathroom. I could hear Stenton's low giggles behind me.

He ran a rather hot bath. I stepped in, trembling from my muscles being delicate. He clicked a wall device next to the vanity and calming music flowed into the room. Before joining me, he lowered the lights. Stenton's long legs encircled mine and I experienced a new level of intimacy. He pulled me back to his chest and we laid in silence. So many things ran through my mind as I examined the beat of his heart.

"Why so quiet, Zo?" his tenor created a rumbling in his chest against my head.

"No reason," I sighed.

"Bullshit," he replied calmly.

Okay. I turned towards him, causing a disturbance in the water. "What we did…" I started, peering directly in his eyes. "What do you call that?"

He examined my eyes for a while before murmuring, "Something I've never done before."

My eyes collapsed shut and I shook my head softly. That wasn't good enough. "Did we make love, Stent?"

"What do you call it?" he asked calmly.

I licked my lips, strangely nervous about putting my feelings out there.

"Would you have done it even if I'd told you I was a virgin? I mean…eventually?"

Still unperturbed, he studied me more before taking me by the shoulders and turning me around and into his chest again. His arms encased me and he reverently kissed my forehead.

"Zo, I can't lie. What you did was foul. I should've known you were a damn virgin," his tone laced with anger. But did he regret it? "You never let a man take you without prepping you first."

I tensed in front of him, separating inches away. "Prepping?"

"Yes." His fingers reached around for my chin and I turned my body completely to face him, my knees up to my neck. And when I did, my stomach flipped at the somberness of his eyes. "You don't think I had my fantasies about our first time together? You ever think about how I wanted to kick off this part of our relationship? The way I crave to taste every inch of your body?" His eyes lowered to underneath my legs. "Especially there."

My gaze dropped embarrassingly and I swallowed hard. I hadn't thought of any of that. I wasn't convinced Stenton even wanted me that way. Suddenly, I was ashamed.

"Just tell me you don't consider me a brute now. Tell me you don't regret me indulging in your innocence and I can admit to you that I had the time of my life inside you for those few short minutes."

I exhaled as I turned my body and melted into him, feeling more secure.

"You think too much, Zo. You didn't have to plot to get me to hit," he murmured.

I snorted, "Oh, really? Like you would've made the first move before my thirtieth birthday."

I felt the rumble of his quiet laughter in his chest against my head. "I was coming. You're just too damn fast."

"Yeah! The girl who kept her virginity until twenty, and had to trick a man by playing *Hide-and-Go-Seek* in his mansion to get rid of it. Picture that." I rolled my eyes into the air.

Stent laughed and his arms held me tighter. We sat for a while. There was so much in the air between us, but I wasn't savvy enough to confront it. The sound of Stent's stomach growling pulled me from my sleepy state.

"You're hungry."

"Yeah," he breathed lazily. "I didn't have my usual protein drink after my run."

I started to get up. "Let me warm up dinner." I don't think I ever sounded so domesticated.

Stent grabbed my wrist. "Relax for a minute. Soak your muscles. I'm gonna shower and change the bedding before we eat."

And that's what we did. We didn't talk much for the remainder of the night. We weren't troubled, just different. I sure as heck felt different. I felt full and…accomplished. I'd finally let go of my virginity to a man I loved. No matter what happened going forward —good or bad—I'd never regret giving it to Stenton.

When we finally crawled into bed that night on clean bedding, I adjusted my body into Stent's hard and warm frame and shivered when I felt his lips kiss my shoulder goodnight.

The next day, I woke up to an empty bed. I knew immediately Stent was off to work out. I slowly made my way down to the kitchen. My body ached in the same manner it did after an exercise when I hadn't for so long.

After deciding on waffles, eggs and bacon, I slipped my earplugs in and got to work. I zoned out, frying bacon, whipping eggs and battering the waffle-maker. I was so engrossed in my head that I nearly dropped the tongs when Stenton grabbed me from behind. I snatched my earplugs out and turned to him, steam shooting from my ears.

"Are you crazy?"

He couldn't stop laughing. He held on to his belly as he hurled over in laughter. I wanted an explanation, but he could hardly breathe. I gave him time to recover as I returned to cooking. He was still sweaty from working out. Stenton looked younger and peaceful when he laughed. Although we did a lot of that, it never got dull seeing him mirthful. I felt my anger about his scaring me ebb the longer he exposed his teeth.

"What are you so engrossed in that you could be scared like that?" He pulled at my earplugs and listened.

It was Marvin Sapp's *In the Garden*, one of my favorite morning worship songs. He looked at me with a sober expression.

I shrugged my shoulders. "Morning worship," I offered while turning over the bacon.

Stent returned a firm nod, being respectful of my unpopular practices, I guessed.

"I guess you're eating in your sweats because breakfast is served in less than five. This food won't stay warm throughout a shower."

He raised his long arms then slapped them against the outside of his thighs. "If you accept me as is, I am."

At the mammoth island, we ate and were successful at avoiding the neon pink elephant in the room. Not only did I wake up sore, I also fought with guilt. What I did was a bit sneaky. I didn't regret making love to Stent at all, just the way that I'd gone about it.

"So, what's on the agenda today?" I asked.

"If we're not playing any more games, I do have some action flicks I'd like to catch up on."

"Are they gruesome?"

"No." He shook his head as he took a sip of his juice. "But considering what you watched the first night we got here, you should be able to more than stomach the movies I have in mind."

"Okay, then I can pick the next activity."

Stenton rolled his eyes, adorably. "What would that be?" He feigned annoyance.

"Teaching you how to cook."

He paused his chewing and gave me a blank stare. "Cook?" he mumbled with a mouthful. "For what?"

"Because we should all at least know how to fry an egg…successfully."

"I don't need to learn how to cook, just work to pay someone else to do it for me," he garbled before swallowing his food.

I shook my head. "You need to know how to cook to fend for yourself in the event you're without a cook, like now."

"But you're here and you can cook."

"What if it wasn't me? What if I couldn't cook?" I challenged.

He held his glass to his mouth as he replied, "Zo, no other female alive could get me to drop everything and come up here on the fly. So I knew like hell you could cook or else we'd starve."

"But you assumed I could cook. You shouldn't do that, Stent. I don't mind cooking. I love it actually, but everyone should know how to cook. You could find yourself stranded with another woman who can't cook. Just look at it as an added skill." I shrugged again and turned my attention to my plate. "Some girls like men who cook."

From my peripheral I could see Stent frozen on his stool. I don't know why I *had* to mention him being with another woman. He was with me and that's all that should have mattered. Then why was I going the jealous route? I'm never jealous.

Does sex do this to women?

No! I will not be that woman.

"Okay," I heard him murmur. I braved a glance up at him. "You can teach me how to cook."

The doorbell rang, stealing our attention. Stent grunted and mumbled some expletive-filled phrase before standing to get the door. I was left wondering if learning how to cook for women was his motivation for consenting.

Silly girl!

I heard mumbling outside of the massive kitchen. Then clear

words grew louder just before Alton turned the corner and entered. He was wearing a black goose, sweats and *Timberland* boots.

"Noooooooooooooo!" he sang, almost in a tormented fashion. My brows knitted. Alton's upper body slammed down into his legs, bringing his athleticism to life, as he continued crying out the word.

He was not the only person surprised. No one knew Stenton and I were friends. It was our secret. In my deluded mind, I was still afraid of Angela finding out and feeling betrayed. *So what she'd slept with Alton enough to forget her strong attraction to Stenton.* This wasn't good for me…at all.

Alton continued with his melodramatic antics, throwing himself into the wall next to him. Falling into the counter, holding his chest. "I can't believe this shit! Why ain't nobody tell me?" He turned to Stenton and cried, "Are you serious, Stent? I thought we were bro-besties, man!" Then his eyes lit up like a Christmas tree. "Fucking Angela lied again! Zo ain't no damn virgin, I see!"

I gasped at not only his brashness, but his knowledge of my virginity. Stenton's neck collapsed and he covered his face with his hand. I was mortified.

"Did she tell you that?" I asked, aghast.

"Yeah, but I kinda believed her. You do come across a little Virgin Mary-ish, Zo. I mean, church girls lose their virginities before their asses are even baptized. Y'all are the best pieces of ass…all freaky and shit! Trust me, I know. Angela was my latest conquest."

"Aye, man!" Stenton growled. "Don't come over here with that bullshit."

Almost at the same time, I grounded out, "The only ass I see here is you, Alton!" I got up to leave the room.

Stenton grabbed my arm at the same time Alton jumped to the entryway in an attempt to cut me off. Stenton protectively pulled me into him, my back to his broad chest.

Alton touched his chest, gesturing his heart. "Aye, Zo, man, you know it ain't no disrespect! We all know you carry yourself with class. It's just that Stent, my man right here, ain't give me the heads up." He lifted his hand to motion to Stent above me.

"I can't believe she told you that!" I yelped, referring to Angela.

That little wench!

Stenton's arms around my wrists clenched.

"Why not?" Alton grimaced. "Everybody knows ol' Ally-boy is trustworthy. I can keep a fucking secret. At least that's what I thought." He threw a nasty glare at Stenton. If I wasn't so livid I would have laughed.

"Look," Stenton spoke up. "I don't give a shit what you think you know or what you thought you knew, I just wanna make one damn thing clear: this doesn't get back to Angela. What Zoey wants her or anyone else to know is up to Zoey. You big ass, loose-lip, don't open your fucking trap."

Alton's forehead stretched as his chin angled towards the floor. "And am I the one who can tell Angela? I know she's even a bigger liar than I knew her to be when she tried to throw a baby on moi." He tented his hands in his chest, pointing to himself. "Ha!" he yelled. "Nisha will have my ass on a skewer! I'm still on punishment behind Angela's lying ass."

I lowered my head, shaking it. "Of course, Alton, you had no involvement in that debauchery," I murmured loud enough for him to hear.

"I didn't! She fuckin' seduced me…each time!" I slightly jumped in Stent's arms, turning to catch his reaction to Alton's usage of the word *seduced*.

Is that what I did to him last night?

Apparently he caught my questioning glare. Stenton's lips twitched up into a knowing smile.

"Y'all was there to witness that shit. I almost called y'all to the stand when Nisha was trying my ass." Alton held out his arms, motioning for me to hug him.

Stent let my wrists go, encouraging this make up session Alton was attempting. I strolled over, hesitantly. I was still seething from Angela's big slip of the mouth. How many others had she told?

"I know I'm an ass, Zo, man. I can't help it," Alton's voice was with less bravado. I was falling for his white flag, hard. "You are good peoples to me. I ain't mean no disrespect," his voice cooed as his arms wrapped around me. "Damn, you smell good as hell. Mmmmm!"

I jumped from his fold.

"I'm just kidding, Zo. Damn!" He laughed as he held his arms out defensively. "Just kidding. You got this dude over here ready to pounce on my ass like a fucking cheetah, man," he jeered as he walked out of the kitchen. "I'm going running downstairs then I'm watching T.V. Holla atcha' boy, StentRo!" Alton called over his shoulder.

I turned to Stenton, not knowing what to say about his rowdy friend. He was pinching his nose trying to control his laughter.

"I can't believe what the wind blew in," I hissed.

"Yeah, and because I slipped up and told him I was in town last night while caught up, playing your fucking game, he'll be here all damn day," Stent informed with amusement in his voice.

I turned in the direction where Alton had just left. "He's going to work out—"

"...here, shower here, and relax here. Yes," he cut me off to clarify. "Thanks to his summer fling, Alton's officially on time out at the order of Tynisha. They live next door in Upper Saddle River. This is his asylum."

"Oh," was all I could say, piecing together the crazy life and relationship between Alton and Tynisha. This had to be a full time job for her, like raising another child. But I wondered why she would be okay with him hanging out at Stent's place. It said a lot about her perception of Stenton.

I felt his warm lips on my forehead, reminding me he was still in the room. "I'm going to take a shower. We can watch a movie and then cook whenever you're ready," Stent murmured before leaving me there in the kitchen.

I went for my phone, prepared to text Angela and give her a piece of my mind. She knew better than to share that with a stranger. Not that my virginity was a big deal to me, but it was private. *What if I told Stenton about all her sexcapades with men over the years?*

I had all my words planned out, but when I picked up my phone

I couldn't do it. I knew Angela was in a bad place with the pregnancy and the last thing she needed was her past with Alton coming up at such a delicate time.

The day progressed. When Stenton was done with his shower, we made the marinade for the chicken we were going to prepare that night. It was cute watching his lanky figure in a massive kitchen, matching his size, but it being the most awkward room for him at the same time. We made a few snacks and took them to the theater room to watch movies with Alton. Alton offered me a beer and Stenton darn near bit his head off. I didn't understand why, but like Alton, I respectfully sat back without questioning it. The doorbell rang again and Stenton jogged out of the room to get it, returning twenty minutes later to finish the movie.

A few hours later, Stenton uprooted from beneath me and left the room. Alton and I remained, watching *Hostel*. After some time, I missed him. Maybe because my temperature dropped and I didn't have his body's natural heat covering me, I'd become conscious of his absence. Then I caught him in my peripheral, and when I peered up, he gave a reverse nod, requesting that I join him. Without hesitation, I rose from the ginormous sofa and strode past Alton, whose eyes stayed glued to the screen.

When I approached Stenton, he took me by the hand and walked me through the house and to the master suite. I noticed immediately the door was closed, which struck me as odd.

We stopped at the doorframe and Stenton turned me at the shoulders to face him. "Zo, listen... Before we go inside, I need for you to consent to something and then make a promise to me."

I nodded dubiously.

Stenton exhaled and rested his arm above his head, on the door, and buried his face in the crux of it. He eventually threw me a strange regard.

"That didn't come out right. Let me say this. Last night was not how I wanted our first time to be." Hearing that warmed me. I didn't know Stenton had thoughts of being with me sexually. "It wasn't my style at all. My sexual style can be a bit…eclectic."

I nodded again, inviting him to continue.

"I want to share with you what I'm into, but I need you to give consent to it first, and then promise me you won't run for the hills after."

My pulse quickened. The jolt of excitement I felt was unparalleled. I'd always been said to be a daredevil, and in that moment I understood why. I would do anything with Stenton.

I nodded slightly, but executed, "Yeah...yeah!" more convincingly.

Stenton's deep and piercing gaze vacillated between doubtful, then desperate, and then finally to convinced. He sighed heavily and went to his pocket and pulled out a strap of cloth. He turned me around to tie it over my eyes. It happened so quickly that I found myself panting.

"You said you trusted me, so I don't want to hear doubt from here on out," he informed throatily.

My mouth was too dry for me to speak, but I don't think Stenton wanted me to. I then heard the unclicking of the door. Stenton took me by the hand and led me into his bedroom. We walked a bit before I felt the coolness of the marble floors underneath my feet making me aware of entering the bathroom. Next, Stenton removed my clothes. He then assisted me into the Jacuzzi where he washed me fully and gently. He didn't speak, and though as unfamiliar with his touch as I was at the time, it felt hesitant. That bothered me.

"Stent."

His roaming hand that was rinsing the soap from my back froze. "Yes."

"I'm okay. I'm not afraid. I'm not unsure. I'm not concerned— curious as all get out...yes, but that's all."

I felt his cool breath hit my wet skin when he exhaled. There was a tentative pause before he asked me to stand and dried me off. Then I stood on the fluffy rug and endured the torment of him massaging a cream into my body, feeling him apply soft worshipful kisses in various places, especially my wrists and ankles. I had mixed feelings when he stopped.

Stenton took me by the hand and led me out into the bedroom.

He stopped and rounded me, pulling his long arms around my waist and into his frame so snug that I felt his erection on my lower back. He buried his face into my neck and inhaled deeply, sending chills down my spine. My breathing spiked.

"Niña…" he murmured adoringly, almost desperately. "I'm going to uncover your eyes." I could feel each syllable he spoke reverberating in my core. Stenton's voice was low, gruff, heavy, and wanting. "Now, if you run like a bat out of hell, not only will you be naked in affluent Alpine, but your skin is still damp and your mom'll tell you that condition doesn't mix well with winter temperatures."

With my mouth agape, I nodded, desperate to experience whatever he was proposing.

When the blindfold was removed, I had to take a moment to adjust my eyes. Everything seemed in place to me. Nothing was unusual or new. I didn't get it. Then Stenton took me by the shoulders again, slightly pivoting me a thirty degree angle to have a frontal view of the bed. That's when I saw it.

In each of the four corners of his bed were long black straps, crossing the bed, with metal chains at the ends that attached to another strap, lined with Velcro. It took no time for me to register the application.

"You're into BDSM?"

I could feel Stenton's chuckle from above as his chin rested on the top of my head.

"Very mildly. Only the bondage."

I steeled in place, shocked that I'd missed it. Stenton had been so passive about sex, leaving me to be the aggressor. I didn't think that was the characteristic of a person with kink.

"Are you going to speak again or run? Because I've changed my mind about allowing you out of here if you decide to, having seen *you* and *those* in the same place." His voice poured out like a pained hum.

Still not in control of my breathing, I answered, "I'm not running. I mean…I won't be running."

Another exhale escaped him. "Good, Niña."

"But why the restraints? What draws you to that type of kink?"

That quickly, I regretted the term.

Stenton's laughter extended this time. I was relieved I didn't offend him.

"I like the idea of having you helplessly at my mercy and direction when bringing you pleasure."

"Me? I'm the only woman you've done this with? Because Mr. Rogers, I don't mind being your guinea pig, but it'll be mighty embarrassing having a firefighter release me from those devices."

"No, but I don't think I've ever wanted it more with a woman than I do with you."

Not able to peel my gaze from the restraints, I shrugged. "Then, let's do it."

My body was roughly turned, completely. Stenton's scowl bore into me.

"You fucking inspire me, Zoey. You're so bold and daring. You have no idea how much of that energy I pull from you when you're not with me."

I gasped. Undulated exhilaration coursed my sensually heightened body. Though my sex was still a bit tender from the night before, I wanted Stenton so bad, pleasure and pain. I jumped into his arms, clamping every limb onto his frame.

"Show me," I found myself purring.

Stenton's lips crashed into mine, his tongue touring my mouth with hunger. His long hands tightly gripping my backside, lifting me onto him, had me eagerly climbing his trunk. He gently laid me at the center of the bed and slowly strapped my wrists and ankles in the restraints, my pulse raced with grave anticipation at the sound of each application.

When he was done, Stenton stepped back and observed his handiwork, forcing me to do the same. My breasts sat high and perky, swollen at the apex. My legs were spread eagle, my sex totally exposed to him. I felt dizzy with longing, so carnal and out of my controlled element.

"You're so fucking beautiful just like this, Niña. You have no idea how crazy I feel right now." The molten look in his eyes gave me an idea.

I felt wholly feminine, paradoxically powerful while restrained.

Turned on by his appraisal and antsy to explore whatever he had coming, I cried out, "Stenton." It was more of a whisper. A plea.

"Fuck, Zo!" he growled and climbed on the bed appearing very feral.

Stenton greedily took to my body with his hungry mouth, devouring my breasts before slowly moving south. I lay there, panting maniacally, and shivering, enjoying every swipe his tongue paid my heightened skin, and each kiss his warm and cushioned lips bestowed on my trembling frame. Stenton was no longer the hesitant lover I'd perceived last night. Tonight, he was the measured and provocative aggressor, and that equally excited and frightened me.

When his face hit my core, my pelvis jolted. Stenton's head rose to give me a moment to relax, and eventually I did. His mouth returned, applying chaste kisses down my slickened feminine lips. Mechanically, I tried closing my thighs, but the restraints prevented that. Then I felt the force of his stiffened tongue move along the opening of my labia. I shivered. He did it again, this time adding more pressure. His tongue moved up and down in patient succession and the more he moved, the tighter the strain I put on my limbs in the restraints. Stenton must have felt my tensing because his head swung up and I could see his questioning scowl.

"You've never been tasted." My belly tightened with tension. It was more of a statement, but one that required confirmation.

I bit my quivering lips.

Immediately, Stenton mumbled, "The fuck was I thinking?" It was hardly audible.

It took agonizing seconds for Stenton to pull himself together.

"Niña, you have to relax and trust me to bring you pleasure. Do you trust me?"

With wild eyes my head bobbed enthusiastically because I totally trusted Stenton and on more than a sexual level. I *especially* needed him to know that.

He caught it. Stenton gave me a slight affirmative nod and deep gaze before he adjusted himself on his knees and lowered his face between my legs then brandished his urgent tongue against my clitoris, thrashing it with wild abandon. In an instant, I felt a wave of heat hit my groin, causing my back to arch over the mattress and my breathing to spike. The sensations undulating my core were nothing my mere mind ever schemed. The grip Stenton had on my hips as he generously fed himself my sex left me little room to escape the pleasure he was forcing me to endure.

I felt a stirring in my groin. It was something I couldn't control, nor was it a sensation I could manage or delay. As the cyclic pleasure built, my hips began to buck wildly. Through my heavy eyes above my heaving chest and tautened coffee nipples, I could see Stenton position himself on his knees as if to prepare to catch something.

A deep, untamed, and obscene cry rumbled from the back of my throat. What I intended to be *Stenton* ended up being a confused plea for something. I yelped from the rolls of unadulterated pleasure that whirled the trunk of my body, causing me to thrust my pelvis into his face as I pulled against the restraints and cried out in blissful insanity.

In the next beat, Stenton was on top of me, his tongue thrashing my mouth, familiarizing me with the taste and musk of my femininity.

Into my lips he murmured, "I can eat you all day. Hearing your cries makes me lose control. You make me crazy, Niña. So fucking amazing." His words were almost incoherent.

Then I felt him breach my sex in a rapid movement. I grunted from the spark of pain that accompanied his fullness. The way Stenton's big arms and hands cradled my shoulders and head made me feel a comfort that was converse to the pressure below. Unlike last night, Stenton's plunges were delivered with increased urgency. He moved forcefully, filling me more with each thrust.

"Lift your hips, baby. I need you to feel me everywhere," he spoke into my ear while plummeting into me.

I did feel him everywhere. There was no room left in me, but I followed his instruction. As I received his swift pushes, I felt flashes of pleasure with each one. But more than that, I felt an incredible vantage point to his essence. Like last night, I felt intimacy with Stenton that his legions of Angela-like admirers would never experience. Sure, he'd had countless partners, but I couldn't imagine him exposing his rawness to all of them. In an instant, I was addicted to this connection to him. I relished in each droplet of his sweat that fell onto my trembling body. I enjoyed feeling his various hard body parts rolling over me, in me, and gripping me. He was using every inch of his taut body he could to work my frame.

"I can't hold out anymore, baby!" Stenton groaned severely into my neck.

There was that cry again. I still didn't totally understand what it meant, but I knew the end result. I couldn't wrap my arms around him, so instead I increased my hips thrusts to meet his. As he bucked feverishly into me, I intersected with a sensation growing from my core that was so powerful it scared me. I held my breath to avoid it and as soon as it abated, Stenton grunted in my ear, stirring it again. My body tensed as I tried to run from it again. In that moment, I'd experienced the most incredible duality of pleasure-confusion and fear. As Stenton suspended his movements on top of me indicating his release, I told myself if I ever met that sensation again I wouldn't run from it; I'd collide with it.

In my rumination, I didn't know when Stenton's eyes appeared on me. I felt how large mine were as I laid there processing all that had just happened.

"I felt you clenching me. Did you come?" his voice was throaty.

"I don't think so." My eyes fluttered at the embarrassment of the topic. "I don't know."

He applied chaste kisses from my jaw, down onto my neck. "No need to feel shame about it. We'll get you there soon."

I was still panting when I whispered, "Okay."

Stenton kissed me passionately again and for so long when he pulled away, he jumped off of me completely.

"Fuck, Zo!" He went for the restraint on my left wrist to release me. "I keep forgetting you're a newbie. I have to take care of you."

I was fine, at least I felt that way. When Stenton was done, he pulled me into his arms and I, at some point, drifted off, blissfully depleted.

I felt the mattress lift. Cracking a lid, I saw Stenton leave the bed for the bathroom. As he ambled there, I saw him carrying the condom. I was glad he was being responsible and protecting me. When he returned, he lifted me from the bed and lowered me into the Jacuzzi. Stenton's touch was just as reverential as it was earlier, it was also more evaluative as he inspected my wrists and ankles. Once again, we found ourselves depleted and in need of food.

I slowly made my way to the kitchen with Stenton just behind me, and we worked together on dinner. Alton joined us, bringing his obtuse sense of humor.

"So now Nisha be on that '*don't forget your diet*' shit!" Alton complained animatedly. I can't eat dairy, sugar, red meat, pink meat —shit, I was like can I eat pussy?"

I cupped my mouth at that one, then threw Stenton an inquisitive and alarming glare. Like me, unable to control his laughter, Stenton shrugged his shoulders.

"I bet if *that* was restricted, Nisha ass won't be playing diet cop!" Alton took to his plate and forked a piece of chicken breast before continuing with his tirade.

This was one event that Stenton nor I minded. You could tell in the glances he threw me the entire meal that he was on the same cloud of love that I'd been savoring.

Alton left close to midnight. Apparently that was his curfew. When Tynisha began blowing up his phone and Stenton's, even I feared her wrath. Alton may have mumbled a few invectives, but he drug his butt out of there wearing a long moue. Stenton and I turned in ourselves. It felt good to be expected to sleep with him in his bed and not having to sneak in like the pesky little sister.

The next day, Stenton worked out first thing in the morning as usual. He had a long conference call that went well into the afternoon. While he was preoccupied, I finally took the liberty of exploring his expansive home. I couldn't believe the opulence—high cathedral walls and ceilings, marble floors and the overall beautiful architectural layout. The place was larger than any of the homes my mother cleaned. That thought led me to call and check in on her and my dad.

When I was done with the call, I found Stenton still in his office, on the computer. I thought he would have come to find me after his call was over. To say we spent the night together, he seemed so distant. He didn't touch me or talk much. I didn't know how to read his mood. I spent most of the morning pondering just that.

Stenton

I was watching the game in the theater room, not really paying Zoey much attention. She wandered out, mumbling about getting something from the kitchen some time ago. She'd been sulking all damn day. She wasn't alone, and ironically, not just for the same reason. I'd been feeling fucked up the entire day, almost to the point of a tension headache. I couldn't believe the sick thoughts that derived from my brain.

What the fuck was I doing with this sweet young girl?

She had the brightest future ahead, unlike any of the birds I'd come up with in Brick City or in the industry. Zoey was smart, strong…filled with substance. She was a damn church girl, for crying the fuck out loud! Again… What the fuck was I doing with her? Maybe it wouldn't work, maybe she had someone…or something looking out for her. Suddenly, my attention wasn't solely on the screen. I was on another planet, hating myself for defiling a young woman who had great things ahead of her.

Unexpectedly, I felt Zoey swing her leg over my lap. With two hands she gripped my face, rubbed her warm nose against mine, placed her soft and moist lips against my mouth and sucked my bottom one. Before I could react, her wet tongue darted between my lips, ravishing me. My dick sprang to life immediately. Her tongue's movements were swift and her lips were firm. I was caught up instantly. My hands gripped her soft ass, pulling her into me. I felt intoxicated. Zoey was turning into a drug I'd immediately become addicted to. She swiped her hand into the breast of her gown and pulled out a condom, handing it to me.

Quickly, she released my lips and whispered hard, "Put it on."

What the fuck? This was the last thing I was expecting.

I was stunned, but without hesitation, I obeyed my Niña's command because I couldn't deny her anything. She lifted from my lap for a minute to give me room to maneuver between us. I'd be damned if before I could remove my hand from rolling the rubber down my dick, she didn't push her little pussy down over me.

"Whoa, Zo! Don't hurt yourself," I whispered, my bottom lip collapsed.

Plunging down again, she tried to take more of me in. Zoey was inexperienced, *so I'd recently learned.* I didn't want to hurt her—or have her hurt herself. I gripped her hips tightly to slow her moves. She removed her busy tongue and lips from me and leveled her smoldering eyes with mine as she ground into me.

"I leave tomorrow…won't see you until god knows when…" She sighed, taking more of me in. "…and…you…don't see the urgency? What am I going to do when I need you?" She thrust even lower and forcefully onto me. "…and you're not next to me? What do I do when *you* need this and have to seek it out elsewhere?"

Fuck! I can only be with you like this, Zo…

She kept moving, mostly without a particular rhythm, but I was able to steady her at the waist. My resolute Niña kept at it and at it, throwing herself into me—her warm treasure, her firm breasts in my face. I couldn't get enough of her. I pulled down the straps to her gown, releasing her mounds. She then tossed her head back as I ravished them. I lifted my hips, pushing deeper into her, turned the fuck on by her sudden boldness in sexuality. This was the perspective I'd had of her outside of sex. It excited me. Aroused me like nothing before.

Zoey's head popped forward and took my mouth again. Something about the determination in her movements pulled me in. Her pelvis plummeted into mine deliciously. In no time, I was balls deep. I grabbed her by the back of the head with one hand and used the other to pull at her right nipple. In no time, Zoey's head withdrew from my face. Her lips trembled. My eyes grew. Her movements went fucking frantic. My mouth dropped. Her breathing turned erratic. My hips bucked wildly into her. Her lips parted and eyes rolled to the back of her head. And then I knew, my baby girl was experiencing her first vaginal orgasm.

Something in my chest burst.

"I love you," I croaked out as I wrapped my right arm around her small waist to piston into her, half past crazy, but not coming yet myself. I just wanted to enjoy this moment with her.

Damn, I wish I could catch this on camera! She's fucking beautiful undone.

"Stent!" she purred so damn femininely.

I couldn't believe my little lady was feeling this ecstasy for the first time. I was so damn happy for her. This was our moment. This was something no one could ever reverse or erase.

I felt the first of my spurt.

"Fuck, Niña!" My heart was pounding so fast, but the ecstasy I felt right along with her could rival anything as I held her so tightly with my ass suspended in the air while my orgasm overtook me.

Everything was perfect. All things felt right. That night, in bed, I held her close to me, because it felt right. She felt right. I slept soundly with her underneath me. Zoey felt like an extension of me, something I'd never experienced in life. I felt peace.

The next morning, as we arose before dawn and left the house, something inside me shifted. I'd started expecting Zoey to change. I found myself, on the ride to Princeton, waiting for her to ask for something: money or a relationship title, all the things that women who sleep with men of my status ask for. However, none of those things came.

When I dropped Zoey off at school, there was another shifting taking place between us. Zoey took a moment to meekly tell me she had a good time and even went to the extent of thanking me for having her. Unbeknownst to her, I got angry. What incensed me was equally as frustrating. It was because I didn't know what to do with the feelings that had been established or the inexplicable ones burgeoning. I hated that I didn't know her angle. Hated that I had no clue as to what was to come with this young woman. Was this a game? She'd already admitted to setting me up. But for what? Everyone had an angle. Everyone wanted something from people like me. I felt suckered.

But damn was it beautiful manipulation.

I fucking told this girl I loved her!

And I did.

Zoey was the only woman, other than my mother, that I'd ever spoken those words to and meant it from the pits of my gut. I felt like I was walking into some shit I knew I wasn't prepared for. It made me feel insecure like a motherfucker. The look in her eyes when she left my Lambo… Was it remorse? Was it an act? Well, time would tell.

As I merged onto I-95 South, I turned up the volume on some old Redman, zoned out and prepared myself for work that lay ahead.

Practice was brutal. It wasn't just the physical exertion that beat on me, it was the questions from my coaches and trainers about my hiatus. It was the stares that I got when I didn't make the shots. It was the sideway glances from my assistant that I received when I wouldn't provide an answer for my whereabouts. It was the images that I couldn't get out of my fucking head of a young woman, laughing, running, and coming in my goddamn face—even into the game that night—preventing me from giving it my all. We won by a mere three points. No one uttered a word in the locker room, not even Al, who knew where I was and with whom.

When I went to bed that night, I checked my phone again and saw no trace of contact from Zoey. I was pissed the fuck off that *that* pissed me the fuck off, too.

Chapter Six

Stenton

The room is ringing with laughter and people greeting one another, and others gushing over the bride and groom. It's Alton and Tynisha's wedding day and they did it up some kind of proper. I mean the ballroom is lined in glass crystals and fancy ass flower arrangements. Wait staff is balancing trays on their shoulders as they serve drinks and refill glasses. *Damn!* I recalled him saying Tynisha's reality show network was footing the bill, but I still cringe at the potential setback of all the glamour.

There are cameras every damn where. I have to do something I've found difficult to do all day; smile. It's difficult for me to do something I'm often paid to do when modeling is a part of my endorsement agreement. What I'm struggling with is how can such a great occasion bring so much fucking gloom to my disposition.

"Excuse me. Excuse me," I hear from the speakers around the room.

I turn from the bar to find Tynisha framed beautifully in lace in her reception gown next to Alton's tiny ass. Short and all, my man

131

looks good in his tan tuxedo and brown dress shoes. His cut is sharp and swag is on blast all day. I couldn't be mad at him. Alton has finally manned up.

"I just wanna thank everybody for making this a happy ass day for me. Nish can speak for herself." He gives Tynisha a salacious once-over and who can blame him? She is finally his. "...but as far as I'm concerned, I don't deserve to be here, standing next to the beautiful bride and calling her my damn wife, man." Alton seems to choke back a cry. "I don't know how I got here. It had to be a damn miracle, man."

The room fills his emotional silent gaps with applause and *awwws*. Ironically, I can feel his sentiment. I know his expressions are real. As much of an ass as Al can be, he really loves Tynisha and wants his family together.

Family. The concept of that is what's put me in a sour mood. That and the sexy ass woman whose assigned chair is next to me at the table. Although she isn't in the wedding, Zoey is seated next to me, torturing me in the sexy ass mini dress she's wearing that has some fancy ass squares colored in hues of blue. Her hair is straight in long curls, and her eyes are dramatically smoky. I can't function sitting that close to her without telling her how fucking beautiful she is. It's what I would have done had she been mine. Her scent makes me dizzy and her glow makes my chest tighten. I can't handle another minute of being so close to her and not gazing into her glowing brown eyes or touching her smooth caramel skin like it belongs to me, so I get up and head over here to the bar. When I left, John Legend and his wife were chatting with Zoey. She seemed to hold court well enough alone, leaving no need for me to stay for small talk.

"But I have to say this," Alton's now squeaky voice speaks into the microphone, bringing my attention back over to him. "I know I haven't been the perfect man to Ty. I'm man enough to admit that. But I was lucky enough to have a friend stick close to me like a brother and didn't judge me. He always showed me love." Alton's chin is to the floor as he speaks, appearing almost melancholy. "My man StentRo always kicks good shit in my ear, and one day he pulled me to the side and told me, *"Fight for your family. There's nothing as lonely in this world as a man with no legacy to leave or one to follow. Get your shit together for your family."*

The room goes up in applause and I have to clear my damn throat. I did recall telling his ass that about a year ago. I can't believe he listened.

"So, next to my lady," Alton's eyes are on me. "...this day is for you, my dude, for believing in me for all these years, man."

I swallow hard. His words hit harder than they would on a normal day. I'd admitted to myself recently my actions in pushing Zoey so far away. Alton here is finally stepping up to the plate, as he should. And my fucking family is as disjointed as a motherfucker. I don't deserve praise for preaching what I don't practice. For years, I've been delaying my own love.

"So, here's to my big dawg, StentRo! Cheers, bro!" Alton and Tynisha raise their glasses in my direction, then clink them together before taking a chug of the bubbly.

I raise my glass of *Maracame Gran Platino* that Tynisha made sure they had on deck specifically for me and gulp that shit down, emptying the glass.

I turn back to the bar. "Another." I slam my tumbler on the bar top.

"Look who we have here!" I hear from just behind me.

I turn around to find Tynisha and a tipsy Alton, with his arm lazily draped around Zoey's neck.

"John is about to perform. Zoey requested *Ordinary People* in our honor 'cause heaven knows that's all the hell we are," Tynisha shouts spiritedly.

"Yeah, boooyeee! And I want my dude to take this plunge with me with this fine ass thang right here, bro!" He somewhat roughly pushes on Zoey to gesture to her.

My eyes go to Zoey, whose expression is sheepish. I can tell she's going with the flow for the sake of the bride and groom. I stand and go for her hand, the way her little soft fingers thread between mine feels so natural. She willingly accepts and we take off for the dance floor behind Alton and Tynisha, receiving applause all the way there. John starts his melodic crooning.

I stop, taking Zoey into my arms, something that is still organic although it's been so long. Her scent saturates my senses, her warm touch gives me goose bumps and in just a few minutes of our swaying, she burrows her head into my chest. The lyrics play on in my intoxicated mind. Zoey and I have lost our way. I've lost her, which is far more difficult than losing an ordinary love. Because we have a child together, Zoey is at my arm's length, teasing and torturing me just the same.

Her head pops up. Her eyes are laden with distress. "Your heart is about to come out of your chest, Stenton. Are you okay?"

I'm drunk. Fuck it. "This is hard for me."

"What?" Her dark eyes do something to my chest. Her narrow yet pouty mouth brings me visions of eroticism that I haven't experienced from her in so long.

"Being so close to you and yet so distant emotionally."

Zoey's eyes bounce back and forth, contemplatively. "Stenton," she begs.

"I know." *Fuck!* "It's just that I'm so frustrated. You and me… we're not done yet, Zo. I've given you time. Now it's time for us to explore *us*."

"Stenton!" She backs out of my embrace.

That was a little more explosive, though it didn't draw attention to us in the middle of the dance floor. I don't know what to say. I know what the fuck I want to say, but it's clear to me that Zoey isn't game. So, I back away, leaving her befuddled there on the floor. It feels like my usual modus operandi. I've always left her standing alone, even though I don't go far. I gait back over to the bar and soak up my self-pity there for a while, in tequila.

"StentRo, we gon' get you home nice and safely, right, Zo?" I hear a familiar voice speak loudly as I feel tugging on my legs. "Shit! Push, Zo, I can't hold his big ass by myself!"

"I'm trying!" I hear hissed through gritted teeth.

I can guess to being stuffed into a car.

"Listen, Zo. I know things ain't on the up and up with you two, but please don't leave him until he can see about hisself."

"Alton," I hear a warning tone. "This is the father of my child. I don't know what you believe, but I can assure you his well-being is of the utmost importance...to my child. I would never put him in a situation where he isn't safe."

"I know, Zo. It's just that I know...him thinking about retirement all, and the depression because...well, you know."

"No, I don't know. What depression?"

"Al, we have to jet now to make that flight. The captain called two hours ago!" That's another familiar voice.

"I gotta go, Zo. Please make sure my dude gets home safely."

"Hold up, Alton!" the first feminine familiar voice calls out. "What did you mean *depression*?" Her tone is critical.

There's a pause.

"Look, man. I'm not supposed to open my big fuckin' mouth, but my man here ain't been the same in a minute. But, Zo, man, dude's fucking depressed about not having a life with you and my godson."

And there's a word that in my drunken state rings familiar. *Depression.*

There's another long pause before I hear a feminine sigh, "Goodnight, Alton."

Seconds later, the car starts and I'm out again.

"Stenton," I hear a strained voice. "This can only work if you cooperate. You were able to make it up from the car…after your vomiting episode, and even help me get you out of your clothes." Her tone is one of exasperation. "You said you have to pee, now pee. Please, Stenton. I'm so sleepy."

It's the *please* that reminds me of better times between me and this woman that relaxes me. I can feel my hands against cold tiles, but my cock is warm, in soft holdings.

"Yes! There you go. Whew!" I hear. I don't process what that means, but continue to relieve myself. "Okay, now let's get you into the shower."

I sense my glide into my shower, but not much after that. Maybe it's because Zoey inviting me into the shower excited me into oblivion, or that my intoxicated mind cannot process much else, but I went out.

The next time I awaken is in the morning. There's only a streak of light glaring through my bedroom. My body lies stiff as I manage one eye open. Immediately, I sense my need to take a piss, but before I can urge my heavy body to move from my bed, I smell her. Then I hear her. Her voice is low, almost a whisper. I glance over and find Zoey leaning against the window.

"Bernard, no. I'm fine. No, I'm not about to leave him here alone. Why? Because he's Jordan's father. Besides, I wouldn't do that to my worst enemy. He could have had an accident in the middle of the night! What do you mean, where did I sleep?"

For some reason, that makes me look to my left where I could clearly see a dent in the pillow and smell her scent.

"I'm not doing this. I'll call you later when I get myself together. It was a stressful night," she grates into the phone, still attempting to control her tone.

So not the thing to say to your man when you're in the other man's bedroom the morning after, Zo.

But then something else hits me. *Why was it a long night?* Then I start turning over memories of last night, at least those I can recall, hoping I didn't say something I'll regret.

Shit! This can't be my life.

"Your Excedrin and water."

I look up to find Zoey gesturing to my nightstand. Slowly, I turn my head to find two white pills and a glass of water. I sigh. So much to get off my chest and yet another reason to feel like shit. I don't want her to see me like this.

Zoey saunters over and hands me the pills and water to take. I do. I don't deserve her charity. She did say she'd do this for her worst enemy.

There's an awkward silence.

I sit up, slowly. "Zo," my voice is scratchy. "I need to talk to you and I don't know how to begin."

"Is it about your depression? Is that why you're talking to a therapist?"

"Depression?"

"Yes."

Why does that sound so familiar?

"Where did you get that from?" Then it dawns on me. "Fucking Alton!"

What's worse than a loose lip fucker is a loose lip fucker with the wrong information.

"No, Zoey. It's just that there are a few things I need to share with you and it can't be on a whim, but we need to talk."

"So, you've not been diagnosed with depression?"

"No." Not clinically. That shit sounds absurd.

She exhales while changing her stance, placing her hands on her hips. Zoey's not the only one exasperated. I exhale long myself and rub the hangover sickness from my face.

"I've always been so fuckin selfish with you." I don't know where to begin, but with that simple truth. "I need to explain some shit to you."

"Stenton, you've been a lot over the years, but not selfish. An asshole of a heartbreaker, yes, but never selfish."

My eyes dart over to her. Zoey never uses profanity. Have I brought her to this point?

Shit! This isn't going to be easy.

Her phone goes off again. And she sighs even harder as she looks down at it.

"Look, Stenton, I have to get to church. We can talk another time. A time when you're in a better state. I'll call your assistant to make sure you get some hangover food." She then comes over and kisses me on the forehead. "Take care of yourself. Okay?"

Zoey issues a long and somber regard. There's a pregnant pause because I don't know how many other ways to tell her we need to sort some shit out. Then she steps into her heels and walks out of the room, leaving me in a stupor, carrying the same fucking load of guilt that I have had for too many years.

Fuck me!

THEN: *February 2007*

Stenton

The morning after I dropped Zoey off at school after our Alpine excursion, just after practice, my phone did ping with a text. It was Erika Erceg. She still wanted to go out. And when she told me she was in Philly and wanted to see me before leaving, it added to my list of irritations. With what Zoey put on me in the past few days, I didn't have room for more bullshit of the female persuasion. But I agreed to it.

We met at *Estia's* on Locust. By the time I'd arrived with Paul, my assistant, in tow, she was there with her male friend, Mehan. Although Mehan likes to straighten up around me, I know he was just as excited and as atwitter as Paul seated next to me, but just not on the surface.

Paul had been my personal assistant for almost two years. He came highly recommended by a Gabonese model I used to fuck. When I decided to get my shit together and clean my image, I did a whole makeover, even in staff. Prior to him, I had three female personal assistants, all of which I'd fucked, making me a not-so-stellar employer. Paul was an aspiring clothing designer, who needed money while getting his business in order.

He had an impeccable eye for detail, could interface well with women, which helped with my sex life. When things went awry with a woman and I needed to separate, Paul would be there with his planner clutched to his chest in one hand, and STOP sign in the other, tapping his foot. He also wasn't afraid to flex his authority over a man professionally on my behalf. The only irony was he seemed to have gotten along with everyone but me. I got ragged on a lot in the beginning by my teammates for having a five foot one inch, vanilla, effeminate man bossing me around off the court. Being criticized for odd tendencies was old hat for me. I never *fit in* in life. I took it all in stride and simply considered how much my life had improved and became much more systematized with his service.

The threesome chatted to their heart's delight at the table throughout the meal. I couldn't figure out why I was there; this seemed to have been a gathering for Paul and friends versus Erika and me. Paul led the conversation, asking about Erika's reality show, the type of makeup her artists used and all other types of shit that had me in my phone rather than in their conversation. Erika would try to rope me in at different points of their talk, like mentioning me cameo-ing on her show.

"You know you want to do it, Stent," her tongue laid between her top and bottom teeth when she finished pronouncing my name. "It'll be great! C'mon." She batted her long dark eyelashes.

"Oh, and I know your mom would so love the cameo. Stent would make her year!" Mehan cheered very heartily.

Paul lifted his shoulders in a heavy shrug as he sipped his tea through a straw. He knew that reality show bullshit was not my style at all. He was bold, but not stupid enough to add to their futile goading. I had built a solid reputation on being a private man over the past few years. It had been easy for me to remain so "elusive," as the media termed me, because I didn't have a large circle. I didn't have close relatives other than my uncle and mother. My cousins that I did keep in touch with weren't all without long prison sentences, preventing us from bonding, and the others I'd never had a close relationship with at all. So, it had been pretty easy for me to lay low.

"Well," Erika sang in her baby voice. "We still have plenty of time to convince you; *E!* isn't letting go of the show any time soon."

I snorted. If she wanted more of a response, it wasn't coming. I waved for the waiter to bring the check. When he did, of course Mehan didn't break his neck to cover it. And even though Erika could more than cover it, she wouldn't dare because in her mind this two hour mind-numbing meeting was a date.

"Well, good peoples, I have to hop on a plane first thing in the morning and still haven't packed," I initiated my departure as I signed the bill.

"I can come over to help," Erika offered with, I was sure, as much lewd intentions as her voice led on.

"Nah, I'm good. I have errands to run before I can do that anyway." I stood and offered my hand to Mehan. "It was good seeing you, M-Easy." His neck heated up a shade of crimson. Then I walked over to Erika, who was still sitting and kissed her on the forehead, catching a scent of her flowery perfume and berry hair.

On a good day, I'd fuck Erika sideways. She was not only fucking beautiful, but she was bad. Her body was molded to perfection. There were rumors of cosmetic enhancements, but if that was true, she certainly got that shit off because her entire package was the truth. What she felt like beneath me would remain to be seen. Now with where things stood with that fiery Zoey— wherever the hell they stood—there was no way that I could go there with Erika, no matter how tempting her butter pecan shell was.

As I was walking off, I heard, "Are you going to All-Star

weekend this year? I was thinking of going with my sister." She didn't even look at me when addressing the reverse invitation.

That was a dumb question. It was like asking if I was going to a mandatory work function. These were the types of games I was accustomed to engaging in with women for my attention.

"Yeah," I snorted as I walked away. "I'll be there."

"Me, too!" I heard her yell eagerly from behind.

"Maybe I'll see you then."

I had a bit of running around to do before I went back to my apartment to pack. I attended a training session that evening before taking it down for the night. When I turned in for bed, it had dawned on me; no call or text from Zoey. Again, I felt annoyed as fuck. I could've just called her, but the hell I was. I'd already let her get underneath my skin, I'd already been making a number of concessions regarding her. I was not about to be a pussy and call her. *Fuck that.* Plus, I needed Zoey to show her hand. I was still confused as to what her game was, or if she had one at all.

Two weeks after we left Alpine, I still hadn't heard from Zoey. Something wasn't right. She wasn't the bug-a-boo type like Erika, but she also didn't have the demanding social life Erika had either. All of my fucking spidey senses told me she was the type that would have called by now—no matter what her game was.

It was the first Thursday in February and I'd just left a photo shoot for *Nike*, and was in the back of a limo with Paul, who was tapping away at his iPad. My team played the Wizards that night and we were headed for the bus.

"Here," I hit *Send* on a text message to him. "Call that number and ask for Zoey. Tell her to give me a call," I called over to Paul who sat across from me.

His phone went off and he immediately got to tapping away on there. Seconds later he returned, "Either you're now afraid to call your women on your own or you think I don't have better things to do than to be played mindless games on," he spoke over his glasses. "The number is disconnected."

Huhn? What the fuck is that?

"Disconnected?" I repeated much to myself.

"Mmmm-hmmm," Paul breathed as he went back to his iPad. "That's what I said, giant."

What the fuck type of game is she playing? She fucks me and then changes her number? I hadn't done that move in years. I couldn't believe when I realized my heart started racing. Something didn't feel right. As much as the word *GAME* had been chanting in my fucking head, a small—very minuscule—piece within my chest was whispering trouble. Why would bubbly and witty Zoey not call me all this time and then change her number? Shit didn't make sense.

As my teammates and I were preparing to board the bus for D.C., I pulled Paul to the side. "I have something I need you to do while I'm away." I rattled off a few things to him before getting on the bus and taking off.

The night before we left for D.C., I'd gone out to a private party in Moorestown, NJ. *Al and the other dudes were all there drunk off their asses, and while I was just a few drinks behind them, I couldn't exactly relax. I had Zoey running through my mind. She still hadn't reached out and I still hadn't been able to figure out why.*

"Shit!" *Alton barked.* "I can't have a fucking life!" *he cringed.* "It's always a text complaining about what I didn't do or an order telling me what the fuck I should do. You's lucky as fuck," *he noted before taking a sip of his Corona.*

"How do you mean?" *I asked, following suit.*

There were women all over the house, some partially clothed, and few even naked. This was the only type of party some of us could do during the season. Ninety-nine percent of the time they guaranteed privacy. The host, Jeremy Booker, was a defensive linebacker for the Eagles and a native of Atlanta where the strippers are bred differently. So, many of us were appreciative of his hosting to protect our privacy.

"You ain't got no lady, no wife, no fucking fiancée, and no goddamn baby-mother keeping track of all your offenses," Al counted off on his fingers. "You ain't got no fucking leash, Stent. Be happy for that shit, bro."

I chuckled. No matter how many years I'd known him, his usage of bro versus mine of bruh was a stark contrast. We were from the same tiny ass state and still had different lingo. With as much of my vocabulary that had worn off on him, 'bruh' wasn't one of them.

"I hear you, Al," I clinked my glass with his without warning. "I feel you, bruh."

That was bullshit. At that very second, I wanted someone texting me something—about calculus, literature…fucking psychosexual development—anything!

Oh, fuck…

I missed my Niña.

"Yo, what's up with Zoey? You hit I see. Y'all still going strong?" Alton asked out of pure innocence. He probably thought since a couple of weeks had past, it was safe to. But to the contrary, it was still a private topic, and as of late, a sensitive topic.

"She good. I'm good," I replied succinctly before taking a swig.

"Here you go with that secretive bullshit. Was she a virgin or what, man?" He pushed on. "I don't believe shit her cousin, Angela, has to say. I know you hit, so spit it."

I looked at him from the corner of my eye. He knew I didn't run my mouth about sex, and I damn sure wasn't about to start with Zoey. If I was honest, I'd admit to it being difficult not being able to have someone to talk this shit out with. It was too fucking complicated. She was so young. I knew the best thing to do with her was let her go. That, however, was easier said than done at this point.

"Okay, well what about Erika Erceg?" Al wasn't giving up. "Man, she been running your ass down for almost a year now. If you don't want that ass, please pass your dick over here so I can use it to handle her. God knows if and when my dick touches any pussy, Tynisha can detect that shit," he snorted almost painfully.

I didn't respond to that. In fact, I didn't utter another word for the remainder of the forty-five minutes we stayed there. We all had an early morning the following day and needed to get the hell out of dodge.

We beat the Wizards; laid them on their asses on their home court. While everyone was wild and boisterous in the locker room, I was preoccupied. I pulled my phone from the locker and found there was still no word from Zoey, but as I searched my phone, I saw there was something in there from Paul. He left a voice memo. Not a voice message, but a memo, using an app. He drove me fucking crazy with these and typically used it when he had quite a few things to share. He said I didn't comprehend long written messages well, but responded to this better. I thought it irritated the fuck out of me to hear his elongated pronunciations, but rode with it.

I plugged my earbuds in and hit play. Paul started with updating me on scheduling and upcoming meetings. It wasn't until he was almost done that he got me to stop in my tracks.

"So, as far as your little mission: I was able to find out where Miss Zoey stays on campus. I called her dorm, but got her roommate, Rebecca, who informed me that Zoey's phone has been out of service for a few weeks and that she doesn't have a new one. I didn't say much from there because you only asked that I try to get a new number for her. So, that's that."

Hearing Zoey's name brought me back to that empty feeling in the pit of my gut. How do you have sex with someone for the first time and not follow up with even a call. I would wonder if she enjoyed herself those few short days, but every time I thought about how tightly she wrapped those legs around me and how violently her body rocked when I sucked between her legs, I knew we'd connected. I just wasn't expecting the sudden disconnect.

I toyed with my phone the entire ride back to Philly. Each time I picked it up to respond to Paul with another move, I put it back down, fearing rejection. What if she'd changed her mind about all of this? She was young after all. Shit, she was entitled. I'd changed my mind on lots of relationships when I was her age. But I wasn't Zo...smart, funny, sexy as sin, and courageous.

Fuck it.

I picked up my phone and typed my next set of instructions to Paul. I had to see this shit through. If ol' girl didn't want to be friends anymore, she was going to have to be mature enough to tell me.

"Are you sure she's in here, P?" I asked as I trailed behind him nervous as fuck.

"Yes!" he jumped and whispered forcefully. He's such a damn crab. "You asked me to get the intel then to get us here. We're here and you don't trust me? You're unbelievable, Stent!" he shook his head as we entered the Lewis Library.

"When did the jawn say Zo would be here? Was that tonight?" I asked, towering behind him.

He abruptly spun around again, this time with his weak porcelain finger pointed at me. "Don't do that! Don't do this, Stent!" he attempted to whisper but turned red while doing it. "You asked me to take on this menial task that I don't like, but I did it because of the broad parameters of my job description—a description that doesn't include private investigation, by the way, but I did it. Now don't get out here and challenge my snooping capabilities, Stent. Don't do that!"

I tilted my head to the side, giving him a warning glare. Paul is so fucking dramatic that I have to remind him who's the fucking boss around here. The last time he pushed me past my limits I had him flying out of the room crying. I was too goddamn nervous to be dealing with his queen persona. Shit, my stomach was in knots.

Nervously, Paul shifted his gaze past me and retracted his finger. "I know what the roommate said, okay? I had to play like I was her World History classmate to get questions answered. She said the Lewis Library; I know what I'm doing here." His tone was much more reasonable.

I followed him through the open foyer, then through the walkway of the main hall and up the stairs, taking two at a time and reminding myself that I was, in fact, following him. All I could think was what if she wasn't alone. *What if she was studying psychosexual development?*

When we got to the private room where Zoey was supposed to be, my chest tightened and my fucking knees went weak. Paul opened the door, and I quickly pushed out breaths to even them before stepping into the doorway.

She was there at the table wearing earplugs with books spread out everywhere. She wore a thick cable knit sweater, looking as angelic as I'd remembered. Her doe eyes were big and pretty with her long lashes and pouty lips that she used her teeth to scrape over. She was surprised to see me.

Zoey…

"You're making that sound in the back of your throat," I noted out of pure nervousness. I didn't exactly have a script planned in case Paul was right about finding her.

At first, I was speechless. I didn't know if this was real or if I'd fallen asleep in the library again and dreamed of him.

He was tall, almost having to duck into the room. Even in the relentless freezing temperature outside, he wore an open jacket with a V-neck sweater, revealing the various patterns of his body art. He didn't crack a smile as he studied me. I immediately grew self-conscious about my appearance. My hair was thrown back into a sloppy ponytail. My blue sweater had been washed so many times the integrity of the blue had dimmed. My lips were dry and I tried licking them discreetly, but who was I fooling. With the depth of Stent's observation, he likely knew the color of my bra. He always saw right through me.

"And you need to step up your defense. You barely won that last game," I murmured, sounding like an idiot.

I knew nothing about basketball, had yet to watch a game. I didn't know what else to say. Paul's brow line narrowed, probably confused by my very false dig. Stenton chuckled.

"Who was the team we played?" Stenton quizzed, his voice low.

"The one with the tall guys on the team. Duh!" I shot back.

He moved closer and my legs trembled beneath the table. He didn't sit, but came unmistakably close enough for me not to miss his words…or his scent.

"You haven't called."

My eye squeezed shut. From the moment I saw Paul, I knew I'd have to answer for my absence. I just didn't know how to tell him my life had gone to pieces from the moment I left his car that day nearly three weeks ago.

"*I*-I know," I whispered before dragging my lip between my teeth again. "It's been a crazy time since we last spoke."

"Really," he snorted. "I guess I would be privy to that had you simply picked up the phone, but it's clear we're no longer the friends I thought we were."

His long calloused fingers skimmed gently over my knuckles that were curled into tight fists. I took a deep breath at the shooting surge of electricity from his touch.

With my eyes closed I whispered, "We are still friends. At least I hope so."

"Best friends?" he pushed.

This time his voice was closer, his minty breath hitting my flushed face. I opened my eyes to find him just inches away, now sitting on the table, hovering over me. It was now Stenton's turn to seduce. Suddenly my breathing hiked and breasts felt heavy and confined. My eyes darted over to Paul and found him with his back to us on his phone.

"Yes," I breathed.

"Then why the distance, Niña?" I heard the plea in his voice; I saw the shadows of betrayal from my abrupt absence in his marbled eyes.

I swallowed the painful tension, hard. I didn't want to trouble him with my issues. I knew I'd thrown a lot on him in Alpine with being deceptive and manipulative. *God, what he must have thought of me.* But I didn't want to lie to him. He was right; he'd been my best friend, in no time.

I trained my eyes to the table and willed the courage to tell him the truth.

"Stent," I whispered. "When you dropped me off, it was early and I thought to drive home and check on my parents' house. I got the mail and saw another foreclosure letter amongst other bills. I stayed there for a few hours, trying to decide if I should call them while they were away at a prayer conference, likely petitioning this very thing. Then there was a knock at the door. It was a certified delivery of the foreclosure notification. I stayed there that night, not wanting the house to be unoccupied. Then the next day my phone was cut off. I forgot that I wasn't able to cover the entire bill this month. Then the following week my laptop broke down. I don't have the money yet to fix it, so I've been coming here a lot." I shook my head, exhausted by it all. "It's just been crazy."

I tried to suppress the tears to the point of developing a burning sensation in the back of my throat. I didn't want to initiate a pity party.

"I guess that splendid idea of graduating and landing a lucrative job isn't working out too fluidly," I choked out wryly.

Stent didn't smile. Instead, his head leaned in and he studied me for seconds long. He then pressed play on my iPod and lifted one of the earbuds to his ear. I heard Ledisi's powerful and soulful voice rip through the tiny pores of the other earbud still on the table. I felt my eyes close again at the longing of her vocals, begging to be found because she needs to love again. Her pleas of needing to be rescued echoed those of my recent prayers. This moment also was shared by the feeling of betrayal. Stenton was getting a glimpse at the side I fought to keep from him.

When she sang the line about wanting to live, Stenton's eyes jumped to mine. I watched as his jaw clenched almost to the point of popping. There was no mistaking the plea in the song that was on repeat. It's all I listened to; one of the two tracks I'd been meditating to for weeks. A part of my soul had been revealed.

"Ewwwwww…that's depressing." I jerked my head toward a grimacing Paul. Stent was shooting him daggers, too. "I'm just saying!" he rustled before turning back to his phone.

Stent's gaze returned to me. "Friends keep in touch with friends so when friends need love or to give it, friends can do just that," his deep baritone rolled over me, caressing my skin like velvet. "Look at me, Zoey!" he rumbled. I did and felt my nose trembling. "Maybe I needed a friend to tell me about my defense, or lack thereof." His full lips quirked up into a smile.

I sputtered a laugh. He knew I had no clue of his game. "No. You need prayer to help with keeping that ball," I continued with his joke.

"Do you even know what position he plays?" Paul's tone wasn't shy of a sneer.

I peered over at him. "Of course I do, silly! Stenton Rogers is a quarterback. Duh!" I doled out while looking straight into Stenton's amused eyes.

I heard Paul gasp, but didn't acknowledge him. I was too caught up in Stent's enthralling smile.

"Paul," Stent called over his shoulder and reached behind him to retrieve something from Paul without removing his penetrative gaze from me.

"Oh, shit," Paul cried, patting himself down. "I'll be right back." He dashed out of the room.

In spite of that weird exchange between the two, I was still caught up in Stenton's presence. My humor died down, smile was fading, and so was his. I'd experienced more happiness in those short five minutes than I had since leaving him that day, weeks ago. He moved toward me, and I leaped from my chair. The heat emanating from his lanky and incredibly delicious countenance was unbearable. I'd spent weeks wondering if I was somehow being punished for what I did with him. To him.

"What the fuck, Zoey?" Stent groaned. His face twisted with confusion.

I was against the wall, panting hard. Ridiculously aroused.

Raising my arm in defense, I babbled, "I-I didn't tell you everything!"

My face set into a grimace as if I was being tortured, and I was; I was tormenting myself with why things had turned so grim for me right after Alpine.

I swallowed hard, and unsuccessfully tried catching my breath. "I Googled you," my eyes darted over to Stenton, whose brows were narrowed.

"Okay…" he supplied expectantly, more or less asking me to continue.

"And I know how much you make. I didn't call you because I couldn't. I couldn't have you believe that after what I'd done to you, I wanted something from you. I'm not one of those girls!"

He inclined his ear towards me, gesturing for me to go on with my point.

I scraped my bottom lip between my teeth. "Stenton, from the night you kissed me last summer when we said goodbye, I knew I'd developed feelings for you that I'd never experienced with anyone. That night, I told myself I was going to give myself to you. I purposely didn't tell you I was a virgin…I left crumbs for you to believe I was experienced, all to…" I was out of breath. Stent moved closer to me, tantalizing my already heightened senses. "Gosh, Stent, I fell in love with you over the summer! Who does that? I didn't know how sex was going to happen, but I knew it would. I knew it was wrong, but I…" I was at a loss for words. "I knew you were a basketball player. Angela told me you were "the man," but I didn't know." I shook my head at my naïveté. "So when I was online researching the foreclosure process in the state of New Jersey, I needed a break from the stressors and thought about you right away. I know we joked about your celebrity and I said I'd avoid your public persona…when I found out, I froze. I thought of the stupid game in Alpine, the way I seduced you for selfish reasons, but none had to do with your wealth. I swear it!"

I was so lost in my discloser that it hadn't registered when Stenton drew closer. Really close. He had me sandwiched against the wall. And his scent. That enticing Bergamot odor, disarmed my defenses, definitely affecting me in some abstract way.

"When all that stuff was happening and I needed someone to talk to, I couldn't come to you. After I found out all about…you know…your net worth, I knew I couldn't come to you with this *convenient* travesty after what I'd done to you." The rough pads of his fingers traced the lining of my quivering lips. I hadn't exactly noticed that right away either. "I didn't know about you when I did that. I think—no, I know I need to apologize for not being lady-like…or Christian-like. You must think I'm—"

Stenton's mouth crushed into mine and the next thing I felt was his tongue near the back of my throat, soothing the burn that afflicted me from attempting to control my emotions around him. Then I felt spikes of pleasure down my groin from his oral move-ments. He lifted my legs, one by one and wrapped them around his narrow waist. My hands found their way into his hair, knocking his baseball cap from his head, and suddenly I couldn't recall what I'd been trying to convey. I could only feel the push of Stenton's arousal against mine. Could only feel the need to rub off the pulsing of my core onto his.

Stenton grabbed my heavy breasts, kneading them through my thick sweater. I could hear my ragged breaths. His big hands rose to my head, holding me in place as if I'd fly away without his consent. My hands flew to the wings of his back, desperately wanting to rub the ink splayed back there just as I did several weeks back. I then felt his hands all over my waist, causing traces of lingering sensations wherever he touched. Our kiss turned hard and fast in no time. When he pulled from my mouth, I was gasping for air. He looked at the adjacent wall for a while, clenching his jaw. I wondered what he was thinking, but couldn't catch my breath to ask.

Then his heated gaze returned to me and everything happened in slow motion. He was channeling something with those marbled orbs as he bore into me with them. His eyes only dropped to watch himself pull at the drawstring of my sweats. My line of vision followed his. My back was against the hard cold wall, my front was against the hard hot essence of Stenton's arousal.

My chest dropped and fell, dropped and fell and dropped in and fell in anticipation. The wild look in his heavy eyes made very clear what his intent was. The only question was whether or not I could be so bold to deliver. The knot was undone and his marbled orbs were intently regarding mine once again. He slowly licked his lips causing my sex to clench. I missed him so much. Just in that short three-day getaway with him in Alpine, I'd familiarized myself with his expressions of desire. The back of his hand caressed the short hairs of my private area. His eyes flickered. He was communicating with me. I then felt his long finger moving lower until I felt it at the juncture of my labia—

"What the hell?" I heard preceded by the forceful close of the door.

I jumped into Stenton's hard chest as he simultaneously grabbed me and supplied a salacious grin. I chanced a glance beyond his left shoulder and found Paul seething, his hands on his hips and bouncing on one foot.

"Were you seriously going to fuck her against the wall...in the library?" Paul gasped.

My neck reversed back over my shoulders and saw the unwavering mischievous smile on Stent's face.

"Uhhhhh...cameras!" Paul whispered forcefully. "Did you think of that, genius?"

I banged the back of my head against the wall at that revelation. *What am I doing?* I lowered my right leg from his high waist, trying to stand, but Stenton grabbed me at the sides of my thighs.

"No!" he growled thickly. My breathing increased again. He lowered his forehead to mine, closed his eyes. There were a few seconds before he whispered, "I don't like not being able to call...to contact you."

I felt myself exhale. "I'm sorry," I whispered painfully. I didn't know what I was apologizing for; it just felt right. His compelling scent reminded me of the private experiences we shared weeks ago. "Well, I *do* have a crisis happening right now," I squeaked remorsefully.

Then I felt an object being stuffed between us causing a sharp pain just beneath my bra line. My head jerked down and saw Paul, pushing a small box and looking pointedly at me. I looked up at Stent and found him rolling his eyes, clearly annoyed. Mechanically, I took it and examined the image of the smartphone on the cover.

"My number is programmed already," Stenton's deep tenor forced my attention. There was strong regard in his eyes, something sobering. "Call me."

This time, I successfully pulled myself down from him and studied the box.

It took a few seconds, but I murmured, "Sheesh! I could always email to keep in touch."

Stenton shook his head. "You seem to have a roadblock there, too, remember?" Stenton reminded me.

And before I could speak, Paul piped in, "And don't think that won't be resolved soon." His tone was laced with sarcasm. I honestly didn't know how these two worked together.

I looked directly ahead at Stenton, expectantly. He returned it with a shaking of his head that gestured I should ignore Paul's attitude.

"We have to go, Stent," Paul warned. "After the stunt you pulled last month with skipping out of town without letting anyone know, you shouldn't be pushing it like this."

"I have to go," Stenton murmured regretfully. "Zo, call me when shit like this goes down. Just call me. All the crazy shit going through my mind these past few weeks..."

"What?" I plucked a brow. "Did you think I was too busy sorting out psychosexual development with Leo?" I gave a mock gasp.

The corners of his lips quirked into a half smile.

"That's cute, but that smart ass mouth is going to get you in a world of trouble with me," he all but whispered with a smirk playing at the corners of his lips before walking over to the door after Paul.

The sad look in Stenton's eyes told me he wanted to stay with me just as much as I wanted him to. It took me a minute to come down. I could still feel the heat from his touch. Could still smell the aroma of his cologne. I collapsed against the wall and fell on my haunches. When I landed, a sharp pinch of my skin had me hopping to my feet. I reached around to my back to assess what caused the alarming nip. I felt crisp paper and pulled it out to find all types of bills; Benjamins, Grants, Hamiltons and Washingtons folded. I went back and sure enough, there were more. I quickly counted over twenty four hundred dollars.

When did…? How?

Then I heard a chirp from inside the cell phone box. I scrambled to the table and opened it. There was notification of a text. I slid the bar and found a message from *"**Niña's Lover**."*

That's all I had on me.

He knew I'd found it.

You didn't have to do this. I collapsed my woozy head on the table. All of a sudden, I felt exhausted by it all.

Yes, I did. Call me…day or night!

I stayed there in the library for at least another two hours. I spent much of it trying to get Stenton out of my head. I couldn't. I was now in a realm with which I had no experience. I felt things for him that made no sense to me cognitively, but my heart—and body —was so easily and naturally inclined to the idea of him. I needed help sorting through my feelings and could only think of one person with whom I could trust this crazed elation. Just at that thought, my stomach growled. I packed up my things and headed to New Brunswick.

"Momma, when did you know you were in love with Daddy?"

I sat at the small kitchen table that I'd spent countless hours of study at, watching her work at a comforting pace as she cooked.

"What was that?" Ruth rudely interjected as she came busting through the kitchen.

I rolled my eyes. "I asked Momma when did she know she was in love."

"Why don't you ask me that question? I may be the youngest, but we all know I got the most experience of the two of us. I'll school you on that." She grabbed a soda from the fridge and swung her small body into the seat across from me.

"Because I'll get the Bonnie and Clyde version of illegal infatuation." I plucked a brow, warning her to back off.

"It's more than you'll ever have, always got that face stuck in a book."

"Better a book than a mug shot," I quickly returned.

"All right now," my mother's voice carried without being too high an octave. "We're not going to start this fighting. Our family is going through enough as it is."

Just then, Ruth's phone rang. She answered it with the biggest and most mischievous smile I wanted to gag at the sight of. The trouble my family had been experiencing had begun because of Ruth and her affinity for thugs. Almost a year ago, Ruth was arrested with her boyfriend when he had been pulled over for bad papers on his car. That minor infraction wasn't the biggest find that night. No. The biggest was the drugs they found in the vehicle. Although they found small amounts of cocaine on his person, she was with him and caught the same charge. My parents had to hire a good lawyer—one they technically couldn't afford—to beat the charges. Unfortunately, they used monies that should have been paid on their mortgage and car for her representation. They'd been underwater ever since.

It had taken months for me to work through my resentment for my sister. I read countless scriptures and books on forgiveness. It had been hard watching everyone in our home be preoccupied with staying afloat except for Ruth. She'd broken up with that boyfriend for unrelated reasons, and moved on to another of the same caliber. It upset me to no end.

"To answer your question, young lady," my mom called over to me, awakening me from my trance, "I knew I was in love with your daddy when I saw a husband in him. I had lots of crushes when I was a young girl. But when I saw myself as his wife, I knew I was in love."

I sighed, resuming my previous source of frustration.

"So, because I don't see myself as his wife it means I'm not in love?"

My mother paused as my gaze was fastened to her kneading hands that were in a mixing bowl, preparing dough. "Is this about that tall young man that came over here Christmas?"

My eyes averted in inferiority. I never lied to my mother, but discussing something that had become so precious—complicated—to me almost overnight wasn't as easy as all of our other conversations. Sarah Barrett was my best friend. There was nothing I couldn't come to this woman with. My mother never judged; only guided and nurtured. I had to get on one accord with her concerning this. I needed answers.

"Elizabeth Ardell Barrett, don't you look away from your momma like you stole the last of the porridge. Spill it, young lady!" Her voice was so firm, yet powerfully controlled. She didn't want to alert my dad or sister.

I rolled my eyes back over to her. "I told him I love him," I squeaked.

Her left hand landed onto her popped up hip. "And if I know my own child, you meant it." It wasn't a question. She knew I'd never been in love nor made it. Her long searing gaze was inquisitive. And as my mother, she knew every answer that didn't leave my mouth by asking the questions that never left hers. She knew I had given myself to Stenton Rogers. "Did he at least say it back?"

I chanced a glance to see her mouth wide open and her brows furrowed. She was unsettled.

"Yes, Momma."

"Do you think he meant it?"

"Yes, Momma."

"How?"

I sighed, feeling my stomach jump in my abdomen, the same

sensation I'd always feel when I thought of Stenton. "Because he looks at me as though I'm the coming messiah. It's hard to explain, but when his marble orbs hit me, I feel a power over him too potent for a mere human being. It empowers me and scares the crap out of me at the same time. Momma, I'm so…"

"Confused." She answered for me. My sister re-entered the room and just when I thought the conversation was over because my mother snapped out of protective mode and went back to her dough, she continued, "And afraid."

"Yes, Momma. Afraid." My voice reduced to a whisper. She understood me.

"Well," Ruth inserted herself back into the conversation. "…if you still a virgin, Zo, you ain't in love, or you crushin' on a man that don't want you 'cause I truly do believe you are going to die with your library card in one hand and your v-card in the other."

"Ruth!" my dad shouted from the living room. "Come turn this TV to my sports channel."

Ruth sucked her teeth, but quickly obeyed as she swung her legs from beneath the table very dramatically and stomped her way out of the kitchen.

"You just make sure y'all be careful, young lady," my Mom whispered over to me with her face contorted. She was not happy, but not judging either.

"We always do, Momma," I fully put it out there to make it clear that she knew about my move into womanhood. I couldn't keep that from her.

She rolled her eyes hard back into her bowl. "Go get cleaned up for dinner. I hope you stayin' for the peach cobbler."

"Momma, I have to get back on campus. I didn't come for dinner. And I keep telling you not to make so much food now that I'm not here. We really have to cut back," I whined. I had been so worried.

I shared the foreclosure letter with my parents when they returned. I even supplied them with information on the process and possible alternatives. While they took the paperwork and promised to look at it, they pushed me out the door and back to campus, begging me to not stress over it. They assured they'd take care of it. It was too late. I'd lost four pounds since then.

"Elizabeth, this here is my home. I gave that foreclosure mess and repo junk to the Lord. He will provide for us. As your mother, I want to encourage you to finish what you started at school. You should be focused on that. Not here with something that me and your daddy is giving over to God through prayer. We gonna survive this." She moved to the fridge. "Now, here. I already packed this up for you. I knew you would be back any day now. You don't ever seem to stay away for too long."

She handed me a Pathmark plastic bag filled with Tupperware. Every time my mother cooked, she would include enough for me. Although she constantly threw my butt out of the house, ordering me back to campus, she would never fail to feed me while away. I was grateful because in all honesty, I couldn't afford to feed myself.

"Thanks, Momma." I wrapped my arms around her voluptuous frame and squeezed all the fortitude from her that I could. I could stay in this woman's arms forever. No one could ever make me feel so secure and loved. The closest to it was…Stenton.

I was almost out of the kitchen when I remembered another reason for my impromptu visit.

"Oh, here. This is for you. Don't tell Dad." I pulled out the same wad of cash Stenton magically planted on my person just hours before.

It was all but $200. Some of that went to gas to get me to my parents' that night, and the rest was for food and a study book I desperately needed, but couldn't afford to get. I shouldn't have said I never lie to my mother, because that night I did.

My mother gasped. "Girl, where did this money come from?"

"*Shhhhhhhhhhh!*" I jumped up and grabbed her at the shoulders. The last thing I needed was Ruth coming in there finding out about Stenton.

"You know I tutor. I mattress all of my savings. I wanted to let it accumulate to have something generous to offer."

"You're always *offering* your tutoring money. I'on't recall ever seeing anything like this, Elizabeth!" At least she kept her volume low on that one.

"I know, but I've been getting lots of referrals. My momma breastfed me and gave me a big brain," I charmed.

"Zo, didn't you say your laptop crashed? Don't you want to use this to get that fixed or your car?"

"I've been spending a bunch of time in the library tutoring, so I use the computers there. Don't worry about me. I've been petitioning God, too." I winked before leaving my mother with an aghast expression.

When I went into the living room, I saw my dad and Ruth glued to the television. It was an odd sight, seeing the two, who were always in conflict, doing something together.

"Zo, ain't this the one you and Angie volunteered with this summer?" Ruth asked.

I shifted towards the television and sure enough, there was Stenton being interviewed my Stephan A. Smith. I couldn't stand Stephan A. He was more emotional of a debater than I preferred in a man. And his tone and accent irritated me to no end, but my dad was a fan, forcing my attention to his on-air persona.

"Yeah. His friend's the one Angie tried to say her baby was by. Foolish little girl if you ask me," my dad murmured somewhat under his breath. The family was just getting over that dud of a scandal.

"You two are both foolish if you ask me. There's no way that summer would have ended with me still being poor. Y'all ain't play your cards right. Dude is fine *and* paid? Yup! Fools." Ruth's tone was resolute.

My dad's head shot back to her. *And there goes the peace.* While my dad gave a rebellious Ruth a piece of his mind, I turned my attention back to the screen where I watched a series of basketball-related questions Stephan threw to Stenton, who was skilled at answering them. Stenton used knowledge and charm as he articulated his answers and responses. The only thing alluring about that segment of the interview was ogling Stenton's heart-shaped lips. They were plumped and even a dim shade of cerise as the top was wider than the bottom, creating sensual perfection. Involuntarily, my sex clenched.

"So, let's talk about something you hate to discuss: your personal life." Stephan provided a disclaimer to prepare Stenton. "You know man, back in the day, the media couldn't get enough of airing your dirty laundry. What has changed? You are an extremely, extremely private man now. Speak on that."

Stenton smiled, squinting his eyes to the point of closing them— something I loved. "I started giving my laundry to the cleaners instead." Stephan belted out a hard laugh, Stenton followed. "Really. I grew up with cameras and microphones in my face. Eventually, I grew rebellious and didn't care what others said or reported."

"And now?" Stephan asked, almost cutting Stenton off. *Indicative of why he irked me!*

"And now, I know the best things in life are things that can't be shared. I now have the advantage of letting people get to know me without the assistance of Google. And I've been enjoying it."

Was that an insider for me? No. It couldn't have been. *Stenton knows I don't follow his career.* But he told me he'd put away his wild and reckless behavior at least two years before meeting me, so why use an insider only I'd appreciate?

"So, here's the question every female I work with," Stephan gestured behind him, "...and am friends with will never speak to me again if I don't ask. Are you dating anyone?" Stephan's eyes grew larger than they usually are.

He annoys me!

Stenton's face wrinkled to express contemplation. "Uhhhh-mmm... Dating? Not exactly."

"Well, what the hell else is there, StentRo?" And there was that name again. Usually only his teammates referred to him as that. That could have only meant they shared some level of friendship, comradery. "I mean, you have to date every woman you have that type of connection to," Stephan goaded.

"This is true, but sometimes these things take on different paths. I'm on a different path right now."

"All right. I know Stenton Rogers and that was a shut-down answer, which means that's all we're getting. Crack the code for yourself and confer with your girlfriends, ladies. That's all the time I have…" Stephan went on to end the interview.

"Hmmmm…you know who he's screwing, Zo? It sho' nuff ain't you. You spent the whole summer with him and probably didn't get him to even look at you," Ruth taunted.

"That's it, young lady!" My dad jumped from his chair. "Upstairs. You go to your room if you wanna encourage behaving like a harlot. Not in my house!"

That was my cue. I kissed my dad on the cheek while he was still fuming at Ruth. I sent a teasing wave her way before I left the house. I had too many things to think about. So much had happened that evening. My mom didn't help much but accepted that I'd been with one of the most respected basketball players in the world. But that didn't help provide resolve with what I was feeling for him. I didn't know how to reconcile that.

Two days after seeing Stenton in the library, a fully loaded *Mac Pro* was delivered to my parents' home. I couldn't believe he went through the trouble…and expense. It took me a few hours to rebound from the shock his gift hurled me into.

Stenton, however, never waited for me to call him; he made sure to text me every day from that day out.

Stenton: **What are you up to?**

Me: **At the Laundromat.**

Stenton: **Doing what?**

Me: **Laundry. Duuuuh!**

Stenton: **Like washing or drying?**

Me: **Both. My parents' washer 'n' dryer are on the fritz.**

Stenton: **Sounds fun.**

Me: **Not when I'm spending an extra 20 cents on the additional ten minutes of a sixty minute cycle that my clothes need to be completely dry. These machines are rigged to make more money!**

Stenton: **Interesting.**

Me: **What? My calculations and theory?**

Stenton: **No. The vision of you in my house folding my clothes wearing a tee and heels.**

Me: **You're a perv.**

Stenton: **Sticks & stones...**

Two days later, I got a text from Stenton while out with a few of my cousins and friends after Wednesday night prayer service at church.

Stenton: **What are you up to?**

Me: **Being grossed out. How was the game?**

Stenton: **We got our asses handed to us. Wait, grossed out by what? Where are you?**

Me: **I'm at Red Lobster. I'm sorry about the game. That sucks. I was really rooting for you in that last quarter.**

Stenton: **Really? Did you catch the other team's name?**

Me: **Yup. The Eagles.**

Stenton: **LMMFAO! What's going on at Red Lobster that's grossing you out?**

Me: **Hang on. I'm going to the bathroom so I can chat.**

I excused myself from the table and ambled over to the restroom to continue my conversation.

Me: **Hey... Well the guy Bernard...our choir director just told me he's attracted to me.**

Stenton: **The McDonald's dickhead?**

I'd mentioned Bernard to Stenton, in passing, a few days ago. I wondered why he automatically went on the defensive about him. Bernard was simply a family friend who directed the choir at my church. He was an aspiring gospel artist and traveled with his band members doing regional performances. I'd hoped he'd hit it big. He was a true talent.

Me: **Stenton! You're more the McDonald's poster child than he is. Don't you endorse them?**

Stenton: **Yup. They pay me for my affiliation. He just wanna be down. Fuckin lame ass choir boy.**

Me: **LMBO! Stenton that's soooo not cool!**

Stenton: **And neither is he. Have you told him you're not interested and to fuckin scram?**

Me: **In a far more polite manner, yes.**

Stenton: **My Nina.**
Last thing. How was your stats & prob quiz today?

Me: **I didn't nail it. Got 8 outta 10. My life sucks.**

Stenton: **Get over yourself Zo. Gotta go. Call me 2nite when you turn in.**

Me: **Roger that StentRo.**

Stenton: **Cut that shit out Zo!**

Chapter Seven

Stenton

"Forbes College is this way, StentRo," Rob called out over his shoulder while we jogged the campus at close to midnight.

That fucking Zoey. Of course that was why my six foot seven inch ass was running through Princeton like a S.W.A.T. on a mission. We had to avoid encountering folks who would recognize me, so I'd only brought two security guards and hoped we didn't look all that conspicuous. Rarely did I travel without armor. I learned that lesson early on in my career. I'd damn near gotten robbed at the first *Summer Jam* I attended after getting signed. Barry and Rob were my main two guys when I traveled. Two guys who likely thought I was crazy for infiltrating the damn Princeton campus, all because Zo said she was struggling with her Probability and Statistics course. I was rusty as hell, but could try to recall what I knew. I was also tired… until we parked the truck. Now, every minute that passed, my adrenaline spiked a notch at the anticipation of seeing this girl.

When we pulled up on campus, I sent her a text asking how

would I recognize her. She said she'd be waiting around the lobby for me. While trekking to her dorm building, I got a text of a picture of her with a big ass afro.

Zoey: You can't miss all this hair.

I chuckled as we approached the building. Barry led us in while Rob stayed behind me.

"Big ass afro," I called out so they'd know who to look for.

The lobby wasn't busy. Just a few stragglers, chatting, reading or on their laptops.

"Ten o'clock, chief," Rob announced.

That's when I saw her. Zoey's big ass afro bounced as she neared me. I'd never seen her hair like that before, but it was cute. She was so fucking cute, even with the bags underneath her eyes.

When she approached me, her arms went directly to my waist and wrapped around my waist. That's when I was afforded a waft her hair. Vanilla. *Mmmmm.* My left arm instinctively went around her shoulder.

"You know you look crazy suspect as tall as you are with that hood on," she joked.

"I just came from work. What the hell do you expect me to wear? A damn suit? I know this is Princeton and all, but you didn't give me enough notice," I complained.

Truth was, she did coax me into coming. The only thing was, what Zoey did likely wouldn't classify as coaxing. She simply asked or suggested and I came running. That's how I felt about her since losing her for those few weeks. Whatever she wanted I would give. She honestly didn't ask for much at all.

"Come on!" she teased with animated eyes. "Let's go before my colleagues mob you."

I always found it funny how Zoey provided a caricature of my already heightened career. She was that clever, and I enjoyed it.

Once off the elevators, we walked past a lounge area.

"You guys can park it here," I called over to Rob and Barry. "I'll only be a minute."

The guys stepped into the room as Zoey and I continued down a hall and finally to her door. As she faced it, she pulled me in to her, wrapping my arms around her tiny waist.

She whispered, "Ready?"

Thinking it was weird, I nodded. Zoey unlocked the door and pulled me in behind her. My long strides were sloppy as I tried to avoid running her little body over in the dark. Once inside, she closed the door and walked me to what I'd soon learn was her bed. She turned around and pushed me until the back of my legs hit the side of the small mattress. When she nudged me back, I fell cautiously onto the bed, hearing the small squeak. Zo sat next to me, snuggling underneath my arm, her big hair tickling my chin.

"I've missed you."

It was natural for me to respond, "Same here." And that was because I did.

Zoey and I spoke daily. I made sure of that. I regularly called at night, around this same time, after a game to hear her voice. My schedule was a bitch and not conducive to a relationship, but I found myself needing to hear her voice. Feeling her near me was much better, though. I couldn't, for the life of me, understand why the damn lights were off if we were supposed to be studying.

"Did you guys win?"

I nodded, forgetting she couldn't see me. "Yeah. Funny thing about prayer. I guess it actually works sometimes."

"All the time," Zoey corrected. "Prayers and requests are mutually exclusive. We may not always get what we request, but our prayers are always heard and we're covered," she whispered.

"I see." There was a bit of a pause and then I couldn't take it anymore. "Zo?"

"Hmmm?" she replied, rubbing her face in my side, almost sniffing me.

Is she inhaling me?

"How can we study in the dark?"

I could feel Zoey's head pop up from underneath me. I felt like a pussy for posing that question. *But really, what is a man of my age and profession doing on a college campus at this hour?* And then with the intent of tutoring? That sounded suspect, even to me—and that was my honest to God intent! I'd even Googled a few statistical formulas to start jogging my memory on the way here.

This fucking frustrating girl! She made me do crazy shit.

"Oh, that," she whispered. "I was able to figure it out. All done and ready for my exam tomorrow."

Her soft hand reached for my cheek and she pulled herself up as she urged my neck down to meet her. Zoey smelled good. Freshly showered.

"I got that out of the way so that we can spend some time doing this."

Her lips inadvertently met my chin instead of my lips, but on her second try she was bull's-eye. When our mouths met, all memoirs of Alpine returned in spades; her scent, her touch and taste. In no time, our tongues twisted with fury. Zo packed a lot into that kiss and I tried to swallow her whole. She unzipped and gently pulled off my sweat jacket.

My dick lifted in my sweats and it was almost as if Zoey instinctively sensed it. Her hands went into my lap and she rubbed my wood through the cotton material. When she moaned my eyes flew open in the dark. I didn't want to alert her roommate. I was treading on dangerous territory, on a college campus, fucking making out with a student. A smart one. A sexy one. And apparently an ablaze one.

Before I knew it, Zoey had her little warm hand beneath the elastic of my sweats and reaching for my cock. I felt her pull on me. My abs lurched at her grip. Evidence of the trance this girl was capable of putting me in, the next thing I felt was her maneuvering her little body between my legs. Now, in my defense, her lips smacking against mine robbed my attention from all other happenings for a while. That was until I felt her withdraw from my mouth and a warm, wet, incredibly soft sensation coaxed the crown of my cock.

I exhaled forcefully, slowly and hardly processing that my sweet Niña was sucking me off. *Or attempting to.* She had no particular rhythm and her grip wasn't strong or fluid, but she was getting busy. Her efforts, though not seasoned, were pleasurable because she was mine. Her every sexual experience belonged to me. And so did her every pleasure. I reveled in her efforts as I tried to relax into it. Zoey picked up the pace and her suctioning staccato snapped my ass back to reality.

Once again, fucking with Zoey, I put myself at risk of scandal. I had to remember, one shot of my genitals being bared to a coed could have my ass in deep water and back in the headlines again.

"Zoey!" I whispered, taking her at the jaw.

"What?" This was the first time she didn't whisper. I could sense not only her slight annoyance, but her embarrassment as well.

"Your roommate!" I whispered again.

Zoey quickly tucked me in and shuffled beneath me. Next, I heard a clicking, and the next thing I saw was the room illuminating. My sensitive pupils darted over to Zoey grimacing. She jumped to her feet and went over to the bed across from me. It was neatly made...and empty.

She sauntered over to me with a glower in tow, her arms crossed angrily in front of her. "Do you honestly think I would even have you over here if Rebecca was here, considering your issues with the public, much less have you exposed?" Her tone and poise expressed incredulity. "Stenton, I told you she left for New Zealand with her class two days ago!"

All of a sudden, I felt like shit. But then I thought again.

"Then why in the hell were you whispering since we walked in? And why keep the lights off?"

"Because I didn't exactly want to do that," she pointed to my rock hard cock, "with the lights on!"

"Did you... Did you plan this?" She rolled her eyes to the ceiling. "Again, Zoey?"

Zoey didn't answer for a while. She stood there, tapping her foot, stubbornly, and chewing the inside of her lip.

I shook my head, fighting the state of frustration against my arousal. "Look, Zoey, I get you're a headstrong woman. And I so love that you know what you want and it's me..." I tugged her toward me. "Look at me when I'm talking to you." Her eyes slammed into mine and immediately, I saw shame. I didn't mean for it to go there, but Zoey needed to let me lead. "If you wanted to fuck, you should have just told me and I would've made it happen."

Her eyes grew large. "How?"

"The way that you tell me how you sort your laundry, or get free detergents by writing detailed letters to corporate, or how much you've saved using coupons. The same way you tell me about things that affect you every day when we kick it. Just tell me."

Zoey was still glaring down on me as I sat on her bed. She was fucking perturbed...and cute. But I didn't give a fuck. She needed to learn. I'd put so much on the line for her just being here. Although she didn't know it, there was nothing I wouldn't do for her. So we needed to get this shit straight right away.

I deepened my stare at her.

"I don't know how to," she spoke through a tight mouth.

"It's easy: Stenton, I want to fuck."

She gasped and right away, I chuckled. "I couldn't say that!"

"I know. But you can figure out a way to convey your needs," I couldn't help my laughter. She was so damn cute. I eventually sobered. "Now, what do you want, Elizabeth?"

She narrowed her eyes, cautioning me. "I want to do what I was doing before I was rudely interrupted."

"Have you done that before?"

Another glare.

"Have you?" I asked again and rather impatiently.

"No!" she snarled. "You know this."

I nodded my head as I mumbled, "I do."

She gasped again. "How do you know?"

"I can show you better than I can tell you," I thought I whispered underneath my breath.

"What was that?"

"Nothing. Zo, we can't do shit anyway. I don't have rubbers. Didn't exactly come prepared for this." My tone was dry. Between my rod being painfully stiff and learning of Zoey's ulterior motives, I was in a bad way.

Zoey turned back to the nightstand, opened a drawer, and pulled out a box of condoms.

"It isn't solely your responsibility to carry these. I'm an equal party in this, too." Zoey poked her lips out petulantly.

"You're acting like a sex fiend."

"And you're acting like an oversized—pun intended..."—she paid a glance to my bulging erection—"...prude. You may be experienced and can even get it in every city, but I—"

I leaped up and threw my tongue in the back of her throat, silencing her ridiculousness. My tongue weaved around hers and lashed every which way, attempting to taste every inch of her cavity. I needed her to know I enjoyed her, but was afraid to reveal my obsession of her.

I pulled back, "I only want it and get it from you, Niña. Nobody else," I whispered directly into her mouth.

Zoey whispered back, her tone less forceful, almost providing supplication, "Well, I want you here and now. I want to taste you, Stenton." Her eyes raked up to mine, much softer and needier than previously.

She asked. And I was totally inclined to meet her request. Slowly, I nodded my head, knowing deep down inside I wouldn't be leaving this room without me being buried deep inside her.

"I'm going to turn off the lights first. I'm not ready for that yet," her voice was still reduced, but her aggressive and determined persona was in full effect.

Zoey turned the lamp off and returned to me, wrapping her arms around my waist lovingly. I reached down to bring her chin up so that I could taste her mouth again. In no time, we were both enraptured again. She lowered my sweats and I kicked off my sneakers when my sweats and briefs fell to my ankles. I pulled off her shirt and rubbed her full perky breasts. *Fuck! Zo has the best tits!* Her body shivered when I pulled on them at the hard apex.

Zoey left my face and dropped to her knees, taking me in her mouth. She used both her little hands to jerk me. I placed mine over hers, applying more pressure. Zoey caught on right away and before I knew it, she was fisting and sucking me to the point of climax. I didn't want one that way, so I pulled her up and wrapped her legs around my waist. With her clawed to my chest, I maneuvered out of my t-shirt, tapped around the top of the nightstand until I felt plastic, and then laid her on the bed.

"Stenton," Zoey begged when I lifted and sat on my knees.

She used the time to doff the remainder of her clothes.

"I just have to put the damn rubber on, Niña," I drawled, so fucking aroused by this frustrating girl.

When I was done, I lowered myself over her and took to her lips again. An impatient Zoey pulled my head in deep right away and thrust her hips upward and onto my full erection. I wasn't even halfway in, but Zoey knew nothing about pacing sex.

"Go!" she whispered into my lips as I moved marginally in and out of her.

"Zo, you're not ready for me to pound you. You're tight again," I scolded, but gently. She felt amazing.

I sensed her nod. "Yessss, I am." She held her breath and pushed up again.

"No, you're not."

But instead of arguing with my Niña during sex, I showed her. I plunged all the way into her canal, pulled back partially and slammed into her again, this time filling her to the hilt. Doing that was a bad move. Zoey's pussy was so warm and gripping, I couldn't halt my dips. Those dips quickly turned into pounding her.

"Stenton!" she breathed.

It concerned me until her fingers pressed into the wings of my back as she threw her sex to meet my thrust. Her breathing increased through her nostrils and I felt soft clenching from her walls below. I was perspiring in no time.

"Open your mouth, Zoey," I grounded out. "Breathe through your mouth, honey." I was fucking shocked at how soon she was ready to orgasm.

I felt her harsh breaths in my face, inspiring my hips to push deeper, grind harder.

I was rewarded when I heard Zoey, "I can't wait, Stent. I can't hold out!" clearly tantalized by my efforts.

"Go, baby! Don't wait for me. I got you." And I did. I couldn't get enough of it.

Zoey proved her need of me with the speed of her release. Her small frame shuddered as her pussy gripped me so sweetly below. I had to control my breathing because I wasn't ready yet. Her lungs drew and suffused air roughly. I pelted into her as hard as my body would allow without climaxing my damn self, Zoey was that amazing.

When she was done, I halted my thrusts, but remained inside of her, doting on her flight. I kissed her insanely, completely consumed by her. I adored Zoey. She truly inspired me. I was proud of her femininity. But I wasn't done with her body.

Abruptly and swiftly, I flipped her body over until she was on her knees. I reared up on the bed and grabbed her ass cheeks, parting them to throw my tongue between. Zoey stiffened, unaccustomed to this position, or the act in the position. I couldn't be so concerned or doubtful. *I* now needed to please her again. I swirled against her lips and then in between, playing on her clit. When she relaxed, I swiped her full slit, tasting her forbidden zone in the rear and used my hand to massage her engorged nub. And when I expected Zoey to flinch and draw back, she pushed into my face and then onto my hand. She kept going back and forth, not knowing which one spurred her pleasure. I increased the speed of both, driving her insane. Zoey's orgasm, this time, was much louder than before. Her cries were so uncontrolled and raucous that I couldn't react to my subconscious that told me we could be heard by those near, possibly even my security way down the hall.

Before she could fully come down, I was behind Zoey, slamming into her with full force. I swallowed my cries by biting my lips.

"Arch your lower back, Niña," I urged by tapping the small of her back.

If anyone would have told me that coaching a woman on how to fuck would turn me on like this, I would have called them a liar. Zoey perfectly arched her back and I plunged into her.

"Hold on to the headboard." I could hear the desperate groan in my own voice.

Zoey did just that as I impaled her hips. I moved hard and swift, no longer exercising patience. I was now turned on by the fruits of my labor. I tried driving deeper and deeper into her. I relished this moment of her supplication; she rarely showed it. But I felt it while bucking into her as she called my name like a fucking plea. I didn't know if she could come for a third time, but just in case I needed to warn her.

"I'm about to bust, Niña!" I grounded out.

"*O*-okay," she drug out dizzily.

I exploded. Completely overcome with her submission, I lost control. I pulled Zoey into me by the hips as my body jerked, releasing my desire for this woman. Once able to move again, I slipped out and collapsed next to her on the tiny bed. After a few moments, I was able to speak.

"Zoey, where's your bathroom. I need to flush this condom."

Zoey moaned, satisfactorily. "Give it to me. I'll take it."

I steeled at those words. Those were the maneuvers of gold-diggers. The type of women I was good at detecting. There was silence for seconds long until I was able to remind myself of who I was with. I won't say I'd suddenly become easy with doing it, but I did succumb to the offer. I pulled the rubber off and double tied it before handing it to Zoey.

The thoughts that raced through my mind while she took off to the bathroom were not of paranoia or doubt that Zoey was indeed flushing the used condom. No. They were far-reaching and just plain ole fucking crazy. Absolutely insane with this young and promising young woman's bright future ahead. Nope! Couldn't continue down that road of insanity.

Zoey retuned next to me on the bed. She wiggled her way into my frame.

"When you were coming, why did you say you couldn't hold out?"

"I don't know," Zoey answered, aloof. "It's what you always say. And now that I can do what you do, I figured that's why you say it."

"Okay, so the word is orgasm. And yes, I say that to you when I'm about to, but that's my role as a man. You're always supposed to come first. It's my job to make sure you do. It's the only way for me to know if you're enjoying me."

"Oh, is that what guys do?"

I chuckled. "I don't know what guys do, Zo. I can only tell you that a real man works for his lover's orgasm before he reaches his own. You never let a man get in the habit of neglecting your need to release."

"Is that my job?"

"Yes and no. Generally speaking, it takes women longer to climax than men. If he's your lover and not just someone you're fucking, it's his job to be patient and help you work toward it. If you're just fucking, you may be on your own."

"You're my lover, Stent," she whispered docilely.

I confirmed right away and vehemently. "You're damn right."

"Wow," she sighed. "I've learned three amazing things tonight."

"What?"

"How breathing affects my ability to orgasm; that my lover is equally responsible for my orgasms; and what you can do with that long and wide tongue of yours."

Unable to control my laughter, I blurted, "What?"

"Yeah, from the first picture I took of you at the diner last summer. I'd been wondering what you could with something that size."

Still laughing, I breathed, "Zo, get some damn sleep."

"Okay," she sighed, contended.

The dinging of my phone woke me. I checked to find a text from Rob, asking if I was good. I searched the screen for the time and saw it was just after three in the morning. I couldn't believe I slept so hard. It was only supposed to be a quick closing of the eyes. I needed to be on a plane in three short hours.

I slowly dragged my cramped body from the narrow ass bed and searched for my clothes in the dark. Quietly, I dressed and just as I located the doorknob to head out, I recalled what I wanted to leave with her. I pulled out three stacks and laid it on the table closest to me. I didn't want to risk knocking into something by going to the nightstand nearest her bed.

The second time I reached for the knob, I heard Zoey slur, "I love you."

Those three words stopped me in my tracks. I wondered if she was talking in her sleep. She hadn't spoken them since Alpine. I'd almost thought they were a part of my active imagination. My stomach turned, but in a good way. Sheer fucking bliss.

"I love you more, Niña," I whispered.

And I did. There was no way she could care for me more than I did her. No way she longed for me the way I obsessed over her. When it came to Zoey, I lost all common sense; tonight was a clear demonstration of that.

When I closed her dormitory door behind me, all I could think of was how soon I could be with her again. When would I see her face again?

So fucking pretty. And such fucking trouble.

About two weeks later, and with much trepidation, I found myself knocking on Stenton's apartment door in Philadelphia. How I was able to make it there with my clunker, I didn't know. I wasn't all that sure if I wanted to be there in the first place.

I didn't expect a strange man to open the door. He was tall, Caucasian, and drunk, so different from the one downstairs who "checked" me in.

"Hi," I croaked out. "Is Stenton home?"

Why did I sound like a child?

The tall guy chuckled and moved aside. I entered the apartment and saw random figures walking about and some even sitting. His place was modest in size and very contemporary with high ivory stained walls and walnut wooden floors, highlights, and features. It was by no means the expanse of his home in Alpine, but it was probably the fanciest apartment I'd ever been in. I entered directly into the living room where there was an open floor plan that blended with the kitchen and dining room from what I could see through the crowd. There wasn't a houseful, but certainly more than I expected, considering I was only expecting Stenton.

It didn't take me long to find him. Once the door closed behind me and I looked to my right, he was there, talking to a woman with platinum hair. His attention automatically transitioned to me and stayed there though he didn't move. His eyes instinctively slanted in awareness of my presence. It's funny how your body becomes aware of certain senses once you've shared it with another individual.

The woman he spoke with melded into the wall, clearly comfortable with her proximity to Stenton. His body language spoke interest to me, but hers said she wanted more than Stenton's proximity there against the wall. I wasn't in the mood for people. I just wanted a bed, preferably mine at my parents'.

Stenton's face transformed almost into a scowl. I didn't see his usual smile when he recognized me. I kind of sort of wondered why, but the wiser part of me knew he was concerned about my disposition.

"Hey, Mascot!" I heard from the left of me. I turned to find Tynisha, holding a fancy, short, and thick bottle that had the word *Mauve* printed across it. This was my first time seeing her off a television or computer screen. I'd guessed she'd learned I was a student. "I didn't know you were coming," she shared stoically, but from her stomach.

"Neither did I, but I'm here," I uttered dryly. "Nice to meet you, too."

I didn't know if Tynisha was coming for me and, just in case she was, I wasn't in the mood tonight. From what I'd seen of her, she was very much a mouthy woman with lots of attitude. She played up her Jamaican roots when she wanted to expose her raffish persona. And when she wanted to present as demure and model-worthy, she'd highlight her Korean heritage. When I Googled her last summer after meeting Stenton and Alton, what confused me was that her father is Jamaican, and her mother is Korean, but she uses her mother's surname, Lang. Pretty pretentious if you ask me.

Tynisha wore indigo blue jeans that fit her like a glove with a knitted halter-top and 5-inch thigh-high boots. Leave it to the fashion designer to wear a summer top in the dead of winter and it be appropriate material. Tynisha always dressed well from what I saw of her: it was her profession. Me, on the other hand, I wore my Chuck E. Cheese uniform top with dark khakis, looking all of twelve. Not that Tynisha was much larger than me, but at least she had style that enhanced her tiny frame. I felt like the very mascot she referred to me as. The only reason I didn't dwell on it was because even on my best day, I couldn't measure up to Tynisha's style. She was a stylist to the stars, for goodness' sake.

"Shit, Mascot. You need a sedative." She raised the bottle, appearing extremely tipsy herself. "Want some?"

I don't know why, but my eyes automatically went to Stenton, who was posted up on the wall with the platinum honey. His eyes were on me…and my brief conversation with Tynisha. He nodded his head firmly. That was strange. When Alton offered me a drink back in Alpine, Stenton vehemently said no. My eyes traveled back over to Tynisha who had caught his notion and grabbed a glass to pour some for me. When she handed it to me I took a huge gulp, feeling somehow it was of Stenton's will. She walked away and went toward the kitchen.

"Everybody out! The host says it's time to call it a night!" I heard someone yell over the crowd.

I turned in an attempt to search for the initiator of that demand, but only found Stenton, towering over me in a greater proximity than I'd seen him with the platinum chick. My breathing automatically increased at the discovery of his all-consuming presence and entrancing Bergamot scent.

"Why do you seem so uptight?" he asked directly into my neck. "You haven't smiled once since walking through that door."

"Neither have you," I whispered, already taken by his company.

"Trust… I'm happy you're here. Now I can relax." I felt the sliver of his tongue on my neck.

"Peace, Stent."

"Goodnight, love birds."

"Great gathering."

"Thanks for having me over."

"Congrats."

All of those messages I heard from just beyond Stenton, whose large frame hovered over mine against the wall.

"Stent," I moaned. "Stop. We're not alone."

"Yes, we are. And even if we weren't you couldn't keep my hungry mouth from you. I've missed my Niña," he growled then his tongue was back on my neck.

"Wait…wait!" I pushed at his hard chest.

His head pulled up and his scowl was on me when he howled, "What the fuck, Zo?"

I licked my lips as I glanced around. People were gathering their coats and heading out the door just a few feet from where we stood. I didn't want all eyes on me while I was making out with him. So easily could I get caught up in his fragrance. Also, I didn't want Stenton getting all worked up for nothing. I found my way back to his inquisitive glower.

"It's just that I don't want to get too carried away. I have to leave soon," I whined. "It's late."

Stenton's eyes fluttered and brows knitted. "You're not leaving tonight." Then his tongue was back on me—in me.

Stenton's masterful tongue invaded my mouth sinuously. My back slammed into the wall, my knees went limp, and my core kindled at his force. I felt the hunger pour from the back of his throat into mine, depositing an untamed desire. I was caught up instantly, but I had to fight against his passion. Still, I couldn't shake my sour mood or my physical disposition. I pushed against him again.

His heavy eyes pried open. "You're killing me, Zo. What the fuck is going on?" he begged gruffly.

I looked around again, noticing the apartment had emptied. I couldn't use the excuse of a lack of privacy anymore. Within seconds, the front door slammed. My chest heaved. My legs quivered. But my belly remained bloated.

"We can't tonight, Stenton," I whimpered, finding it difficult to peer into his eyes.

"What do you mean we can't, Niña? I've been thinking about this—dreaming about this for weeks."

My stomach flipped. "I know," I swallowed. "Me, too…but not tonight. Maybe in a couple of days," I whispered. My eyes were shut tight and my nose ascended while my mouth went south. I couldn't say it.

Stenton retracted from me to study my face and steeled in place. I cracked a lid to find his creased forehead. My eye shut quickly, ashamed. I felt him drop to his knees and heard him take a deep pull of air. I almost died on the spot, overcome with humiliation. He rose again, collapsing his face into my neck.

"Is my Niña on her period?"

My head collapsed into the wall behind me. My eyes still squeezed shut and I scraped my bottom lip through my teeth. I nodded.

"I just need to go home to my Momma. My cramps are killing me. I just need her and her chicken soup," I breathed out.

"No." He took me at the small of my waist, and then his fingers went lower into my pants, grasping my backside until our pelvises touched. I felt his steely erection. "You need an orgasm. The endorphins will help with your cramps. And the last I checked, mothers don't give out those; lovers do."

My mouth swung open, giving away my abrupt aroused state.

"Are you wearing a pad or tampon?" he spoke softly into my ear. I heaved, "Stenton!"

Stenton didn't remove his stance or proximity.

His breath pushed tantalizingly onto my neck. I'd hoped I wasn't chafing at his patience. This was all new to me.

"Niña, I am your lover, right?"

I shook my head enthusiastically.

"You don't have to be bashful with your lover, especially if he wants you in the condition you're in." Stenton paused for a minute, burying his face in the crook of my neck. When he lifted his head he, softly yet fixedly, shared in my ear, "I...need you tonight. I can't explain it. I don't want to have to try. I just need for you to trust me when I say I want you as you are, and I will take care of you, okay?"

"Okay," I squealed, sounding tortured. I was. This was a new venture for me.

"Okay." The strain was removed from his vocals.

"But, Stenton, I don't have clothes for tomorrow, or enough tampons to last."

"What brand of tampons do you use?"

When I couldn't find my breath to speak from the mortification I was drowning in, Stenton removed the strap of my purse that had already fallen into the arch of my arm as the palm of my other gripped the glass.

"My bedroom is upstairs to the left. It's the only room on that side. Go inside the bathroom there and strip down to your underwear and bra. I want to remove those myself. I'll meet you there as soon as I lock up the apartment."

Stenton's face pulled back to meet my eyes, then he slowly pushed off of the wall, giving me space to move. Hesitantly, I shuffled around him and took to the staircase.

I found my way to his bedroom with ease. As he advised, there was just one door on this side of the second level. When I unhooked the knob and pushed the door, I was chary about what I'd find there.

His room was calm, and dimly lit with hues of browns and hunter green. The ceiling was high and coffered. In the center of it was some fancy material, no ordinary sheetrock. The walls were lined with wainscoting, adding to the elegance. Immediately to my left was a small sitting area with a long suede chaise and coffee table with a messy display of sports magazines. His king sized bed against a tall tufted headboard was on the opposite side of the room, not too far from the window that boasted the Philadelphia skyline. Almost directly across from the foot of the bed, was an open door that I soon learned was the en suite bathroom.

I searched for the light when I entered. Upon the room illuminating I noticed it, too, was a margin of the size of the one in Alpine. Yet it was just as intimidating and well appointed. It reminded me of worldly Stenton. I don't know where the audacity came from, but I downed the liquid from the drink Tynisha handed me, not knowing what it was. With lessened reluctance, I stripped.

Man! I wasn't totally settled on sex while on my period, but Stenton was right; I trusted him. And a small part of me—a very irrational and daring part of me—was curious about his desire for me, even in this state.

I wasn't in there too long before I heard the door crack. I refused to chance a glance behind me; I was too humiliated to open myself to the possibility of one of his guests from earlier being there —or worse, Alton. *Nope!* I'd keep my eyes stapled ahead. Seconds later, I heard Maroon 5's *Sunday Morning* pour from the speakers, making me aware he had surround sound here in Philly, too. *This has to be Stenton.* He knew what got me charged to seduce me. I was now more convinced.

But when I felt his erection press against the seam of my behind, I *knew* it was Stenton. It was his length, width, scent and radiating heat that alerted all of my cells and caused them to go atwitter.

"You're making the sound with the back of your throat again, Niña," his thick baritone breathed into my neck.

I froze. I had no idea I was doing it, but it halted in that moment. I needed to fortify myself. If he wanted me this way, I was doing it.

Stenton lifted my chin over my shoulder and kissed me dizzily. He didn't allow me time to ease into it. He took my passion straight from my mouth. His big hands splayed across the side of my face and neck, holding me while he inhaled me. My heart stammered in my chest. Volts of electricity surged through my entire body, springing from the core. For moments long I forgot to breathe. If I didn't know any better I would think Stenton was transmitting his imminent hunger for me through this act. It worked. I melted into his frame behind me. When he pulled back, the cadence of his breathing matched mine, but not his scowl. His scowl spoke of predation.

Stenton rounded me, stopping square in front of my toes. Again, I struggled to stare him straight in the eye. I soon realized he caught on when he gave me a one cheek smile. My eyes shot to the floor. Immediately, I scolded myself for being so starchy. When my eyes started their ascension the first thing I noticed were his bare feet. *Gosh!* Even they were beautiful. It spoke of his confidence.

Then my sight climbed to his extended member, poking through the thin material of his navy blue basketball shorts. He had to be without briefs; the sketch of his swell was too conspicuous. And his shorts hung sinfully low on his waist. *I mean loooow.* It was an illicit spectacle of his private arena. And then his tattoos. *Holy mother of Joseph!* They glistened. Each shade of ink: black, yellow and red— their edges were sharp and dimensional. My tongue itched to taste him. Every morsel of him.

With his thumb, he trailed the length of my clavicle, the innocuous act so intimate, seductive. Then he flicked my right nipple through my bra. I shivered. Still gazing directly in my eyes, he reached behind me and unhooked my bra then peeled it off. *My breasts!* My god, they were heavy and swollen and...attractive. The sight of them increased my arousal tenfold.

One by one, Stenton took them into his mouth, sucking my nipples to the point of pain. *Deliciously painful.* A yelp hurled from the pit of my belly at the starling sensation of his efforts. Suddenly, I felt intoxication increasing in my system from my drink, colliding with that of my humming body. My frame trembled, saturating with a desire never met. A need that I'd never known.

When Stenton withdrew, his inspection traveled the length of my body. Panting uncontrollably, when my eyes followed, I saw I was totally bare. Somehow Stenton managed to steal my attention by disarming my brewing body.

He stepped back and pulled down his shorts. *Yup!* He was commando. And fascinating. I felt a burst of liquid between my legs.

"Stenton," I squealed again. "Maybe this isn't such a good idea; I'm feeling a bit more moist than I should.

He snorted confidently and beautifully. "That's arousal, sweetheart." Then he gaited into the colossal shower, turning it on.

He reached for me and I took his hand, wobbling towards him. When I was close enough, he pulled me into his large inked body and groaned in my ear, "I'm going to make you feel so good, Niña." My breath hitched. "But first I have to secure your hands."

"Why?" I breathed.

"Because I don't want your interference." There was finality in his tone.

He ambled behind me as I steeled in place, anticipating being restrained. I enjoyed it, but wasn't sure how I'd feel about it in my condition.

Stenton never gave me a moment to think. When he returned with a condom fastened between his teeth, he immediately began gathering my hair into a ponytail on top of my head. Then pulled my wrists in a binding device. My heart rate sped again, this time at the sight of restraints. My chest heaved as he meticulously cuffed my neck with a thick, black leather collar that attached to a wide strap connected to a chain by a metal ring. The chains connected to two cuffs that he strapped my wrists into. Stenton stepped back, observing my fists attached to my neck by two inch chains.

"Fucking amazing," he growled.

Then he hooked his index finger through the loop of the apparatus and the sequence of the evening's events sped up as around that time was when my very serious buzz closed in on me.

After being shuffled into the shower by an impatient Stenton, he went to washing my body from my neck to my toes, making sure to reach every crack and crevice. After rinsing me, he immediately fell to his knees and parted my legs. He lifted one over his shoulder and licked me deliriously. Warm sensations spike from my core, shooting to every area of my body almost immediately. My vision blurred and my tongue felt heavy all of a sudden.

When I peered below, I saw him pushing and stretching the lips of my sex with his tongue, being sure to lick every hidden edge of it. When he pressed his slick muscle into the apex of my lips, I saw eroticism like never before. I could no longer watch. It made me feel so out of control. Blissful ripples had me pushing against the restraints, only I couldn't advance in movement. My hands stayed near my face. That stirring in my belly engulfed me and I didn't have a moment to decide to collide with it. Pleasure swept me up and I found myself gyrating ferociously into his face until my one standing leg gave out and I made a short fall into the shower wall.

My head reeled almost as fast as my body when Stenton spun me around to face the wall. I let my cheek meet the cool tiles as I felt a swift pulling of my tampon from me and saw it tossed to the shower floor. The next thing I felt was Stenton slamming into me.

"Ahhhhh!" I cried out. I felt him tremble behind me as I stood on my toes, curving my spine so my hips could yield to him.

"You feel fucking amazing. So warm...so wet and snug for me. Only for me, Niña."

He pulled out and then thrust back in again, causing lightning to thwart my core. It was pain, but an excitable ache. In no time, Stenton's thread of self-control popped and he was hammering me against the tiles. He grabbed onto my breasts to anchor himself, pinching my nipples rhythmically.

"Open your mouth, Niña!" he pushed through my neck before biting down on my flesh in between my neck and shoulder.

That drove me into a tsunami that wracked my body with pleasure beyond belief. With my bound fists pressed against the wall and my head in between, I imploded with a force so powerful. I felt Stenton jerk violently behind me.

"Fuuuuuck, Niñaaaaa!"

Stenton's chest slammed into my back and I could feel his racing heart. Moments later, I felt him releasing the restraint from my neck, then the cuffs from around my wrists. *Who knew orgasms while bound could be so intense and draining?* He mumbled for me to hang on, then I felt cool air replace his heat. I shivered at the loss.

When he returned, Stenton effortlessly pulled me into his arms and carried me to his Jacuzzi. He lowered me into the tub with tender care then planted himself across from me and aligned his long legs astride mine. He then hit a few controls to power the jets behind me. I lowered my body until all but my head was submerged.

"Good, huhn?"

"Mmmm-hmmm," was all I could offer.

"So, about this job," he tossed out with ease. *Job? After what we just did?* "I thought we discussed it and agreed you wouldn't take it."

It took a few moments to command my body to move, but I lazily shook my head, not only shattered, but completely satiated. "I told you I needed the extra cash to fix my car. It's really bad, Stenton. I don't know how I made it into Philly tonight." I mumbled. I didn't have the energy to think about the possibility of breaking down on my way home.

His heart-shaped mouth set into a moue. I was too depleted to address it.

"But how are you going to balance work and classes? What are you averaging in the Probability and Statistics class?"

"I'm up to a B+ now," I yawned as my eyes rolled to the back of my head. I was crashing.

"Zo, that's no good," poured from his heavy vocals. "If you maintain that B+, you can kiss that 3.7 grade point average goodbye."

"Three-point-eight," I managed to correct.

Between being on my period, a long day at a crappy job, the drive here, and two back-to-back earth-shattering orgasms, I had no fight in me or stamina for a full-on engaged conversation. I needed sleep, and where it would be was yet to be determined.

Stenton scoffed, "That, too, sweetheart."

"I'll get through it. I'm good at figuring things out."

"Figuring things out will not get you into Wharton."

That got my attention.

"What in the world is that supposed to mean?" I lifted my body, sitting up in the tub.

"It means you need to stop being so headstrong and let me help out. I can give you a few dollars to keep you straight until you're ready to find a real job."

"Stenton, while I've never turned down anything you've given, you can't expect for me to depend on you like your name is Michael Barrett. We're staying afloat. We always do."

Rejection transfigured Stenton's face as he grimaced. "Don't say shit like that, Zoey."

"Say what? I'm not your responsibility? I'm not, Stenton. I'm hardly my father's. I'm a grown woman and will do what other grown women do every day and that's make ends meet."

This was going nowhere fast. He wasn't letting up, neither did I feel the need to appease his ego—at least not in the manner he preferred. Quickly thinking, I decided to sit up and slid between his beefy thighs until our lips touched.

"Besides, I let you do what you want *to and for* me anyway." I focused in on his marble eyes now that I had his attention. "Look at what we just did."

"Yeah," he murmured coarsely. "But I had to restrain your ass to let me do it."

I pecked his full lips sweetly. "Not anymore. I'm officially down for the red light special, especially if it makes me feel the way I do now. I loved it, Stent. And I love you, too."

I knew I was laying it on thick. Who knew you needed to do so much coaxing with men? That aside, Stenton was worth it. I never lied when I told him I loved him. That was completely true. The flip side to it was I had no clue what to do with the swelling emotions I felt for him. But that wasn't a topic I wanted to take on now. Now, I wanted more of him...and then sleep.

I grabbed him from beneath the water. Stenton's body jerked, surprised by my gesture. In a flash, his eyes went wild, but then retracted.

"I'll tell you what; I'll give you more of what you're asking for if you promise to spend the next two days of your spring break with me."

I pulled my head back and gave him a blank stare. "Sure. And then you'll just put me on a bus back to school, because I won't have the means to repair old Bessie."

Stenton gripped me at the waist, causing me to giggle animatedly.

"We'll discuss the details of your car later. Right now, I want to top your last orgasm."

He lifted from the tub with me clawed to him, laughing hysterically. He paid a few seconds to attempting to dry us off while we were still attached. Then he took me to his bed where he stretched a towel down and laid me on top. All the mirth escaped when Stenton filled me to the hilt with one rapid thrust. That's when the breath left my body. When he moved again, it was at a pace my body couldn't follow, but totally yielded to. Stenton drove me into the most insane orgasm as he pounded me into the mattress. He didn't stop until my last cry of release and then he let himself go as well.

We returned to the bathroom where I watched Stenton discard the bloodied condom. Seeing it that way still made me feel squeamish. We washed again and I plugged myself with a tampon from my purse that appeared on the vanity, out of nowhere. I slipped on a tank and boxer briefs Stenton gave me to sleep in and shuffled into his bed. He left the room for a while and returned with a tray of hot tea, a bottle of *Midol*, and a box of *Kotex* tampons. That brought back my embarrassment.

"I won't be needing these, thanks to you," I smiled teasingly at Stenton, referring to the pills.

He gave me a lopsided smile. "Glad you're feeling better."

I sighed contented. "And how are you feeling, StentRo?"

Stenton snorted. "Don't call me that shit."

Laughing along with him, I asked, "Where did that name come from anyway?"

"You wouldn't believe me if I told you."

He reached over and grabbed the tray while I held the cup, placing it on the nightstand. Stenton then crawled underneath the covers with me, wrapping his arms around my waist and burrowing his face into my abdomen. I had to be sure not to spill the hot tea on him.

"I would believe you. Tell me," I pushed.

"Just before I was drafted, I played in a tournament in Vegas that Michael Jordan sponsored. It was well-known, but not everybody was invited to play. I did and while playing, I went for this dope ass 360 degree layup. When I looped it, I made a spectacle of it, feeling proud. Later that night there was a banquet. MJ came up to me and shook my hand, but being the jokester he is, his words were preceded by StentRo. When he said it, the room lit up in laughter. I guess that was the sound bite of the night because word got out and now people I don't even know call me StentRo, but only those affiliated with sports."

"So because I'm not affiliated with sports I can't call you that?"

"Exactly."

"But I'm a red-blooded American. Of course, I know basketball!"

Stenton's head came up and he regarded me dubiously. "What team did I play for before the '6'ers?"

"Oh, please! That's easy. The Cardinals!"

His incredulous regard made me laugh hard. I couldn't stop.

"That's it. Bedtime for you." Stenton took the mug from me and placed it on top of the tray before turning down the lamp.

"Yeah, because I have to get up early."

I felt Stenton steel behind me. When I turned, I saw his deathly glower.

"You're not going back to that shitty job and that's final, Zoey. I don't care what I have to do to make it happen. I'll sabotage it if I have to. You shouldn't expend energy needed for your studies just for minimum wage."

After doing a stare down for barely sixty seconds, I caved. "Fine! I didn't like working with kids anyway. You may take care of the current malfunction, but now I go back to worrying about the next one that I'll have to figure out how to pay for." I snatched a pillow beneath me and slammed my head into it.

"Again, we'll address that later. Right now we sleep. You have to cook for me tomorrow."

I jumped, turning my neck completely around to face him. "Where's your chef?"

"I told him to pick up a few things from the market and take the next three days off. I knew you'd be coming."

"You didn't know I'd stay!" I noted, taken by his audacity.

"Like hell I didn't." He tackled me back down to the mattress, planting himself on top of my back. "All I had to do was swing my magic wand." He thrust against me enticingly.

His hard body pressed into mine made me delirious. *So crazy*, I moaned. Stenton chuckled as he rolled off of me.

"I hate you," I gritted.

"No, you don't, Zo. Goodnight, sweetheart."

Chapter Eight

Zoey

The next morning I arose early. Stenton was behind me, still fast asleep. When I learned it was just after six, I realized he was sleeping in. I paced into his bathroom to wash up, seeing a toothbrush and fresh towels awaiting me.

Downstairs in the kitchen, I found my instructions, loud and clear. There were fresh whiting and catfish waiting neatly for me. I also easily found grits and the ingredients needed for biscuits. By the time I was pulling the biscuits out of the oven, Stenton sauntered into the kitchen, rubbing his eyes adorably and looking heavenly masculine in his morning state, so unlike the predator he was last night. I quickly returned to the eggs that were frying to finish up on them.

"Morning," he mumbled as he greeted me from behind, wrapping his arms around my waist and giving my breasts a squeeze. "Nice gear."

I glimpsed down at my clothes. "Yeah, well, I didn't exactly come last night, planning to stay over. I had to steal your stuff."

He took a seat at the island. "You look good; your boobs do, at least."

I shook my head as I went for two plates from the mahogany cabinet. While plating our food, I heard footsteps coming up the hall.

"Mmmm! Smells good as fuck!" I knew that voice.

"I'm starving." That croak I didn't.

I peered up seconds later when I could sense them entering the open kitchen and saw Tynisha following behind Alton.

"What do we have here, Mascot?" Tynisha asked as she went for the refrigerator with natural ease.

Did they stay over? How often are they here?

"Uhhh…fried whiting and catfish—"

"I hope you put cheese in them grits," Alton interrupted me. "If not, put some on my plate. Damn! Are those homemade biscuits?"

"I only want cheese in my eggs, please."

I paused from spooning grits into Stenton's and my plates. I was debating on how cold my response would be before Stenton spoke up.

"Y'all done lost y'all muthafuckin' minds if you think she here to serve you."

"Wait! Hang on, big boy. We just tryna' eat. You can't be going Hulk on us this early in the fucking morning, bro!" Alton's words were bold, but his tone was pleading as he raised his palms in a defensive manner.

"It won't hurt her to show a little hospitality when she's been invited to stay overnight at an MVP's place. She should be grateful," Tynisha grated. "She don't want to get cut from *this* team. We winning."

My neck shot over to her. Again, Stenton stepped in.

"Don't start your shit, Ty!" he cautioned her.

Seething, I carried our plates over to the island and took a seat next to Stenton.

"In case you didn't get the memo, you're more than welcome to what I've cooked, but it won't be served."

Alton sucked his teeth. "Man, Ty, get me some food. That shit smell good as hell and look it, too."

"You can ask nicer, boy," Tynisha hissed as she walked to the cabinet for plates.

I could see Stenton's jaw tighten as he chewed. He was livid. We ate in silence while Tynisha filled their plates. I didn't know how I would handle these two, but I knew that I would. I had to. I also knew their animosity originated from Alton's affair with my cousin, Angela, last summer.

As I brooded, I felt Stenton's big hand cup my right thigh. When I looked to my right and saw him wink, I understood, offering me comfort. I wasn't afraid, but I knew I wouldn't be happy until this was addressed.

Tynisha arrived at the island and sat with us. As soon as Alton's plate arrived in front of him, he dug in. The moans he belted in satisfaction were bordering on sensual. Tynisha issued him a warning glare, to which he paid no attention as he feasted.

"Yo, Zo, man, I knew you was smart, but I ain't know you could lay it down in the kitchen like this until we was up in Alpine back in January. Remember that, StentRo? That chicken was the fuckin' bomb, bro!"

Tynisha's neck snapped over to him. Stenton's forehead wrinkled in disbelief of that reference, I'd guessed. I could honestly understand Tynisha's thinking as a woman. Her man just brought up a fond memory with a woman that reminded her of a disgraceful era in her relationship. Anything associated with me would bring my cousin to mind. She didn't like that, and I couldn't blame her. Alton was such a tool. Maybe because of her pride, or simple better judgment, Tynisha didn't respond to Alton's stroll down memory lane. She went a different route.

"What was up with all that moaning and screaming I heard up there last night?"

My eyes shot over to Stenton, who glanced up from his plate and glared at Tynisha.

I reached for the hot sauce as I quickly and audibly murmured, "Funny, I was going to ask what was up with the silence I heard from downstairs." When I was planted on my seat I squared eyes with Tynisha's. "After three kids, the thrill is gone, I see. Lost that elasticity, I guess."

Alton sputtered his orange juice and Stenton choked on his food.

I had to play it cool. I knew how to effectively deal with bullies. I'd always been a target as a kid, between being the devout church girl and highest achiever in school.

"Now, wait on here a minute, little girl!" Tynisha's Jamaican accent was rearing.

"No! You wait. I understand why you would be skeptical of me, but I am not my cousin."

"Thank god hoe-ism ain't in the blood," Alton mumbled.

"And praise Jesus that teams aren't chosen by dick sizes or else you wouldn't wear the same uniform as your boy, StentRo here." This time Tynisha snorted a laugh, and Stenton went for my thigh underneath the table again. "Listen, I get it. I have to prove myself, especially after my cousin...*and* Alton's indiscretions, but I'm no doormat. I will not be the butt of your jokes or your maid." I peered pointedly over to Tynisha. "...or *your* pledgee to haze. If you think otherwise, there will be eventful crossings every time we meet."

I made sure to look them both in the eyes. I was prepared for war. I issued warning shots and now I had to be prepared to annihilate. My pulse raced, mouth had gone dry long before, and my palms were painfully gripping the edge of the island top. I was ready. All they had to do was bring it on.

"Okay. Cool. She's in," Tynisha quickly shot over to Stenton before returning to her plate.

"Yup! She good with me, bro. Pour me another glass of juice, Ty?" Alton swiftly announced his instant change of heart, too.

I was completely mystified by the change in the atmosphere in just seconds. Was this a game to them? Or were they simply putting up guards they felt were needed for snakes trying to gain access to their hut? Whatever it was, Stenton still wore his scowl as he ate. I could tell he didn't have a change of heart.

A few hours later, Paul arrived with several shopping bags filled with clothes. Some fit and others, not so much. My size four frame was hard to call. I was so tiny in all places with the exception of my boobs. Stenton swore I had a butt, though no one had ever corroborated that claim. I was able to put together a few outfits to get me through the next few days.

Tynisha and Alton left for home after the first morning. I learned that Alton and sometimes Tynisha, too, stayed in Philly at Stenton's apartment. The reason was because after so many affairs, Tynisha made Alton sell his apartment and commute back and forth from *Wachovia Center* in Philly to Upper Saddle River, NJ as punishment. She eventually let up and allowed him to stay with Stenton to relieve him of the long drive. It really had to be exhausting trying to keep a grown man faithful.

That afternoon, Stenton took me to meet his mother. It was a weird experience he didn't actually prepare me for it. We drove up to Wayne to a fancy group home where she lived in an apartment-like facility. Stenton clearly treated her well. He introduced me as Niña to his mother who spoke English well, but was insistent on speaking Spanish to him. It was obvious to me that she wanted to exclude me from their exchange. What shocked me was Stenton's ability to return her conversation fluently in the same language.

"Yo se. Nosotros también te extrañamos mamá. Tu solo tienes que estar tranquila para mejorar. Solo quiero verte saludable," he murmured to her, and I saw her eyes immediately gloss.

Stenton hardly resembled his mother. She looked fairly healthy, though I could tell she led a hard life. I couldn't understand why she lived in an assistant living facility. Other than the curly hair and the thick eyebrows he had in common with her, I could assume Stenton was his deceased dad's twin. Call me saccharine, but my heart toiled at the vision of Stenton as a child with no stable parents.

We didn't stay long; their talk was brief, but what I could tell was this woman loved her son. She didn't smile much and I didn't need that for me to discern her affinity for him. It was the way she looked at him absorbedly and the tone used for her responses to him that told it all.

On our way back to Philly, Stenton answered my unspoken

question about his mother's condition. He said someone had slipped her something back in the late '90s when she was at the height of her dope addiction. She'd been diagnosed with paranoid schizophrenia. He said he didn't know if the occurrences were related or mutually exclusive, but it had been a challenge caring for a mother who battled drug addiction and mental disorders concurrently. When he ended his sharing, I didn't push for more. I had loads of questions including about his father who he'd shared a few months back was deceased. Other than saying his parents had a long history with drug abuse, he didn't give much else. I rubbed his long muscular thigh as we coasted the turnpike in peace…and rock.

The next two days went by in a blur. Stenton and I made love, cuddled, talked, ate and made out to our hearts' delight. It amazed me how, when isolated, you got to know small facts about a person: how often they used the bathroom, small grunts they made unconsciously, the way their lips parted when they slept, the slant their eyes form when they're giving their undivided attention to another one of your pointless stories, the expressions made as they succumb to orgasms, and their facial expressions when they're simply contented. This was closeness at its best. It was discovery of intimacy. It was love.

When it was time to leave, Stenton began to act strange. He was less talkative and developed abbreviated communications. It was hugely reminiscent of his taciturn behavior our last day together in Alpine. On our ride down to the parking garage I couldn't help the need to address it.

"You know," I sang lightheartedly. "If this is the way you behave when it's time to say goodbye, maybe I won't visit you anymore."

I couldn't hide my smile. Stenton made me giddy. We'd woken up, rolling all over the bed making love that I didn't know could be so charged first thing in the morning. We even had a quickie after a long nap on his sofa. And from there, Stenton turned sourpuss.

"That's not even funny, Zo," he growled, regarding me square in the eye.

That tore at my patience.

"Then what is it when you walk around like a toddler whose Spiderman was stolen?" I grated before walking out of the elevator.

"This way, Zo!" his tone was short.

I specifically recalled making a left to the elevators, but it had been a long three days, so I didn't argue. Well, not about where I had parked anyway.

"You can be so arbitrary, you know that?" I continued to follow him while giving him a piece of my mind. "Just like when you didn't let Alton give me alcohol in Alpine, but you let Tynisha give it to me here. Now you go into piss-boy mode with your snappy attitude."

"This is why," he remarked a bit stiffly.

"What is why? Why you let me drink the other day?"

"No. This"—he tossed his chin—"is why I've been so fucking pensive."

It wasn't until that moment that I realized we'd stopped walking. "Now you're speaking in code, Stenton. What is why?"

Stenton took me by the shoulders and physically turned my body to face a sleek black compact car. I was lost.

"Any minute now, Stenton!" I had to get on the road.

"Look at the fucking car, Zo."

That's when I noticed the bow.

"I won't be here for your birthday tomorrow. I wanted to give you your gift before I leave."

"What is this, Stenton?" I whispered.

"It's a small 2008 *BMW*. Nothing too flashy, but definitely reliable."

"Stenton...a 2008? It's 2007!" Then I shrieked, "My parents!"

"...don't have to know. And it's nothing grand, just a baby Beamer. Very understated," he spoke with a searing gaze. "Just don't drive it home or to church. Take the clunker."

I started looking around. "Where is old Bessie anyway?"

"At school. I had Paul drive her the night you arrived."

"How? When—" I stopped when I recalled him taking my purse. "That's how you were able to know the type of tampons I wear," I murmured as I pinched the bridge of my nose, overcome with mortification again.

"You're taking the car, Zo," his tone was adamant.

"Okay! Okay!" I gasped. "I see once again I don't have a say in your grand schemes."

Instead of continuing to fight, Stenton exhaled. There was a long pause. We both needed a moment to cool our hooves.

"I knew you'd trip about your parents so it's all in my name, and that can be changed the moment you're ready. The paperwork is in the glove compartment along with a signed affidavit that you're an authorized user of the vehicle. Here." He handed me the keys from his pocket.

Even the fob was elegant. *Holy mother of Joseph!* I have a *BMW*! I couldn't fathom it all. Similar to the laptop, I couldn't muster the proper response.

I reached up and threw my arms around his broad shoulders. "Thanks, Stent, for thinking about my safety." His hands splayed on my back. While still clasped, I murmured, "You're starting to make things weird for us. I'm starting to feel kept like a girlfriend or something, buddy." I pulled back, extended up on my toes, and patted his head like a kid.

"Shit," he scoffed. "Heaven forbid I try holding you to an anti-quated societal title like that," he whispered so low that I almost didn't catch it.

A small grin cracked my bewildered face. Then a revelation dropped in my head.

"Hey, is my birthday the reason why you okayed Tynisha giving me a drink a couple of days ago? You were ready to bruise poor Alton."

He nodded. "You're now a day away from your 21st birthday. I didn't want to be responsible for your under aged drinking back then."

"Ummmm…news flash," I sang from the corner of my mouth, my smile one-sided. "I was still under aged when I arrived here. You're responsible!" I jeered.

Stenton's face didn't break a smile. He was back to being a sourpuss.

"Okay! Really, dude, what's your deal?"

His eyes rolled behind me in the distance and his chin slightly tooted, fortifying himself. "I don't want you to *le*-leave." He exhaled harshly. "I'm not ready to split. I think about you all the damn time and when I'm with you all the other bullshit seems to ebb away." Another deep sigh. "Zo, I haven't seen my mother in almost a year. It's not easy watching her kill herself with those fucking drugs, but bringing you with me made it...feel tolerable." His eyes turned pleading. "I don't know what the fuck I'm doing with you." He ducked his head. "I've never been with a woman so young in comparison to my age, but I feel like I'm fucking addicted to you. I know you have your ducks all neatly aligned and I don't want to interrupt that—" Stenton squeezed his eyes closed. This was hard for him. When they opened he regarded me severely this time. "I don't know how the season's going to end. Just promise me you'll make time to go away with me once it's over. I don't care what you have to tell your parents, just promise me at least a week, okay?"

His pain stricken face tore at my soul. I reached up and kissed him hard and thoroughly. It took him no time to join me. I wanted to cure his angst. To blanket him with the security he obviously wasn't provided in life. I loved him that much. I pulled back first and gave a solemn nod.

"I'll be ready for you," I whispered breathlessly.

The ride back to Jersey was filled with so many questions, the biggest being what were Stenton and I doing together. I had no idea. I'd only known that I had never felt the exhilaration I did with him. He was full of surprises...and confused the heck out of me with his mood swings, like that night I left him.

The next morning, I was awakened by a call from the lobby letting me know I had a delivery. Stenton had a half a dozen floral arrangements delivered to campus. I couldn't fit them all in my room so I ended up giving out half of the ginormous bouquets to friends. I followed his updates on Facebook where Stenton would often post things related to our conversations.

He'd call and text regularly, never skipping a day and always keeping up with the happenings of my classes. He was amazing, even when being annoying.

Stenton: **What are you up to?**

Me: **At a pastor's anniversary banquet with my mom.**

Stenton: **Stiff?**

Me: **Completely.**

Stenton: **Send me a pic.**

I put the phone as low as I could near the table, issued a kissy face, and clicked.

Me: **Cheese**

Stenton: **Damn Zo you got your tits out?!?!**

Me: **LMBO! My mom hates it. Good thing my dad didn't come.**

Stenton: **Fuck! You're about to make ME come!**

Me: **Perv.**

I waited a few seconds as I chewed on my nails.

Me: **What are you doing? Send me a pic…**

Stenton: **I'm about to head outside to play.**

A picture came through and my mouth dropped. Stenton was decked out in a black cowl neck sweater that framed his chiseled chest intriguingly. He rolled his sleeves displaying the heavy ink of his forearms, making the look every bit cosmopolitan. He paired it with what appeared to be casual hunter green riding pants. What topped it off was the black fedora atop his head and gold wire framed sunglasses that hid his eyes. Stenton looked good enough to eat.

And those heart shaped lips…

I figured he decided to put away his rocker boy style for tonight. I just hoped it wasn't for someone of the female persuasion. I felt that unfamiliar pang of jealousy excreting into my bloodstream. Sex does that to people. Or at least it did to me in that moment.

Me: **Be sure to play in the middle of the turnpike.**

Stenton: **LMMFAO & SMH. Lata Nina**.

Jealousy felt crappy.

June 2007

Stenton

"You okay, Zo?"

Zoey's head popped over to face me. Her eyes were big and mouth open, evidently caught off guard by the sudden sound of my voice.

"Yeah, I'm okay. I see you're finally up." She cracked a small smile.

"Yup," I croaked as I stretched my arms and legs, yawning hard and big, tired as fuck.

"Did you sleep through landing?" she asked, still smirking. "I can't believe you were out from the time we took off until now. Somebody's too tired to vacation."

Not too tired for what I have in mind for you, though.

When I learned that we'd be going to the finals, I had Paul book a getaway. My last game was last night. As soon as I got off the court, finished my interviews, took the usual pictures, chatted with coaches and teammates, and showered, I headed home to do last minute packing. Excitement wouldn't allow my labored body to sleep. I twisted and turned with heavy anticipation of the next day.

Before the sun rose the following morning, we headed straight to Princeton to pick up Zoey and then shot up to Teterboro airport. I was drained—physically and emotionally—from this season. I put my all in, pushed myself, and now I needed respite. I used being alone and away with Zoey for a week as my carrot-at-the-end-of-the-stick to perform optimally. And I did. So, I got to hide away and restore in the Cayman Islands…with her.

When Zoey stepped on the plane, I noticed she was a little off. Likely because of the private jet that I chartered. I'd taken several women on their first chartered plane experience and had gotten several reactions; some outwardly excited, some indifferent—those were the groupies who only fucked with dudes with money—and this time with Zoey, it was different. She tried hard to not come across too thrilled, but did admit to never being on a private aircraft. Another new experience for my Niña. This was going to be a great vacation. That, I was sure of.

"You ready, chief?" Rob asked as he and Barry shuffled from their seats behind Zoey and me to get to the main door of the cabin.

As I studied Zoey, I answered, "For sure." She still looked a little askew.

I knew taking this young girl out of the country was crazy, but it was what I wanted. I paid minimal attention to my curiosity as to what tale she gave her family about being away this week, but decided to watch her closely to be sure she didn't freak out. Zoey was adventurous, but still grew up in a bubble and wasn't exposed to the shit I lived. Like now, she was eyeing Rob and Barry as though she'd never seen them before.

I also knew she was still in her feelings about Angela not speaking to her. It had been a couple of months since she had the baby and Angela hadn't even invited Zoey to her baby shower, much less to come by and meet the baby. I'd hoped to shake that depression from her consciousness this week.

I held out my hand for her to take and we exited the plane after them. There was a car waiting just off the runway. As we waited for our luggage to be transferred from the cargo of the aircraft to the car, I checked my phone for emails and texts. On the other side of the car, near the front door, Rob lit up a spliff and pulled from it. I smelled it before I looked up and saw Zo frozen by the sight of Rob handing it over to Barry.

I chuckled. "What's wrong, Zo? You looking like you've just witnessed the theft of the cookie jar."

At that, she tried to straighten her face. "What? That?" she pulled in her chin, playing it off. "Pssssh…whatever!" she turned and looked away.

I pulled her into me by the hand. "You've never seen anybody smoke in public before?" I felt my brows wrinkling, not able to conceal my amusement. She had to be kidding me. *She's from New B!*

"I...of course I have!" She fought hard to hide her face while wrapped in my arms.

"Hold up." I tried to steady her in front of me, pulling tighter on her arms. "You've never smoked before, Zo?"

Zoey kept wiggling in my arms, now burying her face in my chest. I could see her mortified blush. I couldn't help my explosive laughter.

"Awwww...they don't teach you how to roll up in Sunday school, do they?" I teased.

"Shut up!" she mumbled as she laughed into my abdomen.

"Yuuuurp, chief...that's us!" Barry yelled over to me.

I helped Zoey into the car, and we took off to our resort.

The villa I rented was on the outskirts of Grand Cayman, sitting against the ocean of the western Caribbean Sea. I'd always enjoyed the view and vibe of the Cayman Islands. The island never failed to bring serenity to my cluttered mind, and I'd hoped Zoey would appreciate the calming energy as much as I always had. The modest two bedroom unit included a full state of the art kitchen, enclosed dining room, open living room, and a spacious master bedroom with an en suite bathroom. The unique feature of the place was the aquatic deck running alongside the villa with access from both the master suite and the living room. The competitor in me couldn't wait to see if Zoey could swim the distance of the two rooms.

An additional feature of the property was an in-law suite with its own entrance and security, giving us privacy. Rob and Barry would be doing their own thing this week anyway, finding trouble—aka, local women in town—to get into.

After touring the property, Zoey and I unpacked in the master suite. She was mesmerized by the bed, stared at it for what felt like minutes. It was a four-poster bed with sheer ivory curtains flowing in the island breeze. As I observed her entranced reaction, I allowed the excitement to build for how I'd planned to use that style of bed this week. It was not by chance that it was there.

I seemed to have taken more time than she did because at some point, I looked up and she was out on the deck off the suite. When I was done, I decided to check on her. As I came out, I found her at the Jacuzzi with her feet submerged in the water. She had her dress rolled up, exposing her thighs. I couldn't tell if she was troubled or simply relaxed.

"What's on your mind?" I asked, not knowing if I was prepared for the answer.

"You," she answered, looking out into the open air.

"What about me?" I stayed behind her, posted up on the door frame.

It took her a minute to respond, "How different our worlds really are. *You* see sights like this." I could see the corners of her eyes as they moved to observe the tropical landscape. "And I can't even dream about splendor on this level. I never knew this side of creation existed." She turned to me with a reserved smile. A sad smile.

I took my time pushing off the doorframe and squatted next to her. Her skin was like silk, so damn tempting to touch. I hadn't had the opportunity to taste each inch of it, but I planned to before the week was out. I settled for brushing a loose curl behind her ear.

"You're experiencing it now and will be stuck with it and me for one full week," I spoke quietly in her ear.

She turned to look at me with a soft smile. *My Niña.*

"Now that I'm stuck with a dork on a horrible, beautiful, and incredibly romantic island, what next?"

I wanted to kiss her. We were that close. "Now, we go get some groceries. This dork has to eat on this horrible, beautiful, and incredibly romantic island."

I stood for the door, and almost there, I heard, "So, you're going to cook for me this week?" she gushed, a little too happy.

"Hell, no. I'm on vacation. You're cooking for me. Now let's go before I get too hungry and eat you." I kept my stride into the room, but I caught her laughter behind me.

We went into town to grocery shop. It reminded me of the time we went in Alpine, only this time I wasn't falling for the okie doke.

When we returned to the house, she put away the food and called me into the kitchen to help her cook. Although I joked about putting her to work in the kitchen, I really did enjoy having her boss me around in there.

After breakfast, we sat out on the deck on the side of the house and relaxed next to the Jacuzzi. Zoey laid out in the sun on the lounge chair next to mine, finally sleeping while I read Hill Harper's *"The Conversation."* It was peaceful, admiring the tropical and aquatic landscape. It was something I didn't want to experience on my own no matter how much I didn't want to disturb her.

Fuck it.

I got restless and woke her ass up, needing to taste every inch of her. I went over and lifted her from the lounger. I took her into the bedroom, awakened her with my tongue, aroused her with restraints and put her ass back to sleep with several orgasms. Zoey finally saw what fun the restraints could be using those posters.

Zoey and I spent the week sharing, fucking, building, and discovering. It was beautiful and damn, it was so peaceful. Zoey humbled me. There was nothing pretentious about her. She came without guards or motives—other than fucking. Zoey liked that a lot. She was always down for anything. Just when I thought her flexibility inspired me anew, she'd do something else to surprise and please me.

One evening, Rob and Barry were over. We grilled and chilled by the pool. The guys clowned Zoey and me for our music preference, so I tried mixing a little 50 Cent and Fat Joe with Nickleback and Green Day. I was surprised at how quickly and easily Zoey took to them and they to her. I don't know why I was; Zoey was a free spirit. Her quick wit and sense of humor were always a crowd pleaser. What I didn't like was her being seen in that little ass yellow bikini. Her voluptuous tits seemed to spill over her top. Also, whenever her bottoms would crawl up her ass, which was often enough, her dimples would show. I loved those dimples on Zo's ass. They reminded me that beneath the clothes on her small frame, she actually did have a donk, even if just a handful.

I ran to the bathroom at some point of the evening, needing to take a leak. As I was walking back out to the pool, I saw Rob and Barry in the living room, heading out.

"Y'all bouncing?" I asked as I held my hand out for dap.

"Yeah, man," Barry answered as he reciprocated the love. "We got some uhhhh…trouble lined up for the night."

"I feel you. Enjoy responsibly," I advised as I moved on to Rob, giving him love, too, while they laughed.

"I'm gonna get me another one of those sandwiches before we bounce," Rob called over his shoulder.

"Oh, shit," Barry hopped and followed Rob. "Me, too!"

I stayed in place, waiting to see them out. I was happy to be alone with her finally. She seemed so cool with hanging around a bunch of dudes for the better part of the day. From where I stood I could see her out near the water. Her hourglass frame looked fucking unbelievable from behind in the yellow string bikini. I watched as she rounded her neck, stretching out her muscles while the sun set around her. To me, everything happened around Zoey: my schedule lately had been detailed as much as possible around her availability; my thoughts and crazy ass plans for the future were around Zoey and how she would play a part in it; and now the sun was setting around her stunning frame.

She seemed so relaxed compared to when we first arrived a few days ago. It was interesting to observe how Zoey was just as caught up in the air as she was that first morning here. I wanted to relax her even more, though. I went over and changed the station on the radio for a much more mellow speed.

"A'ight, chief! We out." I heard from behind me.

"Aye, y'all got another doobie on hand?" I tossed over my shoulder.

There was silence for a few seconds before Barry tapped my shoulder, handing me a spliff and lighter from behind. I followed them out and locked the door. On my way to the patio, I grabbed a condom and lit up, taking a long drag. I hadn't smoked in a while, so I had to let my lungs adjust on my way out. I sidled behind Zoey, sitting on the big yellow rock that came to my abdomen and brought both my arms around her.

I held the joint inches from her face and whispered in her ear, "Don't do it if you don't want to."

Her scent already had me zoning as I went to nibble on her ear. She didn't move, was calm and motionless, only inclining to me. My tongue then moved to her neck and worked down until I bit the spot between it and her sun kissed shoulder. I enjoyed tasting Zoey everywhere, got off by her response to my touch. My mouth traveled to the other side, adoring every inch of heated silk that it roamed. That's when I felt her grab my lower arm, pulling it to her face as she took her first hit of indo.

I quickly brought my mouth up to her ear and instructed, "Don't take in too much. Close off your nostrils, hold it in the cavity of your mouth before pushing it out." I didn't want her choking.

From beside her, I could see her eyes straining and watering, and nostrils flexing. She did as I advised, only the smoke didn't expel smoothly. Zoey coughed considerably from the potent fumes. I gave her a minute to collect herself, found myself getting aroused by the new slant in her eyes.

I didn't ask her if she wanted another hit and was surprised when she leaned forward and pulled again. She gathered it in her mouth and held it, only this time it flowed with more ease. Something about her willingness to trust me and take my instruction excited me and I roughly pulled her by the forehead with my right hand, turning her face into mine, taking her lips. She yielded right away, melding into me.

I drew her in tighter, appreciating the slight musk on her tongue from her introduction to MaryJane. She accepted my tongue immediately and quickly offered hers. I kissed her like the animal I'm transformed into when around her. She lifted her arm to the back of my head and we wrestled as R. Kelly's "Greatest Sex" blasted throughout the property. *How apropos.*

I pulled away, offering Zoey more ganga. She took it, slowly doing what I instructed earlier. I followed behind her, inhaling. As I held it in, I untied her strings at the neck, then the ones at her back, and allowed the top to drop into her lap. Bringing her face to mine,

I slowly blew smoke into her mouth and watched it release from her nostrils, observing the way her eyes tensed.

I gave her another hit as she inclined into my shoulder. My right hand stroked her breast and twisted her nipple. The smoke flew from her mouth this time as she jerked in my arms. I placed the spliff between my lips to hold while my left hand joined my right on her left breast. Even over the loud music, I heard her groans.

Zoey twisted in place, bringing her mouth to my chest, but I didn't miss the deepened slope of her eyelids. My Niña was high. I pulled her into me and she wrapped her legs around my waist. Then I stepped back until I felt a barstool to park on then took a rubber from my pocket and placed it on the bar behind me. In no time, Zoey slithered from my lap, keeping her heavy eyes on me. She took the blunt from my hand, offering it to me before taking a pull herself. She placed it on a decorative rock, putting it out. I observed the sun setting as she strolled over to me.

It was amazing watching the sun retreat to make way for night-fall while caught up in ecstasy with my Niña. The clouds shifted in almost a choreographed sequence against the blue backdrop of the sky. The sun drifted to my left as dark billowy clouds grouped to my right, filling the sky. Fucking Beautiful.

On her way, Zoey grabbed her bikini top. I had no idea why until she strutted behind me and grabbed my hands to gather and bind it with. When she appeared in front of me, I noticed the satis-fied smile telling me she was impressed with herself.

I've experienced lots of eroticism in my lifestyle. I've had twin sisters and their first cousin, plunging into them consecutively until I released…or them first—which two of them did. Nonetheless, I've never known anything as erotic as Zoey getting high and seducing me like I was a fucking teenager. I was completely at her mercy, yielding to her lead in our sexual excursion.

Before I knew it, Zoey managed my shorts with my help and bent over, taking me into her mouth. Her pace started slow, but quickly moved into quick suctions. My hands moved to break loose from her magnificent fisting. She worked me long and hard. I sucked in my bottom lip as I watched her pleasure me. Her sights were on me, too, and Zoey knew she had me fucking defenseless and damn near crawling up the stool.

When I felt those familiar sensations in my sacs, I gritted out through my teeth, "Stop, Zo. No," as my head rolled.

Zoey halted and looked up at me with an expressionless face. I watched entranced as she untied and peeled off the bottom of her string bikini then felt her wrap it around my arms, too.

She rounded me, still no smile in sight and muttered my ear, "You're being too bossy. Next time I'll cover your mouth."

I snorted, not showing it, but secretly thrilled by her dominance. That's when I caught the condom in her hand and watched her put it on. She then straddled me, letting her legs hang over the arms of the chair, moaning as she took me in. When she started to move, the palms of her hands clasped to my shoulders. I got lost immediately. My hips worked upward while hers slammed down. My tongue flickered her pebbled nipple during her delicious gyrations. Zoey's head flung back as she moaned louder.

When I felt her tighten around me, I warned her, "Don't come yet. I'm not ready. Tell me when you feel it."

She brought her head up and I caught a smirk playing at the sides of her lips. Zoey watched me as we moved together. Her tiny eyes and parted lips had me close to the edge. She kept with her movements and I did with mine. I watched her eyes roll back and her hair swing all over the place, trying not to allow the eroticism to propel my release.

Then her head fell back again, her pussy tightened and her thighs and arms tensed around me.

"Zo!" I barked. "Zo, I'm not ready!"

Her head never came up again and her movements didn't slow. I jumped, pulled tightly at the tiny strings that bound my hands. It took a few tugs, but I ripped those shits in two, and grabbed her by the waist, separating us. Zoey gasped as I turned and sat her in the chair, threw her legs in the air and entered her again. I pumped into her with unyielding force. Zoey brought that shit out of me. I thrust until I felt her walls tightening again. This time I was ready for her.

"Open your eyes," I gritted.

Slowly those eyes opened and zeroed in on me. I could see them go in and out of focus, but she fought to keep them open. I noticed Zoey didn't scream my name, she somehow couldn't. And what I couldn't miss was how hard her body jerked as she came. Even while trying to steady myself on my shaky legs, I watched her little frame shake violently in the barstool. When I was stable, I pulled her into my arms as I stayed inside her, trying to calm her body. I knew she was still in the throes of her orgasm, but still was concerned about her take off. It took her some time, but she came down eventually.

After pulling off the condom and tossing it in a nearby can, I walked us over to the patio lounger, stretched out and laid her on top of me. I would have never tossed a loaded rubber so casually in a nearby trashcan with any other woman. In my paranoia, I made it a habit to leave the room, rinse the rubber out then flush it down the toilet and wait to make sure it didn't resurface. It concerned me how my guard came tumbling down when with this girl.

Out of nowhere, Zoey started giggling. Like...a lot. Her little frame started trembling again, only this time from humor. My face wrinkled.

"What the hell is so funny, girl?" My voice was hoarse.

Zoey lifted her head and let out a full on laugh. The sound grew loud. Her head swung back and her mouth opened wide as she struggled to breathe.

"Zo, man, what the fuck is so funny?"

It took her a while to respond. She made a few attempts, but eventually she was able to speak in pieces. "I'm. Hiiiigh!"

Slowly, a smile pulled at my face.

"Yeah, you are," I agreed.

I tried to give her a few minutes to get past her laughing episode, but it didn't happen so quickly. I lifted Zoey again, carried her into the pool, raised her jerking body in the air, and tossed her in the water. Zoey reemerged without humor. She was pissed.

"Are you serious, Stent!" she spluttered as she tried to wipe her face and keep water from her mouth, then started brushing her hair from her face.

She couldn't see me wading my way over to her. When I reached her, I pulled her into my arms and as she was about to start ripping into my ass, I covered her mouth with a kiss. It didn't take her long to join me. Neither did it take her long to reach her next climax there in the pool.

Chapter Nine

Stenton

The next day, we rose early, cooked breakfast together—or I should say, she gave me another cooking lesson. I made us reservations for dune buggy riding. When we arrived, we started off with a vintage two-seater and I drove us wildly throughout the open wilderness, spinning dirt underneath the wheels. I got a high from speeding on open soil terrain. Zoey seemed to enjoy it and even asked to take over the wheel.

I glanced over at her, doubtfully. "Really? You wanna try?"

"Yeah, why not? Because I'm a girl?"

"Well, yeah, if we're keeping it real," I answered honestly.

Zoey lowered her mask, rolled her eyes, and got out of the passenger's side. I watched as she came over to the driver's and snapped her neck, telling me to move. I pulled out of the cart and got into the passenger's seat. Before she could finish telling me to get ready, she launched. Her take off was jumpy. She had to get used to the accelerator and steering wheel coordination, but she kept stride until she got it. Zoey started cutting short, swerving and busting U-turns before I felt she was quite ready...or maybe *I* wasn't quite ready. On the low, she was scaring the shit out of me, but I would never whisper a word of fear to a woman. When she came to a smooth stop, I was relieved. However, my ease didn't last too long because as I was wrapping up our rental with the manager, I caught Zo staring across the lot at quads.

"No," I spoke adamantly in her ear.

Zoey didn't give me the startled reaction I was going for. Instead, she kept her eyes on the quads.

"We have to," she murmured.

"Have to?"

"Yeah." She turned to me. "You ever met that time in your life where you have this short period of insanity? That small stretch of time where you can do whatever crazy things you want without considering the consequences? It's because you know you'll likely never get the opportunity again. You may never feel the euphoria again, so you just go for it."

I stared at her for a while, receiving so many revelations from the many metaphors she gave. Did she not think she would go away again? Did she not think she'd be with me again? Did she think this was a one-time thing? Or was it simply about riding quads?

"Never mind." She exhaled and began to walk off.

I caught her by the hand and she jerked back to where we were joined, then her eyes traveled up to mine. Our gazes locked and something clicked. There was some crazy type of channeling, and I found myself nodding my head, agreeing to the race.

I knew precisely what Zoey meant, far more than I would admit to her or anyone in that moment. I knew there were things I wanted to do with her, to her, and for her that she may not agree to because she was not ready for it. She needed time to grow and experience life without my influence. She was still young. But I knew. I had completely allowed reality to escape me while out there with her. Hell, I willed it to. I wanted everything I could take in that period of time in paradise with her. I wanted to do shit that I'd never thought of. Crazy shit. Selfish shit. Ill-consequential shit. And I started with this high-speed race with her.

We spent the next three hours on the race course, riding *Kawasaki KFX 700s* where Zoey wore my ass out. She won all but two races against me. To say she walked off the lot that day with her chest out, talking mad shit wouldn't be describing her gloat.

Zoey and I returned to the house for a shower and nap. That night for dinner, Barry and Rob tagged along. We had dinner at a low key restaurant where we took shots and had a blast talking about nothing at all, but finding humor in everything. Zoey fit in like an old friend of ours. She didn't appear uncomfortable being the only female, and so far from home. I didn't mind her drinking, especially after the way she explained her private perspective on being here with me.

After dinner, Zoey asked to go for a walk to get to know the area. I found myself walking hand in hand with her down the festive streets where there were shops and merchandise lining the block, buzzing with locals. Zoey loved to touch. There was rarely a moment when we were alone or in our own private space where she didn't touch me. She'd have her arms wrapped around my waist, her arm behind me while rubbing my back, her face caressing my arm or her hand at my chest or abdomen. This was something I'd never experienced before, likely because I never kept a woman around long enough to be comfortable with someone in my personal space. Nonetheless, with Zo it felt natural in no time.

At some point, we stopped almost in the middle of the road. Rob and Barry were looking one way and caught my attention with a bar that they'd claimed to have not been familiar with, although they'd been coming into town every day since arriving. We watched the patrons go in and out, getting an idea of what type of clientele the place catered to—or at least that's what I was doing and assumed they were, too. Absentmindedly, my eyes roved over to my right to Zoey, whose attention was elsewhere, more specifically across the street on a tattoo parlor. The shots we took had me twisted, damn near wasted, so it took me a minute to figure out what it was.

"What's going on over there?" I bent down and asked in her ear.

I didn't startle her, not that I was trying to, but it just showed how deep in thought she was.

Her arm pulled up and her index finger pointed to the parlor. "I want to go in there."

"Why?" She had no tats, I didn't understand the sudden interest.

Then those doe eyes looked up at me. "Short period of insanity." A small smile played at her lips.

"Yo, Rob...B!" I called over to the guys and pointed to the tattoo parlor as Zoey pulled me across the street.

When we walked in, Zoey eyed all the drawings and sketches on the wall, seemingly amazed. I guessed this was a first for her.

I sidled up beside her and asked, "You picking out a new tat for me?" That was some personal shit. I picked all of my own ink.

Still gazing the wall, she shook her head. "No. You can pick out your own."

Huhn?

I snorted, "Shit, Zo. Are you getting inked?"

She turned to me with a shy smile while biting her bottom lip. "But just something small. I need to figure out just what." Her hands made their way up my t-shirt to my bare chest, softly running over my abs and pecs. "What are you getting?"

"Me?" I looked at her with incredulity.

She nodded excitedly, still biting that damn bottom lip.

I let out a breath. "Shit, Zo. I don't know. You sprung this on me. I usually take time to consider what I want it to express. I've never done it on a whim."

Her hands kept caressing my chest, exciting me, goading me. "You mean to tell me, out of all the ones I'm feeling now..." she rounded to my back. "None of these were done while intoxicated?" And that's when I recognized the slant in her eyes, reminding me of the shots we'd indulged in.

I shook my head.

"Well, I'm not getting one by myself. You pick out one so we can get started." She pushed off my chest and strutted away to talk to the artist.

I took a few minutes to first decide if I wanted this, then when that was done, I had to think of an expression I wanted, forever. That decision took a little longer than the first, but excited me three times as much.

Zoey glanced back at me over her shoulder, I knew, asking for my final answer. When I gave her an affirmative nod, she hopped over to a table behind a curtain to begin her first ink job. I looked around to find the other artist I noticed earlier and saw Rob and Barry, who appeared to be smirking.

"What the fuck?" I asked, my forehead wrinkled.

"That chick got you wrapped around her little finger, chief," Rob snickered and Barry followed.

While at the station getting my latest tat, I thought about what Rob said and realized he was right. Zo had my ass open and there was no need to deny it. I was on that *do whatever crazy things you want without considering the consequences* shit right along with my Niña. It took less than an hour before my art was complete. When I walked out to the small reception area, Zoey, Rob and Barry were there waiting.

Zoey jumped up, bouncing on her toes. "Let me see…let me see!" She was so damn excited.

I was a little nervous…doubtful, and not about my decision, only about her reaction. I extended my left hand and showed her the wide band of black ink on my ring finger, resembling a wedding band. At the top of my finger was the letter *E*, her first initial.

Her eyes slowly traveled up to meet mine. "Elizabeth?" she asked on a shaky breath.

My stomach started toiling. *Shit! She's going to think I'm a freak.*

"Eternity," I murmured as I nodded cautiously, because it truly amended her answer. I wanted Elizabeth for an eternity and had thought of a way to have it.

She didn't speak for a while, didn't move. I saw tears brimming at her eyes. They turned pink. I was not prepared to make this girl cry. I didn't think I could handle that shit. Just when I was about to say something to curb my insane decision, she spoke.

"Stent," she quickly scraped her top lip between her teeth as she glanced away. Then her beautiful brown irises returned to me. She whispered, "*I*-I don't have desires for marriage or...well, I've never desired to get into a committed relationship so young. There are so many things I need to do before I can settle into a life that requires me to give my all to a man. I'm sure I will...but just when I've served my purpose in life and then can commit to him. With you..." She looked beyond me again. "You're... I don't know." Zoey shook her head.

My head and heart were about to explode. Why did I feel like she was telling me I didn't do the shit to her heart that she did to mine? Like I didn't affect her life the way she ruled my universe? How would I respond to this young girl—who I'd involuntarily fallen in love with—telling me that I didn't do it for her?

Zoey extended her hand...her left hand, and although it trembled, I could see the delicate line curving around her ring finger. But when she turned her hand over, I saw the cursive script of the letters *SR*, vertically, spanning from her palm line to the first knuckle line.

I looked at her and saw that her eyes were trained to the floor, lids fluttering. I pulled her into a deep embrace and kissed her forehead adoringly. She quickly wrapped her arms around my waist. I then saw Zoey's artist behind her smiling, understanding my approval. We got our new ink wrapped up and left for the house where we consummated our joint tattooing experience; her first and my best.

The next morning, I woke and reached for Zoey in an empty side of the bed. My mouth was dry and head stiff. I brushed my face with my hands, trying to shake off the heaviness from last night. It wasn't the alcohol that caused churning in my stomach. It was the crazy shit I did that I couldn't take back. The crazy shit I did well after getting an impromptu tattoo. Suddenly recalling the tattoo experience, I got up to search for her. I'd hoped that wasn't a drunken decision that she awakened to.

I noticed the patio door was open. When I stepped into the door frame, I saw Zoey sitting on the step leading to the pool with a sheet hanging loosely from her delicious body, displaying her feminine curves. Zoey looked picture perfect. I caught her as she studied the subtle ink on her ring finger. My stomach turned again. I would hate myself if she regretted that decision, that notion. But before I could get nauseous from feeling disgusted with myself, Zoey lifted her hand to her face and kissed the inside of her palm where my initials were inscribed. Her shoulders lifted as she did and she sighed, seemingly satisfied. *My Niña.* I felt a relieving sensation run through me, but it couldn't rival the guilt still coursing my veins.

What the fuck did I do? I pinched the bridge of my nose.

"You have any regrets?" I asked, my voice raspy.

Zoey turned her head in the direction of my voice, but not completely to look at me. There was a small pause before she shook her head.

"Not an ounce," she damn near whispered convincingly.

Zoey sat there contented. *Unassuming.* She was still feeling that *euphoria that she may never live again* as she put it at the racing lot. And what the fuck was I doing? Was *I* regretting extending my euphoria past this week-long vacation? She was unbelievably beautiful and sexy sitting there, enjoying the view. Zoey was young, but strong and secure in her skin. She was bold, fierce, and unpredictable at times, but stable.

I moved quickly and quietly to get my phone. I had to capture that moment. I didn't know what shit storm was ahead, I needed memorabilia of this *stretch in time*. I returned to the doorway and snapped a few pix, being sure to get a good one. I wanted to always remember her this peaceful, this happy. With me.

"You have any regrets?" she asked with the back of her head to me.

I shook my head right away and eventually answered, "The best fucking birthday I've ever had."

The best birth—

I leaped backwards in my seat to ask why he would keep a birth-date from me. However, Stenton was gone. I wondered why he wouldn't have shared that with me before today. I could have baked him a cake, sang happy birthday or something. That aside, it was clear to me that he if wanted me to make a big to-do over it, he would have shared it in advance. So, I instantly decided to drop it and simply be grateful that it was a great day after all.

That day, Stenton was strange…distant. I don't know how long he stood behind me before announcing his presence. I came out there to meditate. I'd been having such a great time being crazy that I needed a moment of quiet to collect myself, pray, and reconnect. It balanced me, made me feel safe.

When I felt I had enough and was perhaps being rude, I stood to go back inside. Stenton wasn't there. He wasn't in bed either. I was hungry and guessed he was, too. We'd had a bit to drink last night and when we returned from the tattoo parlor, we spent hours making love before showering then crashing into the mattress to sleep. I figured he was probably exhausted from all of that activity. He was in rare form the night before: more vocal with his pleasure, clasping my hips tighter, lying inside me longer, well after our climaxes…withholding nothing. I shook it off as us growing closer in our intimate relationship.

After dressing, I walked out into the living room where I saw him on his laptop with the television going in front of him.

"I'm hungry. I know you must be, too," I called over to him. "You wanna start breakfast?"

He never looked up at me. Stenton shook his head. "Nah. I'm returning emails, this may take a while."

"Okay," I spoke slowly. His response was a bit detached. "Then don't be mad at my selection," I teased as I walked away.

Once breakfast was done, I set it up at the dining room table where we'd been eating since we arrived. When I called him in, Stenton said he was still busy with emails and would eat in in the living room. He didn't even ask me to bring his plate. He came and got it without any eye contact. As I ate at the table alone, I couldn't shake the cold vibes I'd been picking up. Did I do something wrong last night while drunk? I mean, I was pretty intoxicated, but not past the point of sense. Heck, I woke up hoping the tattoo parlor trip wasn't just a vivid dream. I was relieved when I saw his initials on the inside of my ring finger. I hadn't quite worked out what would be my response when people took notice of it, but was ecstatic about my decision and would do it again. My parents killing me be damned.

Not long after cleaning up breakfast, Rob and Barry came over to check in. It was our last day on Grand Cayman and I'd told Stenton I wanted to go back into town to get souvenirs. I didn't work out how I would explain them to my mom, but figured I'd deal with that once back on U.S. soil.

"Stent." I gaited into the living room where he was still seated on the couch. He wore lounge pants and the only thing covering his upper body was red, yellow and black ink. "You want to go into town so I can pick up those few keepsakes we talked about?"

He at least gave me eye contact for the first time today.

"Nah. You can go with Rob and B." He glanced over to the guys. "Wasn't it something y'all needed from there before we bounce tomorrow?"

"Yeah, we can go now, Zo. Come on," Barry waved his arm behind him as he stood.

Rob followed his movements as they headed for the door. I steeled in place, feeling uneasy about that call. Stenton and I had been inseparable the entire trip. Why the sudden need for distance? Stenton never looked up, and I couldn't formulate the words of inquiry regarding his mood without coming off as argumentative, so I decided to head to the back for my purse and went into town with the guys.

We were out there for hours. I was able to find cute trinkets for my mom, Karen, and my roommate. I also found nice jewelry for me. There were two rings that perfectly covered my tattoo until I was ready to expose it to the world. I ended up picking up fish from a market and finally decided to head back to the house. Stenton was likely starving, and I was getting there myself.

When I made it back, I put my things away and didn't see him bumming around in the house. I chanced a peek outside to find him doing laps in the pool. Even doing that, he seemed preoccupied, very solitary. Leaving him out there to himself, I went into the kitchen and prepared lunch. I heard him come inside and pass by, but he didn't stop in. As I was putting the food on the plate, he popped his head in the doorway of the kitchen.

"You got it?"

I sucked my teeth. "How convenient. I'm done. You can grab your plate though."

I handed him a plate and he left out. When I was ready, I grabbed my plate and went into the dining room where I found him waiting on me. I didn't know what to expect after his distance earlier.

As we ate, I had to address his mood change.

"Stent, are we okay?"

Stenton nodded his head over his food. His eyes was trained to the plate.

"I'm just mentally preparing for the shit I'm about to walk into as soon as we step off the plane to tomorrow. This was a real vacation week for me. If I'm not careful, my only for the year." He scratched his eyebrow and exhaled hard. "My manager has so much shit lined up over the next few weeks, into training season."

I nodded my head slowly, trying to make myself believe him. I mean, what did I have to go on? I didn't recall doing anything wrong. This was a bit strange, but I decided to drop it. I didn't want to harp on negativity. Plus, I'd never spent so much time with Stenton. He could have been an introvert for all I knew.

"What's your schedule looking like for the summer? Are you doing *Working Toward the Stars* again?" he asked, still not looking at me.

"Nope," I used the popping sound for humor. "I'll be finishing up with this summer course and relaxing before the fall semester begins and I get swamped." I stretched my arms above my head.

"Are you excited about the coming semester?"

That was an odd question.

"Yeah. It's another step closer to finishing." I gave a wry smile.

Stent nodded his head as he went back to eating. We didn't talk much after that. When we were done, Stenton cleared the dishes and I went to the bedroom to start packing. Our flight was early and I didn't want to forget anything. Stenton spoiled me over the past week. He took me shopping, creating the need for another suitcase.

"Are you marinating that chicken in the fridge?" Stenton's head, top with little curls, peeked in the door of the bedroom. I turned to him. "It's the last thing in there. I can prepare the marinade the way you showed me and soak it."

His inquisitive gaze soothed my gut feeling of their being an issue between us. I'd hoped he was coming out of whatever was bugging him earlier and we could enjoy the last few hours in paradise with our usual chemistry.

"Yeah, knock yourself out. I trust your measurements." I quickly turned my back to him to be sure he saw my crossed fingers behind me. I heard his laughter as he left for the kitchen.

I went for a swim and bummed around by the pool. I was so happy to experience the view, and sad to be leaving the next day. Stenton was around, but still not back to himself. He practically cooked alone and didn't speak much at all during dinner. We found ourselves turning down for bed together, and when I closed my eyes to doze off, I called myself a wimp for wanting to cry. I didn't though; I drifted off with a head full of questions.

Sometime later, I was being pulled while asleep. I felt my pajama slip shifting underneath me. I opened my eyes to the lucent night-lights pushing through the thin curtains covering the bed. I also felt and smelled *him*. I could feel the force of his breath hitting me. Then I felt his warm lips touching mine, not kissing me; just hovering over, parted. My body immediately responded, wanting to taste him.

As he lifted my gown, he whispered, "I'm not ready."

I didn't know what he meant and was still fighting sleep against abrupt arousal, so I couldn't ask for clarity. However, I was reminded of his parting words to me in Philly. Stenton pulled my slip over my head, leaving me completely naked. Then his lips pressed into mine and he swallowed my face whole. That brought me to full consciousness. My hands grabbed the sheet on either side of me. I guess I wasn't used to this functionality of them; more often than not, when we made love in bed, I was restrained. His tongue moved vehemently through my mouth, not really needing my participation.

He pulled away from my face and from the rays of the pool lights outside the suite, I could see his eyes opening. "I'm not ready to leave. I want to stay here...alone with you. Forever," he murmured while reaching his long arm over to the nightstand. I heard the rustling of the aluminum condom package then I felt his hands below, between us. "Why can't *this* euphoria last forever?"

I felt him inside me.

"Touch me, Zo," he drug lazily in my ear.

My hands flew to his head and I combed my fingers through the fine curls of hair. My hips pushed into his pelvis, giving him all I had, hoping it would end his sullenness from earlier. He'd retreated for nearly twenty-four hours and I missed him terribly. I could deal with a little quietness, but not rejection from Stenton. I didn't fully encompass his communication, but each thrust was delivered with force, each kiss landed with reverence, and each word he uttered in my ear was carried with passion. We made love until I tapped out and Stenton came not too far behind me. Almost immediately after, he carried me to the bathroom to shower.

The next day, as we were on the plane and just had taken off, Stenton was brooding again. He had been from the time he awakened. I didn't get it. I thought we'd gotten past this. I'd started to wonder if this was how sex partners behaved. I had no experience. Whatever it was, it didn't feel good at all. Where was my friend? We'd just shared an incredible week in paradise and it ended sourly.

Our plush leather seats faced each other. From across the small table, I observed Stenton's fixation out the window. My heart ripped each time I stole a glance in his direction. Rob and Barry sat in a set of seats behind us, busy with their own affairs.

I had to do something to occupy my frustration, so I picked up a *Sister2Sister* magazine and thumbed through the featured articles.

The distraction must have helped because I was shocked when I felt Stenton's hand reach for mine from across the table. I lowered the magazine and found his gaze.

His expression was pained and apologetic at the same time. It further confused me. He slowly licked those full, heart-shaped lips before speaking.

"Zo," he pushed out hoarsely. "I enjoyed being with you this week."

I felt myself grimace. "Are you breaking up with me?"

"No!" He shook his head. "But that's what I was getting at."

All I could do was stare blankly at him, awaiting something of substance.

"Where do you see this thing going between us?"

"The more you speak, the more you sound like you're ending things." I placed the magazine on the table, giving him my full attention.

He scoffed. "Why the hell do you keep bringing that up?"

"Okay." I jerked my chin. "Speak."

He inclined in his seat, keeping his voice low. "I don't know how to label us. I don't want to fuck this thing up. We started off as great friends and then we…fucked and now…we fuck. I don't know how to label this thing, and I want us to both be aware and comfortable with who we are."

I didn't understand what Stenton was trying to say, but I caught on to his earnest attempt at trying to come to a peaceable agreement about us. I thought.

"Are you afraid that I'll be asking you to be my boyfriend, Stenton?" I questioned with a leveling glare that was meant to humor him—or insult.

He chuckled half-heartedly, but fought to get back on track. "Zo, my schedule is crazy. I just finished up the season exactly a week ago and already I'm headed out of the country to do promos. Then I turn around and head straight to L.A. to shoot a commercial for *McDonald's*. My fucking life isn't mine, and you're not the type to put your life on hold and wait until I get off yet another plane from my latest business obligation. I don't want to give you some half ass shit."

It was my turn to sit up in my seat. "Stenton, if you want to continue to be…friends, that's fine with me. I won't demand anything but your friendship. Everything else is…great, but that's what I want more than anything."

After staring at me long and hard, deciphering I didn't know what, he sat back in his chair, going back to window watching. The man was maddening. I'd hoped I calmed any troubles he was experiencing about my expectations of this thing. I lied about only wanting his friendship; I wanted all of Stenton, but I didn't know if that was too large an order for the both of us at that point.

Covered in his hood, Stenton walked me to the door of my dorm building. He appeared very much dejected. When I turned to him, I tried supplying a smile to buffer his anxiousness. I lifted my left hand to caress the side of his face. The prickles from his fine stubble hairs against the pads of my fingers gave some degree of soothing for me. I wished it brought him the same comfort. I studied his troubled eyes.

"Stent—" I attempted.

"Don't go falling in love with nobody, Niña." His strained voice pulled at something deep within. "Don't give your heart away to another man."

I swallowed hard, fighting back my tears. Feeling pain from the size of the cry burning the back of my throat. The smarting sensation tumbling down to the pit of my belly, all because I fought to keep the tears within. Stenton didn't deserve to see how much he affected me. He was breaking away from me. Disconnecting.

"I can't give away something that was stolen long before I recognized it was gone, or how valuable it was." My gaze directly into his weary eyes was sharp.

"I'm sorry, Zoey," he whispered painfully before giving me a lingering peck on my lips. "I'm so fucking sorry."

Stenton turned and walked off. His shoulders, though high and wide were weighed down with something he didn't want to share. And no matter how self-assured a person I was at the tender age of twenty-one, no amount of hopefulness would fool me into misinterpreting what he'd just done. Stenton had just said goodbye to whatever we made in the Cayman Islands. It was over.

I watched him walk away with my heart in tow.

When my door burst open, I jumped from my bed and into the wall that it sat against, holding my chest. An earplug flew out and my mouth went dry.

"What in the world is your deal, girl?"

"Momma has been calling you for five minutes now!" Ruth managed with all the b-girl attitude she could spew my way. "Could your depressing ass come out of this hellish bat cave to dwell amongst the living for once?"

I ripped the remaining bud from my ear and leaped off the bed, pushing my way into my little sister's face.

"Who on God's earth do you think you're taking that language with, little girl?" I issued the most threatening glare I could. I was prepared to toss Ruth around the second floor of our parents' home.

"Well, now that someone has your attention, I'm talking to you. You've been in this room since we got back from South Carolina a week ago, Zo!"

"You have two-point three seconds to get out of here or you're going to have to have be lifted out," I hissed directly into her face.

I'd never been a violent person. At the most, as children, Ruth and I would shove each other around, but nothing more than that. Until this day. Today, I would make Ruth regret even being born.

"Hey! What is all this commotion going on up in here?" My mother came stomping into the room. She arrived between the two of us. "I know you two know better than to be fighting! Elizabeth, what is going on with you?"

I'd had it. I jerked back, went into my tiny closet, pulled out the overnight bag that was last used for the Cayman Islands. The one I'd refused to unpack before I could understand what had happened. I tossed a few things in there, filling it to capacity.

"Nothing," I answered my mother. "If anyone needs me, I'll be at Karen's, helping with the baby. Then I'm off to school." I made my way to the door, noting Ruth had disappeared.

"Now, hold on just for one second, young lady!" My mother hooked my arm before I could breeze past her in the small doorway. "You've been pouting in this room for days now. This wouldn't have anything to do with that ball player that you been gushin' over, would it?"

Now panting, I realized lying to my mother was pretty much futile. I had been home since returning from the Cayman Islands, because it was a far more comfortable environment that didn't remind me so much of Stenton. I hadn't made love to him here. I'd fallen into a dark pit, a place where I could feel every hollow place, yet had no understanding of how to survive there. I'd never known this chasm of despair.

I leveled my eyes with hers. "Momma, right now is not a good time. I haven't been doing too well with having too much time on my hands from taking just one class this summer. I think sitting with Karen for a few days to help her out will help me."

For minutes long, she just stared at me. I knew she could see right through me, but I made sure not to give her the ammunition she needed to pull the mask clear from my face.

"You be sure to call me when you're ready to talk. I'm your momma, and ain't nothing I don't feel from or for you. Do you understand me, young girl?"

"Yes, ma'am," I returned, barely covering the cry that I refused to release.

On my way over to Karen's, driving old Bessie, my mind churned. It was my first day out of the house since Stenton dropped me off. The day my world turned black. It had been the longest period of my life that I held my breath. I thought the wait to hear back from my early application submission to Princeton was the longest period. Nope. It was waiting out this era of pain. *Because it would leave eventually, right?* I mean time healed *everything*, right?

Little did I know, I'd be holding that breath for years to come.

I spent the first few days praying for the relief. And when I say praying, I mean tarrying. I tarried for days, chanting one word: Please. *Please, God remove this pain.* Never in my life did I feel so bleak. I saw sunlight nowhere. I prayed harder than I ever had in life to remove the weights of my heart and to fill the pit of my belly that echoed its emptiness. I had absolutely no idea what to do with the pain I felt. I had no reference other than Angela, who still wasn't speaking to me. Certainly she felt this when she learned of Timmy's infidelity. How she handled it wasn't something I was up for, but at least she had an idea of what it felt like to have her heart ripped from her chest.

I wanted to talk with my mom. In a perfect world I could, but then I'd have to admit to falling into something that I perceived to be *more* with Stenton. I knew that wasn't the truth. I knew that man loved me. I knew he felt every bit of the love we made each time we did. I knew each time he prepared to enter me when we made love, he held an unvaried admiration for me. I knew the fierce grip he held me in his arms with each time he embraced me after we were done exploding on and into one another was because he wanted to be stapled in that place with me and only me. I knew the way he'd simply speak my name when he called me, that he loved the core of me. He knew me, the real Elizabeth, and not the façade I put on for everyone else. I knew him, the real Stenton Rogers, who everyone regarded as a statue and not a living man.

I pulled up to the garden apartment complex, grateful to find parking. When Karen opened the door the first thing she uttered was, "My god, Zo! You look like you met Satan head on."

Her mouth remained suspended and I stood there, for once, not having a comeback. Karen had beautiful brown skin. She was shorter than Angela and me with a nice set of boobs and a round apple of a booty. You'd never be able to tell she'd just had a baby a few months ago. I hadn't seen her much outside of church. It felt good looking down at her short stature again. I gave a small but genuine half a smile. She stepped aside, inviting me to come in.

"You just missed Angela," she offered from behind me. My heartbeat sped up at that. I hadn't heard from Angela in months. "She left when I told her I'd be expecting you at this hour."

I exhaled long and harshly as I grabbed the bridge of my nose.

"So, BJ is in training for his new job?" I asked, trying to change the conversation.

"Yup, Wal-Mart is promoting him to shift manager." Karen didn't sound so thrilled. "Hang on. I need to check on the baby. Have a seat and make yourself at home."

When Karen returned, she sat on the love seat next to me and went right to it. "My mom thinks you're having some type of delayed emotional reaction to Angela and me getting pregnant and married. She said you're feeling abandoned and possibly even going through some identity crisis. Is that what's going on with you, Zo?"

I closed my eyes and slowly shook my head. "What are you talking about? Why is Aunt Jenny diagnosing me?"

"You know they talk: my mom, your mom and Auntie Bridget."

Auntie Bridget was Angela's mother. I guess she had a point. Word did get around our family like lightning.

"Is it, Zo? I really wanted you over to get into that thick skull of yours. You've been a little distant since my wedding. I don't know if my mom is right, but I do know you've changed. I just hope I had nothing to do with it. I really miss hanging out with you." Karen's voice was almost as pained as my heart was at the time.

"It's not you...or Angela." I licked my lips, trying to garner the nerve to finally open up and share my misery. Next to Angela,

Karen had been my closest confidante. "KK, I…ummm…sort of got involved with a guy."

Her eyes enlarged. "Is that why you've been MIA? I mean, that's a good thing, right?"

I shrugged, feeling that cry at the back of my throat again. "No." I swallowed hard. "Not when you fall in love with him and he up and leaves you without warning or reason."

There were several expressions that washed over Karen's oval shaped face: concern, confusion, relief, and then amusement.

"Well, Zo, I know you've never been the type to fall head-over-heels over a guy, but it's not like it was so serious that you have to call it heartbreak, right?"

"You do when you make love to the first man that causes you to question your values and to want to change everything you called yourself planning for your life," I whispered, unable to look at her.

But I heard her gasp. "Zo!" I glanced up to meet her eyes. "You lost your virginity?"

I nodded while biting the inside of my cheeks.

"Holy mother of Joseph!" she breathed. It was a phrase we all used.

"Well, there goes Bernard's dreams out the window," she murmured mostly to herself. "Does Angela know the guy? I know how tight you two…were."

My eyes slammed shut and my face wrinkled as though in pain. I nodded my head.

Karen gasped. "An ex of hers? Oh, Zo! I know you're not that type of girl." She'd begun to panic and at the same time, mollify me.

"Worse," I whispered, still unable to open my eyes.

"How much worse can it get besides Timmy?"

I did open my eyes to that one. Timmy was Angela's fiancé. I caught Karen's drift. It could only be as bad as Angela's current. But that wasn't true.

"Oh, it's even worse than him."

"Zoey, you're scaring me! Who?"

"Stenton Rogers." The tears I'd been swallowing all week nearly surfaced at the mention of his name.

Karen sat back in the sofa and covered her mouth, looking identical to Aunt Jenny. *Jeez!* I'd aged this girl in a matter of seconds.

"Was it his stature?" She lolled her head in disbelief. "Ang said he's even better looking in person than on television. Even I didn't think that was possible. Did you get caught up in all of that, one thing led to another and you gave him your virginity? I could understand that slipup, you know?"

I shook my head throughout much of her assessment, knowing where she was going with it. "It was more than that, KK. He told me he loved me."

"Well, Zo, you know that's not uncommon for men when they want something. And then with him sensing you were the good girl you are, I'm sure he went even further with his persuasion." She shook her head, suddenly angered. "So, it's taken all this time for you to get over a fling from a year ago. I see now, Zo."

I continued shaking my head. "No, KK. We just ended things a week ago. He dropped me off at home after going away together, and just broke things off for no—" I could go no further or else I'd cry.

I was so confused as to the cause of him ending our friendship. When I thought it was for another woman, I learned I was wrong. Two days after he dropped me off, I went to Stenton's *Facebook* profile and saw he had set it to a picture of me in Cayman the morning after our tattoo excursion. It was taken from behind me. I was naked with just a loose sheet covering my bare breasts, but not my back. My hair was a messy display against my back and shoulders. My posterior was exposed all the way down to the top of my cheeks, revealing such intimacy between Stenton and the woman in the picture. Me.

The caption underneath read: *The moment you meet your perception of perfection is the moment you'll never be the same.* I didn't understand the meaning of that as it pertained to me. The picture got over four thousand likes on his personal page where he had as many friends. How he was able to keep that account from the general public, I didn't know, especially because he didn't go through lengths to hide his identity. His friends knew who he was. Stenton didn't post this intimate picture of me to his fan page where he had millions of followers.

I didn't know he'd taken the picture, but remembered feeling so full and freshly conceptualized about my life after getting inked with him. I looked down at my ring finger covered with a plain wide metal band so that I didn't have to explain it to my parents yet. Couldn't deal with that *and* a broken heart. It also wasn't something I was prepared to share with Karen. But I couldn't help but wonder when he'd posted the picture. That led me to question when he planned on breaking up with me in relation to posting it. I didn't know how long it had been there.

"Well, sometimes they can splurge on their lovers. I mean, it's really no inconvenience; you're staying in the same room. I mean, really. He's just a jerk, Zo."

Still shaking my head, I shared, "I've been to two of his homes. He bought me a brand new *BMW*."

"Is it outside?" In a millisecond, she leaped to her feet and faced the door.

I shook my head.

"Did that punk take it back?"

"No. It's parked at my school where I don't have to worry about anyone bothering it or my parents finding out."

"Oh! So, this *was* serious!" she mused as she took her seat.

Again, I nodded.

There was a long pause, I'm sure Karen was trying to process the gamut of information I'd just laid on her. I was still fighting to make sense of it now that I'd spoken it out loud. Then Karen shot from her seat and headed out of the room.

"You cannot whisper a word to Ang, Karen!"

Karen halted in her tracks. "Are you kidding me?" She gave me a sharp gaze. "I'm about to feed those limbs of yours so we can restore your energy for prayer."

"Been there, done that," I mumbled.

"When two are gathered in my name, Zo! You know the scripture. You gonna need a backup warrior to deal with that Angela. Until then, my lips are sealed…outside of touching and agreeing with you."

In that moment, I couldn't say I felt better, but I did feel like the load was light after having shared it with someone who loved and respected me.

Chapter Ten

"Ohhhh! We so killed it tonight!" Bernard bellowed as he jumped out of the door, at the rear of the church. "Come Sunday morning, folks are going to be dropping to the floor to get their deliverances. Gloraaay!"

Karen laughed hard as she held her belly. She was right behind him and in front of me. Bernard could be funny when he wanted to. Nothing moved that boy more than music. He lived for it. Whenever a new gospel song broke the airwaves, he'd jump to rehearsal to teach it to our choir and execute it the following Sunday. Tonight was no different.

What was out of the ordinary was the fancy Lamborghini parked just outside the door. The lengthy figure leaning against it with his legs crossed was unexpected, too. Just behind the sports car was a conspicuous black SUV with all tinted windows. Right away, I knew that was his security, or armor as he referred to it.

My mouth went dry at the sight of him in army fatigue cargo

shorts, a simple yellow tee and sneakers just as fancy as his sports car.

Stenton's impassive eyes assessed me, then went to Karen. But it was when they landed on Bernard that I'd seen an emotion. He was angry. He pushed up from the car and stood tall—as if he could appear any lengthier. His biceps flexed beneath his tatted sleeve and his jaw followed suit. I swallowed hard.

"Holy mother of Joseph!" Karen whispered, clearly entranced.

That woke me out of mine. But I still couldn't think to speak. As crazy as it sounds, I hadn't counted on ever seeing him again, much less outside of my church.

"Can I talk to you, Zoey?" His eyes darted over to Bernard. "Alone."

"I'll wait here for you," Bernard murmured, undoubtedly starstruck, but exposing his blustering ego along with Stenton's.

"What do you want to do, Zo?" Karen asked, attempting rationale.

Stenton approached us and my heartbeat increased with each step.

"You must be Karen. I'm Stenton. Congrats on your recent nuptials and new baby. Zoey shared his pictures. He's a gorgeous little guy." Stenton extended his hand.

Karen obliged with an ashen face. "*Y*-you know my name...seen my baby? Holy mother of Joseph!"

Stenton snorted. "Of course. Zoey was proud to become an auntie to him."

My body steeled at him recounting my sharing of my elation when I'd first met Karen's bundle of joy. How could he present himself as an intimate friend of mine after dramatically and coldly creating a wedge between us? It was torturing.

Karen blushed herself red. "Oh!" she yelped, regaining her faculties, I'd assumed. "This is our friend, Bernard."

Stenton turned to Bernard, narrowed his eyes and angled his head. "I don't recall Zoey ever mentioning you."

Bernard's mouth went agape. He didn't seem to have a response to that. Neither did I.

"Did you drive?" Stenton asked.

My eyes fluttered as I shook my head, still overcome by his all-consuming presence. "No."

"Karen, I'll give Zoey a lift." Stenton looked directly at Karen, assuming I'd driven with her.

"Zo, your mom is expecting me to drop you off safely tonight," Bernard sheepishly asserted.

He was embellishing. I didn't know what his motive was and simply hoped it was to give me an out in case I didn't want to retreat with one of the biggest names in sports.

"I'll make sure Sarah's wishes are carried out." Stenton extended his hand to reach for me.

"Zo, if you want to come back to my place, you're more than welcome," Karen offered, I was sure she was trying to dispel the illusion of Bernard and me having more than we did. I was grateful for her wit, because I was rendered witless in Stenton's presence.

I couldn't resist him if I wanted to. There was no way I should have gone with him considering how raw and vulnerable I was. However, no matter his audacity, I couldn't repel him. After all, he didn't exactly seem to be well adjusted himself.

I took his hand and he walked me over to his car. I heard Karen's goodbyes behind me. From over my shoulder, I saw them walk over to their respective cars. When they pulled out of the parking lot I turned to Stenton, facing my pain.

"You've been staying with Karen?" He reached over and brushed his calloused thumb over the dark spot underneath my right eye. I winced at his touch, not knowing how to receive him, receive it.

I swallowed, fortifying myself. "I haven't been home in a week. I couldn't continue to have my mom see me like this." My voice was suddenly raspy. That was what this man did to me.

"Why, Niña?" Stenton's shaky tone spilled out.

His question and reference angered me. It made my soul cry again. My body quivered from my attempt to keep it together. I tried to conceal the anger.

"Because if she sees this, she'll hate you!" I finally tapped into my feelings, caved into my misery. After a moment I was able to admit, "I don't want my mother hating you. I'm not ready for that. If she hates you then maybe I will, too. And I'm not ready to hate you, Stenton. I'm not ready to move on from you. From us. And I feel like such a sappy romantic for it. I almost detest myself for loving you!"

I lifted my eyes to control the water threatening to spill. When I raised my chin, I saw Stenton shaking his head regrettably.

"There's no need to hate yourself because of my stupid ass actions. It's just—" His fist rose to his face and slammed into his mouth. "I just—" Again with the fist. "Zoey, I don't know what to do. I don't know how to do this or...if it's even fair for me to ask you to be with me at this delicate point in your life. I've never had to deal with someone as smart as you are and...loving and...so damn tender, Zo." With his fists resting on either side of his hips, Stenton's chin collapsed into his chest.

"Well, I don't know what to say either. But what I do know is I've never felt pain...or loss the way that I have since Cayman. I've lost meaningful relationships...shoot, Angela isn't speaking to me now. But this," I place my hand over my heart. "...and this," I shift both my hands to my belly. "...I've never felt physical pain like this before, Stenton. I don't want this anymore."

When his eyes landed onto my belly, Stenton heaved harshly and quickly shifted away in the other direction, brushing his hand roughly over the back of his neck, appearing embattled.

He didn't turn back to me when he muttered, "I need you to come with me. I need you tonight."

What?

Wait... "How did you even know I was here?"

Then Stenton turned and cracked a toothless, one-sided grin, resembling a bashful boy. "*Facebook.* You said you were starving in the back pew at choir rehearsal. Come on. I'll feed you." He delivered casually as he started his stride back to his car.

I nodded, still dazed.

What was I supposed to say? *No. Absolutely not?* Being young and inexperienced, I had no wherewithal against the object my heart and body were instinctively *and impulsively* drawn to. It wasn't a matter of trust that made my decision; it was a matter of need. I needed Stenton, too.

When Stenton didn't hear from me, he turned back and closely regarded my face. I don't know what it showed, but he correctly perceived my answer when he returned to me, took my hand and walked me over to the passenger door.

The ride was silent. I was trying to think of good phrases, sarcasm, and wit to illustrate the pain I'd been in. I needed him to know and possibly feel it so that he would see only being with him could cure it. On our way up to his apartment, I kept my view at his feet. I couldn't look directly into his handsome face because I'd weaken.

"You're making that fucking sound again," he growled as we ascended in the elevator.

Ugh! My throat! I had to get a hold of myself.

As we exited and sauntered to his door, I frantically rolled over in my mind what I would say. During the separation period, one of the millions of reasons I could think would be the reason he broke up with me is our age difference; perhaps he perceived me as immature. It would be an unpopular opinion, but a reason nonetheless. If this was correct, I needed to carefully gather my words. The last thing I wanted him to do was be reminded of his theory. My pulse raced in panic from the clock ticking. I was losing time.

When we stopped at the door, I heard the clacking of the lock and knob. A tart film coated my mouth. The door opened and I followed the back of his colorful sneakers. The door slammed behind me, then I was being lifted into the air and my back collided with the wall. Stenton's tongue was in my mouth and his big hot hands were all over my breasts, thighs and hips. When my legs were somehow secured around his narrow waist, Stenton sandwiched my head between his hands as if he was trying to prevent me from going anywhere.

His kiss stole my breath, and in no time I was sparring with him. Though I'd kissed him countless times, this one was different. It was feral. Desperate. Unyielding. He sucked on my tongue with fraught hunger. Then I felt his erection press into my core as he grinded into me. I could do nothing but ride to feel friction. My sex gelled with desire and my leg muscles strengthened to pull him into me. Suddenly, I was reminded of what passion felt like, of what he did to me carnally.

Abruptly, Stenton pulled from me. "Zo," his voice was gruff, revealing I wasn't the only one caught up.

I kept grinding into him. "No!" I reached for his face again and all he allowed was a sucking peck.

"Zo, baby, someone is here."

Huhn?

I turned first to the left. No one. Then to the right where I saw a handsome olive skinned man with beautifully laid dark hair and perfectly arched brows, standing awkwardly at the island, trying to suppress his laughter.

My neck snapped back to Stenton. "Who is that?"

"Remember I said I would feed you? This is Jimmy John, a friend of mine, who came on short notice to cook Indian cuisine for you."

My eyes raced in their sockets as I tried to gather myself.

"Do you want to eat now or later?" Stenton gave me a deep licentious gaze.

There was no way I'd muster the appetite to eat after that. I glanced over to Jimmy, who with a broad smile, lifted his hands defensively.

Then I returned to Stenton whose eyes never left me, and mouthed, "Later."

Without time to reconsider, Stenton called out, "Later, Jimmy! Keep that naan hot!" And we were on our way to his bedroom before a handsome Jimmy could reply.

My frame trembled and my skin glistened from sweat. I was

moaning beyond belief, begging Stenton to touch me again. To bring me to another release. My wrists were tied to my thighs, limiting my mobility, but it couldn't stop my squirming. It was a new restraint device and just as the others before, I loved it. I enjoyed giving myself to Stenton for his direction in intimacy. It exposed another side to him; an aggressive one, so contrary to his ultimate approach to me.

"If you don't stop, I'm going to tie your legs up, Niña!" Stenton stood at the foot of the bed, glaring down on me.

"Stent!" I cried out.

My legs were up in the air and my spine couldn't remain still from my thrusting. My nipples were peaked and my clitoris throbbed as if he hadn't just given me two earth-shattering orgasms with his talented mouth. But that wasn't enough. I needed him buried deep, releasing me from deep within.

"It's coming, baby. I just need to record what this looks like. Feels like it's been too fucking long."

Stenton's skin was misted as well. His tattoos came to life under the sweat beads. The tips of the barbed wire inked on his shoulders and upper chest appeared sharper in my hazed view. His appendage hung in the air, bouncing in small increments as he rolled on a condom. I was sure to dissolve at the image alone.

"Please!" I was out of breath, panting uncontrollably.

Stenton froze in place, struck with something internally.

"You still trust me after all I've put us through?"

"Implicitly!" A shiver ran through my spinal column. "Always, Stent. Please." My cries were unabashed.

"Fuck, Zo! I missed you so much. You're never afraid. Never make me feel fucked up about *this* shit I do to you." Now, Stenton's tone was needy. He stood motionless and his voice was low, thick even. "You've fucked me up for life. I swear I can't be with anyone else like this. Only you, Niña." His voice darkened. "Please say I'm the only one you'll ever submit to. Never to another man like this."

In the recesses of my mind, my sarcastic self was screaming, *Walks like BDSM, talks like BDSM…* But I knew that wasn't what he meant. He wasn't into that lifestyle exactly. What specifically he meant, I didn't know, but would agree to anything to extinguish this burning need to have Stenton deep within. To connect with him in a way I never had with a man, or another human being. I'd agree to anything.

I found my head nodding emphatically. "Never! Only with you, Stenton." I was resolute. "Forever *your* Niña."

Whoosh!

That's how the air left my lungs when Stenton dove on top of me and without warning, thrust into me, filling me to the hilt. I cried out in pleasure and pain at his fullness. His plunges were impatient. His touch was urgent. In no time, I recognized the pleasure he ensued on my inner walls. Immediately, I was intoxicated with sensual sensations.

With these restraints, I was still able to push up onto him, meeting him with my needs. Stenton felt incredible, erasing every trace of pain he'd caused with his sudden abandonment and larceny of my heart. While he plummeted, I reconnected with something that made me whole. Not only did I feel physical sensation that my body trembled from, but I could also feel emotional satiation that couldn't be derived from any other form of communication. Once again, Stenton was performing his best. On top of me. Deep inside of me. Ignited something from deep within. My body tensed and mouth collapsed.

"Yes, Niña. That's what I need. Come for me," his strained vocals produced.

And I did. My body shuddered as it was overcome with undulating waves of pleasure that I couldn't control: only Stenton's plunges did. He thrust twice more before his body jerked on top of me and jaw clenched as he tried to anchor his waves of bliss.

When he was able to focus his eyes, I asked, "When did you upload the profile picture?"

I don't know that I was planning to ask him that, and especially at such a precarious time, but I did, and it felt okay.

After giving me a searing gaze for seconds long, he answered, "After I dropped you off, the day we got back from the Cayman Islands."

That answer spoke volumes and confused me all at the same time.

Stenton's big arms gathered my languid frame and pulled me into his chest, resting his hard pecs against my back, making me privy to his calming heart-drum. Depleted, I took a deep contented breath and let it escape with a hum.

"I like this."

I felt Stenton's face push affectionately into my neck.

"Like lying in the bed?" I heard the humor in his thick tenor.

"In your bed...having had you out of sorts like seconds ago," I murmured lazily. "It gives me that momentary belief of being closest to you."

His hold around me tightened. "You are the closest person to me. It may not feel like it because for me, it happened so quick...and unexpected, and I may not have adjusted to that fact, but it's true. You are," his tenor chords rumbled.

Unconvinced, I yawned, "It's the sex. You're still floating."

I closed my eyes to rest. I don't know how long we laid there, I'd drifted off at some point, plagued with exhaustion. I felt satiated and grateful for Stenton's comfort. I thought the silence was agreeable to our mood.

Until I vaguely heard, "My pops was killed by a d-boy and his crew. He stole a whole bunch of their shit from a kid they used as a squatter on their block. It took them a while to find him. In the meantime, he shared their product with my mom. It was bad shit...shit that made her go crazy." I could feel his body steel behind me, revisiting his nightmare. Facing the wall ahead, my eyes bulged in horror. "One day, my mom goes into the hospital, overdosing on the dope. Two days later, my father's body was found rolled up in a carpet behind an abandoned warehouse. My mother couldn't ev—" Overcome with tormented emotions, he choked on a silent cry.

Stenton waited for some time, silence so thick my heartbeat could be heard. "My mother couldn't go to his funeral. She'd just come through when he was put in the ground." Stenton let go of a shuddering breath. "It's hard to trust people with your essence...your emotions—who you really are—when you never had anyone around to teach you how to sort them first. It's hard to admit, but you're the first I've felt this type of emotional connection to. It scares the shit out of me. But nothing has ever felt so right. It makes me want…permanency with you no matter how I can get it." He exhaled harshly again. "Zo, I know that sounds all kinds of… confusing and…fucked up, but—"

My hand moved up to his arm encasing me and clenched it adoringly. It was my way of saying I accepted his disclosure and was grateful for it. He spoke about permanency in the wake of his abrupt breakup, something totally contrary to his actions. We remained that way for countless minutes. I transitioned to an even more peaceful and blissful state than before Stenton shared his turbulent past with me. And I knew in that moment I could never love another man the way I did him. It didn't matter if I were to fall in love a second time with another man; no other man could ever claim my heart the way Stenton had.

Once relaxed and washed, we made our way downstairs. There, I was formally introduced to Jimmy John, who prepared the delicious chicken curry dish. It was rich and well-seasoned, but nothing compared to being with Stenton again. He sat across from me, engaged in his plate.

"So, Indian cuisine?"

Stenton looked up. His marble eyes zeroed in on me, causing my belly to flutter.

With knitted brows he informed, "It's one of your top three favorite cuisines, right?"

I nodded. "After Spanish food," I reminded him.

Then I regrettably watched his eyes return to his plate.

Seconds later, Stenton muttered, "My mom…before she… ummmm…overdosed…she cooked for a Spanish spot called *Manny's* in Newark. She was…ummm…pretty good at it." Then I heard his fortifying cough.

My stomach twisted. Stenton rarely spoke of his parents. It was so bad I'd never ask, not wanting to pry, but tonight he'd been more than forthcoming.

"How's everything?" Jimmy approached the table.

Stenton glanced over at me.

"Everything's great! You're an awesome cook," I gushed.

Jimmy smiled and strode back to the sink.

"We're good, JJ." Stenton then tossed a glance over his shoulder. "If you don't wanna see me devouring Zo, you can bounce. I can have Marie clean up the mess in the morning."

Jimmy nodded humbly. "With what you've paid me, it would be highway robbery to leave your kitchen in this state. I'll clean and then leave, Stent. Just be quiet while you're feeling her down."

I giggled, then it quickly turned into full blown laughter. I had to hold my belly.

Stenton's face sobered and he asked, "You okay? I noticed you look a little pale and thinner."

I rolled my eyes in my plate. "Aside from suffering from a broken heart, I've never felt better."

"Zo…" he started.

"No." I held my hand in the air. "Right now I'm not asking for answers. Maybe tomorrow. Perhaps next week. But right now, I want to dull the pain." I made sure to level my eyes with his. "I just want to breathe again."

With his sight glued to my face, Stenton nodded. I could feel his need for a reprieve from whatever it was that had been dangling over our relationship. I didn't want to try to make sense of everything. I only needed time out of the pit of gloom that swallowed me whole when he left me on the steps of my dorm.

That night, Stenton and I made love well into the dawning of the following day. We didn't ask any questions, make any demands, pledges or promises. We simply relished the magic we made when together.

THEN: September 2007

Stenton

"Are you up?"

I glanced around the room, totally disoriented, trying to come up with a response. I brushed my face with my right hand and rubbed my tight nose.

"I'm good. What's up?" I returned.

"Stent, do you even know who you're speaking to?

What? I found myself grimacing at the phone like *it* was a damn fool. I hadn't spoken much to her since last month when I dropped her off after spending the night with her. I'd been traveling so damn much, fulfilling my contractual obligations and trying to allow her to settle into the new semester.

"Of course I know who the hell you are, Zoey. What the hell is going on?" I asked as I squinted up to the nightstand, inches away, bypassing my *Cartier,* to the clock for the time. It was just after three in the morning here in L.A.

"Don't use that tone with me, *jerk!*" she cried. That last word came out with explosive tears. It was clear to me.

I leaped into a sitting position. "What the fuck is wrong, Zo? Everything all right? Talk to me!"

I heard her sniffles in the phone. Zoey never cried. I'd seen her hurt, depressed, and fucking elated, but never did I see her cry. I was panicking like a motherfucker.

"Zo!" I shouted.

"Stenton!" she screamed. "Stop yelling at me!" she wailed into the phone.

My stomach turned and my throat tightened. She wasn't speaking fast enough. In my craze, I could see her somewhere in a corner, alone, in a fetal position, hurting. And there wasn't a fucking thing I could do to help because she wouldn't just open her damn mouth to tell me what the fu—

"I'm pregnant, Stenton," she whispered through her cry.

Shit! Niña…

In all of my witless planning, not once did I think about this. Suddenly, I felt sick to my stomach. I shot up and raced to the bathroom, barely making it to the sink before throwing my guts up. When I was done, I collapsed against the wall and brought the phone back to my ear.

"Stenton, are you there?"

It took me a moment to answer. "Yeah, baby, I'm here," I breathed out.

I felt enveloped by guilt, stifled by it so tightly I couldn't breathe. In life, I managed to not let a lot of shit get to me. When you're exposed to the public and endure the hot and cold of its fickle support, you learn to develop a hard exterior. I do this even when seasons are good, my efforts align with my output, and we're winning. Even through those times, I try not to let shit get to my core, because whatever affects the inner you controls you. So, I've made it a point to not feel much, and to definitely manage my output in terms of emotions.

This fucking girl… She crept up in me somehow and infected me like a damn virus. She fucking controlled my sanity. That's the only thing that could explain how I was able to lose every faculty and do something so goddamn crazy.

"Stenton," she grounded out through gritted teeth. "What am I going to do? How am I going to tell my parents?" Then her voice elevated with a fresh thought. "Maybe…maybe I should get an abort—"

"Abso-fucking-lutely not!" I was able to find my voice. The bitterness in it matched that of the taste in my mouth from the vomit.

"But what am I supposed to do? I've started my last year of college. I'm on a scholarship; there is no way I can ask for it to be deferred. Opportunities like mine don't come around often at all.

This is it for me. My parents can't afford a baby; they're in the process of losing their home. I don't have a real job, nothing that could help. And what employer is going to hire me only to lose me right away to maternity leave?" she cried into the phone. "Stenton, how am I going to tell my parents that I've disappointed them?"

I gave Zoey time to cry. In my wildest dreams, I had things in place for this one thing I wanted just as bad as I needed air to breathe. I wanted Zoey and this baby. I wanted it so fucking bad it hurt. But it also inconvenienced her. In my wild thinking I didn't intend on that. I hadn't thought of every grievance she'd named. But one I did.

"I'll tell them, Zo."

"*W*-what?" she stuttered. "What do you mean *you'll* tell them? Stenton, my parents don't know you. My family…they're different. They don't tolerate stuff like this. Pregnancy outside of marriage opens up a can of worms that I vowed to avoid. They'll demand marriage and you know how I feel about that! Stenton, it's bigger than my family; it's my church." She was freaking the fuck out. "They won't take this well. My life…my future is over. There will be no me to help. With a baby, I'll be another burden…another mouth to feed—two mouths to feed! Don't you get it?"

Pain ripped through my chest at the cold and harsh tone of her voice. It was one I'd never heard from her. I wasn't expecting her anger. I knew she wasn't ready for marriage, so I'd go with the next best thing. A connection with this incredible young lady forever. I wanted this baby.

"Don't do anything stupid, Zoey." *I've done enough of that for the both of us.* "Just hang tight. I'll take a flight out tonight. Don't sweat telling your parents. I'll take care of that." I didn't know them well enough to trust they wouldn't try to advise her to abort the baby. I needed to play this shit right. "Where are you?"

She sniffled, "At school. I can't keep sitting on this. I have to tell my mom."

"When did you find out? How do you know?" …*what I've done to you?*

"Yesterday. I went to the clinic here on campus."

"And you're just telling me?" My voice was softer than I felt at that moment. "Why didn't you call me right away?"

She sniffled some more. "*Angela* ring a bell? I'm not one of those girls, Stent," she declared through gritted teeth again.

It was sufficient enough of an answer. Angela tried to rope Alton in with a pregnancy she knew he wasn't responsible for. Zoey was nothing like her cousin.

"I'll handle it. Just hang tight."

"Bye, Stenton," she whispered and ended the call.

And I didn't know what that meant. Again, a pain ran through my chest as I laid my head against the wall.

"You ready to do this, homes?" Barry asked quietly from behind the wheel after we pulled up to Zoey's two-story home.

As I looked through the window into the morning sky, I nodded my head. I was as ready as I'd ever be. How do you tell a man you knocked up his young daughter, but you plan on taking care of her? You certainly don't include all the details.

"How you know that fool ain't got no heat up in there? I think at least one of us should roll with you, chief. Man, we 'on't know how 'dis shit gon' go down, ya' heard?" Rob added from behind me.

We'd just got off the plane in Teterboro. When we jumped on the jet right after the last call of the *McDonald's* photo shoot I'd done in L.A., I decided to share why. I didn't give too many details, but offered up some because they knew Zoey and now would really know her. I knew they were concerned about me going in without them, but as a man, I had to do this alone. Rolling up in that man's house with armor to tell him I've fucked and impregnated his daughter would be beyond reckless.

"Nah, I'm good. Give me a min," I called over my shoulder as I hopped out of the *G63* and took a deep breath while moving up the walkway, wondering how many times Zoey walked this exact path, coming and going, over the years.

It took a minute, but eventually Sarah Barrett opened the door with trepidation. I could understand. What the hell is a six-foot-seven-inch tatted giant doing at your doorstep just before eight in the damn morning. Her smile was forced as she tried to recall my face. I knew that expression in my line of work. When folks see you for the first time in person, your features are familiar from the television screen. In her case, I was just in her home the previous Christmas.

"Hi," she squeezed out hesitantly. "Can I help you?" It finally hit me: Her mahogany skin appeared flawless and her eyes were big and expression-filled like the actress Loretta Divine.

"Good morning, Mrs. Barrett. I'm hoping to speak to your husband, Michael," I tried calling on all of my etiquette and vocabulary. These were Christian folks; my normal vulgar nature just wouldn't do. "Is he around?"

"*Su*-sure. *I*-I'll get him. Hang on a bit," she offered, still uneasy.

When she walked away, I turned toward the truck and let out a long and heavy breath. I was tired as fuck when we pulled up, but now I have enough energy to run the entire city of New Brunswick. Rob and Barry's eyes were glued to me. I knew they didn't envy me in this moment. How the fuck did I get into this shit? *Oh, yeah…my brilliant, asinine idea.*

"Can I help you, son?" I heard from behind me, just as curious as his wife.

I turned to see a short and round Michael Barrett, almost shorter than his wife, who stood a few feet behind him. I was sure she was looking for answers.

I extended my hand to him, "Mr. Barrett, my name is Stenton Ro—"

"I know who you are, son," he informed as he accepted my hand. *Is it the tats that give me away?* For the first time, I felt a little embarrassed by my rocker style appearance. "How can I help you?"

"Well, I was wondering if I could talk to you." I looked around the doorframe and behind, gesturing my desire to be invited in. "…privately, if you don't mind."

He nodded, "C'mon in. Have a seat over there on the couch."

I followed him into the living room to the couch he directed me to. As I was preparing to sit down, Sarah asked, "Are you the young man that came over for Zoey last Christmas?" She'd finally placed my face.

I gave a nod and polite smile that seemed entirely inappropriate for the occasion, they'd soon learn.

"Yes, ma'am," I answered then turned to Michael. "And that's the purpose of my unannounced visit. Zoey and I have been friends since last summer. She enrolled in a program that assists a facility where I used to train during the off season." I brought my hands together, begging my words to do the same. "Well, we've been getting along, keeping in touch even during the season. I've grown quite fond of her and…"

"And son?" he pushed. I was being wordy.

"Well, sir, apparently she's pregnant." Sarah cupped her face. And I felt like shit. My nervousness belied my predatory deeds. "…and I wanted to come to you and stand for what's been done. I can offer an apology…if you feel that's necessary." *But I won't mean it.*

I glanced towards Michael to see him stunned into silence. Sarah started to sob quietly while she sat perched on the arm of the chair her husband sat erect in. I quickly withdrew the notion to apologize. It would be disingenuous.

"Where's Zoey?" he grated, alarmed.

"She's in school. She should be home today." I looked over to Sarah's, now, red eyes and repeated, "She should be home today. She needs her mother."

"And what about you?" Michael asked with bravado. His forehead was wrinkled, sharp eyes still daring.

"I need her to be okay. I need for her to be supported by her family," I qualified directly to him.

"And what are your plans for her?"

I knew he was referencing marriage. Zoey's sharing about the girl, Karen, at their church prepared me for this. Zoey wasn't ready for that, and I wouldn't be rushed into shit. That was something I wanted with her in the long run, but now wasn't the time.

"My plans are to support her as well. All the way. I plan on taking care of her and the baby."

"Well, when did this happen? Why hasn't she come home yet?" Sarah cried.

"She called me with the news yesterday. I would have to let her tell you the rest of the details," I answered her then turned back to Michael. "I flew in right away to speak with you. I don't want to start off on the wrong foot, and considering the circumstances, I have a lot to prove."

"Son, I know what you do for a living. I know women love throwing themselves at basketball players." At the mention of that, Sarah's shoulders straightened and she grabbed her chest with an audible gasp, I'd guessed she'd just pieced together who I was. "I appreciate you being a man. I just hope you mean what you say about supporting her. Babies are lots of responsibility."

"Is this like Angela's situation with that other basketball player? Are you going to drag her through court and sue us?" Sarah asked with tears running down her face.

My eyes hit the floor and I shook my head. "No. I'm here to take full responsibility. I know time is of the essence, so to speak, so I wanted to talk to you right away."

Sarah abruptly stood then paused. "Can I call my baby?"

My eyes shot up and mouth opened and closed. "By all means. She's your daughter. She needs you. I just didn't want her to have to break the news alone," I tried to explain.

Sarah damn near ran out of the room, I'd assumed to the phone to call her oldest child. I was right; within seconds I heard her call out her daughter's name as though she was in pain. I heard the barrage of questions that followed, but what I heard loudest was relief. I guess my presence here instead of Zoey's was frightening for her. I couldn't lie and say it didn't please me that Zoey listened when I told her to hang tight. It also made me feel a sliver of guilt for having the trust of someone I betrayed.

I didn't realize Michael was staring me down.

"You came here to offset the lashing," his knowing tone brought my attention back into the living room. He was now sitting with his elbows on his knees, staring right in my face.

"I did."

"Now, I respect the man in you to come tell me about this, but I hope you're being up front with me. Zoey has a promising future ahead of her. This is gonna set her back. I don't have time for no shuckin' and jivin' with my baby girl." He gave me a pointed gaze.

I swallowed hard, and not because I didn't plan on taking care of Zoey and the baby, but because there *was* some shucking and jiving going on to some degree. I'd dishonored his daughter. At that reminder, I started feeling lightheaded.

I stood and extended my hand again, this time to leave. I needed sleep.

"Sir, you have my word, we'll be in touch," I guaranteed.

He waited until I was tall on my feet to reciprocate. His grip was tight and firm, communicating his desire of control. I didn't flex. I couldn't; I'd put myself in this situation. I waited until he was done and withdrew my hand.

When I turned for the door, Sarah came out into the living room. "Wait! You're leaving?" There were still tears in her voice. She looked wrecked. "Zoey's on her way home. Do you want to wait for her?" She and Michael both looked at me expectantly.

I took a deep breath. "No, ma'am. I just got off the plane from L.A. I have my staff in the truck waiting on me. I need to get some sleep. Zoey knows how to get a hold of me. She'll contact me when she's ready. Right now she needs you two to love on her."

They didn't verbally commit to anything, but I knew they would. Zoey always spoke highly of her close-knit family, specifically how tight she was with her moms. I felt like a damn wolf in sheep's clothing. I didn't want to be any more of an imposter than I was.

I walked out and to the car thinking my next move would be calling Chesney to let him know it was time to roll out the plan, starting with his office reaching out to Zoey's family.

October 2007

Zoey

"Do you understand what this means, Elizabeth?"

I broke my trance and glanced up at the tall sandy blond man across the long conference table from me. I must have zoned out again, something I'd been doing since the start of the semester. He wasn't alone. His team outnumbered my parents and me. This man, however, Stenton's attorney, Chesney, was a true spectacle. He was extremely animated with his presentation and communication, effeminate even. I hated the way he stared at me from the time we walked in his New York City office. He used too many inflections when he spoke and thoroughly enunciated words for dramatic flair. Chesney used the word *honesty* and *trust* way too much. That's likely where he lost me.

"I would like to say we're a family, *but I won't give you the illusion of that.* We are *however*, an organization and keep things neat in *our* camp. I know you are in your fourth year at *Princeton*, and understand what girls your age do socially, but I admonish you: *your life is no longer just your own.* What you do can affect an entire organization. You *must* practice discretion."

Those words were followed by a long gaze deep enough to intimidate me. And it did. Chesney sat with his long index finger and thumb at an "L" shape against his jaw. My timid eyes fell towards the table where there were stacks of papers and pens for signatures.

"Now, with that being said, Mr. Rogers has laid out a list of provisions for you, so I'll just get started." He slowly inclined in his chair and gathered a bundle of papers in his hands. "We'll start with the home at 88 Wilson Street in New Brunswick, NJ with the amount of $289,586.68 being owed on the mortgage, including delinquent payments." In my peripheral, I saw my Dad twist uncomfortably in his seat. "Said amount will be paid by the end of tomorrow's business day to Chase Bank. That is what…" Chesney located a document and pushed it towards my parents. "…this form is for. Fill it out completely."

What? Stenton is paying off my parents' home? I was so numb, I didn't know if I should be relieved or offended, but I could sense one thing: *My Dad is going to kill me!*

Then he went back to the papers in his hand and pushed up his spectacles. "Once all the paperwork has been cleared, there will also be $75,000 deposited into your personal account to pay for any repairs needed on the house. There will also be an additional $5,000 deposited into this account every thirty days for food, room, and board for Elizabeth and the fetus."

"Now, wait just a minute!" My dad nearly leaped from his chair. "This girl is my child and I don't need help from Rogers to care for her. She's my responsibility!"

"Michael," my mother cried out as she tapped his arm to calm him. My heart was ready to leave my chest, it beat so hard.

Hesitantly, he sat back in his seat, issuing Chesney a deathly glare.

Chesney appeared unruffled as he returned an impassive one. There was silence for seconds long.

"Now, for you Ms. Barrett: Mr. Rogers understands you are in the middle of your academic pursuits. He also understands that you are in a very competitive program and scholarship agreement. Given that, should you decide to complete the academic year, that is your prerogative. If you decide to take time off to give birth, that is completely at your discretion. However, understanding that you are there on a full scholarship and if you take time off, you lose it, my client will pay not only for the remainder of your academic studies when you're ready to return to school, but also any academic endeavors beyond your undergraduate tenure. And because you're not expected to work throughout your pregnancy and you will likely —*by his estimation*—finish out this current fall semester, you will be given a $10,000 monthly stipend for personal expenditures. This does not include the provisions for the unborn baby. That will be taken care of separately by Mr. Rogers."

I heard my mother's sharp gasp. It was something I would have done if I didn't decide to play possum, somehow thinking it was the only way I'd make it through this humiliating conference.

"Also…" Chesney didn't stop. "…Mr. Rogers hopes you will agree to driving the 2008 *BMW* 3 class series. The paperwork is…" he shuffled through the countless documents on the table again. "…here. You are now the owner of the vehicle and the insurance will be paid for through the year. You are being asked to get rid of your Kia Rio—"

"Wait!" my mother spoke up. I heard the alarm in her tone. "What *BMW* are we talking about here?"

I further shrank in my seat, desperately wishing to disappear from this room. The earth. Maybe Mars had vacancy.

Chesney's eyes squinted. "Oh, I guess you were not aware of Mr. Rogers purchasing Elizabeth a vehicle for her birthday this past February. It is a 2008 *BMW*. I don't know where it is, but I do know there was an agreement between the two that she would drive it everywhere with the exception of home and church as to not alert you to it." Then he looked at me again and murmured real snark-like. "You can drive it everywhere now that it's all been disclosed." If I wasn't decided before that moment, I knew then I didn't like Chesney.

"Now that we're done with prenatal matters, as far as your post-natal care, Mr. Rogers will provide Ms. Barrett housing that is sepa-rate from her parents to ensure adequate accessibility to the baby. A place Mr. Rogers would have free rein to visit the child. This will be arranged at a later date by Mr. Rogers himself. There will also be a yearly stipend paid by Mr. Rogers for childcare in the form of a nanny from the time the child is born until it has been decided by both parents that the child will attend school. Any immediate needs Ms. Barrett and/or the child may have from today, moving forward will go through my office."

He reached for another bonded document. "Here is a list of instructions as to how your requests will be made. Mr. Rogers is open to anything, from clothes, to car repairs." He waved his finger in the air as he scanned the document in his hand. "…he's basically giving you a wide range of items you may desire or need, *down to vacation requests*." That inflection expressed his displeasure. Then it came. "Something I don't agree with, but have to adhere to my client's wishes."

Screw you!

I was in hell and he wanted to cry about his preference to control his heartless clients!

"*I-I…*I don't understand this gibberish. I hear all of this *he's giving…he's giving…he's giving*, I don't understand what he's taking?"

"Yeah, that's my point, too," Chesney drawled out, barely underneath his breath. "…but I'm here to service my client." He rolled his eyes. Then in seconds, he straightened in his seat. "He's *taking* responsibility. Mr. Rogers is saying this child Elizabeth, here, is carrying is his and he will take care of the child *and Elizabeth*." Chesney started pushing more papers towards us. "And as soon as these agreements are filled out with social security numbers, bank account information and nondisclosure agreements are signed, we can implement his wishes."

"Nondisclosure agreements?" I shrieked. That mention reminded me of Alton's handling of Angela.

"Yes, Ms. Barrett. It is very key that we adhere to my mentions earlier about discretion and honesty. These details are of a private matter that we do not want made available to the public. Your business with Mr. Rogers' provisions is not for public consumption. Is that understood?" His tone was the most intimidating it had been since the top of this meeting.

My father grunted. My mother grabbed her chest. And I sulked.

"Now, Ms. Barrett, do you have any questions, objections, or amendments here?" Chesney asked me, appearing bored with this whole ordeal.

I simply sat there, trying not to cry. I felt reduced to a child and embarrassed for me and my parents. I couldn't believe I brought them this trouble. This mess. They were by no means incompetent, but I knew this "mediation" was over their heads. Heck, with my Ivy League status, I was confused by it all. It was well over their class placement, over their educational levels, and realm of life experience. And not because of Ruth this time. No. The culpability of this blunder belonged to me.

Even in all of my self-debasement while there, I wondered where Stenton was. What was he thinking, bringing me and my family into this legal and sterile situation? Why couldn't we have just spoken privately? Why humiliate me like this? I felt even more abandoned.

"I do have to get on a plane to my California office soon," Chesney abruptly informed while checking his watch. "My associate, Whaler here, will assist in explaining terms of any of the agreements. You can take your time and read over some that cause reluctance on your part. We can discuss amending others. My strong advice to you is to get it all signed as soon as possible. It is my understanding that the foreclosure procedure is progressing. The sooner we take care of that, the sooner you'll be relieved of that hassle. Mr. Rogers himself would like to have that settled for peace of mind."

Chesney swiftly left the room without any pleasantries. We sat there in silence deciding to sign away our lives as we once knew them. I secretly questioned if we should have had a lawyer of our own to assist, but didn't speak it. Deep in my heart I believed Stenton would never do anything shady to me or my parents. However, when I glanced down at my still flat belly, I wanted to rebel and refuse to sign anything because of his negligence.

I could only imagine what my parents were battling individually. I'd disappointed them. One day their oldest child was enrolled in one of the most competitive and prestigious academic programs in the country, and the next, they were sitting in a swanky New York

City office with a half a dozen strangers, contemplating signing away their dignity.

"Zoey, dear, are you okay with all of this?" My dad swung his head towards the mountain of papers on the desk. "Is there anything we should know? Anything that you're uncomfortable with? Are there any more secrets?"

I swallowed hard. It was time for me to give an answer for my indiscretions. That was the least I could do. Breaking the news to my sister, Ruth, was difficult—extremely painful. That event was met with an astounding admittance of how much she looked up to me. The memory of her walking away from me with her shoulders slumped toward the ground, weighted with disappoint, will forever be etched in my head.

Now, I had to address it again with my parents. I sat up in my chair, pulled off the wideband ring I wore almost every day while in public since the Cayman Islands, and bared my tattoo, such a reflection of my soul sketched into my skin. Immediately, my mother grabbed her chest and my father mumbled something expressing pure astonishment.

"The only thing missing from this paperwork is this baby was conceived in love. It was not as scandalous as it's becoming or appears. My child was made from love. He loved me. I don't know what happened. I don't know what went wrong, but I can promise you I'm *not* that type of girl. I'm still the Zoey that you raised. I'm still a young woman of Christ. I still have morals. I still have values."

I felt the tears building in my throat. "I would have never *ever* had sex with this man if he did not love me. He. Loved. Me. You *have* to believe me. He loved me. It was not something foolish or haphazard. It was not an infatuation. It was not my imagination. He. Loved. Me!"

That's when I lost the battle with my tears. I broke down in loud sobs and uncontrollable shakes. Another new low for me.

I didn't speak to Stenton as much as we used to after meeting with his attorney. I didn't know how to categorize our relationship after that act of betrayal. So, unless he reached out to me, I didn't contact him.

Stenton arranged for a practitioner that wasn't exactly around the corner from me. Apparently, one that had experience handling celebrity pregnancies and understood the need for discretion. Several times he attended doctor's visits with me. He left with print-outs of the ultrasound.

The first time he heard the baby's heartbeat, he seemed amazed. The first time he saw the baby's image on the monitor and we learned I was carrying a boy, Stenton's head collapsed into his open hands as his elbows rested on his knees. The doctor offered to give us a minute because of Stenton's emotional response. I lay on the examination table with my body so tense. It was the first time I saw a smidge of emotion from him since he broke it off with me the night he served me authentic Indian food at his apartment. I didn't know how to respond. My eyes would occasionally swing over to him, trying to find my voice and then my heart to speak from. But nothing.

Minutes into his silence, with his head still buried, he freed his right hand to find and clench my left arm and traveled down to clutch my palm. He held it for a while; still having no appropriate words, I didn't utter any. I couldn't.

Stenton raised his head and I immediately saw that his marbled orbs were glazed. The rims of his heavy eyes were red and moist. I felt my bottom lip drop.

"I don't deserve this opportunity," he croaked out. "I don't deserve this gift from you."

I bit my quivering lips to keep my tears at bay. Elated that he viewed this thing with me as a gift, my chest lightened for the first time in months. The earnest beam in his eyes was sketched in my brain and heart. In that moment, I could see the loneliness in Stenton. I could feel the concept of this baby being an opportunity for him to extend his almost nonexistent family. I felt like a creditor, granting him a favor so rare. This I didn't quite understand because

I knew there were droves of women who'd donate their limbs just to have a piece of his essence growing inside of them. Why did I feel so revered for doing something as unwise as getting pregnant by him so prematurely?

The look in his solemn eyes told me what I was doing was something good for him. Something that he coveted. From that moment on, all condemnation of my careless actions vaporized. The guilt was mitigated. If I could turn back the hands of time, I would've avoided this pregnancy, but I could no longer carry the weight of the onus that consumed me because of it. Stenton had just extinguished that.

After that day, our frequency of communication didn't improve, but Stenton did attend several more appointments with me. I had to adjust to life in this new place. I was able to finish out the semester, but it was no small feat. I sobbed like a baby the day I filled out my leave papers. Although I knew there were provisions for me to return, I couldn't shake the mentality of failing my family, my parents. Myself. It was a depressing ride home that day.

Chapter Eleven

"You sneaky bitch!"

I leaped from my bed and twisted my torso too fast, causing a shooting pain from my groin to my abdomen. I grabbed my stomach, tensing from the ache. Panting out of control, I finally looked up to find a shaking Angela, seething like an inferno. I was surprised to see her. Last I'd heard from Karen, Angela had agreed to marry Timmy and was planning their wedding. It disappointed me, but who was I to have an opinion considering my recent quagmire.

She was now here, in my bedroom with guns ablaze. My breathing was out of control and my heart was beating wildly. I knew this day would come, just not when I'd finally been able to get sleep in short increments.

"Don't sit there looking dumb and innocent. You are the biggest fraud there is! Now I see what that lecture about forgiveness was about. You only wanted to get Alton Alston off the hook to make yourself look good to Stenton Rogers. You're a manipulative little whore!"

Ruth jumped into my doorway with eyes as big as saucers. *Not now Ruthie!* She stood there frozen.

My weary eyes trailed back to Angela.

"Oh, and all you have is a fucking rolling of the eyes?" Angela inched toward me.

I was able to find my bearings. "Angela, I know I should have told you…and before now. It's just that things have been crazy—"

"Crazy? Yeah, I bet! You fucking ballers who wouldn't normally look twice at your dry ass if it wasn't for me laying the foundation by acting like the thirsty groupie! Did you fuck Alton Alston, too?"

Is she crazy?

One thing that did strike me along with her asinine accusation was how she referred to them by their first and last names, making it clear she really didn't know either one of them.

I didn't realize I was still rubbing my belly until I heard Ruth diffidently ask, "Zo, you okay? You don't look good."

Without looking at her, I raised my hand, needing her quiet and not getting my parents involved. Angela was sharp with the tongue, but she'd never fight me. That thought was just ridiculous.

"I swear to god, Zo, I feel like beating the living shit out of your sneaky ass!" She drew a fist at me.

"Uh-oh!" I heard Ruth shrill before taking off.

"Ang, don't be ridiculous. I didn't have sex with Alton. This thing with Stenton wasn't planned and I didn't manipulate any—"

"Yes the hell you did! And you betrayed me by going after someone you knew I wanted. I know you go all "good girl", but Zo, in the streets you'd get your ass kicked for touching a guy your girl was after."

If her street code jargon didn't give away Angela was beyond pissed, the vein pulsing just underneath her left eye did. This wasn't going to be easy and the pain was still smarting too much for me to defend myself if she called herself hitting me. Angela was no more a fighter than me, but she did crazy things in the name of Stenton Rogers…or anything she was passionate about.

Steady rubbing the pain away, I tried to calm my breathing

enough to speak clearly. "Ang, I'm sorry about all of this, but I think you're laying claims to a man you don't know—"

"*I* don't know Stenton Rogers? Bitch, *you* don't know Stent—"

"What is going on up here?" My mother managed before she even entered my room. "Angela, get your finger out of her face! What is your problem?"

"She is, Aunt Sar! She betrayed me. She's sneaky and grimy!" Angela spewed as my mother shuffled her out of my personal space, making herself a wedge between the two of us. When her eyes landed on my grasped belly she jumped into action.

"Angela, go home and take care of Brooklyn. I understand you and Zoey need to talk, but not like this and not now." My mother took her by the shoulders and urged her to the door.

"I hate you, Zo! Don't you ever call me, speak to me, or look my way! I hate you!" Angela screamed all the way out of my small bedroom.

"Go, now!" My mother yelled, something she isn't known to do.

I heard Ang's threats and rant until she pulled out of the driveway.

Still stunned by the little melee in her home, my mother finally spoke.

"You okay?"

I shook my head. "I was until this," I murmured, as my eyes were trained to the floor.

"Should I take you to the E.R.?"

"No, Momma."

"Zo," she sighed. "You've been doing so much better with your disposition these past few days. I don't want you back in that slump. You have everything to look forward to, only now you have a bit more."

As much as I wanted to take to her every word, I couldn't. I was still blue. I knew I had to face Angela, but I'd been taking the cowardly route by putting it off. I only needed to get out of the black hole to do it. My mom was right: I had been improving. The nap Angela just awakened me from was evidence of that. I'd been restive for weeks now.

"Is there anything I can do to make it better? Can I rub your belly? You want me to pray for you? I can go get my oil."

"No thanks, Momma. I should be fine. I'm just going to lay down and ride out the pain." That didn't apply to that pain in my heart.

She came over to my bed and kissed me. "Call me if you need me. I'll be back to check in on you. I'll call your dad and have him pick up your favorite seafood bisque." I watched her walk out and close the door behind her.

That made me smile…somewhere within. I'd developed a better appreciation for food being pregnant. Eating was something that brought me happiness—temporary bliss, but bliss nonetheless. I'd gained a few pounds and welcomed that, too.

I spent most of my days on my parents' couch or in my bedroom, painting my numbness away. It was either that or church. I felt lonely even there. Being there was especially hard, considering Angela wasn't speaking to me. And eventually the whispers subsided, but the judgment didn't. Our pastor even noted one Sunday morning how attendance had increased in the past few months. I knew it was due to spectators, curious about the rumors of who my "alleged" baby's father was. Although our church was modest in size, it wasn't like I or my parents made a public announcement that not only was I pregnant outside of being wed, but the father so happened to be *three-time MVP*, Stenton Rogers. I didn't know how long we'd be able to keep it concealed, but we agreed that we would.

Nonetheless, after that experience with Stenton when we learned we were having a boy, I didn't hide my face or my growing belly anymore. I was reassured that this child was conceived out of love. It didn't matter that his father's love didn't last as long as his mother's. My child was and would be loved.

February 2008

Time passed and when my birthday arrived, my parents forced me out to dinner. It actually turned out to be a surprise birthday dinner at a buffet restaurant out in Somerset. I nearly cried when the girls awaiting my arrival screamed "surprise" as I approached the rear dining area. There were six jumping girls in total. These were my friends from high school and some from church, including Karen. It was great being reminded that I had friends. It brought a smoke-screen of normal. Stenton, my best friend, and Angela may never return, but at least some sense of normalcy had, in terms of my friends.

We talked, joked and laughed at the table. My parents sat with us throughout the meal, smiling and participating whenever necessary. I noticed no one brought up Stenton. I didn't know how to feel about that. On the one hand, I didn't want the mention of what was painful in my life, but on the other, I didn't want to erase the memory of the love of my life. I was still dealing with a broken heart. Midway through laughing at one of Karen's new-mommy jokes, I decided to bury any thoughts of Stenton for the rest of the night. I needed the break in the agony I felt from my failure.

After spending almost three hours at the restaurant, causing a commotion, we decided to call it quits. I didn't want the temporary relief of elation to end, but I also knew my parents were kind enough to drive me out and I didn't want to belabor their patience. I kissed the girls goodnight and thanked them for the hundredth time, then gathered my small collection of gift bags they also surprised me with and made my way out to my parents' car.

On the drive back home, my mom called from the passenger seat, "You must be tired, baby."

"No," I sighed. "Not really."

I suddenly felt bored. And lonely. Being with the girls for a few short hours reminded me of what it was like to get out without a laden heart. For a bunch of twenty-one and twenty-two year olds, the night was still young. Had my parents not been there, we could have carried on well into the night. I started to wonder what they were getting into now. I knew the girls weren't en route to their beds as I was. Then my mind idly wandered over to thoughts of Stenton. I wondered what he was doing at the moment. I wasn't hopeful enough to allow myself to believe he was thinking of me. I thought of that man every day for long spurts of the day. It was hard not to when I had a piece of him growing inside me, reminding me of his mark on my body. I'm sure he didn't think of me. He had no reminders.

"Well," my mother hummed. "Get all the rest you can now. You're gonna miss these days when you have all the freedom in the world to relax."

"Mmmmhmmm," I acknowledged her, noncommittally as I scrolled my timeline on Facebook.

Minutes later, we were turning onto my street and my Dad muffled, "Who is that in front of the house?"

I didn't look up from my phone with that question. I'd assumed it was my parents, just chatting between themselves.

"Is that—?" my mom asked abruptly.

"Yep," my father murmured moments later as we neared our home.

It wasn't until we pulled into the driveway that I did peek up. I saw the car first. It was a bright yellow Ferrari. Then I saw the tall, lean figure standing just above it. As I caught on to his lanky frame, his eyes rose from his phone and locked with mine while the car was still in motion. I swear my heart leaped as if it were in fear. I guess I wasn't used to those jitter-causing sort of feelings for a man. I didn't know how respond to his magnificent, all-consuming countenance. His stark presence alone spoke volumes of who the man was behind the athlete.

It took a while for me to gain control of my shaky limbs and open the door. My parents were out of the car before I could even pull the handle. As I steadied myself on my feet, I saw Stenton approach and greet my father respectfully with a manly shake. My father was all pinched brows and pouted lips, appearing short and stubby next to Stent. My mother clutched her hands at her pelvis, wearing a wide smile while she waited her turn to be greeted. I noticed his embrace with her was long and was met with him closing his eyes.

In a perfect world...

Then his dark orbs traveled over to me just before he let my mother go. They were penetrating, yet impassive. My heart couldn't have been racing in my chest because I could no longer feel it. In fact, I couldn't even feel the air sloughing through my lungs. Oddly, I did feel the flutter in my belly and intuitively grabbed it. Stenton slowly rounded my mother and gaited over to me. My legs continued to tremble as the distance between us shortened. Then he was standing right in front of me, towering my protruding frame.

"You think I can get a few hours of your time?" poured from his silky baritone.

My mouth collapsed, but for a while nothing could come out. Eventually, able to move, I peered around Stenton and squeaked, "Ummm... Momma, I'm gonna chat out here with Stenton for a minute. I'll be in in shortly."

Stenton's eyes never left me when he corrected me. "Actually, we're going for a ride."

"Oh, that's nice, Stenton!" my mother gushed.

My father chimed in, "You know today's a special day."

"Yes, sir, I do. In fact," Stenton clarified with his marble eyes still locked to mine. I couldn't believe he remembered my birthday. "I'm hoping to spend the last few hours of it with her," he managed to make sound far less sensuous than his eyes relayed...and I wanted to believe.

"If you must," my father drug out, consented as he walked off, leaving us in the driveway.

"Just call us if you're going to be late coming in," my mother threw over her shoulder, following behind her husband.

Once the door slammed shut, I stood frozen, captivated under his gaze. He wore a brown goose, dark jeans and Timberland construction boots. We stood there, gaping at each other. I was still jarred by his presence. I didn't know how to behave around Stenton. I was never really accustomed to being with him. He was still all new to me; I hadn't known him that long. His arm reached out and his big hand cupped my round abdomen. My belly fluttered and I didn't know if it was simply my body reacting to his touch.

"Do you mind, Niña?" he murmured.

I hadn't heard that name in months. Hadn't felt the warmth of the sentiment behind it in just as long. Why was he doing this to me?

I swallowed. "*N*-no." I cleared my throat, trying to calm my shaky chords. "Not at all."

After swiping the globe of my tummy, Stenton reached for my hand and walked me over to his car. With a few grunts, I managed the low drop getting into the passenger seat. Once he managed his long frame inside, he turned to me.

"I guess this wasn't the best car choice of the evening considering your condition." He cracked a wary smirk.

I attempted to let go of a grin. I wasn't sure if my breathing had returned. Stenton pressed a button and the engine came alive, reverberating in my chest. We drove for nearly thirty minutes before pulling up to a valet at a restaurant.

"Glad you've arrived, Mr. Rogers. Our hostess is awaiting you," the valet greeted when Stenton threw him the keys and rounded the car to take my hand.

He laced our fingers and guided me into the restaurant where there was a brightly smiling hostess, welcoming us in by name and immediately leading us to our table. When were seated, the waiter immediately came over to hand Stenton a wine menu.

Before looking into it, Stenton peered over at me and asked, "What are you drinking nowadays?" He gestured towards my protruding belly.

"Water will be fine," I informed the waiter.

"I'll have water as well," Stenton informed the waiter, handing him the menu back.

Once alone, Stenton sat up in his chair and inclined, placing his elbows on the table. "So, happy birthday, Elizabeth," he murmured, his teeth appeared and his eyes squinted in a jovial slant.

"Thanks." I nodded coolly. "I thought you'd forgotten." I don't know why I said that. I didn't want to come off as argumentative.

He shook his head softly. "You're having my baby; of course I know your date of birth. There's nothing I've forgotten about you."

Stenton angled his neck as his eyes studied the crease of my lips. I knew this from the very first day we met. He'd always found fascination with them. He broke down and told me after we parted ways that first summer.

I yanked my head away, suddenly bashful by his attention. Not only that, I was growing aroused under his gaze. I had to gain a hold of myself around him. I didn't want him to be reminded that he chose not to be with me. Thankfully, we were interrupted by the waiters serving appetizers that I didn't order.

As I lifted my fork to decide what I would start with, Stenton informed, "I went with the chef's menu. I hope you enjoy."

I wasn't hungry at all. Not only had I just come from dinner with family and friends, but I had no appetite around this man. I didn't like that I was sitting across from who was once my best friend, Stent. I was having dinner at, no doubt, a five star restaurant with *the* Stenton Rogers, three-time MVP Awardee and four-time NBA Championship holder. I mean, he was sitting right there, just a stone's throw away. I could smell his alluring fragrance and admire his fresh haircut and curly top. His collage of tattoos were hidden underneath the fabric of his clothing, but his full lips looked almost pink against his cinnamon complexion.

"I got the last images of the ultrasound," he shared with a mouthful of food. "I can't believe how pronounced his features are now compared to the last one." I could hear the glee in his voice even as he chewed.

"Yeah," I nodded. "Can't miss that wide nose that we can agree he gets from his daddy."

Stenton let out a boisterous laugh. "Yeah, I thought the same thing when I saw it. So, he'll have his dad's schnoz. He could've gotten passed on a lot worse." In a flash, I saw the melancholy in his eyes. Attempting to brush past it, he asked, "So, you'll be seven months next week. Have you started thinking of any names yet?" His eyes rose to meet mine.

He'd kept up with my pregnancy. *Whoa!*

I sighed as I played with the food in my plate. "Oh, I don't know. I've thought some about it. It's just a huge call to make alone." I chanced a glance at Stenton, who, when he realized I'd gotten quiet, peered up at me. "Do *you* have any ideas?" I threw back to him.

He steeled in his seat for a few seconds then shrugged. "I don't know. You may not want to leave such a weighty decision to me. All I know is ballin'. I'll fuck around and name him Jordan," he snorted.

I chuckled into my plate. "As in *the* Michael Jordan?"

"As in the *legend*, Michael Jordan," Stenton corrected.

"Not that I'd have a problem with it, but his dad is already a legend in his own right," I murmured while training my eyes to my plate.

Through my peripheral, I saw Stenton's head shoot up, but I didn't react. I pretended to cut through my food, unperturbed. We ate in silence. Before long, Stenton cleared his plate, prompting the waiter to our table. I offered my plate as well, not being able to fit anything else in considering what was ahead.

We finally made it to our main course. Stenton must have noticed I wasn't taking in much, so had the waiter when he came over.

"Is everything to your satisfaction, ma'am?"

I noticed Stenton's inquisitive gaze immediately. I fought through my nerves to pat my belly.

"Full house in here. Can't fit a five course in anymore. More like a two," I joked sheepishly.

"I can wrap this to go if you'd like," the waiter offered.

Braving a glance at Stenton, I answered, "Sure. That would be great."

The waiter took off with my plate and I paid Stenton a glance. I'd hoped he wasn't offended. He did, however, seem preoccupied by it.

He shot me a long glance for a few seconds before asking, "Are you going to have room for dessert? It's your birthday; can't forget the cake," Stenton gave a wry smile, but one that was expressed in his eyes.

I only responded with a regretful smile. I couldn't eat. Though I was one of those pregnant women with a robust appetite, my unease countered my need for food.

"So, how are you?" He gestured to me with his chin.

"Hanging on in there, considering the circumstances." I rubbed my belly.

His face turned crestfallen right away. "Are they giving you shit, Zo? All this time I figured you were good…being with your family and all, but if those fucking holy rollers are giving you a hard time—"

"No," I murmured then ducked my chin. I didn't want to think about folks from my church. Yes, they were having a time with the third consecutive pregnancy out of wedlock in our flock, but my parents had been shielding me from much of the scrutiny. "The people will be the people. But my pastor has been great. I know I've disappointed him. Similar to my parents, he thought I was *the* difference. Nonetheless, he's been comforting. He's a bit younger than that *Old Testament* crew who still conduct themselves as they did before the day of Pentecost, but it's no big deal…"

…nothing in comparison to my vacant chest from you stealing my heart.

My eyes traveled beyond him, stalling to think of an appropriate answer to his original question without coming off as angry. I was lonely, big, and tired…all of the time. I felt abandoned and useless. *Why shouldn't I share this? What would I have to lose?* He'd already decided against taking the journey with me. *Or would I do undue damage to what my heart really desired?*

Decided, I looked directly into his eyes and answered, "I'm hormonal."

He wanted an answer, I'd be truthful.

"As in physically?" His eyebrows furrowed.

"Emotionally, often. I wake up confused about my trajectory in life, and I go to bed lost in my reality. I get low from time to time. But yeah, that, too. Physically…my body is a wreck from day to day."

I could see Stent's mind turning over the mouthful I'd given him. He seemed concerned and confused himself. I couldn't torture myself to figure out the specifics of his brain's activity. Moments later, his long arm inched across the table in search of mine, and when he touched me I flinched.

"You're not alone," his tone was soft, sympathetic. If I didn't know any better, I'd think it was laced with regret. "Whatever you need, you know you can just pick up the phone. No matter the expense. It's yours, Niña."

And there goes that pet name again. The name he called me when things were light and...good and uncomplicated. The name he could justifiably call me when I was innocent. It was not an appropriate name for my current state. I was no longer his baby girl. I was a full-fledged woman, about to give birth to a *real* baby.

I quickly swiped the tear that slipped. I let out a snort then a quick sniffle, embarrassed by the slip of emotions. He didn't want to see me weak. It was not a problem his handlers could be assigned to.

"I'm sorry," I rushed my napkin to my face to hide my stream of tears. "You don't want to see me like this," my voice was no more than a whisper.

"No...no! I want to know what you're feeling. Really," his words poured, almost fearfully.

Then he called the waiter over for the check. The next thing I knew, we were back in his Ferrari, speeding the pavement again. We drove and drove, for how long, I didn't know. Each time I'd steal a glance over at Stenton, I'd see his brow line. He was deep in thought. In time, we reached Exit 6 on the New Jersey Turnpike. I knew instantly we were headed to Philadelphia. We ended up in Center City where the streets were aligned with bright lights and the personality of the streetwalkers ranged from stiff elites to the wobbling homeless at that hour. We made a few turns off of South Broad Street and pulled into a private parking garage inside a warehouse.

Stenton reached into the center console and pulled out a large white envelope before leaving the car. He ambled towards my side of the car and helped me out. We entered a high-rise and although I wanted to ask about our destination, my gut told me to be quiet and grateful to be with him.

We walked to the elevator and I could smell the fumes of fresh construction, although the outside of the building looked weathered. The ride up to the second level was short. He grabbed my hand to lead me out of the elevator. We did a short walk down the hallway before he stopped and unsealed the envelope to pull out a large silver key. He unlocked then pushed the door open and invited me inside. My first thought was of Stenton finally breaking and letting me back in. This must be his new place and he's sharing it with me. I stopped in the foyer and observed the lengthy all white walls.

Once he closed the door behind me, Stenton advanced ahead of me inside and swung his arm and hand toward the place, and croaked out solemnly, "Happy birthday, Zoey."

My forehead wrinkled, trying to understand his statement. I looked into his eyes, lost. He inclined his head, inviting me to explore the place. I found myself off, crossing the vestibule. To my immediate right was another corridor leading to a huge kitchen to the right. The room boasted cherry wood cabinetry. The stove was a material I'd never seen, and with gold button-like features. The island was huge and centered the large room. Over in the corner was a small kitchen table for two with a lovely view of the city. Across from the island was a formal table that seated six. It was stunning.

I strolled out of the kitchen and back into the hall until I found my way into the living room. It was a humongous loft with large windows and asymmetric walls. The furniture was contemporary, yet modest in size. Next, I went to the end of the same hall and found the dining room. Fitting with the motif of the rest of the place, it was extremely spacious and contemporary. In the center was a large lacquered table that could seat ten people. Overwhelmed, I turned and made my way out and back into the hall.

When I passed back by the foyer, I continued to the other side of the enormous place. I observed a large closet then a fully decorated bedroom with a queen bed. Across from that was a room with an office setting, decorated with furniture and all. Going back out into the hall, I passed a bathroom larger than my bedroom at home and my dorm. All the way at the end of the hall, I opened the door and lost my breath. It was a nursery. This was clear to me from the crib and bassinet along with the soft green paired with black and white scheme. There was an en suite bathroom decorated with a child's theme causing my belly to flutter with excitement and my heart to melt sentimentally.

Darn hormones.

I had to leave before my tears fell. I closed the door behind me and started my search for Stenton. On the way, my phone went off, alerting a text. I removed my coat before going for my phone. When I checked it, I saw was from my sister, Ruth.

Holy fucking gaud! Did Stent just have a SQ5 delivered here?

What? I replied.

Holy shit, Zo! This shit is on fiyah!

My mouth dropped. I knew enough to know Ruth didn't play Jedi mind tricks. She had to have been telling the truth. I was stunned.

We'll chat when I get home I shot back to her, still needing to finish exploring the mammoth apartment.

Hurry! I want to ride!

I sighed, feeling tightness in my chest. What in the world was going on? Then I made my way into the last room of the corridor. It was nearly three times the size of the previous two bedrooms and office. There was a short passageway beyond the door, making it clear I was entering the master suite. Excitement bloomed in my chest at the ebony hardwood floors against the ivory walls. My eyes immediately went to the large wall mirror in some fancy design hanging above a long padded bench.

My eyes trailed to the large fireplace facing the bed. *The bed!* It was a poster bed, similar to the one I'd fallen in love with in the Cayman Islands. The bed Stenton fastened me to nearly every night and had his way with me. Beyond that was a massive picture window larger than Stenton's in Philly. The view of the city was breathtaking and I'm sure that was by design.

When I finally came to my wits, I heard a familiar masculine tenor, almost whispering. I looked up and found Stenton in the corner on his cell. His coat was off and eyes were already glued to me in a preoccupied fashion.

I didn't catch it all, but I was able to make out, "I wanted to show her the new place for her and the baby when she's ready. Yes, sir. I understand. She may need a minute to take it all in. Yes, sir. I will have her home first thing in the morning. Yes, sir. I appreciate your understanding, sir. Uhn-hun. Goodnight, sir. Give Sarah my goodnight as well. Sorry to have disturbed you, sir."

Did Stenton just inform my dad I wouldn't be coming home? What was this?

He tapped the phone off, dropped it into his back pocket, and gazed at me while posted against the wall.

"You bought me a truck?" I asked stoically, though I was on sensory overload internally.

He nodded his answer.

While it wasn't the most pressing question in my head, neither was it one of priority between the two of us. I asked, "What about the *BMW*?"

"That's up to you. You can keep it or sell it. Just tell Paul what you want to do with it." He shrugged.

Stenton was inspecting me, concerned with my next move. My chest began to heave and my chin hiked to prevent the tears. My breathing was scattered as I fought to hold it together. I felt my face grimace into a cry, but refused to commence the tears. I didn't want to cry. In that moment, I needed to understand. I needed to know if this nightmare was over.

Would I now feel a semblance of the jubilation we'd shared before this pregnancy?

Was he prepared to step up?

"The place is staged," his voice was low, obviously unsure. His marble eyes bounced between mine nervously. "You know...the furniture was added for the appeal. They'll be by in a day or two to pick up everything. Except for the bed." With his chin, he gestured ahead of him to the massive, high four-poster bed against the wall.

Stenton cleared his throat. "That's yours. You can change the bedding or keep them. I didn't know what your preference would be. I have an interior designer on standby if you're not up to decorating all of this." He was rambling, anxious.

As I stood there, visibly shaking, fighting to keep my well acquainted sobs at bay, I questioned him with my eyes. He didn't speak to them for a while, wearing a contortion himself.

Okay, let me try with words…

I was cracking by the second. I could wait no longer.

"What does this mean?" I gritted through clenched teeth, my expression more angry than hurt.

Stenton's eyes glossed. He shook his head and grumbled through his impending emotions, "We're not ready yet." He cleared his throat again. Then his head collapsed into the wall that held up his long frame.

His eyes never left mine, but his message was crystal clear. He was not asking to be a family as I'd hoped. However, his heart was not ambiguous in his expression. We were together, in that moment. He'd just informed my father that I wouldn't be coming home tonight. I could see the swelling against his thigh, could feel his longing mere feet away. With my body still trembling, now humming for his touch, my neck straightened. I was communicating back to him. I needed him. Still.

After long seconds, he pleaded, "I don't know how. I don't want to hurt you."

There was more than one interpretation of his words. He wasn't ready. This wasn't an attempt to reconcile. My heart broke, but my body rattled with overwhelming desire. In that moment—its first occurrence of many over the years to come—I conceded. I consented to overlooking my heart.

"You hurt me by maintaining this distance. You have me question how," I grabbed my belly. "…*this* happened…did it come from love. You wound me by not touching me, making me still feel desired. You cause pain each day you neglect my heart!" The tears finally descended and my shoulders collapsed.

I heard when he painfully breathed out, "Niña…"

In a nanosecond, Stenton was on me. His tongue was down my throat, filling me, pouring the familiarity of the love we once shared. The love that I'd easily forgotten that he carried, too. My hands cupped his face. The pads of my fingers moved against the spikey hairs of his strong jaw as I joined his tongue in a tussle. My breasts grew heavy, my breathing ragged and audible. Stenton's big hands grabbed my rear cheeks in a rough pull, raising me inches above my natural ground. My hands moved up and wildly through his hair, reminding me of old times.

He backed me to the bed. I didn't want to separate from our embrace. Apparently, neither did he when he lifted me from underneath my arms and placed me on the edge. Before I knew it, he was removing my clothes, caressing the goose bumps that cover my skin. I pulled his shirt over his head as he hovered above me, needing to see the artwork of his mahogany skin. My breath caught at the recognition of the black, yellow, and red ink stains that stretched nearly his entire upper frame. His lean muscles flexing in excitement, reminding me of our chemistry.

My hands flew to his jeans, impatiently undoing his belt then button and zipper. I pulled his pants down and without thought pulled him into my mouth. He mumbled something through his teeth that I couldn't decipher because I was too busy expressing my needs. Stenton nearly collapsed backwards, having to catch himself. When he did he roughly pulled my clothes from my body, only using delicate hands around my belly. Once everything was off and we were both bare, I hurriedly scooted up the bed to make room for him.

Some feral sound shot from the back of his throat before I heard, "C'mere!" as he grabbed me at the thighs and buried his head between my trembling thighs.

My back slammed against the mattress and my hands raced to the back of his head, holding him in place. I missed his touch. I was reminded of how his tongue firmly moved in between my slickened lips with hunger. I felt him in every crevice below, licking and sucking and pulling and sparring and...humming. *That's new.* Stenton was droning his satisfaction of my intimate flavor. In no time, my pelvis went from rocking to vibrating beneath his face. Delicious pressure mounted, not giving a moment to brace myself. I screamed my release with one hand on my bulging belly and the other on the back of his head.

My thighs were being pulled back down the bed. And before I could clear the blur from my eyes, I was being pulled from the bed by my arms. I tried clearing my hazed eyes, and when I did, I saw Stenton lowering himself in front of me.

"You're in your 30th week. I don't think you should be lying on your back," he murmured as he placed his head to my bare belly.

I was still out of breath and confused by the sudden change in elevation. I felt lightheaded and all I really wanted to do was lay down and catch my breath. His scent was rousing and didn't help me relax.

"I'm fine," I whispered. "Really."

Stent's big hands were splayed over my bourgeoned abdomen. "No. You grabbed your belly and then I felt the baby move just before you…" he cleared his throat. "…came." His eyes were quizzical as he stared into the distance, feeling my tummy in an examining manner. "Plus, I know at this time, you can be experiencing lots of heartburn. Your mom told me about the episode you had last week when she needed to go out to get you some TUMS."

W-what?

"You spoke to my mother? She didn't tell me," my voice was a bit clipped.

"I speak to Sarah all the time," he informed unperturbed. "I told her that it was about that time. I read the same hormones that cause the heartburn are what assist in relaxing your pelvic muscles when you deliver. A gift and a curse in my opinion." He gazed up to me with a forlorn smile.

"Stenton, what do you mean, you speak to my mother all the time? I wasn't aware of this." My words come out formally, despite his mouth having just been on my vagina seconds ago, because over the past few months, that's the tone he'd taken with me.

"I have to keep track of you and the pregnancy," he appeared confused. "You won't call with updates. You don't even call to say hello."

I'm confused. Was he smoking crack?

"You broke up with me—"

"I'm still here for you, Zo. I'm still expecting a baby," he qualified resolutely and paused to examine my eyes. "I'm excited to be a dad. All these years, I've entertained millions. Brought joy and excitement to the lives of people I'll never meet. This thing," his words pour throaty as he cupped my belly. "This is something I keep for me. This is a piece of happiness I created and doesn't have to be shared with the world; just with the co-creator and those who will cherish it as much as I plan on doing. I would like to enjoy him even now that he's in here, so I call to check in."

And there was the Stenton I knew. The one I'd been spending months wondering if he'd ever existed. The conception was an accident, but this baby was created by love. Still things didn't add up.

"You're doing that thing with your throat again," he informed with a glint in his eyes. I don't know why he finds my irritating habit so amusing. "What's going through that head of yours?"

"Things have become so…clinical between us. You want me to call your *people* for my needs. That doesn't sound like you want to be a part of this with me."

Stenton shook his head. "That's me giving you access to the channels I would have to go to for what you need. I've cut myself out as the middle man. You're the mother of my child; you have access to my world."

"But you haven't called or stopped by to see me." I shook my head, trying to shake the pain from the ordeal.

"Because I know you're still upset by the changes, Zo. You've made it clear you wanted distance. I feel like shit. Your world has been turned upside down. I get that. All that's changed for me is losing my best friend and expecting my first child. You're getting the shorter end of the stick here. I won't push you to tolerate me, but I'm not going far from my baby, and I would like to not have you as an enemy. I will always adore you, Niña. I may have made some fucked up decisions, but I'm not shying away from them. I'm not running from you."

"But sex…" We were here naked, but dancing around the fact that we're not together. "This can't be healthy."

He stood from his kneeling position, bringing up with his stature a glaring erection, and casually kissed my forehead.

"It may not be," he murmured and gently pulled me up from the bed to stand in front of him. He took me at the small of my back, bringing my swollen breasts into his abdomen, his erection stabbing my belly. "But it's been since last summer, with you, and I'm gonna assume it's been the same amount of time for you, too. Please don't say no."

My lips twitched up into a dirty grin and I shook my head. "I've kept company with *Palm*er." I lifted my open palm to his face, fighting a giggle.

He took several of my fingers into his mouth and garbled, "Even my *Palmela* has nothing on my Niña."

Then on a growl, he used his big hand to cup my sex, erasing my silly grin with just one swipe. My legs quivered and lips parted.

"Now where and how will I take you in a way that will keep you and the ba—"

"Jordan," I slurred into his chest, but loud enough for him to hear. His fingers continue to play at my sensitive bulb below, making me delirious.

"Come again?"

I placed my chin on his chest, floating in the intoxication of the spell igniting between my legs. "Your son's name will be Jordan Michael Rogers. My dad would be agreeable to that."

He lowered his mouth to mine, taking my tongue from my face. We kissed like starved animals. After working me to near explosion, he walked me to the floor-to-ceiling window and pushed my hands against the glass. I looked down over the City of Brotherly Love as he entered me from behind.

"*Uhhh…*" flew from my lungs at his fullness.

It had been so long and in my state, my walls felt more sensitive, more swollen. My lubrication was in excess. I felt it in my inner thighs. This is what Stenton did to me. As he thrust I could feel him in places I didn't recall having him before. Stenton held on to my belly until he developed a rough pace, seeming to lose control in no time. As my moist hands gripped the cool glass, Stenton bit that sensitive spot on my shoulder, driving me up a notch.

"Damn, Zo, I'm not going to last," he breathed into my ear.

That's when he used one hand to pinch my extremely sensitive nipple and the other to strum my clitoris, spurring me to climax with him. And I did. My whole body trembled, eyes rolled back, and face collapsed as I collided with pleasure far more riotous than any before. My orgasm was so powerful, tears prickled at my eyes as Stenton offered his last two lunges before quivering at the knees himself.

We stayed at the apartment that night, folded into one another. As I laid wrapped in Stenton's long arms, I studied his heartbeat and breathing pattern. I futilely wondered if that would give me more insight into his enigma as of late. I was so confused about our situation. The only thing clear was that he wanted this baby; probably even more than me.

Another thing decided in my heart was that I loved this man and I knew he loved me, too. It was in the way his body covered mine in reverence and adoration. Stenton loved me. But he wasn't ready for more with me. I wondered if it had anything to do with his inclination to protect himself from the flakiness of human kind. He'd always say people were fickle and they all, in some form, used him. Did he think I'd do the same? Maybe time would prove I was here to stay. To love and provide the reciprocity that no one else had seemed to up to that point in his life.

The next morning, Stenton drove me home. He didn't want to walk me to the door, claiming he couldn't greet my parents considering what he'd done with me the night before and just hours earlier that morning. With a heavy heart from parting from him, I told him I understood when I didn't. I wanted him with me. I wanted to prove to my parents that this baby, no matter how unplanned the pregnancy, was conceived in love, not some May-December romance or summer fling. This was a genuine connection with an unexpected detour.

After kissing our goodbyes, he helped me out of the car and I noticed the Audi. It was black, just like the *BMW*. Just like my life. My desolate feelings returned in spades. I didn't understand the new low. I thought I'd hit rock bottom when he broke up with me, then when I learned I was pregnant, but at this point I felt dejected. After making love the way we did, I should have felt refueled and replenished in terms of my disposition. No. My future appeared as black as this shiny SUV that I could see my protruding image in. I walked into my parents' home with heavier shoulders than I had before Stenton magically appeared and whisked me off.

Time seemed to have sped up rather quickly after that. My due date was quickly approaching. I had so much to do to get ready for this baby and now this huge apartment made it imminent. At first I was overwhelmed at the prospect of furnishing it, but Paul contacted me the afternoon Stenton dropped me off and reminded me that I could hire an interior designer to get the place done before Jordan was due in April.

A designer? What was that?

Then there was Tynisha. She seemed to call more often, offering to assist with shopping for the designer for the apartment and clothes for me. What? I started with soft brush offs, but when she became insistent, I took her up on her offer one day and learned we actually could hit off. She was extremely over the top: high maintenance, unnecessarily loud and ill-tempered, but she really tried to suppress those characteristics when dealing with me. That was until it came to that trifling Alton, who always seemed to be busy getting into hot water behind a woman. She would sound off in front of the Pope when his mess came to her attention. She didn't care who saw her flip side. I didn't understand her attraction to him or his drama. That was too much work. That aside, Tynisha turned out to be bearable.

Church was another story. The word had gotten around who his father was. Yup! My parents and I were able to refrain from confirming Stenton's identity for months. We even threatened Ruth not to open her flap in light of the nasty blathering taking place, but eventually word got out as all gossip does. That's also when things got really interesting. People began smiling at me more, initiating conversations, offering to make and purchase things for the baby. It was all absurd. That's when I got a taste of what Stenton went through. People are only good to you when they perceive you as a benefactor. I even had Doris King, a middle aged woman who ran the youth department, ask if I knew *any* athletes that wouldn't mind speaking to our teens at their next regional conference. She was the main one on the *sit these mothers of bastard children in the back pew* committee! I didn't even dignify that asinine inquiry with a response. I just walked away.

I had no baby shower. I didn't want the attention. I knew it would primarily be my church family in attendance, and after seeing how they did Karen and Angela at their showers compared to women who were married *before* becoming pregnant, I decided to spare myself the humiliation of it all. My mother didn't like my decision on the matter, but respected it. She offered something on a smaller scale to include my friends from school only for me to decline that, too. Stenton had me draw up a list of the baby's needs and send it over to Paul in early March. He himself had things for the baby delivered by the day to the apartment in Philly. I had to ask him to slow down. Hence why I explained to my mother, I had no need for a shower.

And then there was Stenton. He was a busy man, closing up the '07-'08 NBA season. Though we weren't in touch like we used to be, I could tell he was stretched. One night, I stalked Stenton online. I went to Facebook and Twitter, scouring the happenings of Stenton Rogers and came across a couple of clips of him surprising fans with cars for an endorsement deal he had with Toyota. Then I saw "behind the scenes" pictures he posted of his car giveaway campaign. Underneath them I observed the way the women went crazy over him, even read some comments where fans offered themselves to him sexually. I almost gagged. They knew nothing about Stenton. Sometimes I wondered if I really knew him. Since our time together in the Cayman Islands, I questioned a lot.

The closer I drew to my due date, the more I'd see him, but things weren't the same. He made each doctor's appointment he possibly could when his schedule permitted. He'd stop by the apartment in Philly to check on the progress. I chose not to stay there. It was too soon, too big, and every square inch of the place reminded me of him.

We had not been *together* since my birthday. As much as I needed the connection, I didn't want the confusion. I had to prepare for this baby. Stenton may not have been decided on his desire for me, but I had to keep my head clear for Jordan.

Chapter Twelve

Stenton

I rolled my phone in my hand at least fifty times, brooding. My chest was heavy, mind racing. So much shit on me: conflicting endorsements opportunities, disgruntled coaches, angry and fickle-ass fans, pesky-ass managers, shallow-ass friends…and Zoey.

We'd just lost the second game in a row. First to the Bulls and now to the Knicks. Coach was in my face, bitching the same tune. *Get your head in the fucking game, StentRo!* As much as I wanted to provide a rebuttal, I couldn't because I had no idea where the fuck my head was. I'd only known where my heart was and that was with two human beings in one body. I missed Zoey.

My Niña.

In the short time I'd known her, I'd grown accustomed to having a real friend. Her laughter alone did shit to me. And not to mention my heavy sacs. I missed her touch. Her enthusiasm to please me. Her ability to switch from smart-ass teacher, to eager freak. I longed for her eyes to soften and ask me about me; the real me, not the

284

Stenton Rogers everyone pulled on for their own agendas. At night, when I often craved her, I wondered what she was doing and wearing while doing it. I wondered how many people experienced her smile, or her brilliance. If it were not for her being pregnant and that being a repellent for most men, I'd go fucking crazy about her fucking someone else. *But would I still be with her if she was not pregnant?* How would our story have played out if things had turned out differently?

I felt so fucking crazy. I couldn't think most days and even when I did what I loved most, balling, I was in a zone trying to make sense of these feelings I'd had since meeting that smart-mouthed, pretty brainiac last summer.

I knew Zoey was in South Carolina visiting family this week. I kept an account of her whereabouts even though we weren't exactly in touch. I knew she was hurt by my decision to walk away. I was pretty sure I was the last person she wanted to hear from, so I had my assistant check in with her regularly. I also had Tynisha keeping tabs on her. And if Zoey wanted something of significance, I had Chesney be her first contact. He didn't like it, thought it was beneath him to be accessible to a client's baby's mother, but I paid him enough to change my child's fucking diaper if needed.

My days were mechanically played out. I'd rise at the same time, eat my first meal at the same hour, train the same time of the day, rest right after, work, interview, meet, and call it a day. I wasn't living. I was merely floating through life. I could light up the faces, hearts, and lives of strangers, but my beacon was miles away, incubating my baby.

It was still early on a Sunday afternoon in spring. Church was over. I turned the phone over and went to dial. She picked up after several rings.

"Praise the Lord. Barrett residence," her faux high-pitched tone tickled me every time.

"Sarah?"

"Stenton! Hey! How's it going, honey?" She recognized my voice instantly.

"You can ask your husband about that."

"Oh." I heard shuffling around the phone. "Did you play today?"

"Yeah," I sulked. I almost whined—to a woman.

Goddamn pussy.

"Oh, Stenton, it's just a game, dear. It isn't the totality of your existence," she tried.

"Well, it kinda is, Sarah. It's what I'm paid to do."

"But it isn't what you were created to do, son."

Son. She called me son. Even with the shit I was putting her daughter through, was putting their family through with all of the calls of disgrace from their church, she called me son.

"So, I take it you're not going off to celebrate," she teased gently.

"Nah," I sighed. "No celebration when you've disappointed 1.55 million people."

"But you're just one person, Stenton. You can't please all the people all the time."

"I try," I admitted. "I'm going to try harder next time."

"And how do you plan to go about that, dear?"

"I guess go and practice some more."

"Now?" she gasped. "At this hour? That's ungodly. This is the day of Sabbath. You can't work on the Sabbath...can't tear your body down."

I wanted to say, *biblically speaking, the day of Sabbath is Saturday, not Sunday,* but thought better than to correct her. Then I heard her speaking to someone in the room.

"It's Stenton. I'll be right with you. Huhn? No, he just called a moment ago."

I heard Michael's rumble.

"Are you out of town, dear?"

"No, Sarah," Michael answered loud and grumpily. "He just lost to the Knicks!" I winced at the *he* and *lost* mentions.

Yeah...what he fucking said.

"Well, if you have time, honey, you're more than welcome for dinner. I'd rather you do that than tear at your body more than you already have today." I wasn't sure which was more soothing: her voice or the invitation. "I mean, I know you're busy and all," she was being meek in her approach.

It was odd for her to have me over when things were so awkward between Zoey and me. If I had an honest moment, I would say I knew exactly why I called Sarah when I did: I called for reception. I just wanted to be a part of something, not depended on.

"I'll be there in about thirty minutes." I may not have been smiling on the outside, but I was happy as hell on the inside.

I heard her sigh. "All right, Stenton. We'll see you then."

"Sarah," I called out to her.

"Yes, dear?"

"Should I bring something?"

"Just yourself, honey. Everything else is already here."

I did smile that time. I gave the change of destination to the driver and thirty minutes later, I was at the home of the Barrett's. Michael answered the door and gestured me inside.

"Hey, Stenton Rogers." His tone was wry and I could appreciate why. I'd fucked his daughter, impregnated her, broke up with her, and broke her heart. I was lucky to be invited to his home again.

"Mr. Barrett, thanks for having me by."

He turned and glared at me. "Sarah has you by. *I'm* disgusted with my shooting guard." He took off for the sofa and motioned for me to sit across from him.

I scratched the back of my head, feeling self-conscious. I didn't know how to respond to that. I knew we were, and may always be, in a precarious situation when together because of my selfish actions.

"Don't worry; I won't be killing you this visit either," he issued with a straight face. "Although you do deserve two bullets. We know what the first one is for. The second is for those missed buckets you've been in the habit of shooting." His eyes shifted to the television.

"I trust all is well." I tried to steer this conversation. I was uncomfortable already. But what did I expect?

Michael's eyes returned to me. "How do you want me to answer that? Do you want honesty, or do you want generic pleasantries, son?"

That *son* was delivered in direct contrast to Sarah's earlier on the phone. This one was demeaning, leveling.

I opened my mouth, not exactly ready to speak…not knowing how to respond, when Sarah entered the living room.

"Stenton," her voice was low. "Glad you're here. Come into the dining room. You must be hungry." She gave her husband a warning glower.

I followed her sulkily. The delicious smell from dinner hit me when I walked through the front door, but went to a new experience the deeper I went into the house. If I had no appetite earlier, it all changed the moment I crossed over into the dining room.

She invited me to sit at the head of the table and started out of the room as she called out, "Do you eat turkey chops? I fried some up, trying to stay away from red meat for Michael's sake. I seasoned my greens with turkey, too. Please tell me you eat kale."

She was out of the room. I didn't get a chance to answer. If her greens were anything like Zo's, I'd love them. *Damn. Zoey.* There went my chest, tightening again. I was in her home and could suddenly smell her. I could never forget her natural scent. Shit, I'd hoped I wouldn't have to.

Within minutes, Sarah returned with a big ass plate of fried turkey chops smothered in gravy, mixed greens, mashed potatoes, and a big piece of cornbread on a saucer. She left the room again and returned with a tall glass of ice tea. I went in immediately. In no time, I found myself grunting.

"Good, huhn?" She blushed.

As I chewed I attempted, "I didn't think anybody's greens or gravy could top your daughter's."

I didn't know if that was wise to share, but figured *fuck it*: it was the truth.

Sarah giggled delightfully. "Well, that *is* my child." She went over to a drawer in her china cabinet and pulled out yarn and needles then sat next to me.

"She's a really good cook," she murmured.

She's perfect in everything she does.

When I looked up, I saw her knitting a yellow and white blanket. I froze.

"Is that for…" I couldn't finish it.

"Mmm-hmm."

My eyes collapsed. I got that twisting feeling in my damn stomach again.

"Stenton, ain't no need in crying over spilled milk. What's done is done. I keep telling Zoey the same thing." Sarah never looked up from her needling when she spoke.

"Does she… Has she said…" I stumbled on my words.

"She isn't proud. She isn't exactly happy. But she's healthy and so is that baby. That's all we can focus on now." Sarah continued rolling her fingers, moving faster than my eyes could follow.

After a moment I went back to eating.

"So, how have you been? And I ain't talking that ball game nonsense either." She swayed her head towards the wall that separated us from the living room where Michael was.

I took a moment to consider her question. "You want the truth?"

"It always helps." Her eyes skirted up to meet mine.

I dropped my fork and pushed my plate away. I felt high. Like fucking intoxicatingly uninhibited. The only person I could share freely with was no longer around. I'd fucked that up. But her mother, her shaper, her molder and nurturer was here and I felt like making Sarah her daughter's proxy. Would she take to me opening up, I didn't know. But I was so desperate, I gave it a try.

"Last January, Zoey's phone was shut off. Do you remember?"

Sarah nodded, her hands still nimble in knitting.

"I didn't know. All I knew was I hadn't heard from her in weeks and…" My eyes closed, remembering the undercurrent of emotions I felt at not hearing from her after having an amazing time with her that first time in Alpine. "I didn't like it. I wanted to make sure she was okay. I thought maybe I'd said or done something to hurt or offend her. Or worse: that she'd heard something bogus in the damn media. I couldn't talk to anyone about these…fears, because I honestly didn't understand them myself." I shook my head at the memory.

"Anyway, one day I said fu—" I observed the amused smile on her face. "I mean, forget that; I'm going to reach out to her. It took a few days, but I tracked her down in the library, sneaking into a reserved room," I snickered, thinking about how big her eyes got when she saw me step into the room. "She was listening to music on her iPod and I picked up an earplug to hear. A song by Ledisi was playing. *Lost and Found*. I hadn't heard it before, but within just seconds, I could feel the spirit of the song. Feel Zoey's pain. After leaving her that night, I downloaded the track and absorbed it. It's really melancholy...really desperate. The subtitle of the track is *Find Me*—it's that dark." I rubbed my face.

"It's the pressure of it all: the game, the business of it, the wolves in sheep's clothing... It gets so heavy." I brought my eyes back up to Sarah.

Her eyebrows were hiked and chin angled. "And?"

I exhaled. She saw through the bullshit. "And I lost my best friend. I fucking literally *live* the sentiment of that track."

There was a long pause. A cloud over the room being removed. It's hard to speak of those things you can only feel. I didn't feel the need to apologize for the vulgar word I used to express myself, neither would I make a habit of using it. I just needed to be understood.

Sarah swiftly tossed her yarn and needles on the table and grabbed her chest with one hand. She rested her forehead on the other hand balled into a fist. I watched her pant for a minute. I wasn't alarmed. I didn't know what was coming, but for some reason, I wasn't afraid of it.

"I knew it." She shook her head on her fist. "My Zoey's nobody's fool. No one's perfect, but she's been my saving grace as a parent. I knew she didn't fall into this thing without her head."

I chewed on the inside of my lips as I sat back in the chair, feeling a thousand pounds lighter.

Sarah's head rose, her eyes reached to mine desperately. "You loved her—"

"I love her," I muttered, correcting her.

Her mouth dropped. I saw the confusion in her eyes. Could hear the questions she couldn't muster to ask.

"She's so young. She needs to live. To discover. Zoey wants to explore the world, not be locked in a lifetime commitment. She wants to journey alone." I shook my head again. "She can't do that being under me. She doesn't deserve the hot seat that comes with this lifestyle. She deserves the time she needs to make that decision on her own. I don't want this baby slipup to make that decision for her. I can keep her life private—or far more private than I could if she was by my side.

"Zoey wants the same destination any other girl her age desires. She just wants a different journey to get there. She's an idealist. If you don't manage her, she'll slip away."

I shook my head again. "I've created so much of a mess, I don't know how to fix it." I rubbed the pang that ran through my chest. "I don't know what to do with the...pain," I admitted.

Sarah's eyes suddenly narrowed. "Do you want to be with Zoey, Stenton?"

"I want her to choose me. But I never felt I was her choice."

"Seems to me you two need time. Zoey needs to find herself first."

"I just hope I haven't destroyed anything in her," I barely got out. My throat closed up on me.

Sarah's hand cuffed my wrist in a comforting manner. "Now, I know that girl. I made her. She's tough. Shoot, all this time I thought she'd gotten herself into a loveless affair with you, messed around and got an unwanted child out of it. We can't underestimate that girl. She's strong. Smart. She may not be as invincible and sound as she presents, but Zoey will figure it out in the end. Son, give this thing to God and I guarantee things will work out for the best...for both of you."

Call me fucking crazy, but in that brief moment, I wholeheartedly believed Sarah. I even felt a momentary reprieve of the pain I'd been carrying for months. I wanted that peace to last forever.

One thing was for sure; I'd made the right decision in making that call earlier.

April 2008

Stenton

Perfection. There were ten fingers and ten toes—all of which were identical to mine, almond shaped eyes with a brow line just like mine, a cute button nose that we'd already known he snatched from me and tiny plump lips that I couldn't deny came from his mother. His sound and contented sleep deprived me of the opportunity of our first formal playtime, but I was determined to study every inch of Jordan Michael Rogers, who was a touch of perfection. At just three hours old, he made the biggest impact on my life, second only to his mother, who was across the room, asleep herself. She must've been exhausted. It was hell watching her push out this bundle of joy.

When you see your heavily anticipated child, you experience a mirage of lifelong events vacuumed all into just a few seconds. You see his first run, his first time holding a ball, when he leaves for his first date, his graduations, and him holding his first child, experiencing the myriad of emotions you're experiencing with him now. And just to think, before meeting his mother almost two years ago I had no desire for the sheer joy I felt now, holding my son in my hands.

We'd just ended the third quarter against Toronto, and when I jogged off the court, Paul and Travis, my agent, walked over to me with the news that Zoey was in labor. I looked over at Coach DiLeo and immediately caught his affirmative nod. I left the arena, tossing my jersey and pulling on a long sleeved tee and a sweat suit as we paced to the exit. I was nervous as fuck. Paul gave me a blow by blow update from the moment we left the court until we were disembarking the plane at Teterboro.

The ride to the hospital had my stomach in knots at the anticipation of it all. Then it seemed as soon as we entered the hospital, time sped up. A nurse was at the entrance directing my security and me to the maternity level and I had to scrub up because Zoey had to begin pushing.

Zoey.

Her eyes lit up with relief when she saw me. It made me wonder if she thought I wouldn't be here for the baby. For her. I didn't want to go there. Thoughts of the state of my relationship with Zoey fucking depressed me. I grabbed her hand, buried my head in the side of her face and first apologized for my stinking ass, then murmured in her ear words of admiration for what she was doing for me and the baby. I must have told her a million times how proud of her I was and reaffirmed my love for her in spite of our status. That shit was cathartic for me. It worked, too. The next thing I realized was Dr. Henson announcing the arrival of our baby boy. That was a moment I'll never forget.

The fruit of my loins was wrapped in delicate cloth and was snug in my hands. The shit was crazy. I was looking at my legacy, my future. I finally had a familial connection to be excited about. Life to give guidance to. A human being to provide for. Someone that would give me a permanent connection to the woman across the room. I had a family.

"Mr. Rogers," I heard from above me. I glanced up and found one of the nurses—the one I thought resembled Miss Piggy, but was warm and accommodating just as the rest of them—glancing down on me with a pleasing smile. "I have to take Jordan for his vitals, shots, and another weigh-in. I'll be right back with him. Perhaps you can order breakfast while he's away."

Shit. Food. I'd forgotten to eat...*to wash my ass!* My poor baby, having to smell work on his old man.

I nodded and handed my little man over with great disinclination. He was my partner, even in that moment.

When the door closed behind them, I decided to take a shower. Zoey was in a private room, something I made sure to arrange. I wanted privacy for her and Jordan, didn't want to expose them to the media any sooner than I had to. My team worked seamlessly getting me in the place.

When I arrived, Zoey's parents and sister were there. I felt relieved to know she wasn't alone. Occasionally, I'd forget Zoey came from a tight family. She wasn't like me, a loner, which is probably what really drew me to her.

When I was done showering, I threw on fresh sweats and shower shoes Paul arranged to have delivered here while we were en route from Canada. As I sauntered out of the bathroom, I texted Paul, asking him to come and pick up my dirty laundry when he woke up. I knew he had to be somewhere sleeping.

"They miss you already?"

I glanced up and found Zoey smirking. She wore an expression of fatigue, but even exhaustion looked so damn cute on her. My heart swelled in pride at the sight of her. She was a trooper during delivery. I don't know why I expected less; this was Zoey after all.

I tossed a smile at her. "Telling Paul to come get my dirty clothes and bring clean ones for the duration of my stay."

Zoey's brows wrinkled and chin dipped. "You're staying? Here?"

I fought not to take that as a hint of being unwelcomed as I lowered myself in the cushioned chair next to her bed, crossed my stretched legs and plopped them onto her mattress.

"Yup. You couldn't pay me to leave my...son."

I'd almost slipped and used the word family. Because that's what it felt like. Zoey and I hadn't fucked in two months, since her birthday. We were in touch minimally by her design, but I still felt this incredible tie to her. I'd hoped my willingness to meet her need for space would pay off.

"Can you believe we have this tiny creature?" I glanced over and saw raw exhilaration etched into her face. Her smile was broad and suddenly she didn't appear as drained as she was just moments ago. She looked like my youthful Niña. "Isn't he perfect? He looks like you, you know? I see my mom's lips, but everything else is StentRo."

I curbed the initial glare I gave her at the mention of my on-the-court moniker. Zoey was in her element, being the fiery woman that captivated me almost two years ago. She recognized her mother's lips on Jordan, I saw hers. I guessed it was the same difference.

"He definitely has identifiable features," I agreed.

Zoey tossed her head back on the pillows with a big ass smile plastered on her face.

My nose wrinkled. "You're sure a different being from just minutes ago when I walked out of the bathroom."

Zoey giggled. "That's because I'm a medicated momma. See here?" She lifted a device that was attached to tubes. "This is a medication dial. When I feel pain, I turn it up. I turned it up while you were in the shower. My lower back was killing me, competing with my no-no-special place." She giggled.

Why the hell did she have to mention *that* place? Thanks to her, I'd be preoccupied with thoughts of it.

"Your giddiness is reminding me of," I twisted my neck over to the other side of the room to be sure her parents hadn't arrived unannounced. "...your experience in the Caymans."

She smacked her teeth. "Oh, when I was hiiiiiigh?" We both busted in laughter. I grabbed my stomach at that one.

"Yeah. Then."

"Naw! That was a different type of intoxication. The best of my life. I doubt if anything could top th—"

Zoey halted her words. She must have known she was crossing into gray territory. I, on the other hand, was pleased that she at least acknowledged our better days. It made me give myself permission to escape our reality, the mess I'd made.

I sat up in my chair, facing her square on. My eyes were leveled with hers while my back stretched broad, ready to catch whatever she threw my way, metaphorically speaking. I remembered Sarah's words of advice concerning Zoey. She said Zo needed time to figure out what she wanted and who she was.

"So much has changed since then, Zo. I'm sure the pregnancy, and now giving birth have given you a new perspective on life. What do you see for us...you, me and little Jordan down the road?"

Silently, I begged for her to speak of a family unit, something that would include us...together, officially.

Zoey shrugged. "I don't know...I just see me doing whatever I need to, to make a wonderful life for the little guy. I'll do whatever I can to provide, as much as possible, the stability my parents have given me all these years." Then her eyes returned to me. "And I'm sure he'll learn early on that he has one cool dad."

My chin dropped, body sagged as a crisp shiver swarmed over my back, and my chest squeezed at the picture she just drew. I was secondary to her plans with our son. She still didn't want us to resemble a traditional family. Zoey wanted no semblance of tradition. We were still at a blatant impasse. My heart was still on hold.

Just then, there was a knock at the door and right after, Jordan's bassinet was being wheeled back in. That stole both our attention and blocked the somber pit I was about to fall into.

"Let's try to feed again. Come, Jordan," Zoey called out excitedly with outstretched arms. "Come feed from your momma finally."

The nurse placed Jordan in Zoey's arms advising of a football hold. I watched absorbedly as Zoey released her left breast from her gown and placed her dark and enlarged nipple over Jordan's sealed mouth and soothingly cooed words of encouragement to eat. I had no idea what the hell this was about, but I soon saw my son open his little jaw and eventually start to draw from Zoey's breast.

Just then, Zoey's cell chirped next to me.

"Could you check that for me, Stent?" she called back to me, not removing her eyes from our son or sounding pressed about answering the text that came through.

Slowly, I reached for it on the table next to the bed. Even *my* eyes were glued to the event in Zoey's arms. It was weird as shit to watch another mouth on my Niña's boob, even though it was my son's. But he was so damn precious as he wrapped his miniature lips around her and pulled. Zoey giggled happily.

"You're doing it, Elizabeth!" the nurse cheered them on and threw me a happy glance as well.

So fucking proud of her was what went through my mind as I turned my attention back down to her phone. I slid the bar to the text app.

Bernard: **Is it super weird that I want to meet your son? I would really like to stop by the hospital to check on you two. If it's cool send me the info. My prayers are with you two.**

I scrolled up to previous messages. None screamed Zoey had fucked him, but I still felt my anger building. I became aware of my harsh breathing through my flared nostrils, and a wave of heat flushed through my tensed body. Why would this little fucker still be pursuing a woman who'd just had a baby? *My woman!* I knew I didn't like the prick, but this was the moment I began to hate his soft ass.

I had to calm down. I felt I had every reason to and none to be insecure about. I had Zoey where I wanted her. She'd just given birth to *my* child. That made me the permanent fixture I'd desperately wanted to be. I couldn't get hung up on the fact that the Bernard kid was after her ass. I'd laid claim to it when we conceived the life that was now lying in her arms, feeding from her. I had my child.

I officially have my Zoey.

"Who was it?" Zoey paid me a fleeting glance and returned it back to the man of the hour, not wanting to lose a moment of this milestone.

I quickly tapped away, deleting that message from Bernard *the Queen of the Golden Arches.*

"Your mom, checking in," I tossed back at her.

"Oh, she's going to be upset that she missed this." Zoey couldn't hide her excitement.

And I had to get back in the ring to regain mine.

Fuck a Bernard! Fuck kinda name is that anyway?

I placed the phone back on the side table and stood over the bed to watch the festivities. Out of nowhere, I felt a caressing swipe of my cheek. I looked down to see Zoey beaming up at me. Never before had I experienced joy and disappoint in the same event.

I'd have to get used to this. My Niña wasn't ready.

love belvin

April 2008

Zoey

We were discharged from the hospital two days after I delivered Jordan. Apparently, Stenton and my mother agreed that for the first week, while Stenton was relieved of playing, we'd stay at his home in Alpine. It was big enough to accommodate my mother, who would be staying with me. Stenton wanted full access to his son and didn't feel comfortable staying at my parents' where there was no room for him anyway. In Alpine, he could still train while helping out with Jordan.

Things were weird between Stenton and me because we assumed different roles. We were now parenting partners, no longer lovers...or best friends. His good energy was with me, but he seemed more formal and timid. Nonetheless his exuberance around Jordan melted everyone's heart. He stayed in the baby's face, constantly talking about nothing at all.

Two weeks after I had Jordan, I moved into the Philly apartment. I figured the way to go in was head first. I needed stability for my son and that wouldn't happen in good time if we'd stayed with my mother for a few months. I made my bed and had to sleep in it, so to speak.

It was hard because my mother was still working and couldn't stay with us very long. She was killing herself, trying to prepare meals for two households, helping with Jordan and going to work every morning. So many nights I had to kick her out, which was the last thing I wanted. I needed my mom more than ever. She would assign Ruth responsibilities, but at seventeen and with no driver's license, she had to be transported and would keep the same hours as my mother when she visited.

The upside to the isolation was the bonding that took place between Jordan and me. He was the most beautiful baby I'd ever seen. It amazed me how I could soothe his cries with just a diaper change, burp, feeding from my breasts, or simple cuddling. I never imagined what I'd be like as a mother; it had all come so soon, but Jordan forced me into this realm of love I never knew existed. And while I thought I loved and appreciated Sarah Barrett before this experience, I could now honor her with a fresh perspective. I'd been a mom for two short weeks and could see what the fuss was all about every year, leading up to the second Sunday of May.

Jordan slept a lot. He was still a newborn, and with having to be prepared for his every demand, I couldn't exactly relax. That bull crap about sleeping when the baby sleeps was the most invalid advice anyone could give. There was always laundry that needed to be done, food that needed to be prepared and other household chores. I'd wipe those things out and then look for more to do before Jordan's next scheduled feeding. Sometimes I moved too fast for my own good and became antsy.

One night, I stalked Stenton online...again. I went to Facebook and Twitter to see if I could catch up with him. We still weren't as communicative as we once were. Now, everything was about Jordan. I'd set it up that way. I had to protect the place of emotional stability I'd been able to find vacancy in. As I did my social media voyage like a fan of his, I clicked on dozens of pictures of Stenton, posing with our newborn son. If the number of teeth he exposed in each picture could measure his elation, the amount of them he shared made his joy palpable. He was revealing his private life, something he was reputed for not doing. His beaming smile in the hospital, next to an hour-old Jordan in a plastic bassinet; his sheer happiness when holding a sleeping Jordan on his bare chest covered in graffiti, were all telling of his absolute contentment. In the last photo of them skin on skin was the perfect contrast of purity against rugged art.

In the numerous pictures Stenton appeared to be happy, on top of the world. How could this be when I was still suffering from a broken heart? From failure.

When I Googled him like an overzealous fan, I found a clip of Rosci of 106&Park, who was clearly smitten with Stenton, ask probing questions, "We all know you just had a baby. How you were able to hide that from the world is beyond me. So, the *woooooorld*," she emphasized the word, "...wants to know, who is the woman worthy enough to have Stenton Rogers' baby?" The crowd went up in a roar, rooting and whooping.

Stenton smirked, but I knew him well enough to know he was uncomfortable. Stenton Rogers never minded attention on the court, but a telescope into his personal life brought about high levels of anxiety.

Trying to calm the boisterous crowd, Rosci hushed them before continuing. "I mean, we all know you're a private man. You're rarely photo'd out with anyone. But you were able to slip this past us. How?"

Stenton snorted, causing another round of *oohs* and *aahs* from the crowd, "By doing what I'm doing now: not speaking about it."

This reserved and confident man I was observing was far from the yielding, excitable, and eager lover I experienced making the baby in question. If I was less stable, I would question my knowing the man on my computer screen. The spotlight made him super-natural.

The chorus of regrettable *awwwwwws* came. Rosci joined them.

Where is Terrance J?

"C'mon, Stent. You gotta give us something. You know these

ladies aren't going to let you out of here without something—*I'm not going to let you off the stage without a legitimate answer!*"

"I can tell you this: the next woman you see me photo'd with will be someone I'm *dating*, but the only woman you'll hear me speak of will be my wife."

That set off a heavy applause and I cocked my head to the side wondering why. Was it because the audience got the riddle or because it was *cute* to hear Stenton Rogers refer to his future wife? I was then able to see just what Stenton meant when he said people don't *see* him; they see who and what they want to see.

"Wow! Okay!" Rocsi, too, seemed moved by that ambiguous comment. "But I have to push a little here, Stent. You and I have a mutual friend that didn't even know you were expecting. I had to ask him if she put some kind of spell on you to cut the line."

I gasped.

Stenton seemingly found that one humorous as he laughed. I didn't agree.

"Nah. No spells, no potions. Just awesome chemistry that produced the cutest and most adorable little prince. I'm a very lucky man. He has the best mother."

That was issued without humor. Did he mean that? Was that a ploy to appease his legion of crushees? Did Stenton feel something more for me than the young girl that was so inexperienced, she got pregnant by him? Was I overthinking this?

The sounds of Jordan stirring next to me in his bassinet stole my attention.

And there was my life: me and this precious new being, forcing me to learn new things about myself and propelling me to develop others. When you have a baby to care for, you reflect on the times of leisure before the baby when you thought you had no time and realize you had it in abundance. You wonder when you'll be able to get back to some level of normalcy or whether you should say goodbye to what you knew as normalcy and expect new normalcy. You wonder if you'll be able to relax and not always be on guard for a disgruntled baby.

You also wonder if you're providing the best for your child. I had Jordan outside of the cushion of a marital partnership. It was just the two of us. Yes, Stenton was around as much as his schedule would allow—and sometimes when it didn't; he made so many concessions in his schedule—but he wasn't here every day. Ultimately, it was me and my baby boy. Don't get me wrong, I thoroughly enjoyed exploring this new life. I took joy in observing his ever changing features the first weeks of his life. We'd get out for doctor appointments and walks when the weather permitted. My mom, sister, and Karen would come by when they could, but the distance isolated us. Yes, we were closer to Stenton and his job, but it was a complete culture shock not having family just a stone's throw away.

Angela still wasn't speaking to me. That hurt when I thought about it. Thankfully, I didn't think about it often. Having a baby will prioritize your mind, and Angela wasn't a part of my day-to-day struggle. I didn't go to church for the first few weeks of Jordan's life because I wasn't ready for the fanfare, seeing everyone was aware of whom Jordan's father was.

I was completely hormonal eight weeks into my postpartum self. I'd become awfully high strung and too idle with my time when Jordan slept, which was increasingly less, but still a lot. At one point, I started planning his christening. I didn't want a big, lavish event; only to get it over with and rededicate my son back to Christ. I consulted my mom on the minor details that it would take to pull off what I had in mind and before I knew it, the day had finally come.

June 2008

The soft and melodious rifts of the organ rang to fill the air as Pastor Whitaker ran down the latest announcements. We'd already sat through the official announcements portion of the service that

Sister Brenda does each Sunday as part of her job as the announcer, but Pastor Whitaker would always come behind her and emphasize the ones he felt were of high priority. He also took the time to shout out his seven-year-old daughter's birthday. It amazed me that I could recall when she was no bigger than Jordan, who rested in his car seat next to me, on the floor.

Jordan. My latest obsession.

"We have a dedication on this morning before I bring forth the word," Pastor Whitaker announced, drawing my attention from my prince. "Could we have the participants come to the pulpit please?"

My stomach roiled. I knew this occasion would be difficult, yet a necessary occurrence. This was for my son…and my commitment to Christ. We always christened our children as an act of worship. It is a way of returning, through ritual act, your child to Christ whom entrusted you with the child in the first place. I wanted to do right by Jordan, who I secretly felt I'd let down already by conceiving him so prematurely.

As I walked down the outer aisle with my baby nestled in my arms, my body went cold and trembled. I heard and felt the hardwood hidden beneath the aged tan carpet creak, and I quickly wondered how many times had I traveled this aisle over the years. The number didn't matter because none of those times were as terrifying as this moment. There were never the stares and silent throws of judgment that were being cast at me and my innocent child right now. Never had I been so closely regarded as I took the walk. I told myself during the journey to the altar that it was for Jordan. He was pure and precious. I had nothing to be ashamed of or uncomfortable about. He was conceived out of a love that some of these hypocrites wished they had a day of.

I made it up to the foot of the altar and observed Pastor Whitaker's comforting smile as he descended the pulpit.

He continued, "Amen." Then he turned to the crowd and asked, "Who will stand with this mother and child?"

I ducked my head at that portion of the ceremony. It was customary, but today meant much more. Usually the father, mother and, baby arrived first and he'd ask, *Who will join this man, his wife, and child?* But that was not the case. Even Karen and Angela had men with them to carry the burden of scrutiny. I was alone. I had no husband. My focus then became my beautiful sleeping baby.

My father, mother, sister, and Karen joined me. There was no man by my side, which was odd in this church. I glanced over to my parents who held their heads high, supporting me once again. There seemed to have been a long stretch of silence. I held my breath, waiting for that moment to pass. I glanced over at Angela, who still wouldn't look at me, but pretended to play in her baby's hair. That hurt.

Then I heard movement from behind me. I turned to find Bernard clearing his throat and smoothing his skinny pink tie as he stood and made his way by my side. The act would have been noble if he wasn't so dramatic about it. Bernard loved attention and this was furnishing him with plenty of it. Standing with an unwed mother and her bastard child? That'll garner him some respect. In all honesty, I didn't want him there. I wanted to do this alone. I'd prepared for it. It was my life. My choice. My consequence. My blessing. My child. Bernard didn't have to stand with me to help me save face, but there was no way I could relay this to him in that moment without being rude.

I sighed my frustration. *Yet another circumstance of not wanting traditionalism.* Not wanting marriage. *I'm a single mom and here's my path. This is the road I have to travel.* I would make the best life for Jordan… along with his dad, wherever he was.

And then I heard commotion down the middle aisle, leading to the doors of the church. A door was yanked open and the first one crossing the threshold was a pensive and jumpy Paul. My stomach churned. His petite frame looked formal in dress shoes, fitted black slacks, dress shirt, textured vest and a skinny tie just as pink as Bernard's. In fact, they were identical. Noticing my quizzical glare, Paul shrugged with his hands in the air, almost apologetically.

Right away, I knew what that meant: *Stenton's here!* My heart dropped into my belly and the wind had left my lungs. Twice I'd consulted Paul about this occasion without exactly telling him what it was. I asked him about cute christening gowns for boys. I didn't want one made, which is what a woman in our church did for our babies for a small fee. I wanted to involve my church as little as possible. And since Paul, by default, had become my go-to person, I'd asked him. I also inquired about a shoe store for babies. The ones my mother recommended in New Brunswick were with outdated styles or closed down.

Did he tell Stenton?

Then I saw familiar faces mixed with those that I was less acquainted with. Alton's short frame came through with Tynisha in six-inch heels, and their children in tow. I saw Barry and Rob in the mix of people piling in, looking for seats. Then I saw an older gentleman whom I recognized as Stenton's uncle. There were at least thirty people who arrived before Stenton's tall frame entered through the doors. He wore the most perceptible scowl as he perused the room and eventually came up to the altar.

I'm in trouble…

I knew he was angry. Most people would sensibly think he was looking for his child. But I knew Stenton well enough, knew those eyes. Knew the way they roamed. And when they landed on me I felt even worse. My feet felt heavy. I couldn't move to run.

Stenton, unlike his guests, gaited gracefully, straight up the aisle toward us just as natural as a member. I was granted a delicious and generous waft of his cologne that warmed my core—there at the altar. *Jeez!* It was as if he knew his place because he stood right across from me and threw the coldest regard to Bernard. I swallowed hard.

He extended his hand to Bernard. "Stenton Rogers…Jordan's father. Are you a blood relative?"

Bernard looked as if he'd seen Christ himself as he shakily took Stenton's big hand. I saw the yanking Stenton did when they touched. Bernard wasn't prepared for that. His mouth hung open for a while before he could speak. Stenton was being passive-aggressive. He knew who Bernard was. Bernard knew who he was—they'd met. I had no idea why they both played this role. Perhaps because Bernard would've never imagined Stenton setting foot in our church. I don't know, but this was weird for everyone. No one spoke. You could hear a feather drop.

"*N*-no," Bernard sputtered. "I'm a friend of Zo's."

"Well, I appreciate your support today, but I don't think it's necessary for you to stand with Jordan's blood relatives, do you?"

Holy mother of Joseph! Nooooooo!

An aghast Bernard looked over at me and when I couldn't give him anything, his sights went to my parents, then to Pastor Whitaker. They couldn't provide anything either. So, he paid Stenton one last parting gaze before backing away reticently.

I was mortified. The last thing I wanted was Bernard by my side, but Stenton had some gall running him off!

Stenton straightened his shoulders as he shifted into place. He greeted my parents, sister, and pastor with a nod, but wouldn't look at me. He did, however, gently take Jordan from my hold, raised him in the air reverently as he always did, and kissed him before placing him at the crux of his arms. Once that display of his doting was done, Pastor Whitaker continued the ceremony.

I felt like crap. I mean, like the gum stuck at the bottom of a runner's shoe. During the prayer portion, I got a chance to take in Stenton's countenance starting from his leather dress shoes, heather gray suit and up to his stark white dress shirt where the top two buttons were left undone, exposing the ink on his neck. That ink did things to me, tantalizing things. I observed his knuckles that were tatted as well. Stenton looked urbanely gritty and it turned me on... there at the altar, in front of a couple hundred people. Then my eyes roamed up to his lips. Those lips that were full, wide and shaped like a heart. They were perfect and so teasing that my pupils dilated at the sight of them.

That's when I noticed his eyes and realized he'd caught me staring. He didn't smile. Didn't smirk. His nostrils however did flare. It was as if he was telling me to back off, so I did.

We made it through the christening with Stenton participating seamlessly. When we all moved back to our pews, I sensed Stenton right behind me, holding a cranky Jordan. I was relieved because it was time for him to eat. Almost perceptively when we sat, Stenton went straight to the Gucci diaper bag one of his associates had sent as a gift, and retrieved Jordan's bottle and burping cloth. I loathed the bag, and thought was unnecessary, but felt just as foolish for wearing it as I would for wasting someone's money. He draped the cloth over his shoulder and gave the baby his bottle just in time to miss his cry.

As the service continued, I furtively watched Stenton with Jordan. My chest tightened with guilt at how Stenton knew to stop Jordan midway through his feeding to burp him, even though Jordan protested for a half a minute. Once he belched, Stenton returned Jordan to the crook of his long arm and continued his feeding. When the bottle was empty, Stenton burped the baby again then put him to sleep. As I marveled at how attentive and involved he was a father, I could only ask myself one question: *How could I have excluded him from this christening?*

He allowed Jordan a few minutes before placing him in his car seat to continue to nap. I had to fight for that with Stenton over the past few weeks because he'd hold Jordan all day if he himself didn't have to use the bathroom. Babies don't need to be held while they sleep. They'll get spoiled. It was bad enough he was a breastfed baby. Stenton's obedience to that request further spurred my guilt. Even after putting Jordan down, Stenton refused to look at me.

I don't know how much of the sermon Stenton took in, but he kept his eyes straight ahead. I, on the other hand, couldn't focus on anything but this man whenever he was around, especially today during this awkward encounter. Stenton remained locked and still. At one point, I heard Tynisha scolding Alton for being on his phone in the house of worship.

When service was over and Pastor Whitaker directed everyone down into the dining room for food in celebration of the christening, I noticed most of Stenton's crew headed in the opposite direction to the door.

Stenton finally turned to me and murmured, "I have to leave, but before I do, I need a word with you outside."

I nodded my head keenly. As we left the pew, my mom appeared with a warm smile. Stenton asked her to take Jordan while we spoke.

She agreed and Stenton kissed a sleeping Jordan, who ironically smiled. That caused a pang to rip through my chest.

"He's going to need a diaper change really soon. He didn't have one all service long," Stenton informed my mother as a responsible parent should.

Yup! I feel like crap!

When we continued outside, I didn't know what to expect. Stenton and I had never really fought. We hadn't really argued since our initial interface when we were forced to spend time together while Alton and Angela had their short-lived affair. Other than him breaking my heart, we had nothing to fight about.

On our way out, Pastor Whitaker stopped him.

"Mr. Rogers, I'm so glad you were able to make it. I apologize. Had I known you'd be a little late, I would've waited for you. I know today's a busy day for you," he offered genuinely.

Stenton shook his hand and offered an amenable smile. "That's all right, Pastor. I'm just a mere man; no one to wait on. That was made clear to me today."

My mouth swung open as Stenton tossed me the nastiest glare. Pastor Whitaker must have caught on as he cleared his throat and swiped his nose.

Stenton then amended, "Pastor, I appreciate your service in christening my son and the hospitality shown to my friends and family today. Although I know you're not in the business of making money, I'm insistent on speaking with Zoey's parents to discuss an appropriate donation to your congregation. With the years I've missed in tithing, I know I can cough of something to show my appreciation."

"Well, you don't have to do that, Mr. Rogers, but we would appreciate what you do give, even if it's only your time for the Word." Pastor Whitaker extended his hand again. "Thanks."

"Yeah, well, I appreciate the support you've given Zoey during a time when an unexpected decision had to be made. Thank you for not being as critical as the masses." Stenton gestured to the church and I died a thousand deaths. Again! "That went a long way with me."

I noticed Stenton never referred to Jordan as a mistake. No matter how unexpected, Jordan was a blessing from God.

"We love Zoey. And we now have Jordan to love as well." Pastor Whitaker nodded. "God bless your family," he spoke to both of us with a gleam in his eyes before walking off.

Stenton directed me down the church's steps, to the sidewalk, and almost to the corner before he stopped. I noticed Rob and Barry trailing a few feet behind us, but distant enough to give privacy. With each step, my heart almost raced from my chest in anxiety.

He then abruptly turned to me, placing his fists on his waist. "Let me tell you something. I don't know what the fuck you thought you were doing today by not—"

I sucked in a breath as my eyes felt like they were being pulled from their sockets. "Stenton!"

"Don't fucking *Stenton* me! Zo, you know you could have told me that my fucking son was going to be christened today—"

"Stenton!" my throat shrieked in alarm. "You are in the middle of the championship!"

"FINALS!" he shouted at my ignorance. "They're finals! And yes they are important, but nothing is more important to me than my son and supporting you." He pointed his long finger over my shoulder towards the church. "If this is the shit you're into then I'm into it, too! It means something to me!"

"Well, Stent, it's not like we're together." That felt juvenile as soon as it left my lips. I tried amending it. "I know you have a life."

"Yeah, and I'm putting myself and several of my teammates, who came today to support me, at risk of being fined for showing up late to practice. A practice in Boston we may not even make! But I'm here for my son. It's not just you, Sarah, Michael, and Karen!" His face morphed into a grimace. "And then you had the nerve to have that…Bernard…" Stenton turned and punched the air as he mumbled a string of expletives. He returned to me. "I don't know what type of feminist bullshit you're on—"

I gasped. "Stenton, you know I'm no feminist!"

"Bullshit!" He drew closer to me. "You're so fucking independent. Zoey, you may be a single woman who's a mother, but you're no fucking single mother. I'm his father. I'm an equal partner in this! When you make decisions like this, you need to involve me!" Stenton took a moment to breathe. And just when I thought he was done, he continued, "Let's not act like I'm not footing the bill for the food they're in there partaking of right now. Let's not act like I'm just a sperm and financial donor. I am Jordan's father!" he stabbed his chest with his index finger. "I am here. I am *your* partner… whether you like our setup or not, we're going to make the best of it. You will not pull shit off on me like this. And if you continue to, Zoey, I swear to fucking god you will feel every bit of it! I will not tolerate it. *I'm. Here!*"

Shocked. Shamed. Embarrassed. Foolish. Those were some of the words that could best characterize what I felt in that moment. I couldn't speak. Had nothing to follow up with. The *Queen of Comebacks* had no comeback. He was right. Even today, during one of the lowest moments of my life, he'd shown up for me…uninvited and all.

I stood there and widened my eyes in an attempt to keep my tears inside. My chest heaved and nose flared. Stenton pivoted again and that's when I saw my mom just beyond him. Stenton must have caught her in his peripheral, too, because he turned completely toward her then let out another string of profanities under his breath. I knew he didn't want her to have caught his tirade.

As my mother approached us I noticed the plate she held in her hands. She had her loving smile in place. A smile that could sooth anything…up until that moment. My heart was still bleeding.

"Stenton, I came out here because I know you love my cream cheese pound cake. I was told you don't have time to eat with us, but I know you'll always make room for this." My mom handed him the plate.

Unable to look her in the face, Stenton took the plate and murmured, "Thank you, Sarah. I appreciate this." A few beats later, he croaked out a low, "I'm sorry." And I was aware he was exclusively speaking to her.

"Son, there's no need to apologize." Her voice was so calming as she gently took him at his broad shoulder. "I was not aware of this, but I will be talking to Zoey about co-parenting even though you two are in a precarious situation." Her eyes turned restless, she was disappointed in me. "You're a great dad. You go on. Get to work. We don't want you in any trouble behind this. I'm glad that you showed up for your son today. Thank you for showing up for my child, too."

My child? I'm a grown woman!

Stenton walked off to his waiting truck, tossing me a last glare before getting in. I turned my head and inadvertently collided with my mother's feverish glower.

"He's just so frustrating! I don't get him. You know how I feel, Mom. You know what I've been through. You said yourself, you don't like the confusion taking place between us."

"I said I don't like confusion, honey. Stenton doesn't at all seem to be the one confused." She gave me a searing gaze before walking off herself, leaving me, just like Stenton did moments before.

Chapter Thirteen

Zoey

"What are you looking at? I thought you came over to help me sort this laundry." I laid Jordan's fresh onesie in the pile with the rest of the white ones on the dining room table.

Tynisha glanced up from her laptop and rolled her eyes. She sighed, "Mascot, what you need is a damn maid, not someone to *help* you. Have you looked me up lately? Do you not know what I do for a living? It's a little awkward when I don't even do my own."

"But that's what you said when you called to tell me you were stopping by."

"That was just to get me in here. God knows you won't come out," she hissed as she went back into her screen.

"Anyway," I exhaled. "What are you doing?"

"I'm...ummm...looking up Alton's activities to see if he's been cheating."

"Huhn?" My jaw fell to the table.

"Yeah. There's this small production company out of Delaware

312

—run by some guy Alton went to high school with that moved down there—who has been doing a documentary on him for years now." Tynisha's voice was low and the cadence of her words staggered as she was so engrossed in what was on that screen. "They're recording him like my camera crew does me, and uploading small clips on their website to drum up anticipation. And *I've* been watching to catch him in the act."

Tynisha and I had been relatively cool for months, but never had I felt comfortable enough to inquire about the policing she does with Alton.

"How would video footage prove anything unless it actually shows him in the act?" I knew Alton could be a bit dumb, but even he wasn't that foolish.

"Look." Tynisha flipped the laptop so that I could see the screen. "See, I know Alton. If he's fucking this bitch, he'll avoid looking at her in public. He doesn't want anybody to know. In his mind, he thinks the best way to fool people is to not acknowledge her at all. Because Alton can't keep his dick in his pants, he naturally stares at a woman with his tongue hanging from his mouth. So, I'm looking to see what he does with this one girl," she points her perfectly manicured nail at the grainy image of a woman on the screen walking down an alley with at least six other people alongside Alton.

"So, what is he doing?"

"I haven't figured it out yet. This is my twentieth time watching and I see a little eye action on his part, but I can't quite tell."

"Does that method really work? Is your theory even valid?"

"It works. It's how I was able to tell he was fucking your slutty cousin a few years back when she tried to say he got her popped. I looked up the footage and saw he wouldn't look at her when y'all was leaving the country club and diners. He doesn't even know how he gives himself away. I could also tell that Stenton was fucking you because he kept stealing looks your way. Alton is the exact opposite."

That stopped me in my tracks as I held a burping cloth midair. "Tynisha," I shook my head and tried stifling my laughter. "Stenton and I weren't involved back then when Alton was sleeping with Angela." I decided to ignore her labeling of Angela, realizing it would be futile in correcting. She was understandably upset by the situation. "We didn't start…you know…sleeping together until well after that summer."

"Well, whatever. My point is every woman has her method of telling if her man is cheating. Every man has a rhythm. I know Alton's. Like, I always try to make sure to give Al the snatch before one of us leaves town. When I can't give it to him, it increases the chances of him getting it from somebody else."

I rolled my eyes at that utter bull crap. *Men who want to cheat will cheat!*

I sighed and wrinkled my face to fortify myself. "Ty, doesn't that get a bit exhausting, always checking up on him to make sure he's doing his part in keeping with fidelity?"

She looked up and into the distance, considering my question, as elementary as it was. Tynisha shrugged, "I don't know, girl. I've been doing it for so long, I have no idea."

I scoffed. "It would get a bit tiring to me."

Then her eyes narrowed. "Well, it beats sitting here doing laundry like you're getting paid for it. What are you doing with yourself?"

I fought my grin as I shook my head at Tynisha again.

Tynisha's neck snapped back. "Mascot, don't judge me! I'm sure you know Stenton's rhythm and you try your damnedest to make sure he doesn't trip out on you, especially with Erika Erceg sniffing around his balls. Him having a baby recently has not slowed her chase at all, in case you didn't notice."

I'd heard of Erika. She was a drop dead gorgeous woman of Syrian descent and had been almost an overnight household name for a sex tape of her and a rapper that went viral a few years back. Erika was also a reality television star like Tynisha. I got the distinct impression she didn't care for her competition. But I had no idea she had something for Stenton.

I tried shaking that scenario from my mind and resumed folding clothes. "Stenton and I are not together."

Tynisha didn't skip a beat when she observed, "According to you two, you were never together, but baby Rogers back there," she flicked her fingers to the back of the apartment where a napping Jordan was, "…would claim otherwise."

I chuckled while shaking my head. That's when I noticed Tynisha staring at me dubiously.

"What?" I narrowed my brows.

"You and Stenton ain't sleeping together?" Her already slanted eyes, contracted even more.

"No!" I snorted. "Stenton and I haven't been together in ages."

"I'm sure since the baby…"

I shook my head. Not that I was exactly comfortable with sharing about my sex life or lack thereof, but I felt I could be candid with Tynisha. She was a celebrity herself. What public figure didn't appreciate confidence?

"No. I haven't been with him since well before I had Jordan."

"You better be careful. I know Stenton's a freak. I've heard he's into that kinky shit…chains and whips and shit."

I let out a small chuckle as I shook my head at her musing.

"Damn, he is! Isn't he?" she blurted in a revelatory manner, lustful even.

"I didn't say that."

Tynisha continued her examining, staring at me. "You didn't have to. The color in your cheeks is telling me that he is. Not only that, but look at how hard your nipples are all of a sudden." I re-draped my silk—and apparently thin—robe. "What the hell's going on, Mascot? Okay, you guys haven't exactly been in an official relationship. I can't judge that. Look at Alton and me: we've been engaged for three years and have as many kids and all we have to show for it is countless scandals." She took a breath. "But you two… Stenton's never wavered in his feelings for you. It's clear that he's crazy about you."

I huffed. "Well, I can't tell."

"Well, yeah, because men can be so fucking retarded with the way they express themselves. But trust me, I know. That's why I've been chilling with you. Not because you're my speed. He's made it clear that you should be treated as a part of the circle." She shrugged again. "I don't know…" She then went back to her footage.

That only lasted a few seconds. Tynisha popped her head back up toward me as I stood over the table, folding and sorting.

"Mascot, you're here with the baby. He comes by and you guys don't go at it?"

"No. He spends time with his son. He has a room in the back for when he can't come until late at night, and even when that happens, he takes the night shift to let me sleep. We've been doing a much better job at co-parenting since the christening."

What a fiasco that was. It was hard coming back from that. Stenton would still come over for Jordan, but hardly looked at me, much less conversed with me. It took some time for me to officially apologize and offer to do better at including him in all decisions made regarding Jordan. I'd tried to play it safe with Stenton since then.

"I'm just so damn confused." Tynisha wouldn't drop the subject.

"About what? What's the confusion?" I returned with just as much frustration, and snorted, "If he wanted me, he would've made that clear long ago, and we'd be together. I respect his wishes and will give him time to decide what he wants. Life goes on, right?"

In all honesty, I was simply happy to be in a better place from the breakup that occurred nearly a year ago when he dropped me off and said goodbye for no reason at all. Being pregnant with Jordan eclipsed that, and having him around pushed it to the back burner, but there was still an ache in my chest from his decision.

Tynisha shook her head. "You around here doing laundry… first of all, you need to start with getting a damn maid, then a nanny." She snatched a few items from the laundry basket. "Then you need to get your back blown out. There's no way a woman can function if she's connected to Stenton Rogers, but not being taken care of. He's running around here flossing it up for everybody else, but you ain't getting a piece of the pie. You young girls need to learn how it's done. Because I guarantee you if he was getting some of that snatch, there wouldn't be any confusion in your relationship. You, unlike my dumb ass, would probably be married by now."

That hurled me into a pit of confusion. I stilled myself, processing Tynisha's new theory.

"Well, anyway, once we're done I'm gonna call my guy to come over to take your measurements. What are you...a size six now? I have some fun pieces that you would kill in!"

I let Tynisha ramble on, too stuck on the mention of marriage for me and Stenton.

Then: August 2008

Stenton

"You don't know? What does that mean, Stent?" her voice purred harmoniously, a little too sweetly.

"Nah. I got some things coming up. You know summers are just as crazy for me with endorsement work, and I have to steal all the time I can with my kid. My schedule is pretty tight now."

"I know, but...Stentiiiiiiiiin," she enunciated my name fully as she called out. Erika was laying it on thick, but I wasn't ready.

As I traveled Alton and Tynisha's hallway while chatting on the phone, I thought about how I needed more time for Zoey to come off her independent bullshit and tell me she wanted a family with me and Jordan. I didn't want to force her or influence her on that. So far, everything I set up for her and the baby had been met with her willingness. She hadn't fought me on child support or the monthly stipend I'd arranged for her. She never oscillated much on the cars or the apartment I bought her. Neither had I heard a complaint about the money I'd given her parents as rent while Zoey and my unborn child lived there. I knew she wasn't the type of woman easily influenced by money, but she hadn't resisted anything. She just went with my flow. Well, why the fuck hadn't she expressed the desire for me?

"Why don't we do this: let's wait until the season begins, give me a few weeks to settle into it, and we'll see when and where we can meet during my away games. Deal?"

Erika sucked her teeth. "I'm not happy about it, but I'll take what I can get. Don't be shocked when we finally get together…and alone if I ask to see all your tats. Rumor is you got a new one below the waistline and that's the one I have to get a close look at. I'm near-sighted, you know."

Shit! She was coming with it. Lately, she'd been more aggressive with her flirting. She'd just made it clear that she wanted to suck my cock. *Goddamn.*

I turned the corner and headed into the kitchen. Under any other circumstances, I would have played along with the seduction game Erika seemed down for, but my life wasn't that simple. I was fucking stuck on another woman. One that didn't know if she wanted me or to conquer the damn world.

I chuckled, "Funny thing about them fucking rumors: they're not always fun, once discovered, as they were in theory. I'll check you later, E."

"Bye, Stent."

"Mmmmm…" Alton purred as he snuggled into Tynisha's neck.

Charmed by it, she stroked the side of his face with her free hand as they leaned on the marble countertops in their state-of-the-art kitchen. Unlike the rest of the world in television land, I was accustomed to seeing this public display of affection between the two of them. Alton had some shit with him, but he was as tender as they came, off camera.

We were tired. I wouldn't even necessarily say sleepy, perhaps drained. We'd just gotten off a rigorous training streak with the next few days off. We were at Alton and Tynisha's in Upper Saddle River in their kitchen doing small talk before I headed over to Alpine for the night. It was early August and the weather was more or less conducive to outdoor adventures, rather than trekking back and forth from North Jersey to Philly as we were doing.

"I know the kids are happy to have you home for a day or two," I shared with Al. Then I was hit with a thought. "Are you shooting at all?" I asked Tynisha, whose head rested on top of Alton's on her shoulder, referring to her reality show. Their schedule was off the damn chain with cameras on them all the time.

She nodded contently. I knew I needed to move. I needed to start making my way to the car. Rob was out keeping the *G63* running for me. No matter what I needed, I knew resting was not in the cards for me over the next few days before I boarded the plane for Atlanta for a *Nike* commercial shoot. I was excited beyond compare, nonetheless.

I exhaled. "Let me get my ass on. Besides, Al's looking like I'm raining on his damn parade."

"Yeah the fuck you are," Alton shot back, stifling a yawn.

"And what are *your* plans for your time off?" Tynisha's neck popped and her eyes widened at that question. Her glare was expectant.

What the fuck is that?

"You know my plans," I returned.

She and Zoey had grown tight over the past few months. She knew I was headed to Zoey's to spend time with Jordan. I'd been looking forward to feeling his warm milky breath yawning into my nose. It had taken no time at all for me to fall in love with that kid. Even if he had pissed and shitted on me more times than I could count because I'd been too slow putting fresh diapers on him.

"I'm going to dote on my legacy between practices." I'd wondered what the fuck was up with her line of questioning.

"You need to be doting on more than JR. You need to be *working* his mother," Tynisha spit rather harshly.

I wrinkled my forehead and angled my head.

Alton's nostrils flared as his eyes rolled while laying on her.

"Fucking women. Speak fucking English please."

Tynisha rolled her eyes herself at that statement and then returned her scowl to me.

"What I mean is, Zoey's in need, too. You need to handle that!"

"In need of what?" So many things ran through my mind. I felt anger mostly, wondering who couldn't be playing their part, making sure Zoey had everything she needed.

Tynisha's daggers zoomed into an area below my waist. My dumb ass followed her gaze to my crotch.

"She just had a baby, Stent. Her hormones and self-esteem fluctuate more than Alton's steal stats. Mommy's body is jacked with nurturing that baby, and needs a fine tuning," she so cleverly articulated.

I knew shit about a woman's hormonal makeup postpartum. However, Tynisha's message was loud and fucking clear. It reminded me yet again that I hadn't thought this shit through. I'd pledged to myself to always meet Zoey's every need. This one was unique, but damn sure wasn't one I was going to shy away from.

"Really?" I asked dumbfounded.

She sighed as she shook her head. "You men need a damn manual for everything female related," she mumbled as she left her position, upsetting a comfortable Alton. "I'm going to bed on that note. I have an early morning tomorrow, starting with hair and makeup."

I said my goodbyes to Alton and Tynisha and left their crib. The moment I crawled into the back of the car, headed to Alpine for the night, I pulled out my phone. After a few rings, she answered.

"Hey." Zoey sounded subdued.

"Did I wake you?" It was still a little early, just after ten at night.

"No. I just fed, burped and put Jordan down."

I chuckled at the sound of his name. *Such a cool kid.* "How long will he be out? All night?"

Zoey snorted. "I wish. Try about three hours."

My expression turned serious as I gazed out the window, not focused on anything in particular. "Are you getting enough sleep?"

"Stenton, I'm the mother of a four-month-old baby. I don't

sleep; I survive from day to day."

I rubbed my chest as if literally nursing the pang that ran through it.

Shit.

"About that. How are you feeling…physically?"

She sighed long and hard. It was almost like I'd opened Pandora's Box. "I don't think you're prepared for that answer," she murmured into the phone.

"Damn it, Zo, I told you I would be here for you. If you don't talk to me how am I supposed to help?"

"Jordan's fine, Stenton. He has more than what the average baby has…"

"And you?" I wanted to cut the bullshit.

"*I*-I…" She groaned, regrettably. "My needs are beyond what you've agreed to do regarding him."

Feeling my frustration simmer—more at myself for putting her through this shit—I took a deep breath and tried to refocus myself. With my head lowered toward my lap, I whispered, "I wanna help. What can I do?"

"I just need to get myself together. I'm sure what I'm feeling… the body changes are typical for—"

"Are they physical needs?" My tone was terse, impatient.

"Well…yeah and…"

"Related to your emotions?"

"Yeah, but again, I'm sure it's typical for a woman who has recently given—"

"I have a photo shoot first thing in the morning. I'll try to keep it short and will be over for Jordan…and you," I breathed into the phone, hoping she caught my drift. "I'll have a few things delivered there, and Eligia will be there first thing to take over with Jordan for a couple of days. Please give her a chance so you can have a break. It'll be for just a couple of days while I get you sorted out."

There was an extended pause on the line as I pulled up to my home. I'd been short enough with her, but I needed to go so I could put plans in motion. I waited. All I could hear was her deep breathing. My cock twitched as my mind processed the memory of her doing just that in my ear as I rocked into her. I couldn't lie, all these months, I wondered what Zoey felt like and tasted like after giving birth. Some dudes say it's different. I wanted to know how. I also wanted that connection with my Niña again, but wouldn't dare ask. I was growing in need just thinking about it.

"Zo," I called out.

"O-okay," she pushed out lightly. That was all I needed. Although her response was timid, I knew when I showed up with what I had in mind, she would be down.

"Goodnight," I endeavored and ended the call without a response from her. I had calls to make.

Stenton

The next day, just after noon, I pulled up to Zoey's condo with bags in tow. I came alone knowing I'd be here for a couple of days unless things went horribly wrong. I knocked on the door and seconds later, Ruth, Zoey's younger sister, pulled it open. Immediately, she looked me up and down, not missing the shopping bags I had in both hands.

"What the hell is all this?" She pointed to the bags. I walked past her and into the foyer. "Shit…and a duffle, too?" she asked incredulously behind my back, I assumed after seeing the *YSL* duffle that was strapped around my chest and rested against my back.

I turned and glared at her. "It's a fucking shame that Michael and Sarah spent so much of their efforts into properly training up their first offspring that when their spawn came, they had very little to offer. You had better not be using that fucking filthy mouth around my muthafuckin' seed."

Ruth gasped, but she wasn't too taken aback. This was our relationship. There was always vulgar banter back and forth between the two of us. We only managed to keep it clean in front of her parents. In front of everyone else, we let it rip. It was a true love/hate relationship. I knew much of her resentment of me came from being a protective younger sister. I'd disrupted Zoey's life and confused her. I had to accept that, even if I didn't show it to Ruth.

"The shopping bags, I can understand. Most of those are obviously for my JR. But the stuffed duffle bag, damn roses and *Le Perla* shopping bag is a whole 'nother damn mode." She waved her pointed index finger in a circular motion. "Wonder if it has to do with why my sister hasn't let me into her damn room for the past thirty minutes." Ruth issued a penetrative glower, and I returned it.

"I see that skirt you're wearing, and it's Wednesday...noon-day prayer at your church, right? The high cut of it is a whole 'nother fucking mode to me."

Ruth sucked her teeth and rolled her neck, begging my pardon. She then closed the door.

"My nephew is in his nursery with this *nanny* you sent over. I don't think it's a good idea, but what say does the auntie get in his life?" She turned to leave out.

"Bye, Ruth," I bade casually before laying the flowers on the hall-table, there in the foyer then headed towards the back of the apartment for the bedrooms.

My first stop was to JR's room—Jordan Rogers had turned into JR, as we affectionately nicknamed him. I dumped some of the bags against the wall in the hall and slid out of my sneakers before I entered. His room was fairly large. So large that I had to look around once inside to find its dwellers. There they were, near the bay window, in the rocking chair.

Eligia's eyes lit up once they recognized me. "Mr. Rogers!" she gasped quietly.

I placed the bags down, out of the doorway before crossing the room.

"Eligia, I'm glad you were able to show on such short notice——"

Jordan's little head popped up in search of me and then he wailed loudly. *Shit.* In all my excitement of seeing him, I forgot how much my presence roused him. Eligia gasped again, not able to hide her amusement about my son's keenness. It was crazy and I enjoyed it, though this time I was hoping to divide my time between him and his mother.

I held my index finger up, gesturing to hang on for a bit. "I need to wash my hands," I whispered before taking off for his bathroom there in the nursery.

When I returned to them, Jordan was still fussing, wanting to get to me. Almost the moment I took him from Eligia and gathered him in my arms, he quieted.

"Hey there, lil man. I got you," I murmured to him.

His little eyes gazed into mine a while before he made the sniffling face and sound, resembling more of a stinky face. He then brought his hands and mouth to my face discoordinately and landed a wet kiss on the left side of my cheek. It was more like his warm milky breath hit my face first, panting wildly, then his wet tongue followed like a soft smack.

"Hey, kid, you're going to have to get your kissing game up for the ladies. That was sloppy!" I giggled. Only my kid could make my grown ass giggle like a woman.

I loved his attempts at affection towards me. By all accounts, he wasn't this demonstrative with anyone else, and knowing it brightened my heart.

Eligia handed me his pacifier. "I was just putting him down for a nap. Are those bags for him?" She pointed to the small pile I'd dropped. I nodded. "Would you like for his mother to put them away to see what you've bought or should I do it?"

I guessed she asked because for some single parents, it can be important for fathers to show off what they contributed to their children for appearance sake or accountability. In my case, I had to hide most shit. I spoiled this little guy to my heart's delight. I'd had his nursery packed here, at my apartment, and up in Alpine. There was nothing I wouldn't do for him.

"You can put them away. I don't want to get in any trouble while I'm here," I answered Eligia as I adjusted Jordan in my arms to start putting him down for his nap. I could tell he wanted to play as we usually did, but I didn't want to prolong his crankiness and needed to put him out of his misery. Plus, I had his mother to tend to.

In less than five minutes, Jordan was out. I laid him in his crib and cracked the door behind me when I left his nursery. I headed out to the kitchen where I knew Eligia was, and could smell the seasoning of her cooking.

"He's out," I informed her as I clicked on his monitor.

She nodded and I looked for a vase for the flowers I brought. I left the sole black rose out of the bouquet and headed out of the kitchen.

"Everything set?" I asked before stepping past the threshold.

"Yes, Mr. Rogers. Everything is here." She nodded assuredly with a warm smile. "We will be just fine."

"Cool." I tapped the doorframe. "I'll see you in a few."

I grabbed my duffle and the remainder of the shopping bags on my way to the back. When I arrived at Zoey's door, I stood listening, for what I didn't know. I guess I was a bit nervous. Finally, I knocked softly.

Within a few beats, I heard, "Come in."

When I entered, I quickly closed the door behind me and glanced up to find a nervous Zoey in a black sheer baby doll slip that opened in the front with a thong.

"Is that for me?" she asked trying to hide her shaky voice.

I nodded and I assessed her body as I sniffed the black rose. She was a few inches thicker and wonderfully filling out the lace cloth. But there was more to her stunning appearance: her legs wobbled in her nervousness just as her eyes bulged.

I tilted my head to the side. "I don't recall you being this nervous when you forced yourself on me for the first time in Alpine." My voice was just above a whisper, not giving away my excitement.

Zoey's eyes bashfully shifted from me and her cheeks heated. I thought I'd finally beat her at her wit. I was wrong.

Without looking at me, she pointed to my pelvis. "And I haven't seen you this attentive since that day either."

I glanced down to find my rod stiff and visible through my sweats.

I shrugged. "What can I say? It's been a while."

I then jerked my chin towards her, my heavy eyes raked over her barely contained breasts that were peaked at the apex. "Someone else is a bit excited, I see."

She glanced down at herself and rolled her eyes nervously, unable to hide her embarrassment. "I'm fat."

"You're fucking gorgeous," I countered without finesse. Her eyes flew to mine in disbelief. "You're just being polite," she whispered, her eyes glossed.

"I'm not. You're unbelievably sexy with the extra pounds, Zo." I dropped the bags, feeling adrenaline flowing all over. "I'm known for a lot of things, but lying isn't one of them." I gently laid the duffle bag against the wall there in the small corridor of the expansive master suite, needing to get closer to her. "And it's my plan to demonstrate to you how you're still the most attractive and desirable woman in the world, and a few extra pounds doesn't detract from that. You're sexy as hell and I'm so eager to prove it to you that I'm afraid I'll hurt you." My voice turned hoarse, belying my calm demeanor.

After tossing the rose on the chair to the right of me, I stepped closer to her and pulled my t-shirt over my head. I found Zoey's molten eyes and knew she understood what time it was.

I bent down and traced her ear with my tongue. She smelled of vanilla and her skin resembled silk. My senses were in a frenzy at the memory of this proximity. All morning I fought with myself, saying I couldn't do this for her. I couldn't do this to me. I loved this girl and was borderline obsessed with her. I didn't need a relapse in our progression: my plan. But the insatiable, selfish asshole in me couldn't deny myself of Zoey. Ever.

"I'm about to devour you like it's my last opportunity." *And I pray it isn't.*

I heard her breath catch and felt her body tremble. I backed up to look into her eyes. Her chest heaved and she attempted to lick her lips. I reached for her face and sucked in her bottom lip, instantly reminded of what they felt like. I did the same with her top lip before pushing my tongue into her shaking mouth and darting at her suspended tongue. *So sweet.* It took no time for Zoey to gain her senses and join me. We kissed thoroughly, exchanging tastes and forgoing breathing to do it. Her small hands rose up to my chest and her nails raked down my abdomen.

"Pull my pants down," I groaned into her mouth. "Keep your mouth where it is." And my tongue thrashed her lips, into her mouth again.

I felt Zoey's little palms push down on my drawstrings to loosen them. She gripped my boxers and sweats and pushed down until they stopped mid-thigh. My wood sprang out wildly. She then lifted her foot in the crotch of them to push them down to the floor, pooling at my feet. In two rapid movements, I stepped out, kicking them away, stepped, and rammed my pelvis into her bare belly. I pulled her closer to me by the back of her head and deepened the kiss. The tips of my fingers gripped her scalp against the wavy roots of her hair as I devoured her. Zoey's hands rounded me and grasped my wings. I began to grind into her. My tongue swirled and swirled. I sucked on her lips as though they were my last meal because with Zoey, I needed to savor each taste. She was a fleeting fantasy. A dream I could never seem to catch up with. I needed her to feel my unrelenting desire of her.

A groan from the back of her throat erupted causing me to grind harder against her belly that though was relatively flat, I could still feel the extra cushion, remnants of her pregnancy. She felt wonderful. I reveled in her femininity, feeling connected to her passage into womanhood. And she felt me, felt every inch of my need for her as she pulled me in, clinging to me even tighter. I leaned in so close that her back bowed reminding me of Zoey's nimble limbs. It wasn't long before I spilled out in between our pressed bodies. I groaned hard and deep, feeling my frame jerk roughly, but felt comforted in her small arms.

When I was able to, I pulled from Zoey and aside from her swollen parted lips, I saw her tight eyes trying to focus below to our torsos. I followed the trail down and saw my essence splattered in some places and dripping in others, mainly on her belly. My dick twitched at the processing of that. With her lips still parted, she glanced up at me.

"I had to get rid of that one for what I have planned for you," my voice was raspy.

Zoey visibly held on to control by a thin thread. I felt her body teetering with need as I patiently loosened the tie of her lingerie. Her breasts spilled out, making Zoey wince in shame when she moaned. If I wasn't so intoxicated in lust, I could swear she was close to tears.

I tilted her chin with my index finger as I aligned my eyes with hers. "There's no need to be embarrassed with me. I'm enjoying you already, and I plan on making you feel incredible."

She sucked in a breath and her eyes rolled to the back of her head. I covered her mouth with mine and made love to her face. Within seconds, Zoey crawled up my body. She was now demonstrating her impatience.

"Take me, Stent," she panted against my lips. "I can't wait."

I grabbed her ass, inserting my hands in the tiny straps of her thong. "Niña, you're trying to play director again," I growled, telling of my unyielding need. "Besides, I have to get a rubber somewhere deep in my duffle." I gestured behind me where I'd dropped the bag.

I grabbed her at the back of her head again, not able to get enough of her sweet lips. Zoey pulled back hesitantly.

She licked her lips and murmured so close to my face that she had to adjust her eyes to catch mine, "You said it's been a while for you. How long?"

My face wrinkled in a flash, then it was my turn to smile embarrassingly. I chuckled as I set my eyes to something in the distance. "Your birthday."

As abashed as the fact was, it was true. Erika had been dying to fuck, but I couldn't. Not yet. I still had Zoey in my system. I couldn't understand why my son being so young and his mother being stuck in my psyche affected my libido—apart from Zoey.

"I'm on the pill," she whispered into my face as her fingers caressingly rubbed the back of my head.

I knew she was on the pill, learned about during one of JR's doctor visits when breastfeeding was discussed, even had mixed feelings about it, but never thought about going raw. My heart expanded in excitement. With her clamped to my frame, I mounted the bed and gently laid Zoey on her back. I roughly swiped all of the decorative pillows off the bed. I then looked down on her squirming underneath me.

"I can't, Zo. We need to use protection. It's the responsible thing to do."

"Stent..." she begged.

"Just wait up." Her shoulders sank as I strolled over to my duffle, windswept through it until I found the box of condoms. "See," I murmured in her ear while I pulled it on underneath her hips after returning to the bed.

Then I cast my line of sight down at her full breasts. I couldn't give a damn what changes her body had undergone, Zo was flawless. And mine.

My tongue trailed the seam of her lips, down to her chin and chest, and then my mouth greedily nibbled on her breasts. Her nipples swelled while suctioned between my tongue and lips. Zo had the best tits. Full, round, and perky. I felt her bow from the bed, feeding them to me. I swelled even more as her moans turned uncontrolled.

I pulled my hand down between her trembling thighs. *Fuck, she's wet.* She was warm as hell, too. When I saw she couldn't last, I lowered myself between her thighs. Zoey tried thrusting upward to capture my erection. My frisky ass Niña was coming alive.

"Calm the hell down," I scolded low in her ear. "You're tight. I'm trying to revive your femininity, not go ape shit on you."

"Stenton," she panted with her eyes closed.

I knew I didn't have much time before she would become irritated. I lowered myself, breaching her lips, hardly giving a full thrust before I felt the friction. Zoey sucked in a breath, feeling penetration. She was extremely tight. So tight, my thrusts weren't making much advancement. I thought quickly.

Descending my upper torso, I brought my mouth next to her ear. "Tell me your travel fantasy."

"Travel fantasy?" she asked, trying to calm her breathing.

"Tell me about an exotic place you want to visit. What do you see yourself doing there?"

"Oh." Zoey tried to pull her hips up to meet my marginal pushes inside her.

"Let me do this, Zo. We have plenty of time," I breathed into her ear. "I don't want to hurt you."

"Okay," she moaned. "Ummm…travel fantasy. *Br*-Brazil…I'd love to take the cog-train to visit the Cristo Redentor. I'm sure it's beautiful. And—ahhh!" she winced. I pulled back. "View the sun setting from the Two Brothers Mountain."

I could feel Zoey relax as her mind took off with thoughts of Rio de Janeiro. I continued with my gentle thrusts, happy to have had a release already because there was no way I could keep this mild rhythm and disposition without it. Even at this pace, I was reminded of how incredible it was to experience Zoey this intimately.

"Two Brothers?" I grunted.

"Yeah…" she breathed. "It is the perfect viewpoint that allows you to witness the social contrasts in Rio de Janeiro. The sunset is *s*-said to *be*—huhh…" she groaned. "…romantic."

I felt leeway. Zoey was just about where I needed her to be.

"I'm going to take you there. As soon as you're ready, you'll see everything Brazil has to offer," I whispered in her ear as I picked up my rhythm and switched angles in my hips.

Zoey's mouth collapsed as she tried to focus her heavy eyes on me. She caught on to my promise. The next thing I knew she pulled my face into hers and wildly threw her tongue into my mouth as she pushed her hips up to meet mine. My Niña was fucking me back, telling of her renewed confidence. In no time, her moans increased in volume as did her breathing. I was giving her all I had without attempting to break her in two. She felt incredible.

The moment my mouth lowered to her left breast and pulled her nipple deep into my mouth, Zoey's body tensed. I knew she was preparing for her release. And she did. Zoey threw her pelvis into me with rough upswings that animated the fuck out of me. I brought my head back up to witness her soar, and damn was it beautiful. Her eyes were wild and her mouth slacked as she sang octaves that pleasured something deep inside of me. I needed to at least hear it again.

So, as soon as I was convinced she was done, I abruptly pulled out, backed up on the bed and buried my face at the apex of her smooth thighs. My tongue twirled, my lips rubbed and sucked, and my nose teased. I lost all control, inhaling her sensual musk that intoxicated me, deluded me of any conflicts we may have had. I ate Zoey like a starved man, because I was. I'd missed her terribly, but didn't know how to convey it to her.

When Zoey's hands cupped the back of my head and her pussy pumped into my face, it was my turn to moan. We cried out together, though only one of us orgasmed. I'd never experienced anything like that in my life. *Only Zoey.*

While waiting for her breathing to calm, I showered a trail of kisses from her thighs up to her belly where I kissed and licked and caressed with the side of my face, worshiping the incubator that gave life to my son. To me. I whispered into her skin messages of admiration and appreciation of her plight into motherhood. Her hand came down, fingering my scalp, and I glanced up at her. Her eyes were zoomed into the ceiling and I believe she was fighting to keep her tears from falling. We lay there in silence for some time while she came down from her flight. I struggled not to get caught up. It was damn hard.

I scooped her up in my arms and took her into the shower where I paid more homage to her body. When we were done, I moisturized and massaged Zoey then instructed her to get in bed to nap. Her eyes were heavy and not in a salacious manner.

As I rolled the covers over her, she muttered, "But you didn't...you know." Her eyes went down to my semi-erect penis.

I gave her a one-cheek smile. "This isn't about me." Then I

stilled, abruptly sobering. "You okay, Zo?"

She gasped and her eyes widened in reaction. "Are you leaving already?"

I chuckled. "No. I'm going to check in on my kid while you nap."

Her eyes softened. "You look like you could use a nap, too."

I couldn't help but smile at her muffled yawn.

"I'll sleep later, Niña."

"Here? With me?" She didn't attempt to mask her desires. That was Zoey; she left all pretenses and games out of the equation. I'd always admired her for that.

Amused, I scoffed, "If that's allowed."

She nodded softly before turning over to find sleep.

Zoey

I slept for nearly three hours. That was unheard of with an infant around, especially one you're nursing. Speaking of which, I knew it was time for Jordan to eat. In fact, it was an hour after his feeding time. With heavy breasts, I leaped to the bathroom to relieve myself and wash the sleep from my face. Stenton was in my apartment somewhere and after what he put on me earlier, the awareness of my appearance had resurfaced.

I tried to wrap my mind around what his visit meant. Paul called me with instructions that made it clear what Stenton's intentions were. The manner in which he informed—not requested—for me to welcome Eligia into my home and to my son, and to wear a piece of sexy lingerie that had been delivered first thing in the morning gave an indication of his intention to have Jordan cared for while we had other plans. Intimate ones. I didn't know where the gesture had derived, and even hesitated with going with the flow. However, I had to quickly get honest with myself about the loneliness I'd been plagued with and how I teetered on the edge of depression. As arcane as Stenton had been, he'd never been callous.

When I gaited into the living room where I heard voices, I saw Stenton's long legs sprawled out on the floor, bouncing Jordan on his thigh. Those two were always a sight that swelled my heart.

"Hey, look who it is!" Stenton announced excitedly to Jordan. "Food!"

With a pleased smile, I smoothed my housecoat and sat on the sofa above them. "I expected to come out here to his fussing. It's time for him to eat."

Just then, Jordan started to cry for me. Stenton handed him over to my outstretched arms.

"I've been a successful distraction. I was trying to give you ten more minutes before we disturbed your much needed nap… Oh, wow. He's ready," Stenton observed as he watched me uncover my left breast to feed Jordan.

Jordan's little hands reached up to grab me into his pouted mouth. He was beautiful. His need of me to eat was a phenomenon like none other. It strengthened our bond that much more. I glanced over to Stenton to find his eyes dark and heavy.

My nose wrinkled. "Does this arouse you?" I couldn't believe the look in his eyes.

"Everything about your postpartum state seems to arouse me," he informed hoarsely and I couldn't miss his quizzical expression. I guessed that odd fact surprised him, too.

I cocked my head to the side, stirring the pot. "What about my pre-postpartum body?"

Stenton snorted sexily, "That, too." He was adorable when slightly embarrassed.

"Wonder where that will leave me when I'm done nursing." I murmured that while peering down at Jordan.

I heard Stenton exhale. "I don't imagine much changing. You're a very attractive woman, Zoey."

Not attractive enough for you to want more than friendship.

I didn't speak those words out loud for fear of ruining what he'd been trying to accomplish by being there.

We sat in silence as Jordan fed himself into a sleepy stupor. He was just about done when Eligia appeared, gingerly waiting on him to finish with a cordial smile on her face.

With her hand crossed in front of her, she informed at a comforting volume, "Lunch is ready. I can change Jordan and put him down for another nap when you're done."

Initially, I dithered, unaccustomed to someone else caring for Jordan. Only family assisted with him, but they were limited due to our distance. Ruth stayed over last night because she was meeting friends here in the city, so she helped, and that was a bit out of the norm. Stenton was extremely familiar with the care of Jordan, so when they had their time together, I pretty much stepped back, giving them their space.

When Jordan's suction broke, I knew he was done. I wasn't exactly empty, but realized since Stenton kept him busy for so long, the kid was exhausted. I chanced a glance over to Stenton, down on the floor to the right of me. He gave me a warm regard and I couldn't be rude to his help after that. Besides, I was having second thoughts about having help.

I handed a dozing Jordan over to Eligia who thanked me after arranging him over her shoulder to burp and paced to the back of the apartment.

"Time to eat," Stenton announced cheerily, breaking my attention from my baby being hauled off. I couldn't help but believe it was by design.

Just off the main area of the kitchen, next to the floor-to-ceiling window, was a table set for two. It smelled even better in closer proximity than it did permeating the apartment all afternoon. We sat down to eat.

"What's this?" I asked, feeling my stomach growl. "Smells awesome."

"Bacalao Encebollado," Stenton curled his tongue around like a Caribbean native as he fixed his napkin on his lap. "Stewed cod fish, rice and beans, and plantains. Eligia said the fish will help with your breastfeeding. Something about the baby's brain development."

"Oh," I squeaked, stumped by her thoughtfulness. "Funny that you mention her extra mile. I've been having second thoughts about childcare."

Stenton's eyes rose. I was sure I had his full attention.

"About a week after I had Jordan...while I was under an insomniac spell, I reapplied for school."

"Where?" he asked almost desperately.

"Princeton, of course."

I could see Stenton visibly relax. That was weird. He motioned for me to continue.

"I'd put it to the back of my mind after doing it. Then a few weeks ago, my old advisor emailed me, excited about my application. She assured me that Wharton would still be interested if I could jump right back into my undergrad career. I know she's trying to discourage a long break. I've struggled with my decision, but..." I bit my bottom lip as I observed Stenton's eager posture. "I think it'll be best for me to go back...this fall."

His eyelids fluttered and he sighed deeply. "Is that what you were stalling to share? Why were you so afraid to tell me you're ready to go back to school? I couldn't be happier for you. I support your decisions, you know that."

I still held on to my breath. "I mean, I know in the agreement I signed it said a nanny would be paid for in full as well as tuition, but..."

"Zo, that's for wherever you decide to go."

"But Princeton is expensive—"

"It's also where you were when your plans were disrupted. It's the least I can do."

I rolled my eyes at nothing in particular, feeling frustrated by the glaring topic once again. This "situation" haunted my private thoughts, relentlessly.

"Stenton, it took the two of us to make a baby. I don't want you to take the blame for the consequence of something I consented to, wholly." I made sure to align my eyes with his.

His expression morphed into a scowl, making it abundantly clear he was annoyed.

"You had to live through disappointing your parents and community, put your career on hold, carry a baby for almost ten months, experience your body expanding, being isolated, and then deliver my legacy. Me? I still work, still continue with pretty much all the activities I've had since before Jordan, and add to all of that, be congratulated by the President of the United States for having a child. Doesn't sound like a fair trade off to me." He lowered his chin. "Go back to school, Zo. Resume your career path. If all I have to do is write a damn check to grant you that, it's a drop in the bucket compared to what you've been through over the past year."

I was speechless. When he put it that way, I forgot how disconnected it felt like we'd been. It made me reconsider the cave I'd been alone in while everyone else went about life. Stenton was offering me an opportunity to make a life for my son and me. He was giving me the tools to continue the journey I thought I'd derailed.

I bit back the cry that begged to be released. I'd never been much of a crier, but lately my hormones had been off the charts.

I nodded softly. "Thanks, Stenton."

His thick brows peaked as Stenton shook his head categorically. "No. Thank you."

Slowly, an assured smile worked its way onto my face. "Now, let's eat. You need to restore that energy you exerted earlier."

He laughed. *God, I've missed that.* It warmed something deep within...this time carnal.

"In that case, you need to clean your plate for what I have in store until I board my flight on Thursday." He sounded sober with that one.

"You're staying until then?"

His brows met. "Yeah, Zo, damn! What's so hard to believe about that?"

I smiled broadly. A goofy one. A goofy smile I couldn't contain. And it felt great.

Chapter Fourteen

THEN: *August 2008*

Zoey

"Zo," he cried out lazily as I rested on my haunches with my head in his pelvis.

Stenton's head rolled back and forth, spurring my inspiration to keep pushing him into my mouth and pull him out with a suctioned jaw.

God I've missed this.

This expression. This communication. This interaction. His vulnerability. His need of me. While in his lap, I forgot about the loneliness, the exhaustion, the confusion, and the waiting game I played for Stenton's ultimate commitment. When I felt the sweat beads from his thighs against my arms, I knew he was nearing.

"Zo, baby, not like this. I don't wanna come like this," his throaty cry was raw and so…masculine. I missed having a man in my bed, at my mercy, in my mouth—and suddenly in my body.

I released him from my mouth with one final suction. When my eyes met Stenton's face, I saw his bottom lip between his teeth. His tattoos were all glistening, his chest lifted and dropped with hyper rhythm. And his long and lean arms were raised above his head where his wrists were tied together.

Stenton agreed to me tying him up tonight. Having had more than an amenable day today since our heart-to-heart over lunch yesterday, we'd had a wonderful time talking, playing with Jordan, and even ended the day by going out to a quiet dinner alone. Eligia kept Jordan while we continued catching up.

When we returned, Stenton gave Jordan his bath, I fed him then handed him back over to his dad to be put down. For the first time in over a year my heart didn't feel so weighed down. We paid my tuition for the upcoming semester, sealing the deal for me to fulfill my dream. Stenton seemed just as excited as I was. What better way to celebrate than with our sweaty bodies rubbing against each other in passionate fury?

When I handed Jordan over to Stenton to put down, I threw the question out there with little expectation of him agreeing to letting me tie him up. In all the time Stenton and I had been together he'd only entertained me a couple of times. After our lunch together yesterday, he pulled out the restraints from one of his bags and we played for hours into the night.

Tonight, I had him in simple nylon restraints using one pillar of the bed. With the way he wriggled underneath me, I didn't know how long he'd stay this way, so I quickly grabbed a condom to sheath him before sinking down on him.

"*Sssssss…*" he blew through his teeth, feeling the friction.

I was too excited to go slow. Something about having him tied up made me appreciate his reasons for inclining to this particular kink. Stenton's muscles bunched and even rolled at times as he pulled against the device encasing his big wrists. I moved up and down on him, enjoying the fullness of him inside of me. Stenton started to move with me, flexing his hips up from the mattress as I pushed down on him. I saw the tip of his pink tongue peek between pinched lips and decided I wanted to feel that, too. I lowered my torso to capture his lips and rolled my tongue around his mouth as I rocked my pelvis against his. Stenton felt amazing and I could feel my orgasm stirring.

Suddenly, I needed his hands on me, so I quickly rushed up his long arms to release the swivel snaps of the D-rings and separated the restraints. This wasn't the easiest feat considering how tall his is. It was somewhat like climbing a tree. It was such a far reach that Stenton had to thrust alone as I released him.

Before I was completely done, Stenton yelped, "Fuck, Niña! I'm about to come! The shit you do!"

Then his big hands slapped my skin as he clasped my hips, ramming into me. My eyes slammed shut as I felt pleasure spikes shoot through each corner of my frame. My orgasm hit me quicker than I expected, and abruptly I was engulfed in immeasurable bliss. As my body began its first waves of euphoria, gyrating uncontrollably with pleasure, I grabbed the post he was once attached to and could hear Stenton's ragged breaths beneath me as we met our release together.

The best!

It was magical, the things he did to me. His ability to make me feel so reverenced and valued. I floated above earth. Felt stronger than I had in a long time. In that moment, I collided with the clarity of my future. Felt like the old Zoey. The one that could take on the world.

Then I needed to see him. Experience his eyes. When I settled my sight below I wasn't prepared for what I saw.

"Holy mother of—! Stenton!" I yelped.

Licking his lips, he smiled. "It's okay. You're good."

"No! Nooooo!" I straightened and covered my breasts. "I'm so sorry!"

"Don't sweat it. It's all good, Zo," he assured as he wiped my breast milk from his face.

Stenton's teeth were on full display as he smiled. His eyes were tight from his recent ascent and his tongue wouldn't stop swiping his mouth. I shuffled off his body, wincing at the disconnect, leaped into the bathroom, turning on the shower, and barely felt the ice cold water against my still hyper-sensitive skin.

"Zo... Heeey..." Stenton soothed as he entered the shower and wrapped me against his hot hard frame, a stark contrast in temperatures, making my body jerk. He lowered his mouth to the side of my face. "Calm the hell down."

"I *d*-don't think I've ever *f*-felt so mortified," I attempted through chattering teeth, I was freezing.

I felt Stenton steel behind me. He cupped my chin so that I could meet his eyes. While his face was wrinkled, there was a comforting smile playing on his heart-shaped lips.

"Zo, this is me here. I'm no stranger. That milk feeds my son." It took a few seconds for me to calm, but I eventually nodded, willing myself to believe he was okay with having my breast milk splattered over his face. Slowly, I turned to face him. I mean, it was Stenton and no random one-night-stand. My arms rounded his waist and I placed my head on his chest. "Besides, I'm not new to your bodily fluids. Remember, I'm the one who proved you can enjoy sex even when you're menstruating."

I cocked a brow. "You're the only man I've had sex with while menstruating. You're the man who took my virginity." I made sure to include cynicism in my tone.

Stenton angled his head, "Ummmm…I didn't take anything. I was actually forced to catch it if memory serves me correctly."

I slapped his chest. "Stenton! Is that what you tell people?"

"Yup. Everyone who interviews me. And I make sure to include how perky your tits were the first time I saw them." As I laughed he cupped my cheeks from behind, pushing me into him. He rubbed his nose against mine as he whispered, "You look even better now with the weight. You're incredibly sexy, Zoey. Don't doubt for a moment you're less than what you were before Jordan. You're even more attractive now."

I believed him. It was easy to. There was no way Stenton was lying to me when I considered the gleam in his eyes as he spoke to me and held me to his frame. We were so close that I could detect the rhythm of his heartbeat. I took him at the sides of his face and kissed him tenderly. In that moment, I knew there was no other man who could love me or enrich my spirit the way Stenton did.

A few hours later, I couldn't find my way to sleep, so I stayed up with the television on at a low volume while on my laptop. I joined a few chat rooms for my upcoming classes, wanting to know who I'd be spending my semester with. I was happy to be able to hook up with a few old friends.

Stenton was fast asleep beside me on his back with his arms and legs stretched wide. All I saw was a tatted octopus in my bed. He was exhausted. This was supposed to be a restful few days for him before he did a circus round of commercial and print ad shoots and then go right back into training.

My eyes started to get heavy, so I logged off my laptop and my attention unconsciously wandered over to the television where a rerun of the Wendy Williams show was on. I caught it as she introduced her next guest, Erika Erceg. The crowd went up in applause as the buxom beauty strutted out in a white fitted midi dress with five inch gold heels. She was beautiful: shiny jet black tresses, olive skin, long and thick eyelashes, plump pouty lips, and the perfect set of hips and booty. Erika was sinfully striking, which was the crux of her success. She didn't sing, act or dance, but made her family's surname a brand. She was also Tynisha's nemesis for some reason: solely diva issues if you asked me.

"So," Wendy started her question while fluffing her hair. "What's this I hear about your progression with your big crush— wait…how long have you been crushing on this man, Erika?"

Erika's flawless face falls into the perfect bashful expression. Her cheeks heat up visibly, and in the same moment, the crowd goes crazy over the picture that appears on the back screen of Stenton Rogers. I use his formal name because that is who the crowd sees, who she sees. There, in fact, were several pictures that flashed on the screen. One with him in his team's uniform, another of him posing shirtless, and one black and white photo of him in a pushup stance in the rain.

Another thing I observed was how Stenton was drop-dead gorgeous in all of them, completely stunning. Don't get me wrong: even his sleepy face lasciviously stirred something deep within, but gosh! The producers hit the mark trying to demonstrate him being crush-worthy. Even I'd suddenly seen him in a different light. I experienced the lust Erika did.

The last picture to flash was with Jordan about a month ago. That one stung. It was personal, of my child. I had to quickly remind myself that Jordan's father was a public figure and he'd be as exposed as Stenton would allow.

Erika's gushing broke my daze.

"It's been like…oh my god…all his career. He's always been so hot. When I would see him years ago, I would completely freeze, couldn't even speak."

Wendy laughed along with her receptive audience. "So, have you talked with him or been out on a date with him?"

"We've been out, but not like…alone. We've definitely been chatting a lot lately on the phone," Erika offered.

"Awwww…" Wendy sang. "That's too cute." Erika's cheeks flamed again. "So, when was the last time you saw him?"

I couldn't believe the amount of airtime being devoted to a crush.

"A few weeks ago at an event. We didn't get to talk for long. You know he's always being swept away somewhere."

"Yeah, Stenton Rogers has the most endorsement deals in the league, I've been told. You think you can handle that with your busy schedule?"

Erika licked her lips before nodding her head animatedly. The audience went up with that one, too.

"Okay! I don't know about you all," Wendy pointed to the audience. "…but I caught that." She laughed along with Erika. "Okay, so when was the last time you talked on the phone with him?"

"Two days ago."

Two days ago? My body jerked in bed. Then my neck snapped over at an undisturbed Stenton.

"And was that conversation promising?"

"It actually was. We agreed to spend more time with each other this coming season. I wish it could be right away, but I understand he's busy and all."

"Yeah!" Wendy nearly shouted. "Busy with a newborn baby!" she screamed to the audience. "Does he talk about that? I'm sure that's probably why he can't start anything new. You should be careful with a man who's just had a baby. That baby momma has rights, honey!" The audience clapped in agreement.

Erika smiled placidly. Was she an airhead or something?

"And you, missy," Wendy continued. "Are you and Shirez over with? That was a pretty bad breakup less than a year ago. You know, Stenton is over thirty. He's probably thinking with his head up here." She pointed to her head near her brows. The audience agreed with their raucous applauses. "What was the last thing you said to Mr. Rogers?"

Seriously?

I don't know why that question stabbed me in the gut. In fact, the longer this conversation went on, the more anxious I became. Stenton and I had a glorious two days together and although we were not solid and had no plans on extending it, I didn't want the bliss to end.

"Well, I told him when we do get together, I want to see how far down his tattoos go, and that I'm nearsighted."

The room went up in a roar far more than at any previous point during the interview. My belly lurched and my arms wrapped around my waist. I found myself staring straight into Erika's brown eyes, feeling vindictive. My eyes squinted and nose flared.

"All right! On that note, we'll be right back with Erika Erceg, talking about her new makeup line!" Wendy announced as the theme music began to play, alerting of the commercial break. Wendy turned and double high-five'd Erika as she giggled like a sexy vixen.

My stomach was now rolling over with nervous energy. I knew it was a direct reaction to my rare case of jealousy. I wanted to wake Stenton up to ask about his relationship with this exotic socialite. I wanted to ask him if he called her before or after he called me the night before he arrived at my apartment. I wanted to ask him what his feelings were for her. If he found her just as sexy as every other man on this planet seemed to. I wanted to know if he believed all of his praises of my postpartum body, which he seemed to be infatuated with, and if they came close to how he perceived hers.

The most lewd curiosity was if she could make him lose control like I did. If he would claw her hips, shoulders or the back of her head the way that he did mine when I drove him crazy between my thighs or in my mouth.

Suddenly, I needed to recall myself.

I clicked off the television with the remote and turned toward Stenton, straddling his muscular frame. Creating a trail down his torso with my tongue, I shuffled down past his belly button and then his wiry bush of hairs until I hit the base of his penis. I felt him stir beneath me, even heard a moan. That incited my need to arouse him, to drive him crazy in the area Erika was so curious about.

I twirled my tongue around the bulbous head of his penis, loving the feeling of it swelling in my mouth. The smooth and thin skin encasing his steely erection felt superb against my tongue. As my hands wrapped around the base of him, the tip of my tongue probed at the opening of his head, tasting the first discharge of his pre-essence. The creamy taste of his viscid fluid that I spread around him before swallowing drove me wild.

"Fuck, Zo," Stenton stretched out, awakening from his reposed state.

His big hands curved around my bobbing head. And when a groan escaped him, I suctioned harder, sheathed my teeth even more. I worked him further in with each dip I took.

"Zo," he cried out again and I felt supreme. It was petty of me, but I didn't care. I needed to feel that I wasn't a young amateur who seduced him and became an unexpected dependent by carelessly getting pregnant, changing his life forever. I wanted to be a skillful lover worthy of him being in my bed, so I took my time pleasuring him.

"I'm going to come, Zo. Come here," he demanded through gritted teeth.

"Unn-unn!" I moaned. Then I pulled his wide crest from my mouth. "I want it here." I countered and quickly took him in again, working him even more.

I didn't want his release just yet, I was having too much fun controlling his continence. His wide thighs rose and fell around me as he fought, squirming, and his pelvis strained beneath me trying to contain his pleasure.

"Zo…I don't know about this!"

I did. And suddenly I did want his release now. I wanted to snap his source of control.

"Elizabeth," Stenton's upper torso shot from the bed as he moaned.

The rope snapped and he gave me exactly what I was looking for. He called me Elizabeth, a name I'd always shunned, believing it was more fitting of an old woman. I wanted a youthful name, hence my self-appointed moniker, Zoey. For the first time in my life, I appreciated my name. Yearned for it to come from this man. I craved to know he viewed me as a real woman. A woman he didn't need to tolerate or care for, but one who could be viewed as an adequate partner. I longed for that validation from him, believing it to be the reason why he'd never chosen me. With this revelation, I jerked him more fervently and suctioned with more of a grip in my jaw.

Then his hands roughly pushed on my head as his hips drove into my head. My breasts felt heavy, but this time not ready to express milk. I could feel my excitement at the apex of my thighs. He was ready.

Within seconds, hot, virile, creamy fluids shot into my mouth. I had no time to think. I could only relax my tongue and let his release spurt into the back of my throat, reveling in my ability to render him undone in this manner. His breathing was harsh, rough air sloughing from his lungs as he trembled most vulnerably at my ministrations. There was nothing better.

When he was done, Stenton reached down to pull me up and clutched me into his arms. As I lay over his hard chest, I could hear his racing heart. The heart I wanted into so badly.

August 2008

"Good looking out, Paul." Stenton ended the call next to me at the island in the kitchen. He glanced over to Eligia, who was standing in front of the subzero refrigerator unit, waiting for him to finish. "You're good to go. They can have your things moved in tonight. A driver will be here at noon. As far as meal preparations and scheduling, I'll leave it to you two to settle that. I know Zoey will need some time to study outside of classes. Let me know if you need anything else."

Eligia nodded her head before excusing herself. It was official. I had a nanny and help around the apartment while I returned to school full time. *But is that all?*

"There's that damn clicking sound again. At least I have confirmation that something's up," he noted. "You've been brooding all damn morning. You sure you're okay with this?"

I wet my dry lips before scraping them in between my teeth. I never demanded anything from Stenton when it came to our relationship since he broke up with me after the Cayman Islands. I needed to finally confront this thing between us—or lack thereof. I didn't think long before going for it.

"How soon before you'll have Jordan around other women?"

Stenton's expression quickly turned jarred. In all fairness, I couldn't blame him.

As he examined my eyes, his head slowly rolled left to right and then left to right again, ruminatively.

"I can't answer that question. It's not a bridge I've thought to crossed," he spoke slowly, and I could see the cogs of his mind churning.

"But you will…soon, I'm sure."

"Zoey, I don't know where this is coming from. Perhaps if you can tell me what's going on in that busy head of yours, I can provide a more adequate answer."

My eyes dropped as I tried to think of my next move.

"The christening…this whole period since our "break up" after the Cayman Islands," I used air quotations because we were so far removed from that time; so tightly intertwined and yet I still didn't feel as close to Stenton as I did before I got pregnant. "…the reason I've not kept in touch is because I need a barrier from you. I need to protect myself from the pain I feel from when you stole my heart. When I hear your voice or when I'm near you, I feel things that delude me. It makes me want to be with you like we were before my stupid…" I bit my lip.

Jordan is a blessing. He's not a mistake.

Stenton's face wrinkled and he visibly heaved. I tossed my gaze away from him until the tears rescinded and I could speak again.

"I want to be like that again. I want to be your best friend and… lover. I want you to want to be with me, not just take care of me," my words turned inaudible as my emotions peaked.

Stenton's mouth dropped.

"I saw the Wendy Williams show last night. I saw Erika." I looked him deep in the eyes. That's when I lost him. Stenton actually rolled his eyes and they didn't immediately return to me. "Is she the woman you told me about when we first met? The one you said was a hook up by your PR teams?"

Stenton swallowed with a clenched jaw. "Yes."

"Why haven't you been with her all this time?"

"I've been kind of wrapped up in something else in case you haven't been awake for the past two years or so."

I ignored his quip. "Are you going to date her?"

Then his eyes met mine again. "So, I now see the inspiration behind the superb blow job in my sleep." My eyes jumped to his, cautioning his audacity, and his pierced into me, not backing down. "But why are you asking about her? Why is she of any fucking consequence to us?"

I jumped from my seat, quickly angered by the direction of this conversation. Maybe I didn't think this through, but I realized I was at a pivotal place in my life. Yeah, I'd had a baby, but my career track was about to resume. My life would have traction again. I wanted it all, including Stenton. My best friend. My lover.

"Why can't we be together?" I turned to him.

He shifted in the bar chair. "And do what? Live together?" He snorted. "Get married?" I nearly leaped in his direction at that. "Tell me what you want and I'll make it happen, Zo! I'll go out and get the fucking ring right now. We can be at city hall in two hours! Just tell me, what do you want?" Stenton yelled angrily.

My body trembled, my eyes glossed and my hands balled into fists. His words were elementary, but his tone was derisive. "I don't know!" I grated through gritted teeth, meeting his volume. Never had I felt so infuriated by not being able to articulate my feelings, being misunderstood.

Stenton stood and got into my face. "And *that's* why we're not *together*," he grated, his voice eerily low, searing me with the depth of that revelation. "You have no fucking clue as to what your *together* means." He violently yanked his body away and then stormed off to the floor-to-ceiling window just a few feet from me.

We stayed that way for long minutes, trying to bide time to allow tempers to cool. I was shaken by his argument, but couldn't deny its validity. It still stung. I may not have known what exactly I wanted to term us, but I knew I wanted him with me every day. I wanted more. I wanted his intimacy that went far beyond sex and yet I wanted that, too. I was so in love with this man that I couldn't think straight. I was once again deluded by his presence after just two days.

"Listen, Zoey." I turned to his back as he still faced the window. "When we started this…shit…you were so young. Privately, I struggled so damn much with your age. You were tender and inexperienced beyond your virginity. But when I was with you, all of those doubts, fears, and reservations fell by the wayside. I tossed caution to the wind and got swept up by your beauty, aptitude, ability to be transparent, your forceful spirit…the way you squared your fucking shoulders and kept your chin in the air against harsh winds."

Stenton turned to me. "The way you challenged me, and forced new lenses to my eyes…the way you always ride for your family, and the way you love me with no pretenses, seeing past all the bullshit of my lifestyle." He stopped and furrowed his brows. "I mean, you've never asked to go to a game. Have you even watched one yet?" My eyes swept the floor. "You and Sarah; you two don't give a shit about what I do on the court. You make me feel valued off of it." Facing me, Stenton lowered himself, aligning his head with mine. "Shit. That's not something I can get from a fucking Erika Erceg. I've been in the league thirteen years and I've never come across a woman who saw past the ball in my hand or the bank account that follows it."

Stenton then cupped my face with his hands. "I'm not going anywhere. I swear on my life that I will always be here for you and Jordan. No one could ever replace or compare to what you two bring me. I don't know what this next step will be for us. You're going back to school and I'm starting a new season. One thing I do know is that I'll be here for you and for Jordan." He exhaled and closed his eyes before opening them again. "I love you so fucking much, Zo, it scares the shit out of me. But I will not force you to make a call before you're ready. You need to experience life, conquer those goals you told me about two years ago. Go off and fucking take over the world. If you realize it's me you want when it's all said and done, I'll be here waiting."

The tears fell from my eyes, and mucous from my nostrils. I felt the emptiness once again, however this time I had answers. He wasn't ready. Stenton still wasn't choosing me. Oddly, I did feel he wouldn't go too far while I *"grew up."* Maybe there was hope after all. Maybe we'd one day be together.

I nodded in silence. My eyes were to the floor because I couldn't look at him. I couldn't face him with the tears and snotty face. It would add to his reasons for thinking I wasn't mature enough for him.

Stenton's phone pinged on the counter. He exhaled, exasperated, as his lids slowly closed. He placed his forehead on mine.

"That's my driver. I have to run home and pack for my flight. I'll be back in a couple of weeks. My schedule is going to get crazy, but I'll be here as much as I can, even if that means sleeping here more than my own place. I know you're about to be busy preparing for school." He used his index finger to lift my chin, forcing my eyes to meet his. "Zo, if you ever need anything—I don't give a damn how small or...personal the request—reach out to me. I don't like the distance. I've not done well with it. I want that to change. Okay?"

My answer took a while to surface. I'd never been much of a liar. It was actually something I preferred to be absent from all close relationships I had. This thing with Stenton though was entirely different. It was a miscellany of emotions—contradicting ones—I'd never experienced. I knew I needed the space. I needed to work on me to become the woman Stenton needed, not the girl he perceived me to be. School would help with that. I had another start and I was prepared to take it. I had a lot to prove.

"Okay," I murmured as I gently removed his hands from the sides of my face to swipe my tears and running nose. I forced a smile as I backed out of his person, grabbed a napkin from the center of the island, and started to clean my face. "You're right. I have lots to do to prepare for this new phase of my life. You go ahead and say goodbye to Jordan, and we'll see you when you get back into town." My voice was less shaky than my belly as I lied through my teeth. My smile was still in tow as I exited the room without saying another word.

From that moment, I had a new charge of pulling out that *old* Elizabeth, and polishing her anew. I had to chase my future in order to find me.

Now: July 2014

Stenton

"You heard me, Dad?"

"Huhn?" My head jerks toward Jordan.

"I asked which one I should choose; Mariah or Marie?" Jordan asks, tussling with his wrestling figurines on the bed next to me.

I wrinkle my eyebrows, trying to recall previous conversations about these girls. "Mariah is the Puerto Rican girl and Marie is the Haitian, right?"

"Yeah."

I shrug. At least he's an equal opportunist. "I really don't have an answer for that. How about neither? What's wrong with being single?"

My son is only six and talking about girlfriends, not just me teasing him on the subject like before. *What are they teaching at that preparatory academy?* My attention goes once again to the muffled voices I can swear to hearing beneath my room.

Is that her?

"I know. I told them both that, but they keep saying everybody else is hooking up—"

"Hooking up? What the hell, JR?" He has my attention again that quickly. "You know about peer pressure. Your mother and I both talk to you about leadership. There's nothing wrong with blazing your own trail. You don't need a girlfriend to be the man."

"That's what I told everybody in the class. I said my Dad is the coolest man on the planet and he ain't got no girlfriend."

"Doesn't have."

"Huhn?"

"Your Dad doesn't have a girlfriend," I correct. I'm not paying out the ass in tuition for my son to speak like he's from the fucking Westside of Brick City.

There's a knock at the door.

"Come in," Jordan calls out.

The door cracks and in seconds, I see her tentative smile as she scans the room while walking in. She's wearing a simple fitted white tee with light gray cropped jeans and flip flops. Zoey's mane is pushed back with her long hair falling onto her shoulder blades. Her face is naked and her visage is breathtaking.

"Mommy!" Jordan jumps from the bed and is in his mother's arms in milliseconds.

Lucky kid.

Zoey giggles. "Whoa! If this is how you are after just two days, what's your summer going to look like, kid?" She smiles without guards just the way I met her seven years ago.

Jordan is clasped to her small frame, being silly. Zoey's eyes trail up to me. "Hey."

I fight my excitement at seeing her and offer her a one-cheek smile instead. "Glad you made it down safely."

"I did. Even survived Bernard's snoring on the plane." She attempts to pull JR from her.

Bernard. I forgot he was coming.

"Mom said you guys made it in this morning. I'm jealous," she calls over to me, then drags her body with Jordan still clamped onto her towards me on the bed. "I'm sure she cooked for a castle."

"Yeah, she did," I confirm. "I'm sure there's more left." Zoey stumbles. "Jordan, off your moms, dude. She just got in," I chide. I know he's happy to see her—shit, *I'm* happy to see her. Zoey has that effect on people. Her presence lights up a room.

"Mom, come look at these new wrestlers I got." Jordan hops back on the bed.

Zoey follows and tosses herself on the bed as well, at a close proximity. I haven't shared a bed with her in so long, which could likely be the reason my heart rate just increased. After paying a few minutes of attention to Jordan's animated talk and fight with his action dolls, she turns towards me.

"So, Mexico this summer?"

"Yeah. I have a photo shoot out there and I figured I could take JR to Punta Mita."

"Nice!" She beams.

"Mom, you should come," Jordan calls over his shoulder.

"I wish." Zoey pouts playfully. "I have work and meetings. Tynisha is still holding rehearsals for her fashion show, and Bernard has a gig in Baltimore next weekend. I don't know when I'll be able to slip in time to sleep."

"You could always sleep here," I murmur slickly.

Zoey's head swings in my direction and the first thing I see is her collapsed jaw.

I don't speak and neither does she. She caught my fucking message. I can tell as my eyes descend to her engorged nipples. She follows my line of sight and when hers return to my face, mine stall before meeting them. I see her mask slip. I still affect her. All Zoey has to do is say the fucking word and I'll be whatever she wants me to be...or do whatever she wants me to do. I don't give a damn what she does with Bernard; he can't fuck her the way I can. I'll make sure of it.

"Well...well...well, if it isn't my favorite lady with...her son and...his dad."

I glance up to find Bernard's pseudo-cocky ass, standing in the doorframe, smirking smugly.

I say pseudo because his arrogance doesn't drip naturally to me. It seems so contrived. I've always felt it's what he feels he must offer to Stenton Rogers, the father of his girlfriend's child. He's one of billions that only see the ballplayer and not the man...a detrimental mistake for a man who's proposing to govern the house my seed lives in.

Like that shit'll ever happen.

Zoey jumps off the bed and nervously leaps over to him. His arrogant smile broadens as he takes her at the small of her back.

"Oh, what's up, B," Jordan murmurs noncommittally.

Bernard's neck jerks back. I stifle my laugh. Zoey gasps.

"It's Bernard," Zoey lightly scolds. I notice her nipples are no longer taut under her man's arm, *under his touch.*

"Yeah," Jordan returns, his eyes still below on his toys.

A boy after my own heart. I've never kicked Bernard's back in to JR. Real men never do. Let's just say he can sense his Dad's enemies.

"What's wrong, young fellow?" Bernard perks up. "Your mom told you the news about us moving?"

"Moving?" Jordan and I croak out at the same time.

"Yeah. I can't stay in another man's place with my bride. We need our own space, to make room for our newly formed family," Bernard proudly announces.

My chest tightens and I can feel my nose flare. Zoey's eyes shoot to me. Her anxiousness is obvious.

"Well, that hasn't been decided yet, Bernard. You just broached the topic last night." Zoey runs her hand down his chest onto his belly, causing my abs to flinch. I hope no one picked it up.

"I'm sure once you two come to an agreement, you'll discuss it with me." I look Zoey directly in the eye.

She nods emphatically. "Of course."

"I'm tired, sweetheart," Bernard prompts.

Zoey gasps nervously as she tosses a glance my way. "Well, it's off to bed we go. It's been a long day." Her plastered smile is so contrived. Then her attention goes to Jordan. "You," she calls out pointedly. "Make sure you brush your teeth thoroughly before turning in."

"I know, Mommy," Jordan whines.

"Goodnight, pumpkin," she bids then waves to me before turning for the door.

Bernard gives a dramatic gaze after she leaves the room. Do you know that feeling of having the asshole who's fucking the love of your life throw you a pompous glare? I do. I want to crack Bernard's fucking face. But my hands are tied in more than one way.

"Goodnight, JR," Bernard finally offers.

"Jordan," my son calls out to him as his attention is still devoted to his wrestling men.

"*P*-Pardon?" Bernard stammers.

Jordan's head rises from the bed and he looks directly at Bernard. "My name is Jordan. Only my family calls me JR."

My unwilled smug grin appears. *My fucking seed.* Internally, I beg Bernard to try to check my son. I'd be two milliseconds on his ass.

"Ah... Oh...okay. Good night, Jordan." Bernard appropriately responds. He gives me a respectful nod that I return before he follows Zoey.

I have Jordan wash up for the night and I'm right behind him. He's sleeping in my bedroom tonight, on the pullout, because Alton is staying in his until tomorrow when Tynisha is due to arrive. We're all at Zoey's parents' vacation home in South Carolina for two days. Sarah's having a big birthday celebration tomorrow night. The following morning, Jordan and I will board a plane to Mexico.

Being here with Zoey and Bernard is harder than I realized. He goes boor in my presence all the time. I'm not sure if he can sense my desire for her, but he damn sure makes it clear that he's the leading man in her life. For the moment.

I toss and turn all night, preoccupied with thoughts of Zoey being with another man. The first couple of hours are spent ear-hustling the sounds of their room down the hall. I can hear faint sounds of Zoey's giggles and their conversation. I don't pick up actual words, as they are down the hall and not next door. Nonetheless, I could recognize my Niña's voice from miles away. If I told the truth, I'd say I waited to hear signs of them fucking. I know Zoey fucked Bernard. She made that clear some time ago. However, witnessing it would destroy me. I lay in bed, stretching my ears beyond the walls.

When Sarah sat with the builders for special features on this home that I gifted her for her birthday a few years ago, she dedicated a smaller suite on the opposite end of the house from her own to me. She said I'd always have an open invitation no matter what. I now wonder is Bernard that *what*.

I can't sleep thinking about the finality of Zoey and me. I can't be so unreasonable as to think Bernard will stay in the place that technically belongs to me back in Philly. I mean, is he going to fuck his wife on the bed where I've blown my load in her countless times?

The thought of it makes me sick. And Jordan. Bernard would have more access to my little man than I will. Giving up Zo would be life altering for me. Sharing Jordan would be the death of me.

I don't know what time I fall asleep. My night and day blends so well that I can't tell when one ends and the other begins. I do feel it when a groggy Jordan, with his funky ass breath, is in my face, petitioning my consciousness for something to eat. At this point, I have to get up and start my day.

Kids.

By the time we quickly wash up and head downstairs to raid his grandmother's refrigerator, Jordan and I find her kitchen filled and busy with Sarah, Ruth and Zoey. I glance around the room and see a tight faced Alton, sitting patiently at the table, waiting to be served.

He had to have just rolled out of the bed. I stroll over to him.

"Did you even brush your fucking teeth before sitting at Mom Duke's table?"

Alton's neck jerks back, feigning righteous indignation, but before he can come back, Sarah shoos, "Oh stop being territorial, Stent. Alton has been waiting patiently for the past thirty minutes." She rounds me, standing on her toes, she lands a kiss on my cheek. She knows it warms me. "Besides," she whispers to me. "Everybody knows I only have one son."

Sarah giggles as she watches my squinted eyes soften.

As much as his brutish ways annoy me, it feels great having my man here with me, especially considering this shit with Zoey and her bum-ass boyfriend weighing my shoulders.

When breakfast is ready, everyone sits for the big spread in the dining room. Sarah pulls no punches. She and her daughters cook every damn breakfast item I can think of. She's trained them both well. When days were brighter for Zoey and me, she'd always make sure I had a full and hot meal without request. It was as if it was her innate charge. Today is no different as I sneak my glances of her while she moves swiftly, making sure everything is laid out.

The first plate Zoey makes is Jordan's. What fucks me up is when she serves Bernard his food next. I almost lose my appetite when it lands in front of him. My plate has been in front of me for a while, courtesy of Sarah. She was able to do this because Ruth fixed her father's. Then Sarah serves Alton his food. It's all orchestrated and no one is slighted. But me. Seeing Zoey serve another man and totally skip over me burns the shit out of my pride.

I feel eyes on me and look over to my right, across the table. Alton's eyes are imploring me to chill. I acknowledge him, but don't acquiesce. I'm fucking pissed.

"Ah, Mr. Barrett! You sho' got you an assembly line in here with these women cooking like it's for Master White!"

That was Alton's attempt to break the tension. It's somewhat successful because the only two who do not bust out in laughter are me and Jordan, who doesn't get the slave-themed joke.

Fuck my life.

After breakfast, the guys are sitting outside of the back of the house, killing time. Michael's best friend, Fred, joins us just as we finish up breakfast. As it seems, he and Alton hit it off well with their coarse personalities in common. It would be perfect if Bernard wasn't present. His ass makes my skin crawl. Alton acts as his buffer. It's almost as if he knows how close I am to losing it.

Sarah and Ruth are to the left of us, underneath the carport, talking over Ruth's iPad. Michael is speaking about the evolution of the black man in America and how there's been regression in our development. Fred chimes in, often agreeing with his boy. It's an insightful lecture, but I'm pleasantly distracted by the sight of Zoey, horse playing in the massive green yard with Jordan.

Seeing my life in one place, interacting gleefully does something to my core. It reminds me of my reason for living. My world. My elation isn't only sentimental, it's physical as well. I'm fighting my erection as I watch Zoey's ass jiggle in her short shorts, and her breasts bounce in that stingy tee-shirt. It brings my mind back to the

Zoey I met seven years ago, whose curves weren't as plentiful, and hid beneath her loose clothing. The weight gain over the past few years has enhanced Zoey's appeal. She's even more beautiful…and especially arousing.

In the back of my consciousness, I hear Michael excuse himself. Spouting something about an aging bladder as he pads off. My eyes never leave my family.

"Damnnnnn!" Alton growls while holding his sack. "Seeing Zo's ass out there reminds me about my piece, coming down here child-free. I can't wait to drown myself in that ass."

Alton is a bit more dramatic than he's been down here, at the Barrett's. I don't flinch because Michael is out of earshot. And not for nothing, Zoey's natural sexiness had me entranced long ago.

"I know, man, I can't wait to be able to say that myself. As soon as she's official, I'll be drowning in that all day."

As my head snaps over to Bernard, I notice in my peripheral, so does Al's.

"What the fuck?"

"Say what, young man?"

Alton and Fred damn near shout at the same time. Almost immediately, Bernard's expression turns sheepish. It's clear to me he didn't realize the jewels dropped when he did.

He isn't fucking Zoey?

"Yo, bro!" Alton yelps, and instantly, I see the mischievousness in his eyes. "You mean to tell me you got one of the sexiest women in American pop culture…purely for who she's affiliated with, and you ain't fuck yet?"

Fred's expression matches Al's. My curious glance doesn't provide relief. Bernard's eyes shut, easily giving away his embarrassment. His slip up. *He's not fucking my Niña!* My somber mood since he left my bedroom last night suddenly turns triumphant.

"Well, we tried once…" Bernard tries to explain, but that attempt is weaker than his slip up. He failed big time, intensifying my excitement exponentially.

I know Zoey; she likes to fuck…and a lot. She's also very straight forward. If you're hitting it right, she'll come back. If she's not pleased with you, in any manner, she will figure out a way to avoid displeasure.

Bernard doesn't know how to fuck.

"Trust me, son," Fred pleads with Bernard. "It don't matter how religious they come. If you make 'em feel good, they gon' keep coming, ya hear?"

Bernard glances at him ghostly. I can tell he's registering that he's gone against man law.

"Shiiiiit! I know enough about *that* ass," Al points directly to Zoey. "...to know she likes to be handled, nah I mean, son? She one of those that makes her wishes known, nah I mean?" he cups his sacks. If I didn't know my man, I'd think he's disrespecting me, my son, and his mother. But Alton is communicating territory to Bernard. He's telling him that I've fucked Zoey, properly.

Bernard gives a half-confident snort. "Well, she is sporting *my* rock, right?" He takes a sip of his drink.

"My man," Fred calls for his attention. "One: That ain't no rock. Two: a ring don't equate to love for a woman who ain't being touched right."

When Alton leads his and Fred's laughter, I almost feel sorry for Bernard. But when I catch a glimpse of Zoey's ass perked in the air, mimicking a three-point stance along with Jordan, it all dissipates.

Fuck Bernard. I need to handle Zoey.

The small banquet hall where Sarah's birthday dinner is being held is nice. It's modestly decorated with silver, pink, and deep purple Mylar balloons and the tables are covered in pink and purple tablecloths with exotic flower arrangements as centerpieces. It's understated elegance, precisely indicative of the honoree. Her and Michael's table is centered. Seated with them are their daughters, grandson, and me.

I wouldn't feel so awkward if Zoey would at least look at me. It's not that I make much of an attempt; my mind is still turning over the fact that Zoey has no sex life. There are so many revelations to be gained from that.

Angela is in the building with her daughter, Brooklyn. Karen and BJ are here with their two boys as well. I still can't believe they're expecting a third. There are a few faces I recognize from being with Zoey's family over the years. What's telling of the ones that I don't know are the stares and attempts to take pictures of me. They are being handled by the security that I have to keep around me, even if at a distance. For the most part, Zoey and Sarah managed their family regarding the fanfare over the years, asking that they not make a spectacle of my presence. That quelled the unnecessary conversations and requests from people I don't know.

Bernard left for a show in Greenville after his monumental miscue this morning. Tynisha met Alton here, and afterwards they'll be headed to Key West for two weeks. That'll be his restoration vacation before the season starts.

Although the venue is small, the service is excellent and dinner is served promptly to guests. There are presentations given to the birthday girl including a soloist performance. Sarah seems happy. She's a modest woman, one who doesn't ask for anything but for people to live their best lives. She deserves this and more. Zoey put this together for her mother. When I offered to help via email, she declined, leaving me to think of a birthday gift all on my own.

When it's time, Jordan and I take to the podium to present Sarah with her gift from us. Jordan starts with a poem he created and memorized for his grandmother. It's short and sweet, yet beyond what you would expect from a six year old. But that's JR. He has a seasoned soul. Sometimes I wonder if his maturity is due to him being exposed to so much and being an only child. I'd love to give him siblings, but refuse for it to be with another woman. I don't want that type of set up.

After the applause dies down, Jordan looks up at me. I lower my body to the microphone.

"Good evening everyone," I clear my throat, uncharacteristically nervous about speaking publicly. The room goes up again. That, I'm used to. It comes with the celebrity. "I couldn't let this little player steal the show. Sarah may be his grandmother—a super grandmother—but I often feel she belongs to me as well. I'm not a man of public display..." Laughter. "...unless there's a ball in my hands, that is." I have to chuckle myself for stumbling over my words. "But for this woman I'd endure the embarrassment to tell the world how great a woman she is and what a..." I lick my lips, braving myself. "...blessing she's been to me and my fam—my son." My eyes go to her. "Sarah, I don't know any mother who loves as hard or extends herself as much for her den. There isn't much I wouldn't do for you...although you never ask. Thanks for..." I bow my head to control my emotions. It's bad enough that I'm bent over, talking into a fucking mic that is as low as my knees, but my damn emotions are trying to surface, too. "Thanks for being an extraordinary grandmother to my son and a...an unexpected mother to me."

I quickly stand and pat Jordan on the shoulder, providing his cue.

"Now, Daddy?" he looks up at me.

I nod.

"Grandmom, our birthday gift to you is a cruise..." Jordan looks up at me again. "What kind again, Daddy?"

The room laughs.

"Mediterranean."

"Yeah...and a coupon—"

"Voucher," I correct.

"Voucher for a pool in the backyard!" Jordan shouts his joy because, while Sarah has expressed wanting one, he knows he'll benefit from it most.

The room goes up louder than they have all night. Folks stand from their seats. Jordan jumps in place, soaking up their response, not having a true appreciation of what he's just gifted his grandmother. Sarah grabs her chest and cups her mouth at the same time. I give her a wink, having fun with her modesty.

Then my eyes land on Zoey, who's just as elated by our gesture as everyone else. Her eyes are wet and nose is red. When we leave the stage, Jordan flies into his mother's arms. She whispers something directly in his ear. I hear him say thank you, but not much else.

Then her eyes rest on me and for the first time in years, I don't see acrimony. I see pride, similar to when I met her.

"I have someone I'd like you two to meet." Zoey does a reverse nod, summoning me to follow her.

We walk a few tables over and come across a table full of people. Because I know Zoey understands how I feel about meeting strangers, I'm at ease. Yet I'm still curious about who this person is.

"Aunt Lucinda, this is my angel, Jordan, and his dad, Stenton," Zoey initiates.

An elderly woman with smooth unblemished sable skin slowly turns in her seat and lifts her chin to regard me. Judging by her languid movement, I didn't think she heard very well.

"You's a tall boy, ain't ya?" Her dentures are stained, but her smile is bright.

I give her a slight bow then offer my hand. "Nice to meet you, Aunt Lucinda." She takes it shakily, which is indicative of her age. She must be eighty or so years old. I then turn to Jordan. "Greet your aunt, kid."

Jordan smiles as he offers his hand. "I'm Jordan Rogers."

As she takes his hand, she jeers, "You must be if he's Stenton. Your momma only introduced two people."

Zoey and I chuckle. Seconds later, Lucinda joins in.

"Now where's ya' other family?" Lucinda tosses over to Zoey.

Zoey's expression matches my bemusement.

Other family?

"This is it. You're looking at it, Aunt Lucinda." Zoey's soft rub on her aunt's shoulder mirrors her soothing tone.

The lady must be a bit senile at her age.

"No, honey. Ain't you engaged, too? Where is that lucky fellow?" Lucinda clarifies. The whole table is quiet, raptly watching our exchange.

Shit! That answers it. *Fucking Bernard.*

Zoey's eyes rise to mine. It is clear that concept is as foreign to her as the ring she wears. She then subconsciously thumbs the underside of her left ring finger…where my initials are stained into her skin. I shrug my shoulders as my brow line rises. This is for her to answer. She scrapes her bottom lip between her teeth.

Rebounding, she gleams, "Well, nothing's official 'til I say I do, right?" Zoey gives her faux chuckle. This time I don't follow suit.

"It was nice meeting you, Aunt Lucinda. God bless," I bid cheesily. I need to get the fuck up out of this cypher.

I take Jordan's hand and tread toward our table. That's when I see Sarah ambling our way. Her smile falls as she nears.

"What's wrong, baby?" she asks.

I'm about to answer when I hear, "I'm not feeling too well, Momma."

I turn to find a distraught Zoey. I didn't realize she was on my heels. She didn't look good.

Sarah wraps Zoey in her arms. "Is there anything I can get for you, dear?"

Zoey shakes her head. "I just need to go lie down. I think I've pushed myself too hard this week."

Just then, Jordan lets go of my hand and takes off running to his grandfather, who waves him on from a distance, not at all clued in to what is taking place.

"Okay, honey, but you shouldn't drive."

"I'll just see if Ruth will drive me," Zoey murmurs sulkily.

"Ruth is handing out favors." Sarah glances up at me. "Stenton here can take you home. Right, son? Jordan can ride back to the house with me and Michael."

It's posed in a manner that I can't decline. Zoey's eyes ascend to me. I don't know what this means.

"Sure." I pull out my phone. "Let me notify security."

Less than five minutes later, we are in the truck, heading to the house with security tailing us. I take the opportunity to chip at Zoey's brain.

"So, are you two officially engaged?"

"We're committed." Again, Zoey grabs her left ring finger and rubs at my initials, not the "rock" Bernard gave her.

"So am I to my team, but that isn't an engagement."

She shifts in her seat with wide eyes and grates, "What are you getting at?"

I stare at her for a few seconds, admiring her beautiful angry face. Her features have matured over the years, but she still has the innocence-and-purity aura she did when I met her. This anger she's throwing my way is what I've caused, so I won't push her. My eyes go back to the road.

"Since you and Bernard are talking about moving, I'm assuming you're moving forward with the engagement."

"Well, you shouldn't assume."

"It's hard not to when you're wearing that." I nod toward her left hand, referencing her ring.

"Bernard shouldn't have asserted that. We only talked about it briefly." Zoey shakes her head, clearly frustrated. But that's who Zoey has become over the years when I'm around. "I have things to sort out before I can make that move with him."

"Shit like what? You took the ring—"

"I told him that I would accept his desire for a commitment to me!" That came out nastier than I'm used to with her. There's a subliminal message, I'm sure.

"What the fuck does that mean?"

"It means..."

"Means what, Zo?"

I hear her sigh. "It means more than you ever gave," she murmurs.

I cringe, surprised by her candor.

"So, you settle?"

With her arms wrapped protectively across her chest, she clarifies, "I'm not settling. I'm simply being smarter about waiting things out. Before, I waited on you, now I'm waiting on me to make sure this is right for my son and me."

Ahhhh... So, we finally address the real issue! *But what does that mean?*

I turn it over in my mind as I pull onto the Barrett property. Zoey's out of the car and slams the door before I can stand to my feet. I follow her into the house and through the kitchen. The farther we go, the more I believe I'm losing my footing with her.

"Zoey..." I call after her.

She keeps her stride going for the rear staircase.

"Zo!" I leap to grab her.

She jumps and her back meets the wall. Her mouth drops open.

"Tell me what you need from me and I'll do it," I murmur, internally feeling that isn't an adequate offer.

Our lips are so close. Closest they've been in over a year. I've missed the scent of her, the feel of her warm breath shooting onto my mouth at this proximity. My dick twitches its need.

"What do you need, Niña?" I breathe onto her pouted lips, ready to devour them. I can smell her desire for me. It's been a while, but I now know she's in need. I've never pushed her this hard to see her so raw. I didn't want to defile her if she was sleeping with another man. But I now know she isn't, which means her pussy belongs to me. Again. "Fucking. Tell. Me." I whisper into her mouth.

Now, I see her chest heaving beneath her chin as I tower her. Her face grimaces into a frown, almost like an impending cry.

"Stent!" she croaks out then flutters her eyes.

That was it. That is her consent. I crush her lips with mine, immediately dipping my tongue into her trembling mouth. Within seconds, Zoey joins my tongue in wild and impassioned swiping. Her tongue. Goddamn I've missed it. Zoey tastes so fucking good. So sweet. It's instantly intoxicating. Her hands are all over me, pushing me in a 180-degree pivot, frantically perusing my shoulders, chest, and when I feel them below my waistline, my abdominals leap. Feeling her little hands fumble with my belt dizzies me.

When she pulls back, she whispers with closed lids, "All. I need it all."

The back of my head collides with the wall behind me. Zoey drops to her knees and takes me into her mouth without a moment for me to process it all. Her hot, wet mouth suctions my painful erection and her tongue twirls at the head, making my mouth go slack.

This is the Zoey I've always known; no pretenses, no coyness, no games when it comes to sex. She sucks me fervently and jerks me with both her hands wrapped tightly. Suddenly, it feels like the first time for me. The sensation urged by her inspired twirling and draws shoot straight to my groin. It doesn't take long for me to feel my orgasm.

"Niña," I whimper because I have no gumption in me now to put bass in my voice. It's all in my pipe, ready to shoot into her mouth.

Her eyes jump up to mine and she simultaneously starts to swirl her tongue faster and pull her wrists with more enthusiasm. When she moans, I know she's giving me permission. I let go and detonate. My knees fucking quiver and my hands grip the back of her head as I hold my hips suspended, waiting to come down. All of sudden, Zoey brings my banked liquids up to the head of my cock, displaying my essence then sucks it back into her mouth. My eyes damn near pop out of my head. I watch her mirror my actions as she swallows hard.

"Stenton!" she cries before jumping on me, pushing my body against the wall. "Only with you. Only for you. Only you bring that out of me," she pushes into my ear.

That plea unleashes something within. In seconds, I have Zoey on her back, panties torn, her legs hooked over my shoulders, and my face buried at the apex of her legs. I lick, suck, and spar with inspiration. Zoey isn't happy. I know this because I know Zo. She needs to be pushed and challenged beyond what she advises. She presents as so confident, solid, and well versed. And after all these years, I realize deep down inside she's made up of the same thing every woman is. She has the ability to be led and to submit. In this moment, all things are made clear to me.

Having Zoey like this—bare, on the steps of the back stairway in her parents' vacation home, screaming insanities of pleasure—the essence of her soul is sound. She needs to be taken, to be loved. Zoey needs that *wow* factor that I've always given. I was just so fucked up by tying her down at such a delicate age that I let her slip between my fingers. I've caused so much pain for the both of us by my tepidness about my ultimate commitment to her.

"*Stenton!*" That cry, pouring from her lips as I catch her shooting liquids in my mouth confirm my revelations. "*Don't. Let. Me Go!*" she cries. As my hands cup her ass, I know I could never let this woman go.

I could never be without her. I've always known I've had an unusual preoccupation with Zoey since we met, but so many truths are being revealed in this act. Almost too many for my brain to process.

When she's done, I crawl up her body until our mouths meet. I lift her onto the wall with her legs curled around my waist and mouth dancing sensually with mine. I enjoy her this way. She's raw, stripped of that fucking know-it-all shield. She's just my Niña.

"Do it, Stent!" I barely recognize the cry in her tone. She's breathing harshly in my face. "Please." Zoey cups my face, petitioning my eyes. "Do it."

I reared and pushed into her pliant lips with one swift movement. She didn't have to beg; only make clear her need. Zoey tosses her head back as she squeezes her eyes shut and grips her hips around my waist. Her lips are separated as if she wants to scream.

"Go!" she demands, challenging my attempt to be gentle. She's tight as fuck.

But I don't want to lose her in this moment. I need to remind her of who we are together. What desire is like. Our passion. I go slamming my pelvis into her. I make sure to serve Zoey every inch of me. She fits me so well. Even if she experienced a bit of discomfort when we first started, Zoey is making room for her pleasure now. I feel her clamp on my waist even tighter, rocking into me, needing me to bring her to that next echelon of pleasure.

All this time, I thought she had another path. One that didn't require a man next to her, giving her the partnership that I've wanted with her. I thought Zoey was a species different from any other warm-blooded woman. Her Teflon exterior had me believe all these years she had no emotional need for me. I've always felt I've been a mere option to her; one that she purely entertained. In this moment, while I ram into her like I'm fucking king, I have dominion. She yields to me and I bring her there. I finally realize

I've been delaying my own love. My life and commitment to Zoey.

"I can't hold out any more! I need to pull—"

"Don't stop! We can do it...together!" Zoey breathes forcefully through my ear.

I start to plummet into her with such force that I feel an escape from my body. My mind floats somewhere when I see the grit of her teeth and feel the arching of her hips as I rub against her erogenous zone within. The minute Zoey cries her release, mine ignites an explosion too great for me to contain, and I cry along with her. We hold on to each other like rabid animals, needing each other to survive this fiery bliss.

At some point, my ascension must have been a spectacle for Zoey because as she comes down she regards me, eerily, while still in my arms against the wall. I don't want regret to settle upon her. I need her to stay with me.

I don't give a fuck. I have nothing to lose. "I love you. I've never stopped. You've been the only woman for me. When you're ready, I can prove how." My tone is the most desperate I've heard of myself.

Zoey slowly unwraps her limbs from around my torso. It's troubling along with how she's looking at me as though I'm an aggressor, a total stranger. Something isn't right.

Zoey

My body teeters on the ledge of post-coital bliss and unadulterated shock. My head's nearing explosion as it fills with memories of his hinting admissions over the years. *I need to talk you about something ...what I've done to you. I don't deserve this opportunity. It's the least I could do considering what I've done to you.*

My lips tremble with a combination of disdain and disbelief. I'm in utter shock. It all makes sense now.

"I know...*us.* Believe it or not, I can recall and narrate each time we've made love since the first time. I can tell you every sensation I felt and every expression of ecstasy you made with me. Trust me, I can; it's tortured me to imagine which ones you've shared with Erika...and Jenna over the years. The only times you've glided in and out of me without the...feel of rubber was in The Cayman Islands."

Stenton pulls in a sharp breath, too hard. Too quickly.

"I may have been high one of those days and somewhat intoxicated a few nights, but I recall vividly what we felt like together. I remember how smooth your penetration was." Then my eyes narrowed while zoomed into his that were now wide. I felt daffy and melodramatic for going there, but those feelings couldn't rival my sprouting revelation. "Did you not use condoms with me that week?"

Flashes of the ambiance of Cayman course my fuzzy mind that's still clearing from my recent orgasm. Rapid visions of the master suite catching the fluorescence of the moon when I was able to open my eyes from the bliss I floated in while Stenton was behind me, plunging deep. Or the rays from the early sun piercing my closed lids while he rocked on top of me during a morning greeting. All those times he was more verbal with his ascensions, yet less talkative in coaxing in my ear. Those sessions were far more intense, though shorter.

His translucent fluids are now spilling from me, something I've never felt. Then I recall how during those times, he'd always carry me to the tub or shower, immediately. I catch and swallow back the bile shooting up my esophagus.

Once I'm able to speak, I breathe, "You deliberately didn't use condoms. You got me pregnant on purpose."

"Hold up. Wait. Wait!" Stenton barks then squeezes his eyes as he grimaces. But with each passing second, my premonition gets stronger and stronger.

"Why haven't you asked for a DNA test?"

"Excuse me?"

"You've gone through all the formalities of apologizing to my family and paying them off for renting my pussy...made generous arrangements to compensate me for my condition, but you never once asked me to verify Jordan is your child."

Stenton looks sick. Like really sick. Like sick enough to vomit.

And he does, right here on the steps.

Holy mother of Joseph!

The end...of ***Love Delayed***.

Zoe Barrett
I have a question that you can't be offended by.

Stenton Rogers
I'm game. Do you.

Zoe Barrett
Ummmm... Are those your real teeth?

Stenton Rogers
What the fuck Zoe? LMAO

Zoe Barrett
DS! They're kinda of big...too nicely aligned.

Stenton Rogers
And so are your boobs but you don't see me inquiring about authenticity.

Zoe Barrett
Don't be pigheaded, you dork.

Stenton Rogers
Don't go getting all prudish. I used to get teased a lot as a kid about my big ass choppers. Trust me when I say I've grown into them.

Zoe Barrett
I don't believe you.

Stenton Rogers
Don't believe what?

Zoe Barrett
That your teeth are real.

Stenton Rogers
I'll prove it to you.

Zoe Barrett
How?

Stenton Rogers
I don't know. I'll think of something. And them you'll pro.... are real.

Zoe Barrett
Dude! I'm poor. My parents can't afford a boob job!

Stenton Rogers
But you studied around rich people. Who's to say you didn't have a sponsor?

Zoe Barrett
Touché.

I wouldn't speak on the sensation that flashed in my core at his comeback. That was private along with the rest of the inexplicable things he caused me to feel without his hands...or mouth.

LOVE Delayed

~And
_____

Wait! Where's the drama? Does Stenton get with Erika? Who is this Jenna woman? What type of professional career does Zoey take on? What happens next, Love? Will Zoey marry Bernard? Does Stenton and Zoey have their happily ever after?
Find out all that and more in…

Love
Delivered

Book 2 of the *Waiting to Breathe* series

#PenningWithoutParameters
#ImGonnaMakeYou*Love*Me

~Love Acknowledges

Karras Jordan & Ariel Meredith – You two have been amazingly generous with allowing us to use your images to give the readers visuals of Stenton and Zoey. Thanks for letting me doctor up your professional shots as well as your selfies on social network. It took the fun out of stalking because I had permission, but it took my imagination to another level when I was able to coordinate them with the storyline. I so appreciate your talents. You two specifically are skilled with your range of images. Because of the timeline of this story, I was able to go through your pictures and _select_ Stenton and Zoey at their respective ages, and still have more to choose from. Phenomenal!

Love's Betas – Angela Jennings, Yorubia McNeil, Corinne Baker, and Juaquanna Gaines-Sams. I appreciate you guys' feedback and your time! Shumethia Seal, thanks soooooooooo much for tolerating my literary babble. I appreciate the research you did to help bring these characters (you hate) to life. You are an awesome individual! Sabrina S. Scott, your nurturing tone and zeal has been felt and greatly appreciated. You took this baby and made it your own. I hope to continue to hold your interest. Christina C. Jones, OMG, Love officially has an author-buddy...or bae (insider)! I appreciate you being a sounding board for all my frustrations of this indie world. Thanks for the feedback, enthusiasm, confidence, professionalism, genius, and your friendship.

Karen Rodgers-McCollum: You keep saying, "It's okay, Love." *But it really isn't!* You have been an angel throughout this entire process. Your patience and nurturing spirit has been a blessing! Thanks soooooo much for your super proficiency and professionalism! You rock!

In-house editor: Zakiya Walden of **I've Got Something to Say Incorporated**: Thanks for your quick turnaround on this project...and right around your 30th birthday! (It's today) I'm so grateful for you, chica!

Juaquanna Gaines-Sams: Thanks for all of your coordination efforts, your consultation on the cover and the marketing of all the LB projects. Thanks for your brutal honesty as well! You're the bomb! Hopefully we're one project closer to me getting an assistant. Teehee!

MDT: You've yelled, kicked and screamed about this timeline, but we delivered. Thanks for your guidance...and money to roll out my second project. LOL! *And another one!*

To my ***Master***, my ***Jireh***, my ***Rohi***, *1 Peter 4:10*. I bless You for the opportunity to share my gift. May You receive ALL the glory.

~Other Books by Love Belvin

***Love's Improbable Possibility* series:**

Love Lost, Love UnExpected, Love UnCharted & Love Redeemed

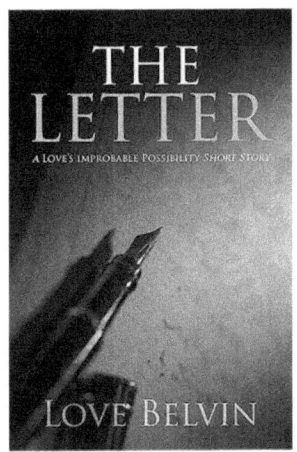

***Waiting to Breathe* series:**
Love Delayed & Love Delivered

Love's Inconvenient Truth (Standalone)

Love Unaccounted series:
In Covenant with Ezra, In Love with Ezra & Bonded with Ezra

The Connecticut Kings series:

*Love in the Red Zone, *Love on the Highlight Reel, *Determining Possession, End Zone Love, Love's Ineligible Receiver, *Pass Interference, Love's Encroachment, & *Offensive Formations (*by Christina C. Jones)*

Wayward Love series:

The Left of Love, The Low of Love & The Right of Love

the *Wayward Love* series

Love in Rhythm & Blues series

The Rhythm of Blues & The Rhyme of Love

LOVE IN RHYTHM & BLUES series

The Sadik series

He Who Is a Friend, He Who Is a Lover & He Who Is a Protector

The Muted Hopelessness series:

My Muted Love, Our Muted Recklessness, & Our Reckless Hope

The Prism series:

Mercy, Grace, & The Promise

Low Love, Low Fidelity (Standalone)

~Extra

You can find Love Belvin at **www.LoveBelvin.com**
Facebook @ **Author - Love Belvin**
Twitter **@LoveBelvin**
Goodreads: **Love Belvin**
and on Instagram **@LoveBelvin**

*Join the #TeamLove mailing list on my website to keep up
with the happenings!*

See visuals from the series on my website – www.lovebelvin.com